The ORBIDDEN

The Forbidden

A VAMPIRE HUNTRESS LEGEND

L. A. BANKS

 ST. MARTIN'S GRIFFIN ✠ NEW YORK

www.stmartins.com

Library of Congress Cataloging-in-Publication Data

Banks, L. A.
    The forbidden : a vampire huntress legend / L. A. Banks.— 1st ed.
        p. cm.
    ISBN 0-312-33622-5
    EAN 978-0-312-33622-6
        1. Richards, Damali (Fictitious character)—Fiction.   2. African American women—Fiction.   3. Women martial artists—Fiction.   4. Vampires—Fiction.
5. Occult fiction. gsafd   I. Title.

PS3602.A64F67 2005
813'.6—dc22   2004065825

10 9 8 7 6 5 4 3 2

This book in the series is dedicated to the concept of redemption—that if we simply believe, we still have a fighting chance. Much has happened in the world since this series began. There are signs everywhere that we might all need to take heed and pursue a more spiritual path. The earth even stopped in time for microseconds after a disastrous tsunami. This tells me that there is a power out there greater than my tiny human brain could ever hope to conceive of, and therefore, anything is possible. But one thing I know for sure is redemption was a promise.

May you choose wisely and pause to think about things greater than we can fathom.

ACKNOWLEDGMENTS

To my agent, Manie Barron, who continues to bring brilliance to projects; my editor, Monique Patterson, whose tireless dedication can be felt on every page; to the team at St. Martin's Press, who are like family; to Eric Battle, for his wondrously creative renderings of the characters (his art is da bomb!); to Vince Natale and Michael Storrings, who continue to blow me away with their cover art and designs; to Chris Bonelli, a saint who keeps the Web site fresh; and, of course, the Rowdee Black Giants, who always inspire—*go, brothers*— and to Zulma Gonzalez, an angel whom I am blessed to know.

The Forbidden

CHAPTER ONE

ALL WAS still on level seven. A clawed hand held embryonic life within it. Golden green glowing eyes misted over black as they looked up to the vast expanse of nothingness that mimicked a vaulted ceiling. Trembling with anticipation, a shaky finger extended a hooked talon that prodded at the bloody mass of dormant life . . . life that could be molded into its own image. A hissing coo filled with gentle adoration warmed the small cluster of cells, making them glow red and begin to pulse.

"Oh, soon, my son," a passionate voice whispered. "Very, very soon."

Sydney, Australia . . .

Dread tightened Damali's chest as she watched Carlos's eyes. Visceral emptiness filled her, making her clutch her lower belly. His once-serene gaze now darted to her face, then to the faces of her teammates and to his surrounding environment like a man displaced and confused. The sensation was so overwhelming that it threatened to choke her heart to a standstill. Her man, once confident, suave, and smooth as black silk, had come up out of the unknown looking crazed and wild in the eye.

Suddenly she felt a strange sensation that fluttered in her womb. She pressed her hand against her abdomen. *What was that?* But she had to shake off the weird feeling. Too many issues competed for her attention right now and the most immediate was Carlos.

The Light had brought him back, had actually reconstituted his form from the burnt vampire ash left by dawn, and now it seemed as though he didn't know where he was, how he'd gotten there, or whom he was with. Beyond all that they'd had to contend with, this was perhaps the most frightening experience of all: Carlos

Rivera's mental state was in question—tears, screaming, ranting, fighting against the hold of friendly hands. Damali turned away for a moment and swallowed hard.

A head on a silver platter would be her bride price. Yeah. She and the chairman had unfinished business.

She reached out her hand to touch Carlos's face, and he jerked away from her, unsure if she were a mirage, a vampiric illusion, something evil and vile that would start his torture all over again. His fear rippled through her and rattled her bones. It sent a chill through her like a knife. It drew her mouth into a tight line as she fought not to scream. She saw what they had done. A head. *The head of the bastard who'd done this,* was the only acceptable answer to levy the debt paid in full.

Down in Hell they had a phrase: Fair exchange is no robbery. Then so be it. A head for a head, a mind for a mind . . . and an eye for an eye and a tooth for a fucking tooth—the chairman's fangs mounted on her wall mantel. This was war.

Damali could feel her eyes narrow to slits as her man tried to stand, and then tried to get away from her and her team. Oh, hell no. They'd raped his mind and stolen his dignity. And for that unforgivable offense, she'd blow the Vampire Council's doors off the damned hinges. In her mind's eye, she could see the pentagram-shaped table surrounded by dark thrones, and the chairman's smug expression. But Hell had no fury like a woman scorned. Her thoughts frayed and descended to the pit.

Fuck you, Mr. Chairman. This time, it's just me and you.

Carlos could feel his eyeballs roll backward beneath his lids as consciousness ebbed and flowed like a reluctant tide. One moment he had been sitting on the ground, naked, awed, and so profoundly moved that he couldn't speak, and in the next moment, he was being hurried away by many hands and clamoring voices all trying to get him into a vehicle and onto hallowed ground. Were it not for Damali's hand firmly holding his and her voice cutting through the mêlée, he would have tried to escape them all.

For the first time in his entire existence he truly feared he was losing his mind. Something was very wrong. He'd gone into the

Light—more accurately, had been propelled into it, summoned by it, sucked toward a bright, indescribable iridescent wonder that had a pulse, a center, and held the heartbeat of the universe. Beings of unfathomable strength had hurled him forward, their silvery light sabers cutting at filaments of dark tendrils, holding him, burning him to ash. The heat was so intense that his bones had liquefied, his skin had blackened and crumbled away, his eyes had melted and had run down his cheeks like gory, oozing tears . . . but silver metallic wings with the texture of satin had shielded him from the furnace blast beneath him. What were they and who'd sent them?

Healing warmth had entered him, coating his burning insides with instant peace, quenching the sun's fury against his skin. One being had parted to become many with raised golden shields that seemed as though each held a living, moving orb of sunlight until he was encircled by them, each ball of molten, living, golden light fusing to become a ring around him. The ring had covered him, entered him. . . . All he could remember now was that they came and then in a fluttering cloud they'd dispersed, shooting away so quickly they'd left only a blinding blur of white light in their wake.

But perhaps the powers-that-be had messed up somehow. Maybe they didn't catch his soul in time, and how did a man turned vampire return to the sun?

He couldn't hear. Everything was coming at him in muffled tones. People spoke in indecipherable guttural fragments. Everyone seemed to move in slow motion. It was like moving through mud. His mind was a slurry of confusion. He was nearly blind, each friendly face blurred beyond recognition until it was breath-close to his face. His skin felt thick and dull, the sensation of hands soothing his shoulders, rubbing his back, bundling him into a coat, but all of it took seconds to register. Breathing was an effort that consumed his concentration. The most troubling aspect was the heaviness he felt in his limbs, as though his muscles were too weak to lift his own body.

What had the Light done to him?

Carlos leaned forward and covered his face with his hands. The sensory overload was too much—rather, the lack of sensation and the ability to perceive his surroundings was horrifying.

"I think he's going into shock," Damali said, drawing him against her body closer as the Jeep careened through the streets. "We have to get him inside, out of the sun."

"I'm gonna fry," Carlos croaked, becoming more disoriented as the vehicle barreled through desolate streets in a town he didn't know.

"We'll be at the church in just a few minutes, kiddo."

Carlos slowly removed his hands from his face, training his attention toward what he remembered to be Rider's voice. "To a church?" Instinct made Carlos begin struggling against Damali's hold. He could hear his voice rising with panic. "No! I'll burn!"

Many strong arms held him. In a distant part of his mind he heard Father Patrick call out to him.

"You've stayed with us on hallowed ground before, Carlos. We have to keep you safe. Remember the woods, the cabin? The dark side cannot know you've come back. You won't burn."

"No!"

More hands held him down as he grabbed at the door handle . . . but these were human hands, hands that shouldn't have had enough power to hold him, even in his weakened state. He needed to feed and find shelter!

"Stop fighting us, baby," Damali urged. "It'll make it worse. *Please,* Carlos, trust me."

"We're taking you someplace safe," an old man's voice said. It was a familiar voice.

In unsteady increments memory came back to him. Father Patrick . . . that's right. The monks. They had a prayer barrier that only he could cross. Yeah. He remembered. The safe house. Damali trusted them. This was her squad. All right.

Carlos stopped struggling and closed his eyes. He could feel Damali's cool hand stroke his brow, wiping away the sweat. He ran his tongue over his incisors to retract his fangs, lest he frighten his benefactors, and then froze. He touched his mouth, running his fingers over his upper canines. Tears sprang to his eyes so quickly he didn't even have time to blink them back. He glanced at Damali, then away, lowering his hands from his face, staring at his palms in disbelief. He'd been neutered. He wanted to vomit.

He curled his hands into fists. He shut his eyes tightly and hung his head. He could feel Damali's hand stroke his back and he jerked away from her touch. "Don't."

"It's Jose, man. Don't you remember?" A young, soothing voice cut into his consciousness. "You burned and came back. You said you saw angels, *hombre*. You sat there looking at the sun. You spoke to us, looked at us, sat quietly with D and said you were free."

Carlos shook his head with his eyes closed, pressing his fingers to his temples. "No. I don't remember. Shut up, you're confusing me!"

"Ease off, Jose," the voice he knew as Rider's said in almost a whisper. "Father Pat, Marlene, either of you guys got something for dude—something to help him bite the snake that bit him?"

He felt hysteria rising in him. Carlos chuckled, but he kept his eyes closed. The sound was hollow even to his own ears. Rider. That's right. *Hombre* was human and had brass balls . . . had been chained to the ground as bait while the harpies pulled out his guts. Crazy white dude yelling at Hell's worst nightmare, talking trash with no weapon in his hand, trying to divert the predators away to give him a chance to beat the rising sun. Very cool of Rider . . . he wouldn't forget the debt. "You drink Jack Daniel's, right? Add a little color in it for me and I'll buy you a drink, man. After what we just went through on the docks—you buy; I'll fly. Cool?"

Silence in the vehicle surrounded him. No one but him was laughing. He could feel the vehicle slowing down.

"Get him inside, Father Pat," an older woman said from somewhere within the Jeep. "He's delirious."

A pair of strong arms threaded around his back and nearly lifted him off his feet. What seemed like a battalion of clerics wearing long black robes and white collars accosted him with phalanges of holy water, striking at him in the sign of the cross, making him cringe, as he turned his face away to protect it from the assault, to no avail. Relentless, they swung heavy brass pots filled with smoking frankincense at him as the burly brother hoisted him over his shoulder and advanced up the cathedral steps.

He could feel several hands dressing him . . . someone was anointing his head with oil. Then he was being moved again, up what seemed like an endless spiral of stairs. Footsteps, many, many footfalls, rushing like a military SWAT unit, followed him. The sound of choppers in the air, bright sunlight filled his eyes and touched his face, but like the incense and holy water, it didn't burn. *Why?* he dimly wondered.

Confusion tore at his brain. Blurred white birds of metal with a crest on the side . . . blue, a crown of thorns, a sword, a bleeding heart—just like Father Pat's medallion—opened at the side, filling its belly with humans that eagerly climbed in and dragged him with them.

This was a vampire's true Hell. The chairman had indeed had the last laugh. The choppers were flying toward the sun! Carlos braced himself against the pain once again. How long would the chairman continue to torture him?

Pilots wearing dark aviator sunglasses never turned around as he begged them to release him from the Sea of Perpetual Agony. He suddenly feared Damali's touch; what beast would she turn into? An Amanthra? He squeezed his eyes shut, refusing to watch her gorgeous brown eyes change into slanted, glowing orbs while her beautiful body transformed into a serpentine menace. Or maybe the chairman would be particularly cruel and she would become a were-demon. It would be a painful taunt to remind him of his brush with that entity in the Amazon; Hell always beat your ass down with past mistakes in the place where there was no such thing as forgiveness.

Carlos's thoughts scrambled, trying to figure out an escape, a way to negotiate a shorter sentence. Hell was eternal, so peace and the lack of acute pain had to be measured in milliseconds. For every minute that passed where no direct pain was being inflicted, he had a chance to rest, maybe regenerate, just enough to be able to withstand the next assault that was destined to come. If he wasn't in pain, he could think. If he could think, he could bargain. But what aces did he hold? What could he barter with at this juncture?

When the choppers touched down in a deserted section of airport runway, and the illusion of humans helped him toward a crest-bearing private jet at the end of the landing strip, he had to wonder just what the chairman had in store for him now. And could he bear it?

Carlos opened his eyes, his breathing labored as he tried to form words. He searched the impostor Damali's face as she led him by the hand with Big Mike on his flank helping him walk. "Where?" was all he could manage to get out.

"Ethiopia," she said quietly, tears shining in her eyes. "Baby, we have to get out of Sydney and go to a Christian stronghold there. It's said that is where the Ark of the Covenant is held. The clerics all agreed this is the safest route. By nightfall, the Vampire Council might send a cleanup crew to look for your ashes that don't exist, so we have to leave *now*. Then, we'll take a transcontinental flight to Algeria . . . the mosques there are old, but we have to avoid the site of the pending Armageddon, the Middle East. Understand?"

None of what she was saying made any sense.

The big brother—an international courier?—was pulling him down the tarmac with the impostor of Father Pat jogging beside them to keep pace. Knowing that resistance was not an option within the inquisition chambers, which only seemed to steal his strength faster, Carlos stopped struggling against them. He had to be strategic.

"As soon as we get clearance, we have to get you behind the walls of the Vatican," the cleric said. "Until they're sure of what you are . . . all the Covenant can do is keep you on the move, from fortress to fortress."

Carlos cocked his head. He didn't believe that the chairman knew how the Covenant operated, not at this level of detail.

Carlos peered at the man who'd spoken, then looked at the one who was supposed to be Rider.

"Dude, the Vatican is like the Pentagon for the guys with the collar—just like Asula can't just waltz you into Mecca until you're checked out, dig?" the supposed Rider said as they walked up the jet's narrow steps. "So, they're gonna have to take you to their hideaways in the hills . . . sorta like being an alien and getting shuttled to Area 51 till ya spec out. Now why we all have to go along for the ride with your boy, Berkfield, is beyond me. I, for one, know I didn't get bitten, although Damali's case is a little—"

"Everybody get on the plane," a tall brother with locks said, his gaze lethal. His tone made the group stop walking as he slowly pointed to each person. "Damali has already been compromised. Jose and Damali had a twister of harpies on their asses, and came into the church bloodied and beat up. Jose, Dan, J.L., and Rider were also riding in the VIP vamp limos, alone, with what was then a council-level master vamp—Rivera. Me and Mike were on the yacht, like the others eventually were, and in unseen, dark corridors away from the group at times long enough to get nicked. Mar, Father Pat, Father Lopez, Monk Lin, and Imam Asula were all on standby, in speed-boats, out in the open, in the dead of night. My point is, any one of us could have gotten nicked. You think the powers-that-be are going to let us roll up on the pope with who knows how many vamps and a potential daywalker in our midst?" He shook his head, then turned his back to the teams and strode up the jet's steps. "Our side ain't taking no chances, and I don't blame them."

"Shabazz is right," the woman named Marlene said in a weary tone. "Life as we knew it has just ceased to exist."

The names began to link with the faces as the memory of what had happened came back to him in fits and spurts. The past came back in snatches of quilted memory. Without resistance he slowly walked up the steps and entered the jet, noting the somber expressions around him as everyone took their seats. Again, he searched Damali's face for confirmation that the truth had been told, and found it.

She clasped his hand and led him to a seat, one hand touching the small Isis dagger at her hip. "I've got your back," she said, her eyes holding his. "They've got mine. It's gonna be all right."

He nodded, slowly beginning to believe that this was all real. But as he fastened his seat belt with a click and slowly turned to stare out the window at the sun, Marlene's words rang in his ears. Her truth permeated every fiber of his being, and with that sudden knowledge, an acute sadness that he dared never share with another living soul entered his being; life as they'd known it was null and void.

CHAPTER TWO

Los Angeles . . . same night

HUNGER TORE at Yonnie's insides as he held on to the edge of the bar in the plush VIP basement section of Club Vengeance. What the hell was going on? Earlier in the evening, the contents of bottles on the shelves had turned to sludge, as though the blood within had suddenly aged.

All third-gen vampires and below had rolled. But to where? Even most second-gens were lying low. No human wannabes would come near the club tonight. If he and his squad wanted to feed, they'd have to go out hunting, old school. Where was Carlos? Concentration was impossible. The master's beacon was nonexistent. Something was very wrong. If Carlos had been exterminated, he should have immediately felt the jolt. But there was simply an eerie void, an absence of power and presence.

He looked up slowly, watching the club's top-shelf reserves begin to rattle, flames consuming the labels, peeling them away, as black bottles began exploding. His second-gen bartenders instantly collapsed into a pile of ash.

His longtime friend, Stack, stood up with effort. His squad got to their feet, their eyes taking in the horror as the building began to deconstruct, deteriorating into an old, dilapidated structure. They were so tired they could barely stand. The atmosphere felt thick, heavy, as though daylight were creeping in.

"Oh, shit," Yonnie murmured.

"Resources are drying up, man," Stack said, breathing hard. "Rivera musta fucked up, big-time. Maybe another master smoked him and the territory is realigning?"

"No," Yonnie said quickly. "A new master would be building assets, not destroying them." He held his hands out before him, feeling the vibrations, trying to search for a power pulse within the empire. He lowered his arms slowly and glanced at his five-man squad. "Feel it," he whispered. "I don't sense *any* master."

"Git the fuck outta here," Stack said, panic making his voice tight. "Rivera's rank just got knocked down a notch, maybe, but—"

"Feel it!" Yonnie shouted. "Lock in on the females. Where are they?"

Stack slowly opened his arms, palms facing out toward the crumbling walls, and he turned in a shaky circle. He blinked twice and balled his palms into fists. "Ash." Swallowing hard, he tried again. "The seriously old, fine ones are . . ." Stack's voice trailed off as he watched his hands darken and his arms fall away before his eyes.

Yonnie stepped back from his two-hundred-year-old friend in horror. Stack's expression of terror became frozen in a face that crumbled away as the others in the squad hit the ground beside him, leaving only their recently tailored suits.

For a moment, Yonnie couldn't move. He brought his hands to his face, wondering why he hadn't disintegrated along with the others. Feeding now was imperative. Yet he couldn't muster the energy for flight or transport. Breathing was more than an effort; it was nearly impossible. His hands went to his face, feeling its skeletal remains. Then he spotted a pair of golden yellow orbs low in a shadowy corner.

Yonnie immediately bulked up. His strength was severely compromised and he knew he was in trouble. The predator in the corner suddenly lunged. Huge were-demon jaws narrowly missed his face as he leapt back, but the claws of the beast opened five deep gashes in his chest. He gasped at the pain. In his weakened state, he was no match for a were-demon.

Sections of wall gave way as the were-demon slammed against support beams, pillars, missing Yonnie as he dodged with what was left of his vampire strength and leapt up to a ceiling beam and held on. However, exhaustion was rapidly slowing him down, and the were-demon seemed to sense that. It waited for a moment with a leering smile on its wolflike face—the form it had chosen to take. Its elongated fangs glistening in the full moonlight that now shone through a missing portion of the left wall, it stood on hind legs, flexing in a spectacular display of strength and power, clearly challenging Yonnie.

"Now, what's your strategy—since the Vamp Empire is mere ash?" a snarling, low voice asked.

Yonnie stared at the creature from his perch on the high fragile beam. *What the hell had happened out there?* He needed to keep this dumb motherfucker talking. The portals to level five were wide open.

"Who said we ain't running shit?" Yonnie said through a snarl. "Just because you caught us on a slow night don't mean we won't have your ass seen."

The were-demon laughed and dropped to all fours and began circling beneath Yonnie. "Where's your master, bitch?"

The question taunted Yonnie. He gripped the beam tightly, his fingernails digging into the wood.

He glanced around, knowing that were-demons, especially those of the wolf persuasion, usually traveled in packs. But he couldn't detect any others. He could only assume this one was walking point for those soon to follow.

"I thought so," the stinking thing said with a sneer. "I told them your forces were vulnerable, now I know for sure. It's just like all your other vamp hidey-holes. Vulnerable throughout the empire." The beast laughed, vicious and triumphant, as he threw his head back and released a long, bloodcurdling wolf wail.

Knowing that he had only seconds to act before the place filled with were-demons Yonnie concentrated every last ounce of his strength. He felt his fingertips ignite. Every shard of broken, jagged glass behind the bar magnetized, drew together, and became an airborne blade that he sent flying into his tormentor's throat. Yonnie watched with no small measure of satisfaction as the wolf's call was abruptly cut off on a gurgle of blood and the stunned expression still remained on the were-demon's hideous, distended face when his head fell to the floor. Black demon blood spattered the walls.

Acting quickly before the beast began to smolder and combust, Yonnie leapt down to the floor. He needed to feed, and the shame of eating from the belly of a beast was beyond him. But this was about survival. In one deft move he slit the beast's abdomen, knowing that it wouldn't have attacked without feeding first.

Reaching in, he extracted a human arm and a section of torso, siphoning what undigested human blood he could from it, then cast it away in disgust, careful not to allow any remnants of the demon's foul blood to intermingle. Then he got up and ran, hearing the sound of wolf calls in the distance.

A team of hunters would be on his ass with the quickness to seek retribution for their fallen comrade. He needed someplace to lie low. If old lairs were compromised and graveyards were impenetrable due to prayer barriers, where could he go? Who was left? Why did all but him burn? If a master went down, the whole line and all its assets didn't torch. *At least that was myth.*

Tears stung his eyes as he kept moving. His master was dead; he had to be. Then what was the point of survival? He'd been an underling for years working for other ruthless masters. Rivera had been the only one to treat him with respect and dignity.

Yonnie stopped abruptly when he found himself in front of Carlos's Beverly Hills lair. The night became his cloak as he pulled it around himself and remained invisible. He closed his eyes, opened his arms, and slowly dropped to his knees. His emotions crashed down on him and he wept. Carlos was missing. Stack and the squad were gone. Their assets had disintegrated. He had been reduced to a carrion feeder.

"Where you at, man?" Yonnie asked the night. "If you go down, we all go down!" His voice hitched on a bitter sob. In a short time, he'd come to love Carlos like a true blood brother. No matter what had happened, who had won, he knew he'd follow Carlos into the very sun.

"Whoever did you, I will smoke," he promised the night. "Whoever stole from you, I will rob. We go to war, man. For you."

Silence answered Yonnie, the stars above teasing him with their glittering faces. It wasn't fair. Rivera had had it all. Yonnie stared at the abandoned lair, despair filling him as he yelled his master's name. *"Carlos!"*

Carlos watched Marlene go to Damali's side as soon as the captain had turned the seat belt sign off. The older woman moved with a slow grace, her steps measured, her expression grave. Damali turned her head away, and Marlene stooped beside her, taking Damali's hand gently within her own.

"Why don't you come to the ladies' room and let me help sponge you off?" Marlene's voice was low, gentle, but also contained a plea, when Damali shook her head no.

"I have fresh clothes for you." Marlene's eyes met Carlos's for a moment and then she turned back to Damali. "You don't want that all over the seats."

Neither woman needed to say it. They both knew speaking of the miscarriage was off-limits right now.

Carlos watched Damali nod and close her eyes. For the first time since the surreal had begun to unfold, he saw it—her condition, her team's condition. The awareness and memory of her pregnancy slammed into his brain. She'd survived the unthinkable. Tears of heartbreak stung his eyes and nose, but he refused to let them fall. The chairman would pay. Carlos tightened his fists and stared out the window for a moment. This *was not* over. The sight of Damali's blood-caked, tattered dress stole his breath and shredded his soul.

He turned in his seat and moved a lock off her damp brow. "I'll be all right. Go with Marlene," Carlos said quietly, ashamed that he'd been bugging so hard that the obvious had never occurred to him. Each member of the Guardian squad was dirty, bloodied, gashed, and seemed to be hanging on to fatigue like it were a life jacket. But Damali's condition made him want to weep. He kept his eyes on her grime-smudged face and allowed his gaze to travel down her disheveled clothing, stop at her blood-streaked thighs, and he was forced to look away.

He watched tears well in her eyes as she stood with effort. His abdomen clenched, and somewhere within the recesses of his mind he knew that her body was riddled with a pain he could only imagine. It was a pain that no man could know. The dark side had clawed life from her womb, and her uterus was contracting, purging the life it had once held . . . his baby girl was bleeding, horrible cramps making her steps unsteady while she held her head high and passed her Guardian team. Each male lowered his eyes and let out a slow, quiet breath, almost as though he could feel the sharp contraction stabs as Damali and Marlene made their way down the narrow aisle to the bathroom.

Shabazz, Lopez, and Dan, the tactical sensors in the group, were nearly ashen in complexion as Damali approached them. Rider and Jose had practically stopped breathing, the scent of blood now too much for the team's noses to absorb within the tight confines of the plane. J.L. broke down and silently wept; Big Mike allowed quiet tears to stream down his huge face and simply leaned back against the seat with his eyes closed. Monk Lin and Imam Asula were hunched forward in a silent, but urgent, prayer.

A new level of respect and awe entered Carlos as he watched how Damali bore the burden like a true warrior, only a grimace giving any indication of how badly she hurt. And he also knew that the pain went beyond the physical. It was a deep gash within her psyche that might never heal. It wasn't supposed to go down like this.

He could barely stare behind her as Marlene escorted her down the narrow aisle past her team. They had murdered his baby and cut out his woman's heart in the process. Yeah, it was all coming back to him—very clearly. There wasn't a place on the planet the chairman would be able to hide, and council chambers weren't far enough under the earth to protect that old SOB.

Steadier now, Carlos breathed in slowly and let his breath out with concerted effort. Father Pat was now at his side, and Carlos almost retched when he looked at the pool of blood Damali had left in the leather seat. He could feel the team watching the elderly cleric as Father Patrick murmured a prayer and used paper towels, holy water, and an airsickness bag to clean off the place where Damali had been sitting. With reverence, the old man folded away the debris and dried the seat, constantly murmuring prayers, then sealed the top of the plastic bag with holy water.

Defeat claimed Carlos as Father Patrick walked to the trash chute, stopping at each bloody footprint Damali had left in the carpet to strike holy water in the sign of the crucifix upon them, and then made the sign of the cross over the small plastic bag he disposed of before he returned to slide into a seat beside Carlos. But Carlos didn't look at him. He couldn't. The remains of the dark side's damage had been reduced to gore and had been deposited in the jet's trash bin.

"I don't have the blood hunger," Carlos said quietly. "I thought I was supposed to go into the Light, to some kinda place of peace—at least that's the hype you gave me when I made my deal with you guys. You reneged."

From the corner of his eye, he watched Father Patrick lean forward and stare at him. Their eyes met.

"No, I didn't renege, Carlos," the old man said. "I don't know what's going on, either. This is beyond all our comprehension. We all saw you go to ash in broad daylight and then regenerate under that same sun. And, yet, now you don't bear fangs. We don't know what that means."

Carlos nodded, no longer angry at the cleric, just weary. "I can't smell, I can't taste, I can barely see. I can hardly walk. Surely *that's* going to change when the sun drops."

Father Patrick nodded. "Have you ever considered that you *can* see, can smell, can taste and hear—just not with a vampire's acuteness? Maybe you're just . . . human."

Carlos stared at Father Patrick in horror. He kept his tone low and controlled, fury nearly stealing the words forming in his mind. "Have *you* considered how fucking insane it is for me to be a Joe regular now with everything that's about to jump off? There's gonna be hell to pay for the bullshit that was done to Damali alone!" He held the cleric's gaze, a fragile part of him dangerously near the breaking point. "No, Father Patrick. If that's why I'm like this, then there was no *point* in bringing me back—'cause I'm only gonna live a very short time. You *know* I'm going after that bastard, right? Human, daywalker in rehab, whatever it is they brought back, I have one mission. To take the chairman's fucking head."

The elderly cleric's eyes burned with a quiet rage that matched Carlos's. But he kept his voice low, his expression tight, as he spoke. "No, Carlos. *You* need to get very clear, son. If *they* brought you back," he said pointing upward, "then there is a higher purpose for you. Even what had been your kind can't bring back the already extinguished. The Light has interceded through the hand of Christ, who only did that once, to my knowledge, and his name was Lazarus. You think about *that* and focus on *that* while Marlene is helping Damali. You work for *Him,* now—just like I do. Our teams have been through enough. Damali has been through enough. You need to think about what that young woman, our Neteru, just experienced and is going through, instead of your own rage and need for revenge just so you can satisfy your own ego."

Father Patrick glanced over his shoulder at the dozing team. "I'm sick to death with all of this, too, Carlos. You have no idea how traumatized we all are."

When Carlos didn't respond, Father Patrick looked back at Carlos. "My advice is that you give a quiet prayer of thanks for being returned to her, in whatever condition. Say a resounding *thank you* for being delivered from a torture chamber in Hell, and count your blessings instead of your losses." He nodded toward Jose and Father Lopez. "Be thankful that the ones left in your line were moved by instinct. That through their faith and choice to follow the Light, they gathered your ashes and prayed on your behalf—as we all did. That the Neteru cried out to Heaven for your redemption and return. That the angels heard her cries and that she gave up *much* for your salvation. And that now we are being transported to safety under the protection of the Vatican! Therefore, we follow the orders that come down from On High to the letter, from this point forward. We wait until we get a sign from On High before we act. Deviate, and I'll kill you myself."

With that, Father Patrick stood up, his tattered blue robes swishing about him as he walked back to his seat, sat down, and closed his eyes.

CHAPTER THREE

THE SIMULTANEOUS loss of five masters had devastated his empire. Three councilmen had been exterminated, leaving only him and two weakened councilmen at his side. Topside, second-level vampires had returned to feudal law, and were-demons were making violent inroads into all territories, which would radically reduce food supplies and block transports to chambers.

For a while, awaiting the inevitable inquiry, the remaining members of the Vampire Council had spoken in nervous whispers and intermittent hisses as they continued to discuss the empire's vulnerabilities, but soon, even their essence would begin to expire.

It had already started. Just like that. Instant evaporation of what had been. The Light was dredging them; he could feel it as day set the planet above on fire. The chairman drew from the reserves of night, wrapping it around his embattled chambers like a dark, woolen cloak to protect his dying loyalists. Somewhere on earth, it was always night, making it perpetual. But silence had replaced his remaining councilmen's hoarse, starving murmurs. Blood was slowing in their veins, making it a thick and putrid slurry that robbed their vitality. He could painfully feel the stringy clots congeal within his cold body as though gelatin set to mold.

Yes, it was inevitable. Soon, without food, they would have to ration, reduce themselves to ashen stasis and suffer, where they'd all be forced to lie prone, crumbled to near dust, waiting on the table to quicken again with resources—fresh blood. In just one night, their outer vaults had been pillaged and burned by the weres. Council chambers now were filled with dark, charcoal-hued smoke as each elderly vampire slowly wasted away.

The chairman sat quietly, plotting. To risk surfacing topside to make more masters was too risky right now. He summoned patience. Second-generations from all the regions were unstable, and three attempts to telepathically elevate second-generation lieutenants had been disastrous. They'd torched on impact. The Light had intervened. Even those he'd sent a transport cloud for had perished in the care of weak couriers that were vulnerable to upper-level demon incursion. His summons in order to elevate the weaker generations to master status in chambers had failed. And yet Yonnie remained. Why?

It made his black heart burn that even destroyed, Carlos Rivera had left behind a master who was not beholden to the empire. Carlos had made Yonnie with good intent. A council-level vampire's turn bite had been used for *the Light*? To help a man, to save him from sure extinction, to give him *his due*? Compassion and empathy were in the bite, not greed or power-lust? Horrified, the chairman sat numbly looking off into the vast caverns. Never in all his thousands of years of rule . . . never was there a provision in the black tome that sat beneath his crest for such sacrilege against the empire! Empathy in a bite? Never.

His councilmen glanced at him and then shut their eyes. They also had come to the same conclusion. No wonder their resources had slowed to a mere trickle. Even dead, Carlos had bested them. The Neteru was a poisonous variable and no less formidable. Maybe even more so, because it was the Light in her that had ruined a good vampire. Yes, he'd submitted Carlos Rivera to the sun, had clawed out his woman's insides and broken her spirit. He wondered if she'd died. That was a hopeful thought.

He kicked at a withered, expired bat that had dropped at his feet. The once screeching, swirling, gorgeous mass of red-eyed creatures had barely enough energy to cling to the rafters. The chairman glanced at his fellow councilmen in despair. Their onyx robes were beginning to show signs of age, the hems becoming tattered, and their crests had begun to collect particles of dust. It was wise to sleep and save their energy as much as possible during this fallow time in the empire. Yet he hated that their breaths were now foul, their skins decaying, cracking, and peeling, festering with gangrene.

Substantially weakened by the civil war, the Neteru's successful attacks with Carlos Rivera against their empire, and the subsequent investigation into their failures by the level seven, forced them each to remain very still upon their marble thrones. The inquisition into their failures had been so vicious that it had barely left them enough energy to merely think, let alone move. Speaking was a waste of energy, unless absolutely necessary. Breathing had to be done in slow, measured sips of air, inhaled with great effort.

The chairman kept his expression unreadable as he and the others sat with their eyes closed. A thin veneer of calm masked his smoldering rage. There had been blood famines before. He and his kind would rise again.

The chairman made a tent in front of his mouth with his fingers and drew a ragged breath to steady himself. He peered down at the table, exhausted. His fellow councilmen were so frightened and weary that telepathy was impossible. Their minds were guarded, each sure that he would siphon them for their last reserves of strength. He briefly closed his eyes. It had come to this. Cannibalism in chambers. He never thought he'd witness that during his reign. To put their fears to rest, one last debate before stasis was in order. Council had to remain united; no assassinations at the table to further dredge the empire of power. "We must act, now."

"Rivera had been groomed for greatness," the councilman to his left said. "That loss is not replaceable in such a short time."

The chairman nodded very slowly. "But it also gives me great pleasure to know that infidel, Rivera, burned layer by layer in the sun." He let his breath out slowly, the memory of Carlos Rivera's duplicity still haunting him.

"The Neteru vessel has become beyond problematic," the councilman to the chairman's right said. "Do not underestimate this millennium Neteru's effectiveness, despite her youth. That has, to date, been our weakness."

"We may have to detain her in Hell for the next six years until she ripens again, then fill the territories after her abduction." The chairman drew a shaky breath. "The were-demons, Amanthras, and all the upper levels are slowly coming to realize that the hour of dawn is upon our empire. They do not respect nor fear us as they should."

"To take her hostage would be risky," the councilman to his right said cautiously. "With our forces weakened, warrior angels may come for her. I wouldn't put it past them to breach our borders and with the Armageddon so near . . ."

"Yes," the councilman to his left said quickly. "I say that we cannot afford another harpies inquisition. The response after losing three council thrones, plus our most formidable topside sources, have drawn horrendous questions about our level-six leadership capacity, to the point where—"

"I do *not* need to be reminded of our position," the chairman spat, rubbing his hands down his face with frustration. "We can torture Damali Richards's spirit to keep her from exacting a heavy toll on our remaining empire. Seal her body in disease, keep her womb inviolate, and make her a—"

Both councilmen shook their heads, stopping the chairman midsentence. The bolder of the two took up the argument, however his voice was frail with fear and the need to feed.

"We all know that to ensure that the Neteru conceives, she must willingly accept our seed. But if her spirit is damaged and her body is—"

"Enough!" the chairman shouted, his façade of calm shattering as he expended precious energy. "If we cannot find a seducer, she is of no use to us and I want her heart in the middle of my council table! I want her to writhe in agony as the harpies did to us in these very chambers! The fucking harpies were wrong!"

The two councilmen drew back from the table, setting their thickening goblets of blood down carefully. The chairman stood, eased away from the table, and held on to the back of his throne, knowing he'd spoken too loudly and without enough reverence when he mentioned the harpies.

Immediately, the floor just inside council chambers quaked, the marble cracking and yawning a huge fissure that shook the walls, made the few torches that were lit extinguish, rumbled furniture out of place, and made the weakened transport bats clinging to crags in the high ceiling above the pentagram table try to fly and seek cover.

The chairman held his breath as yellow sulfur smoke billowed up in a furious volcanic hiss. He waited with dread, knowing the foul little gargoylelike creatures would soon slither over the edge of the gaping cavern. He knew in seconds their vile black tongues would lacerate him and the two remaining councilmen, siphoning information from their skulls, through their ears, noses, and every orifice on their battered bodies, just as they'd done for nearly four relentless hours well into dawn and beyond it, refusing to allow them to regenerate.

The councilman to the left of him clutched the edge of the table, bracing for the small gray-green bodies to fill chambers, rushing in like a putrid wave, leathery wings flapping, spiked tails slashing everything in their wake, their razor-sharp black horns a torment to the frayed hems of their once-majestic vampire robes. His eyes filled with tears. The more junior councilman who always sat to the chairman's right put his head down on the table and wept as his bowels voided. The chairman set his jaw hard, preparing for the onslaught. Never, except once, in his entire existence had he ever experienced such personal and professional humiliation—and right after the Paradise fiasco, it had not been before subordinates like this.

However, he knew he had to be hallucinating as he trained his unblinking gaze on the pit that had opened in his chamber floors. Instead of harpies rising in a swarm from it, a familiar face did.

She was gorgeous, just as she'd always been. Her smooth, olive-toned complexion looked like refined glass. Her dark, smoky eyes were mysterious and seductive, set above perfectly chiseled cheekbones. Her presence was mesmerizing, her mouth lush, begging one to taste it. Her shoulder-length wavy black hair seemed to be spun from velvet. Her body was that of a goddess. She was sheathed in an iridescent black gown, the neckline a deep plunge to reveal her ample breasts, the slit up the side showing her shapely legs as she sauntered forward. She smiled, giving them a discreet quarter inch of fang.

"Mr. Chairman," she crooned, "it has been a long time. But you should measure your words if you are going to speak so loudly."

"Lilith," he murmured, "I am so glad it was you who came."

"Actually, I haven't yet this morning, but if you can bring yourself to clear chambers . . ." she said in a sultry voice, her eyes now glowing red as she motioned to the other councilmen.

Without waiting for the chairman to tell them to leave, the two high-ranking officials stood, nodded at her with appreciation, and then vanished to the private inner chamber vaults. Their need to regenerate, and eagerness to get away from any potentially bad outcome at the table, left a residue of fear in the room.

"Mr. Chairman," she said, coming to the table as he slowly rounded it to meet her.

"*Dante,*" he said, his voice dropping seductively to match hers. "There have never been any formalities between us."

He turned and filled his goblet for her, then transformed into a more youthful version of himself, and handed her the offering of blood. She was worth the energy drain, even if his two councilmen starved later for it.

She accepted the goblet he'd offered with grace, yet sniffed it with disdain, and set it down on the edge of the table. Her hand went to his long, dark brown, curly hair, and she traced his bronzed cheek, then allowed her soft caress to slide down his strong, bare shoulders and down his hard chest. She glimpsed the swath of white linen that hung low on his narrow hips.

"Dante, you know I always liked your rendition of the Sistine Chapel lovers . . . it's so sacrilegious. But, what has happened to your resources, darling? This isn't you at all. Frankly, I'm shocked."

Embarrassed, he clasped her hand and kissed the center of her palm, offering an apology. "Had I known you were coming, I would have sent for a body, topside," he said with false bravado, and held her gaze, searching it for an alliance. "Our resources have been extremely strained lately, but that will soon be rectified."

"That's why I'm here to help."

She walked away from him and looked at his three thrones left vacant by extinguished councilmen. "May I?" she asked, gracefully waving at them.

He nodded, his gaze raking her. "You can sit in mine, if you'd like."

She smiled. "No, darling. Business first, pleasure later, especially given the mounting tensions in level seven."

He nodded and found his seat opposite hers across the table. "How bad is it down there?"

"My dear, it's never good if they send me up after the harpies. You know I'm normally the final step before permanent detainment."

The chairman rubbed his hand across his jaw and then took an unsteady sip from another councilman's goblet. He forced a laugh after he'd swallowed hard. "Well, at least it's good to see that my father still observes the old protocols—giving a man one last indulgent sin before his reign is over." He set the goblet down, trying to keep his hand from trembling.

"My, my, my . . ." she said, making a little tsking sound with her tongue as she leaned back in the throne and released a long sigh. "It must be horrible, because you're not even picking up on what I said." She smiled broadly and opened her eyes, mischief glittering in them. "I said *normally*, lover."

"Speak to me, Lilith," the chairman whispered hoarsely. "In all candor, I am taxed beyond my endurance for mind games."

She sat forward and folded her hands on the table, leaning on her forearms. "*You* can't play mind games? How . . . impotent of you." She sat back quickly. "Do you want to get us *both* exterminated?"

He held up his palm. "I'm sorry, but you can see how—"

"Listen to me," she said fast, cutting him off. "They've sent me to exterminate the Neteru, and I cannot fail, if she is still alive. The problem is, I cannot find her. Your father is truly displeased. Were it not for the coming Armageddon and his preoccupation with the creation of his new son, he would have come up himself. This is really bad, darling."

The chairman stood and put his hands behind his back, and walked a path behind his throne. "He would destroy our daywalker vessel, if she lives? Would eliminate our opportunity, which is only a mere six years away, cut off his nose to spite his face and banish my empire to complete darkness for another thousand years—simply because a few thrones were lost? Is he mad?"

She chuckled when he stopped and looked at her hard. "Absolutely out of his mind. But insanity has no bearing on genius; we both know that. You and I also both know that he has cut off his nose to spite his face when he's gotten into a real rage. But, alas, it does regenerate once he's calmed himself." She shook her head. "You've considered killing the Neteru yourself." She wagged her finger at him. "Did you already destroy her? Is our conversation moot?"

"I've only considered it. I have not acted upon the impulse."

"Good." Lilith reached for the goblet that she'd refused earlier, leaned back, and took a small sip. She wrinkled her nose with disgust, and ran her index finger around the rim of the goblet of clotted blood, then looked up. She gave him a sexy grin. "Even he won't go that far. I was just testing you. He needs daywalkers to assist in the final war. But he does want me to kill the male Neteru that they may have made. 'May' being the operative word." She sighed. "You also may not have six years to deliver, since we never know when my husband might want to begin the Armageddon."

The chairman paused and then slowly found the edge of the table to lean against. "There is no male Neteru. Only that infernal female one."

"Have you been so consumed by your own problems that you have not been watching the stars? Didn't Mars, the planet of war and male energy, recently pass the earth the closest it's come in sixty thousand years?" She took a healthy swallow from the goblet, then set it back down on the table hard and leaned back deeply into the throne.

"Yes, but with the female Neteru topside, our forces in tatters . . . I assumed that the forecasted war was the one waged against us already."

"There's a little ditty; to *assume* makes an ass out of you and me." She inhaled sharply, closed her eyes, and shuddered. "He's not at his apex yet, and I will most assuredly have to kill him before he does. The absolutely brilliant cunning this one possesses will compromise my judgment, if I don't get to him before he hits his prime. He's magnificent."

She opened her eyes slowly, her breaths coming in irregular spurts of raw desire. "Oh, Dante, how did you let him get away? I can see why the female Neteru completely lost it and got herself compromised for a bit. He would have been *so* perfect for the job of impregnating her. I'm definitely going to have to fuck this one before I take his head off . . . I'll do it with tears of regret in my eyes, however, trust me."

"Who the *Hell* are you talking about?" The chairman's voice thundered and bats began dropping from the rafters. "There's no topside element like that in my realms! There's not even any topside master vampires left—"

"He had a throne in your chambers, you foolish bastard!" She stood quickly, her black gown swishing as she approached the table and slapped the chairman's face so hard his nose bled. She pointed her finger at the throne she'd just abandoned, her fangs growing two inches as she railed. "Carlos Rivera was one of your masters! He was even a councilman, damn you! He was a dark Guardian, and you had him in your grasp, and you idiot, you allowed his soul to get snatched and dragged into Purgatory! Your own fucking councilmen tried to warn you, but you were blinded by ego, and if I dare blaspheme this chamber, by some misguided, twisted compassion—"

He grabbed her by both arms, halting her words, and pushed her away so hard her backside slammed against the table. "Bullshit! I did a thorough harpies inquisition on him, dredged his mind right over there on my walls," he shouted, pointing where Carlos had been tortured. "He was chained to the rocks, and demons impervious to light ate his innards until the sun came up!" The chairman came close to her in a flash, almost nose to nose as he yelled. "He burned with the sun for his betrayal. He was a dark Guardian, yes, but not a Neteru!"

Trying to wrest his dignity back from the outburst, the chairman took a deep breath. "Lilith, you tell my father that on this one, he's wrong."

She shook her head and laughed. "Oooohhhh, noooo. I *never* tell your father he's wrong." Her gaze narrowed and her voice lost its amused tone. "Especially when he's *right.*"

"Then how?" Unnerved, the chairman folded his arms over his chest.

"He went into the Light and came back," she said, studying her long, manicured red nails. "It's a hunch, but the Guardian team and the Covenant are rebuilding, adding more players to the game. Their behavior is peculiar. I haven't located him yet, but I can feel him somewhere very near. He's still—"

"No! Impossible!" The chairman raked his fingers through his hair and ripped his scalp.

"Love will do it every time." She smiled, but it was an evil one, as she looked up and held his stunned gaze. "The female wept for him. The angels heard that pitiful shit and responded. All they needed was a catalyst. He burned, Dante, reaching for her and calling her name—not begging for the pain to stop . . . not even calling The One who will remain nameless down here. He had diluted vampire lieutenants in his ranks. Some eighth- or ninth-generation near-imposter vampires that went down the side of a fucking mountain and collected a handful of his death ashes and gave them to her! He had two of them helping to collect his remains; in fact, and one was a cleric. They brought Rivera's ashes up to her and she wept into them, creating a trinity. She cast Rivera's ashes on fertile soil, took off a diamond ring that had a ten-carat stone in the shape of a heart . . . an engagement ring of betrothal for the *hoped-for* blessed union of holy matrimony one day—but prior to that, she was a *councilman's wife.* Any of this frightening you, yet?"

Lilith sucked in a deep breath to keep from spontaneously combusting with rage. "And this ring—which you did not take back when you stripped his powers, because you were thinking like a man, not like a woman, because you lost focus . . . you wanted her to twist . . . didn't realize the strength of a woman's tears, so you let her keep the ring. It was a fucking crystal amulet, an ice-blue crystalline section of his actual heart that had all his hope and love for her in it when he gave it to her, you stupid sonofabitch! Normal quartz crystal is powerful enough, but a ten-carat diamond rock made from our DNA, are you insane?"

She folded her arms over her chest. "But you wanted her to keep it, because you thought you were getting even by letting her have something hurtful to remember him by. So, you left her a treasure that she could wrap warm memories around from her soul, something supercharged when he took her to the vanishing point." Lilith shook her head with disgust.

"He took *a Neteru* to the *vanishing point* with a diamond on her hand, and didn't permanently turn her . . . a master vampire?" The chairman covered his face and breathed slowly.

"Well, she remembered him all right," Lilith said, ignoring his question. "Yes . . . she remembered down to her pure soul, crying all the way to his ash pile. Then she plunged the Isis blade into the earth to bury her dreams, and made it bleed. Our harpies saw it all and reported the whole sordid incident to me, not you. She got him right in the heart in spirit, and he was escorted back into matter form by a *battalion of angels*. This is what is rumored and suspected, because none of us can see that deeply into such bright light. But my job now is to substantiate the facts and tie up any potential loose ends."

She paused and looked at the chairman hard, her gaze narrowed to a withering slit. "That's why you, in your level-six stupidity couldn't see him when he came back. Only the most advanced realm got word of it, level seven, and even we just got that late-breaking information . . . since the male Neteru's vibrations are lowered. He's stopped behaving like a monk. He likes the things of our realm, grieves the loss of power. But when he first came back," she shook her head and whistled, "he was squeaky clean. Was off dark radar and we had no trace. If she's been trying to corrupt him and make him remember their union, to no avail, what chance do you think we have? Normal forces of darkness won't work, because this Neteru male has been to Hell and back, and knows we are real—not illusion. If he hadn't begun craving the things of the world again, we might have been blindsided, and the seventh-realm empire may have taken severe casualties. The only reason we suspect Rivera is because of the vibrations this male Neteru is casting. . . . Power-lust, a deep desire for revenge, and a general's strategy. If I find him, his head is mine. Both of them."

When the chairman didn't respond, she leaned into him. "Are you hearing me?" She screeched. "This was all done before a clerical team from the Covenant, plus an entire Neteru Guardian team with a mother-seer present—all of whom were praying for a *master vampire* to get a second chance! *Never,* in my whole existence have I seen such a convoluted case of familial and Eros love mixed together in such a horrifying display of pure human compassion. Oh, so help me, Dante, I'll kill you myself for allowing such an indignity to come from your level!"

When he opened his mouth to speak, she held up her hand, then pressed her wrist to her forehead and waltzed away seeming near faint. Males were so easy to manipulate. Her strategy was foolproof. Have father and son go to war against each other, while the embryo that slipped so beautifully into Hell was lodged safely within her womb, ticking away like a time bomb.

All she needed was one hit of *Oblivion,* the raw essence of Neteru passion and love to ignite dark life within her. Rivera's brilliant drug had practically felled an empire. Too bad he'd used the last of the substance for folly. But the drug was what could make her dead womb spill forth life again. Damn the angels that had slaughtered her children and rendered her barren. They would pay. This grudge was between her and them, and even the Devil couldn't stop her. He never cared about his children anyway. Just another deadbeat dad. Now, the key was to bait Dante into helping her locate Rivera, if he was still alive. If she could find Rivera, then she would find *Oblivion.*

She glimpsed the chairman and fanned her face as if she was still too overwhelmed to talk. Yes, Dante was still strong enough to locate his own turn, if Rivera existed. Knowing that was critical. Her impromptu visit confirmed it when he'd transformed and was still able to cast illusion. Very good. The fact that he was rattled and his mental barriers were down was even better. It made him sloppy. A coup was so titillating.

The essence of one male and one female Neteru's union was all she needed. The Light's greatest strength would be its greatest weakness. This hadn't been done since Eve had carried Cain and Able, one demon embryo and one pure human one. Dante's fixation on revenge had eclipsed the opportunity from his mind. Stupid bastard. Her husband was also just as insane to believe that she would allow him to choose a human vessel to carry the heir apparent, the Anti-Christ, just to make a point that he could still pollute what those above had created, even at the final hour.

No. Not on her watch. Not after all she'd given her husband, the years of suffering in his lair and devotion to his cause, only to have it all snatched away from her. Never. By the time father and son figured it out, *her* heir would be born. In Lucifer's fury, Dante's realm would be decimated, and her biggest competitor along with it—the chairman himself. By the time her husband came to his senses, she would possess the critical link to his war . . . correction, *her war*—and when she won it, *she* would rule level seven—not the beast embroiled in useless politics.

Lilith finally sighed and peered at the chairman as though near tears. She almost laughed at his stricken expression and the way he'd held his breath, waiting on her to continue as she allowed her voice to tremble then slowly escalate for dramatic effect. "Oh, yes, your father is spitting crucifixion nails over this one. There hasn't been a young, fertile, male and female Neteru combination levied against us in the same era since Adam and Eve!"

"What can I do to fix this?" he whispered. "I swear, Lilith, I never meant to—"

"Silence, so I can think!" she yelled, pacing up to stand close in his face. "Do you know what your father has done?" she asked in a quieter, more lethal tone.

He shook his head no and foolishly reached to touch her cheek.

She slapped his hand away, enraged. "Do that again without my permission and you'll draw back a nub that won't regenerate." She placed her hand over her heart. "Your father," she said, her voice calm, quiet, the words seething from her lips slowly, "has called for an open-level bounty hunt. Whichever level wins becomes his favorite. That is why your blood resources dried up so quickly. Haven't you wondered why your inventory evaporated, was pillaged so easily, why vampires have been turning to ash in record numbers overnight? You should have been able to live for *years* down in chambers without replenishment."

"We couldn't understand—"

"He's really pissed off and willing to let the other levels try to correct what you've botched, and they all know it. Vampires are under siege across the board. The were-demons have sent their ruling Senate up to go after your weaker generations, casually wiping them out while they hunt for the male Neteru. *Your father sanctioned it all.*"

"He didn't." The chairman leaned against the table to keep his knees from buckling.

"He did."

They both stared at each other.

"I'm the chosen assassin to represent the vampire nations, sent to find this new male nemesis to our way of life. He doesn't trust you to handle it, especially since you couldn't handle the female one."

The chairman pushed away from the table and began to pace, thoroughly humiliated. "I could have handled it."

"He wasn't leaving any more to chance. You didn't even have enough power to get past the chest brand the female put on Rivera to rip his heart out. Dante, that's pitiful." She sighed as he glared at her. She swallowed away an evil smile, and allowed his ego to eat him alive, further strangling his objectivity in the process. "Your father is giving the were-realm a shot at killing him. Not the big cats, even though they are stronger. He's opted for the wolfen clans. Rivera is connected to North America, which is the werewolves' primary territory, as is Europe."

She walked back to the table and hopped up on it. Dark blood soaked into her dress and she doodled in it with her finger. "The Amanthras can only send up one of their best serpents. They missed the opportunity with Nuit to make daywalkers and they've been duly chastised, but you know your father has a weakness for the serpents."

"What about the upper levels, the poltergeists and—"

"Yeah, yeah, yeah. They each can send up an assassin. Only one, though, because they are usually so ineffective. But the ghost gangs won the bid to participate by agreeing to partner to send up a single succubus and incubus. The concept intrigued your father."

"A succubus *and* incubus?"

"Don't underestimate them. A good succubus can drive a man to his death, if she knows what she's doing. We want him dead. We aren't picky about methodology."

She stared beyond him at nothing for a moment. "The Guardian team and the Covenant have been traveling without either a male or female Neteru presence in their midst. However, we think one of the teams will lead us to them. We need them as bait for the moment. After that, they're expendable."

He looked at her hard, a slow smile crossing his lips. "Lilith, I have known your wicked ways for a long time. What's the *real* bounty . . . because if I'd offended you that badly, you wouldn't be disclosing all of this to me."

"I don't want to lose," she said in a falsely demure tone. "What else would there be, darling? I obviously cannot rule level seven—your father does not share power, and while I adore level six, he has forbidden me to reside here, as you and I well know. The other levels are interesting and I can rule all of them, which I have a fair shot of doing—if I win this little joust. So, I've made my peace with the available options."

"What's the real bounty, Lilith?" he asked again, casually coming up to her to trace her cheek. "We're too old for games."

"Winner takes all," she said, lapsing into their native mind-bending tongue of negotiation. "Why don't you trust me?"

"And my cut if I assist you in besting all your opponents?" He'd breathed the question against her throat in *Dananu,* and let his hands trail down her arms.

"Wouldn't the satisfaction of killing Rivera be enough?"

He chuckled and kissed her neck. "Not hardly."

She leaned back and scooted away from him so that she sat on the table's center crest, then made her dress vanish. She chuckled as she opened her thighs and allowed her wetness to ooze down over the symbol of his realm's power. "Why are you determined to haggle with me tonight?"

"Impressive, but not worth half the world." He laughed with her.

"Touché. I'm getting old and must be losing my skills."

"I miss sparring with you, Lilith. You haven't lost any of your skills," he said with honest appreciation as his gaze swept her curvaceous body and settled between her legs. "And I haven't lost any of mine."

She smiled a crooked smile and let her head fall back. "Half the world? You drive a hard bargain."

"Half the world," he said, dematerializing the white linen cloth around his waist. "And I want the female Neteru delivered to me with her mind bent and willing. I have a little gift for her."

He climbed up on the table and crouching above her on all fours as he kissed the gully between her breasts, his breath warm against her cool skin. He suckled one of her nipples and looked up at her with a wry smile. "Do we have a deal?"

She shuddered. "What is this gift you have for the Neteru?"

He chuckled and shook his head no, evading her bite. "My father is old and obsessed with power. He doesn't do this to you very often, does he?"

"You know I've always had a weakness for vampires," she breathed, arching up to him, and allowing her question to fade away for the time being. They both knew she'd revisit it later, but enjoyed the game of pretending she wouldn't. "Topside has been pathetic this generation . . . I've been meaning to visit council for a while . . . but I've been so preoccupied."

"All you had to do was call me."

"You know how he gets when I come to see you. It's ridiculous, but you're the only one he gets really jealous of. You're evading my question."

"Does he know you're here now?"

"No, you know, as they say, the Devil is always busy."

"Do we have a deal?"

"Seal it over the crest," she whispered, nearly panting with anticipation, and then slapped him hard. "And act like you mean it. It's been decades." Her eyes went to near slits as she arched again, waiting.

He smiled, touched his cheek where she'd opened a gash in his face, and came away with black blood. Bringing each digit to his lips, his hand trembled as he sucked them one by one while the gash slowly sealed and disappeared. Suddenly he slammed her wrists down hard over her head, bloodying his fists in the oozing marble table as he brutally entered her. Then he dropped ten inches of fangs and ripped out her throat.

He missed the look of cunning in her eyes.

CHAPTER FOUR

DAMALI WALKED silently before her mother-seer, swaying from the mild turbulence of the plane. She could deal with this. What choice did she have? Millions of women had known this heartbreak, and theirs was probably worse than hers. She'd only been pregnant for twenty-four hours.

That's what she told herself as she clutched her abdomen and kept moving forward. It wasn't like she had felt life move within her. Nor did she have to face the horror of disease or senseless tragedy taking her child.

But she'd been robbed, nonetheless. The sense of loss was profound. She tried to shove it to the back of her mind; she just couldn't. Her hopes for a child with Carlos had been torn away. She'd been violated—*they* had been violated.

It was a damned vampire! Mild hysteria overtook her for a moment and made Marlene put a hand on her shoulder.

"I'm all right," she told Marlene as she straightened her back. "Just laughing at my own insanity." Now she knew how Carlos felt. Laughing to keep from crying. Losing his mind slowly right before her very eyes. The psyche was a fragile thing. Get to a body and you could bend a mind. Get to a mind, and you could co-opt a body. Damage a spirit, and you could take it all.

Yeah. She had work to do, the timing had been bad, and the whole situation was messed up. That's what she had to remember. Now she'd have to allow frightened men, doctors, to invade her body, and perform the barbaric act of a D&C. She wondered, if men could conceive and miscarried, would medicine have advanced beyond the scraping out of their wombs? Probably.

The murky thought made her weary. But the strained expressions on everyone's faces really wore her out. It was time for a change. She'd been a lightning rod, bringing all sorts of calamity their way. She needed space, not the group-home living arrangement. Once they got back home, she was moving out. They needed peace; she needed peace. There was nothing left to fear now. Her aging team didn't need to be put in harm's way, and she wasn't afraid of the dark.

But even a bad ass needed a mom at a time like this. God bless Marlene. Damali briefly shut her eyes as they entered the tight confines of the bathroom. Marlene hadn't said a word as she lowered the toilet lid and climbed up to stand on it, motioning for Damali to step into a small plastic food container from the jet's kitchen that had been placed on the floor.

She needed to cry so badly, but no tears would come. She was all cried out. Determination filled her. A crippling contraction almost doubled her over. She would slaughter the chairman first.

Her mother-seer filled the sink with warm water, making suds from the liquid hand soap on the wall. She placed paper towels and a new kitchen sponge on the sink. Damali carefully laid the Isis dagger on the edge of the sink as well and removed her blood-soaked clothes. Marlene took each piece from her before it hit the floor. Each woman worked silently in unison with complete comprehension.

Then as gently as though she'd just been born, Marlene dabbed cleansing water on Damali's face, her throat, her hands, and her arms, intermittently breaking the silence with a soft murmur as she rinsed off her back. The older woman's voice was a soothing balm, reinforcing with gentle whispers that this too would pass . . . the Father had a plan. Damali desperately needed those words, just as she needed Marlene's gentle ministrations and the light cluck of her mother-seer's tongue while older female hands passed a nasty war gash, wiped away demon gook and splattered innards, battle residue, and took away the ache from the surface of her skin.

"The next plane has a bigger bathroom. I'll wash your hair once we're on board, baby," Marlene reassured her. She paused then said into the silence, "It's gonna be all right. If this happened, then something was wrong with what you carried, and this was the most merciful outcome. If it were normal, the Light would not have allowed it to be taken."

Damali stared at Marlene for a moment. "I know," she finally said. "Make sure you burn everything when you're done."

"Don't worry. We've taken further precautions than mere fire. We've prayed over every drop. The darkness will not reclaim it, or be able to resurrect it."

Damali simply closed her eyes again as Marlene refilled the sink with fresh water, patted her with the sponge, cleaning that only someone who has given birth to one should. Yes, God bless Marlene for serving as midwife to a miscarriage. It wasn't supposed to go down like this. What had transpired in Sydney was her miscarriage of justice as much as it was her miscarriage of flesh. With that thought came the first wave of real tears since Carlos had bubbled back to the surface in a new crimson beginning. The Light had been kind; had heard her cries . . . but the trade still seemed so terribly unfair.

Silent tears coursed down Damali's cheeks, and the older woman who knew healing told her to let them fall like rain to wash it all out. It was done. Soon Marlene applied creams to her skin as though that could smooth over memories . . . Marlene kept talc in her bag, but it smelled like what a baby would have, and knowing that made her cry harder, but more privately, as the pure scent became almost too much to bear. She knew Marlene must have seen some of this coming. Marlene was always prepared; her bag was a deep, magical chasm, like a reservoir that contained whatever was necessary to heal the fallen. Now they shared yet another female loss that bound them more tightly, the loss of a child.

And as Marlene worked on her body, and by extension her spirit and mind, she also knew that Marlene's loss of her own child was much more profound than what she was experiencing now. How did a woman cope with losing the flesh of her flesh after nurturing it in her womb, bringing it forth to the Light, suckling it at her breasts, watching it grow? That was so different than it being taken before ever feeling it stir within. But that was intellectual understanding; it was a knowing that didn't completely remove the sense of grief that quaked her with each ebbing contraction.

Damali sucked in a deep breath, allowing newfound respect and understanding to strengthen her. Even with all that she'd been through, her mother-seer had been through so much more and had kept the faith. Damali drew on that strength, watching Marlene's wise eyes. No words were necessary for the telepathic transaction; one woman's mind and eyes said, *Thank you, I'm blessed, despite it all.* The other's said, *Ashe, I love you, dwell on it no more . . . pain is relative. I am your mother, and this hurts me for you more than you can know.* They both nodded.

When Marlene offered her a pair of clean, white cotton panties and a pad, Damali accepted the items as the gifts they were. She kissed Marlene's temple then her hands. "Thank you," Damali said quietly. "Guess you're never too old to need a mom, huh?"

Marlene just stroked her hair as she pulled on the shield.

"I have a dress for you," Marlene said in a quiet tone, offering yet another balm to her senses.

Damali accepted the soft Egyptian linen from Marlene and donned the long sheath with bell sleeves. Marlene dried her legs and feet, dropping a towel for Damali to stand on as she dumped the red water from the food container into the toilet, said a prayer over it, and flushed it away.

"Put on these sandals," Marlene murmured as she handed Damali soft, butter-almond-hued leather, and then fetched a long, white gauze wrap from her bag. Moving methodically, Marlene wrapped Damali's hair in a regal twist of fabric. "Queen daughter," Marlene whispered, "today you wear unbleached white. It is a new day. We are about to go into lands where women wear their hair covered, their arms covered, their legs covered. We will honor the traditions of old in a very old land, where a people have been independent for two thousand years. Rest and I will guard the Isis blades until you need them again."

There was no struggle in Damali's countenance as she allowed Marlene to do what was culturally correct. There was no more fight left in her, and she didn't want to think about why women had to cover the natural gift of their bodies, why men got to do whatever they liked, and why there was so much injustice in the world, much of it aimed at the majority of the species. Women.

Battle weary and near broken, she put on the flowing gown that had replaced her torn, vampiric one, and stared at the bathroom door. She refused to contemplate the depth of her rage and heartbreak. Mending would come later and would take time; that much she'd learned from Marlene's quiet brand of strength. Right now, all she wanted was to get horizontal.

"I have to lie down," Damali admitted in a subdued voice. A slight shiver ran through her. "I feel like I'm going to pass out."

Although her movements were steady, Damali could feel a level of frantic energy just beneath the surface of Marlene's skin as the older woman ushered her from the bathroom and into a seat beside her. She didn't question Marlene's seating choice as Marlene lifted a window shade to put Damali in the sun beside her.

Clasping Damali's hand, Marlene reached around her, fastened a seat belt and reclined the chair for her.

"I'm going to bring you some special tea, an herbal mix from the motherland." Marlene stood and left Damali's side, and returned quickly with a piping hot brew.

"Sip it slowly," Marlene said, stroking her back. "Then, if you can hold that down, water, plenty of it, and then we'll clean you out with fruit."

Damali took the porcelain mug and did as she was told, her gaze never traveling toward Carlos. Her mind could only focus on one problem at a time. The sweet elixir had a hint of ginger in it, but she knew Marlene had more in the concoction than that.

When Yonnie opened his eyes, he was looking down the barrel of a sawed-off shotgun. Exhausted, he gave into his fate. Extinction was eminent, and death by hallowed earth–packed shells was far more merciful than being torn limb from limb by werewolves.

"Just do it," he murmured to the female staring at him, her finger flexing on the trigger.

To his amazement, she lifted the barrel and stepped closer to him, and then offered him her wrist.

"We have an hour till dawn. Feed quickly and then transport us to a place I'll show you. Look in my eyes to see where."

Confusion forced him to stand. True, she had silently rolled up on him as only his kind could, but how did she dare to carry hallowed earth–packed shells? Even more troubling was the thick silver-and-turquoise necklace she wore. No vampire could wear that without it burning a hole into her chest. For a moment, neither moved. Yonnie allowed his gaze to ruthlessly assess the woman who stood before him. She appeared to be in her early forties, her long black hair streaked with strands of silver-gray. Her dark eyes smoldered with the knowledge of his realms. Her body was lithe, curved, yet was sleek with muscle. The body of a soldier.

"You're a fourth-gen," Yonnie said, his gaze going from her throat to her weapon.

"Yes. And we don't have time. Feed," she commanded. "At my level, I do not have the power of transport, but when Councilman Rivera made you a lieutenant in his inner circle, you acquired that power. Take us both to safety and don't be foolish. We're the only ones left in the zone."

"How can that be?" Nervous, Yonnie stepped back. "It could be a trick sent from the new master that—"

"There are no more masters topside," she said with a too-peaceful smile. When he didn't immediately respond, she let out a hard breath of frustration. "Carlos obviously made you a master. Didn't you feel it as he was swept away into the Harpies tornado near dawn? I was the only female he trusted with his SOS beacon. My orders were to find you. Now feed."

Too stunned to move, Yonnie just stared at her. Deep sadness mixed with guilt, respect, pride, and sudden elation flowed through him. His boy, Carlos, must have known he was gonna die and sent this last quiet gift to him so he could continue the line. Tears filled Yonnie's eyes, but in front of this unknown female, he blinked them away. Suddenly he remembered the strange surge that had rippled through him just before everything in his world went to ash. He had thought it had only been a power spike from his master who was kickin' some ass. But Carlos had elevated him before he died. Carlos had loved him like that . . . and even sent the last female in his territory to *him*? There were no words. A quiet vow that went beyond mere revenge for Carlos's death filled Yonnie's mind. No matter what, from this point forward, he would do his boy proud, would honor all of Carlos's pacts, protect every mark, whatever foundation of Carlos's that had been destroyed, he'd resurrect. It was the least he could do.

Astonished, he held his hand out for hers, the smell of the blood within her veins too intoxicating to resist. Wary of the heavy silver near her throat, he took a submissive stance and lowered his head to her wrist. For a moment he studied the pattern of everlasting life that moved just under the surface of her honey-brown skin, then scored her flesh in one ferocious slash, greedily sucking from her veins until she struggled to break his hold. The click of the gun hammer ripped through his awareness, as did cold steel positioned in the center of his chest.

"Don't be stupid. You bleed me out and flat-line me this close to dawn, we'll both fry. Be advised, there's only one safe place for us now, and only I know how to enter it." She glanced at Carlos's abandoned Beverly Hills lair. "That's a death trap. So are all his other lairs."

Yonnie wiped his mouth with the back of his hand, feeling his body begin to regenerate. He looked at his skeletal fingers, and watched them become covered with the even, brown, tight skin of an eighteen-year-old youth.

"How can a fourth-generation carry hallowed earth, wear silver, and know of the only safe place in town? Sis, if you're a vampire wannabe, you just brought yourself a ticket to a very wild ride." Yonnie shook his head and walked around her in a circle. "If you want me to fuck you good for the rest of the night, not a problem. Done. But you need to stop drinking deer blood and soft-packs from the Red Cross, trying to front like the real thing. That shit will get you smoked one night, and even at your age, you're too fine for that with your black Cherokee self."

He watched her eyes narrow and become glowing, golden slits of fury as her fangs lowered. "Listen, you dumb bastard. I have aged in a few hours to what I would have been if I had not died at eighteen. You have aged to what you would have been, were you not Vampire. Every seal that was set by Carlos has been torched. Every member of his circle has aged to the point of progressive time. Only you and I are left standing, although I'm not sure why."

She was definitely not human. Her eyes and fangs confirmed that. However, her words inspired a slow, smoldering terror within him and left many unanswered questions. Revived from her blood, his first impulse was to make a run for it, solo. But if she knew where Carlos was, or what had happened, he needed her to tell him more.

"The silver," Yonnie said, motioning to her throat. "How?"

"My grandmother was a shaman seer," she said simply. "It was mine when I was destined to be a Guardian. The energy drain hit me . . . made me feel . . . I thought I was dying and went to her home where she's buried. The Neteru's light was gone. My grandmother must have known, seen the end of days. Her spirit had left it hanging on a tree beyond the hallowed-earth perimeter. Maybe she wanted to protect me, knowing that everyone who might have given me haven would perish. I don't know. But with nothing to lose after I felt the one Guardian I'm linked to snatched by Harpies, I began the death chant of my people and put it on . . . to die with honor. I didn't want to be taken under the reign of a new master. Carlos was the only one I'd serve—he allowed me at least my dignity. Any others would not. Now I'm afraid that he's gone, too."

She blinked back tears and cast her gaze toward the blackened sky. "But I didn't burn," she whispered. "Then I heard your call. Your love for him was a beacon; it may have saved your life. You seek the one I'm now supposed to guard and we have to find him before they do, if he still exists. That's all I know."

"Guardians? Are you delirious? Carlos was a councilman when he made me a master. Who's they? If you heard a master's call, then—"

"Yes. I'm something we cannot explain at the moment. And *they* are to be discovered. But you just ate from my—"

"It was venison!"

"Correct. Because never since my turn have I befouled a living human being. Blood from stolen packs, deer, but never feasting from the living . . . that may be the only reason I'm still standing. But I am not about to tempt the sun."

Yonnie nodded. It was the first rational thing she'd said that made sense since she'd rolled up on him. "Were-demons, the wolfen clans, have compromised every place I know."

She smiled. "My people have a long history of dealing with the clan of the wolf." She stroked her silver necklace that he now knew to be an amulet. "Look into my mind. You'll see a cabin in the woods. Even council cannot breach it. The barriers are formidable and many. There's only one way into it. The perimeter is hallowed ground, and has been littered with wolf bane. I keep silver shells packed with hallowed earth for insurance." She tossed him a Glock from her shoulder holster. "It'll heat up your hands. If you don't shoot yourself, you'll live."

The weapon felt like it was searing his palm as he caught it, but he appreciated the gesture and held it steady, the barrel pointed skyward. "Thank you," he murmured, now appraising her once again. This woman was fine, brazen, and would make a wonderful lair companion. Although a little old for his tastes, she was stunning in her tight deerskin pants and the suede halter was slaying him. Her figure was awesome, not an ounce of body fat on her petite frame. He felt a smile tugging at his mouth. Maybe Carlos wasn't dead after all. "Later on, you've gotta lose the silver collar, baby, if you want to go to the vanishing point."

She smiled. "Go to Hell. I'm spoken for. Try my throat and your ass will fry."

Yonnie shrugged and chuckled. "Okay. I'll chill. Why didn't you just say you were Rivera's from the jump?"

"Because I'm not," she said, tossing her long, velvety hair over her shoulder as she retracted her fangs. "I'm Rider's."

Yonnie blinked twice and cocked his head to the side. "That Guardian dude on Rivera's 'do not touch' list?"

She glanced at the sky. "Yeah, and you're burning moonlight. I need to take you to the safe house."

"What? A Guardian compound? Are you—"

"Do you want to survive?" she asked, drawing each word out slowly. "Yes or no?"

"Yeah," he said, no longer in the mood to argue with her. "You know we could both be getting set up in a Guardian rig?"

"Or we could both see what effects dawn might have on us. You in or out?"

"I'm in, but Rider—"

"Has had my back for over twenty years."

For a moment, he just stared at her. "And Rivera was cool with that going down in his territory?"

"You and I both know that Carlos has always had a soft spot for that team."

Yonnie nodded and began to gather the transport clouds about them. He concentrated; it was taking longer to generate the swirling winds than ever before. "I don't know if I can do it," he whispered, closing his eyes tightly, summoning the energy for their dematerialization. Humiliation and rage filled him. The sun would be rising soon. He redoubled his efforts to no avail.

He looked at the lower-generation female, the panic in her eyes clear. "I may need your help," he said, shame singeing his tone. "Whatever is being sucked out of the territory is weakening my powers. Has anyone ever moved you through the night? Do you know how to summon the winds? Command velocity?"

She shook her head sadly. "I've never been taken by a master, and can't tell you much more than you already know." She walked in closer to Yonnie and placed her hand in his, her eyes searching his. "But I know I was sent to find you. There is purpose in our being together. We are from the same lands, from the same stolen tribes; our human bloodlines intersect with Carlos's. My people were native to this earth, just like his . . . yours were brought here by force, just like mine were forced into near extinction. Draw from that. Summon the wind. Take us to the place that I showed you. I believe in you . . . you're all I have left to count on."

His eyes never left hers as he felt a current bind their hands. He literally felt the energy of the ground beneath his feet pulse alive within the small spot of earth where her feet were planted, issuing forth concentric circles of fluctuating power. He locked into that power and rode it, seeing the real beauty of her face for the very first time. Aware of the silver at her throat, he leaned in close to her, nearly brushing her mouth as the winds gathered and swirled, the energy connecting as their bodies began to disintegrate. "I know you're spoken for, pretty shaman," he murmured as the winds howled and picked up, "but tell me your name."

"Tara," she whispered as they disappeared.

Struggling to sit up, Berkfield scanned the room in panic. Small windows, narrow confines, medical equipment everywhere, flashes of the laboratory that began his nightmare entered his mind while he stared at two men in white lab coats. If he could just reach something to use as a weapon. Then slowly he comprehended what he was seeing. The doctors were taking blood, not injecting him. Vials were being placed in a silver box with a religious crest— a crucifix. This was not the work of vampires. Sunlight streamed through the windows. The man speaking behind him was a cleric.

Tears came to Berkfield's eyes when he saw the heavy silver cross hanging from the man's neck, his white clerical collar, as he prayed in an Australian accent.

"My wife, my children," Berkfield croaked. "I have to get off this ship before dark falls again."

The cleric kissed his crucifix and came to Berkfield's side, wrapping his shaking hand around it as both men grasped it and held onto it for dear life.

"They are in the Vatican, Richard," the cleric assured him. "Father Patrick flew them to Rome when they showed up at his safe house. You're on a plane and are going somewhere safe until you can meet them again. The Darkness no longer imprisons you."

Slowly Berkfield relaxed and nodded as his memory came back in jagged pieces . . . being submerged in jasmine-scented water within the cathedral font. Frankincense. Dousing. Incessant liturgical mutterings as his clothes were stripped and burned. He looked at the cleric and began to sob. Doctors joined his side.

"This man has been under a lot of stress," he heard one voice say. "Do you want us to give him a tranquilizer so he can make it through the long flight? He's near collapse."

"No," the cleric said. "Our orders are to just give him water and some clear broths, fresh fruit, something to nourish him and make him comfortable—but *do not* pollute his blood."

The moment the cleric mentioned his blood, Richard Berkfield was off the table and fighting against the many arms and hands that held him. Screaming for help, he punched and kicked at his attackers. "No more blood!" he yelled. "Get the beasts away from me!" His voice rose, shrill with hysteria. "I won't let you take me to them! Get off me! Get the hell off me!"

A hard slap across his face. Dazed, it took a moment for him to respond, but it was long enough for the cleric to say quickly, "I'm sorry my hand has offended. We are men of God. We mean you no harm. We protect you and your family. You've had the Lamb's Blood within your veins and must be kept from all harm. Stop fighting us so we can help you." Two large tears rolled down the cleric's weathered cheeks and he drew a shaky breath. "No human being on the planet has ever held the honor . . . I've never witnessed such a miracle in all my years of faith. There are so many questions I want to ask you. *Please.* Trust me."

Totally stunned, Berkfield watched in awe as the cleric went down on his knees, shielding his face in his palms and began sobbing. By some odd twist of events, the doctors now assisted the elderly, white-haired man with the collar, giving a male nurse instruction to get a needle ready with a tranquilizer injection.

"No. Don't," Berkfield said, clarity coming from some unknown source despite the chaos still roaming through his mind. "The poor man is just overwhelmed, like all of us. Let him sit down and bring him some water." He bent and helped the older cleric up, but that seemed to make him sob even harder. Every place that Berkfield's hand landed in assistance, the cleric touched in awe and reverence, and began wailing anew.

It took almost ten minutes for the man to collect himself and then rise with the help of Berkfield and two doctors, and finally become calm enough to sit down in a chair facing the table that Berkfield had been lying on. For a long while, the cleric just sat, simply staring at him, holding a cup of water without drinking it. Berkfield sat on the gurney staring at him, waiting.

"When we touch down in Manila, they have military facilities with state-of-the-art equipment to give you an MRI, full set of X-rays, run a battery of tests, and—"

"Hold it right there," Berkfield said, his voice tense as he stared at the doctor who had spoken. "I don't do military nuthin'. Been there, done that. Sick militaristic SOBs sold their souls to develop new weapons, and I'm not trying to be their lab rat ever again." Fear tore through him as he stared at the cleric. "Father, don't let them take me there. Please."

"We have equipment in Rome," the cleric said, finding his voice and his strength. "Do as he asks."

To Berkfield's surprise, the doctors deferred to the older man.

"As you wish, Cardinal," one said.

"We meant no harm, just wanted to get him to the most modern facilities possible, as soon as possible, in case his body had been harmed in some way, given his ordeal. We didn't want him to have to try to get any tests done in Ethiopia, where their medical facilities are strained beyond comprehension," another doctor said quickly, trying not to further offend. "It will be such a long flight, and he cannot be left injured. What if there was internal organ damage or hemorrhaging that we didn't discover?"

Berkfield's eyes widened. "You're a cardinal?"

The cleric nodded but averted his gaze toward the floor. "Yes, Your Eminence. And these doctors are also men of the faith— clerics. No one but those of the order has touched you. That I assure you. Their concerns are real, however, and I'm no doctor."

"What did you call me?" Stunned, Berkfield stood slowly, but held on to the edge of the ambulance gurney for support.

"Your Eminence," the cardinal whispered and then bowed with the others as they stood within the tight confines of the aircraft.

"Wait, wait, wait," Berkfield said, becoming agitated as he waved his hands. "I'm not Him, by any stretch of the imagination, and you guys need to let the boys in the Vatican know that. I'm just a regular Joe that got caught up in something really bizarre."

One by one the bowed clerics peered up at Berkfield, awe still filling their expressions.

"Are you sure?" the cardinal asked, seeming so disappointed that fresh tears glittered in his eyes.

"Yeah," Berkfield whispered.

"Do you feel any pains? Soreness? Nausea? Anything that might suggest there's an injury we haven't treated?"

Berkfield looked at the frightened medical team and slowly shook his head no.

"But you've had the Living Blood within your veins. No human being has ever—"

"I'm just a regular guy who misses his wife and is scared shitless." Berkfield let out a weary sigh. "I want to go home, hug Marjorie, tell her it's gonna be all right." Tears threatened Berkfield's composure. "I wanna kiss my daughter and drop her off at the mall, and yell at my son for playing his music too loud." His voice broke. "I want to drink a beer and wave at my neighbor while I'm grilling burgers. I don't want to be on the run for the rest of my life, or have my family live in the shadows. I can't live like this!"

"The first shall be last and the last shall be first," one cleric said above Berkfield's sobs.

"When the stigmata occurred, is it possible that it all came out of him and soaked into the holy robes?" the cardinal asked, going to Berkfield to place a comforting hand on his shoulder.

"Whatever soaked into the robes, Cardinal, evacuated itself into the challis as soon as those clerics entered the cathedral," another said. "That's been sent directly to Rome on a separate charter with a clerical army on board to protect it."

The cardinal nodded. "I was given orders to follow your lead . . . to grant you whatever you asked. We were told we would know from your words what to do, because the pontiff believes that a man cannot experience the Ultimate Light without being subject to profound change." He looked at Berkfield, his aged gray eyes searching for answers. "There is so much that we want to know about what it felt like to have His grace enter your cells, to fill you up with the Light. We have lived all our lives hoping to experience a small measure of that . . . yet a man with no particular religious zeal, no special gifts, nothing other than a good heart has been so blessed." He chuckled sadly and turned to one of the doctors and sighed. "Just as it is written, so it was done . . . as it has always been. The least likely is given the highest honor."

"But where are Carlos and Damali and the rest of the team?" Berkfield cried. He looked at the faces around him, fear, anger, and frustration colliding to become one emotion.

"I don't know how many of them made it," the cardinal said, fingering his cross and then taking it off, holding it out for Berkfield to accept. "If they don't turn, or weren't polluted . . ."

Berkfield's eyes went to the cross, but he didn't take it from the cardinal's hand. "You should have seen the way they fought! They were on the front line and got their asses kicked. Do you hear me? I've seen that same shit when I was doing my bid in 'Nam . . . young kids on both sides, barely out of high school, haven't even lived, but slaughtered. And for what? Same thing is going on now over in Iraq, same thing has been going on over and over again in world history. Call it Desert Storm, the Gulf War, Korea, or we can go all the way back to the beginning of caveman versus caveman, the Crusades, whatever. For what? Nobody wins. Wrongs get done on both sides. Mothers and father bury their children, blood soaks the land, the women wail, and all of humanity suffers. Don't you guys get it? People have to stop fighting each other. We have to go after the real enemy, or it never ends. And I know where he lives . . . about seven levels underground." Berkfield held his head in his hands as a wave of nausea suddenly overcame him.

Unable to speak, the clerics bowed. He could almost feel their shame of wanting a safe haven mingling with their misplaced reverence. He wasn't the Most High; they didn't need to bow to him. In that instant he felt it with clarity, as though someone had called him by name. These men of the cloth had been hiding behind safe walls, while the world suffered. They ate well, lived well, had been sheltered from horrors, and their deep resources had kept jets flying and spectacular cathedrals as monuments, while people begged in the streets. They lived in oasislike compounds while the common man lived in a spiritual and physical wasteland. This one sect of faith wasn't the only guilty party. Every major religion had done no less. But they all had seemingly forgotten that the battle was in the streets, their prayers necessary, that until one's body was out on the front line, it didn't mean a damn.

As soon as the thought ebbed, Berkfield felt his body slump from sudden, inexplicable fatigue. But his new awareness made him bold as he looked at the men before him.

"I can't tell you how I know, but I do. The vamps can kill me, but they can never bite me. If I die fighting for the side of good, I go into the Light. So I don't need a cross, it flows through my veins these days. Thanks, anyway."

The cardinal nodded. "Forgive us and don't judge us so harshly."

"I don't judge anymore," Berkfield said, stretching out. "I've seen too much to do that." He reclined and closed his eyes.

"Then, what would you have us do with you?" the cardinal asked, confusion slowing his response.

"If any of that Guardian team made it out alive, I'm going with them. My family is going with them. I don't know what else to do. I can't go back home and act like none of this ever happened. There's no safe place to put your head in the sand and hide. This whole thing is about to blow. So, I'll wait for a sign. Got it?"

CHAPTER FIVE

CARLOS CONTINUED to stare out of the jet window. He needed a moment to think, put everything into perspective, and figure out his next move. In his currently weakened state, with all his most cherished powers stripped from him, what would be his strategy now?

He was glad that silence had fallen over the cabin. The only sound that punctuated the oppressive quiet was the low drone of the engine and Big Mike's snoring. Then he heard someone opening a bottle of water. The sound of deep swallows suddenly made him aware of the burning dryness of his own throat. But he'd declined the water offered by Monk Lin. He wasn't ready for the reality that he might, indeed, be able to drink it without color. He wasn't ready to face that until he was someplace private.

There was a surreal comfort in knowing the rules of the game, whatever game a man played, and he'd played Hell to the bone— literally. For whatever it was worth, at the moment he allowed himself some small measure of pride in having bested the most ruthless bastards at their own game. Problem now was, to what end? Maybe he'd played himself.

Carlos sighed and kept his eyes trained on the sun, remembering how he'd finally embraced his fate and how delicious the power had been. True, he'd been in Hell, but what a ride it had been. . . .

He shook his head slowly, quietly admonishing himself for the perverse thought. Yeah . . . the Light was awesome, but on the other side, the women, the cars, the villas, walking on air, the clubs, the money, the sex . . . damn, it had been good, and when Damali had turned, there'd been nothing like it.

A new, frightening thought made his chest tight. He was now, possibly, just an average human being. Again, he was trapped in a situation with no money, unable to use the full range of his personal power, and probably owed a higher authority, just like before. They hadn't approached him, but he knew it had to be coming sooner or later. There was always barter, always a payoff. Nothing was free.

True, being a council-level vamp had been a rush, but he had to remember all the heartbreak that came with it. His brother, Alejandro, and his boys had all perished. His mom, grandmom, Juanita—all hidden away from him, lest he turn them in a moment of bestial lust. The torture, the blood, the insatiable hunger. He had to stop being sentimental about it. Had to stop romanticizing the past like an old man who'd done a thirty-year prison bid, thinking about the good times and laughs and not about the lack of freedom, shit food, and the destruction of one's personal dignity in the process. He remembered those old drunken fools, and how as kids they would shake their heads and laugh at their stupidity when they'd come back to the corners talking about the joint, and how they ran the yard, as though they'd been down to the Bahamas. Crazy. Had he already become like them?

Maybe the old padre was right. Father Pat was a deep old dude, and had always made him stop and think about choices and consequences. No good was going to come in the long run from the vampire life, he told himself. He had to stay focused and convince himself that this change in circumstances was for the best, that it would be cool, or else he'd go nuts. All he had to do was remember the baby that was clawed from Damali's womb.

Now, he had someone who really depended on him, but he had no income, was dead with no assets, according to the cleanup Berkfield had done before on his behalf, and the chairman had it out for Damali. How was he supposed to be the Neteru's man? How was he supposed to protect her, even if he didn't go seeking revenge? These were the types of things the clerics never dealt with or thought about.

In his human world it was still about resources, and to be turned out with nothing to his name was a position of vulnerability. He hated that predicament worse than death. At least death was sort of final, even if one did come back on the other side. But in the coming back, resources were available, either from the Light or the Darkness, whatever side one happened to find themselves on, of that he was sure. But what was an average guy supposed to do—a dead man walking, with no formally recognized education, no work history, no nothing? Go work at a convenience store for minimum wage and no health benefits? What, after having great cosmic power and the knowledge of the history of the world and all its technology within one's mind . . . he'd seen too much, experienced too much, and knew too much to ever go back to a normal life.

Even if he hung with the Guardians, they all had special powers, extra juice to their games. It would take him forever to learn martial arts, how to swing a blade, or find an expertise that could be of benefit to them. He wouldn't be running shit on the team; Shabazz was the male leader—position already filled. Mike was the strong man, J.L. the tech whiz, Dan the business ace, Rider the sharpshooter, Jose the master tracker, Marlene was the healer, and his baby girl was all that and then some. He definitely wasn't the religious type who could fit in with Father Pat's boys on the Covenant squad. He wasn't no cop, so he couldn't even roll with Berkfield as a partner. So, what the fuck was he? Assed out.

Carlos refused to glimpse at Damali and struggled not to turn his head to do so. It was so strangely cool between them when he was what he'd been and she was what she was—the vampire and the virgin. Again, he almost laughed to keep from crying.

What the hell was he going to do now? She had only known one man in her life—him—but as a council-level master vampire. His woman had known him at his apex of power, and he'd marked her, rewired her sexual circuitry to only respond to the most acute sensory lock with him. And what did that mean? Truth be told, what could he deliver as a regular guy? He damned sure couldn't take her to the vanishing point again. Carlos closed his eyes. They might as well have driven a stake through his chest. His woman had been turned out by the baddest motherfucker on the planet—him—and he was no longer that. She liked it rough, could take a fang drop in her jugular like a pro, and could still get up and walk on the beach at high noon. So what was a mere male supposed to do when his woman became the baddest mutha on earth without him?

No, it definitely wasn't supposed to go down like this.

Carlos opened his eyes and stared at his hands. To him, they were dead. They contained no special powers. He couldn't transform a room, gather the winds, he'd never be a panther again—not even on a whim to feel the thrill of a hunt. He'd have to use a door with a key. Carlos shuddered at the thought. He couldn't walk through a wall at will or rip out an enemy's heart with a glance. Damn, this was beyond fucked up. And his woman had a team of martial arts boyz . . . hell, she could fight like a demon herself, and was poetry in motion. When he really thought about it, she could probably outrun him; she had the Neteru speed and the endurance to match it. He hated to admit it, but she could probably go round for round, pound for pound, and might just be able to kick *his* ass . . . given she knew all that fly kick shit that Shabazz had taught her. And if she'd been made a junkie for vamp bad boys, by his own hand, then sooner or later she'd want what she was missing in him . . . might go out one night and take a walk on the wild side. He'd never be able to live with that, if she slept with another man, especially another master vampire.

The thought was so unsettling that he jettisoned it from his mind as he stood to go get a bottle of water. Another man? A bad, smooth, fly, Hell fiend that could make her scream his name? Never. His hands were shaking as he retrieved a cold bottle from the jet's kitchen, broke the seal, and guzzled it. Some *hombre* that could stand in his face, laugh at him, and outright challenge him for Damali, and could beat his ass down so hard he'd die of humiliation before he died from the attack.

Carlos grabbed another bottle of water, threw his head back, and downed it quickly. As he brought his gaze level with the seated teams, he saw that everyone was staring at him. He glanced at the bottle in his hand and then hurled it at the trash chute, missing it, then sulked to his seat and flopped down. Why did they ever bring him back? This was no gift; it was a curse . . . pure punishment, if ever he'd witnessed it.

Damali quietly watched Carlos from her seat next to Marlene. Her mother-seer only squeezed her hand in acknowledgment of what they both now knew was true. Carlos was human. But what did that mean?

She checked the back of her dress to make sure she hadn't bled through onto the light fabric, and started to stand, but Marlene's grip tightened on her hand.

"Give him some space," Marlene said in a barely audible tone. "Brother is tripping right now, and as a man, has a lot to think about."

Damali stared at Marlene for a moment but didn't argue. "Third eye or common sense?"

"Common sense," Marlene replied in a whisper.

Damali nodded. "I'm just glad he's alive."

Marlene nodded. "But he isn't, and that may take a while. Let Rider or Shabazz talk to him until he finds his place on the team."

Damali settled back in her seat and closed her eyes. "I can't worry about that right now."

Marlene stroked her hair and followed suit, closing her eyes with a weary sigh. "I know. So, don't. Get some rest and steady your nerves. The problem will be there when you wake up."

Damali glimpsed at Marlene and yawned. "But what the—"

"It's drama as old as Adam and Eve," Marlene said in a low, gentle voice without even opening her eyes.

The plane's rapid descent once they reached Brisbane roused everyone from their slumber. Slowly, bleary-eyed passengers sat up straight, stretched, and yawned.

"I'll be glad when we get on the flight to Manila," Shabazz muttered. "Seven hours or so will do us all good."

Rider nodded through a loud yawn. "Yep, just like when we

were touring. Sleep in the air, rock 'n' roll on the ground. Whatever, as long as I get some shut-eye during the day."

"You put touring in past tense, man," Big Mike said cautiously. "Any special insight you trying to deliver?"

Rider looked at Mike, dumbfounded. "Did I say it past tense?"

"Yeah, *hombre,* you did," Jose said, staring at Rider.

The teams looked at Marlene and Father Patrick for confirmation.

"We don't know what's going to happen," Marlene said. "Let's stay positive and not freak ourselves out."

"Mar," Dan said, glancing around the now-standing group. "All of her commercials have been taped and are done. I hadn't signed her to anything beyond Sydney, because we didn't know the situation. I also never inked any movie deals, because going into Sydney, we didn't know if Damali could cast a reflection. We don't have any upcoming concerts committed yet, but residuals from commercials and the Sydney concert, plus royalties on all the CDs should float the team for a while. However, given what could be after us, my suggestion is that we put her portfolio of income in some unmarked accounts in Swiss and Cayman Island banks."

"Yo, Dan," Shabazz said, his tone surly and flat. "Let's get our teams to a safe house, then we can sit down and start thinking about money and whatnot." Shabazz released a weary sigh and moved into the aisle.

"He's got a point, though," J.L. countered. "We used up a lot of ammo, lost a lot of gear, and we don't know what we'll face when we get back to the compound stateside. We have to be thinking about public relations and damage control, if we have to stay on the move and underground for a while."

"That's what I'm trying to say, 'Bazz," Dan added, coming into the aisle with Shabazz. "When we get on that flight, we need a team meeting about next steps—before everyone goes to sleep, before it gets dark, and before we lose another day when I can make some calls and make some wire transfers."

"Yeah," Damali said. She stretched her back and kept her eyes on Dan, fighting not to look at Carlos. "We have to handle our business. Without resources, we're sitting ducks. Until the Covenant gives us the green light to move this squad in relative safety, we need a cover story about why I've suddenly dropped from the scene."

Dan nodded. "She's at the apex of her career, man. I have to feed the media vultures something to keep them interested in what Damali will do next, and to keep her fans hungry for her next move. I can play this sudden drop out of sight as her going on a religious pilgrimage or something, mix the truth in with the fiction . . . which will also make the dark side think she was so torn up that she can't perform."

For a moment, no one said a word. Dan's comment was so close to the bone that it almost cut when he'd said it. Damali drew in a silent breath and spoke with a steady voice.

"Yeah, Dan is right. That is very close to what happened. Tell them that after Sydney, I'm going to . . . hmmm . . . Tibet." She smiled. "Cool?"

Dan smiled and the group relaxed.

"We'll be headed in the opposite direction toward Africa and then Europe, so if anyone checks that we flew into Manila, it will make sense. They'll be roaming over Tibet while we're getting papal clearance to enter the Vatican on the other side of the world." She smoothed the front of her gown and entered the narrow jet aisle with Shabazz and Dan. "Hopefully, by the time we get through all of this, I'll have some slammin' new cuts, inspired from wherever we go. Maybe."

Monk Lin moved to her side slowly. His expression was grim, but his eyes were gentle. "This is the right course of action, Neteru. Therefore, in Manila, my journey ends. I must go prepare my brothers for a possible attack."

"Hold it, then," Damali said quickly. "I wasn't even thinking that a mention of Tibet would send a search-and-destroy team your way! Let's pick someplace else to use as a decoy." Her gaze frantically searched the group for answers but only blank stares returned. Damn . . . where would she send the vamps? She didn't want any innocent blood on her hands in any country.

"There is no safe place to turn the bowels of Hell upon, Neteru," Monk Lin said calmly. "Tibet has been bloodied at the hands of human destruction, but is spiritually sound enough to take an invasion. As a member of the Covenant, we are to accompany you to points along your path, and you have made a wise choice. I will be waiting for you in Tibet when the time comes for you to journey there. For now, my remaining brethren will accompany you."

Panic seized Damali's voice as she looked at Monk Lin's resigned, peaceful expression.

"My journey ends, Neteru, in Algeria," Imam Asula said. "You have learned well. Our task is nearly done. Only the Guardians will soon be necessary. That is why we stop there."

Her gaze shot around the small cabin and landed on Father Patrick. "Tell me you're not leaving us, too? You and Father Lopez. . . ."

"Child . . . our Neteru, we lead you to the Christian strongholds, then my work is most likely done. From there, Father Lopez will be your link to us, but we will never be far away."

"You sound like you're dying," Carlos said, interjecting himself into the conversation for the first time since they'd entered the aircraft. His voice hitched without censure. "Man, all of you are family. You just can't up and leave. It ain't right."

"The winds of change are upon us, son," Father Patrick said gently. "Monk Lin and Imam Asula have been sent visions instructing them where they need to go now. My impression of what I'm to do is still hazy, even though I am the father-seer for the group. But I promise you, I will not just up and leave," he said with emphasis, "without telling you. We've become too close for that."

The groups looked between Carlos and Father Patrick, and no one spoke until Carlos's shoulders relaxed and he nodded.

"All right. Cool."

Father Patrick's gaze was tender, his voice warm. "I will not abandon you. I promise."

Carlos nodded and moved into the aisle. He kept his head held high and his back very straight and faced the door. Damali watched the muscles in his jaw working, and for the first time since the hellish nightmare in Sydney concluded, she realized that she wasn't locked in on his thoughts. It wasn't that she was blocked; there was simply no connection. The awareness made her chest heavy. She wanted to reach out to him and hug him, but knew better than to do that just now.

Sensing the tension, Marlene faced the group. "Father Patrick, this is your convoy. How do we proceed?"

"We will board a knights of Templar jumbo jet. All identification as diplomats of the church have been processed and are in order. The plane has already passed security clearance. But that brings me to another very critical point."

All eyes were on the senior cleric as he paused, took a deep breath, and continued.

"No weapons."

"What!" Rider shouted. "We've got senior levels of Hell on our asses and no weapons?"

"Marlene has a sea salt and herbal compound, and we have a bottle of holy water for each of you. Before you get on the plane, we will go to a private hanger that has been outfitted for VIPs. You will shower, get the blood off of you, will scrub your bodies with Marlene's compound and rinse it off with holy water, and get out of these military fatigues. We will put on the white cotton embroidered dashikis, pantaloons, and crocheted knit caps of the faithful Ethiopian. You will travel as pilgrims led by clerics. You will be unarmed, and pose no international threat when we go through the heavy inspection in Manila and upon arrival in war-torn Ethiopia. The only weapons on board will be the Isis dagger and blades—which I will say have come from the Vatican . . . which, they did at one time, so technically, that is not a lie."

Rider opened and closed his mouth, but no sound came out. Carlos never even turned around.

"When we get to Algeria," Imam Asula said calmly, "there will be weapons stashed on the aircraft brought in on the food contain-

ers. You will be informed of where they are, as well as each given a
new roll of clothes and toiletries. With the death of the Transyl-
vanian, Europe is hot."

"Hey, ain't no friends in this game, brother," Rider said. "We
smoked masters from Africa, Asia, Australia, and Europe; and our
boy, Carlos, who was representing the U.S. and South America, also
got smoked, so to speak. So why is Europe any hotter than Africa
or Asia right now?' Rider's gaze settled on Asula after it briefly
scanned the group.

"Europe had been the most recent epicenter of world power,
with other forces diverted to the Middle East," Asula said in a patient tone. "That was the dark empire's most severe blow, and
where they will most likely reconstitute quickly, just as they will
have to redress the loss to the U.S. territory. Therefore, you may be
able to travel in relative safety on the mother continent and Asia,
for now, but Europe and the United States are in total chaos after
this most effective strike."

"Why does that make sense, but not make me feel much better?" Rider said, although he nodded to signal that he would re-
lent. "Makes me want to just go fishing in the Caribbean and call
it a day."

CHAPTER SIX

⚜ SHE HAD been prepared to melt under the hot water in the shower. She nearly passed out from the relief as Marlene massaged grime out of her scalp. She had been prepared to just want to drop from exhaustion and terrible cramps. She had even been prepared to feel the lump of anxiety forming in her chest as she got her nerves ready to say good-bye to dear Monk Lin in only a few hours once they arrived in Manila.

However nothing could have prepared her to see Carlos step out of the men's room, freshly showered, wearing a stark white-on-white satin embroidered knee-length dashiki, flowing white pantaloons, his feet shod in handcrafted leather slip-on sandals, his hair wet and slicked back under a crocheted skullcap, his jaw set hard, his eyes hidden behind dark shades and staring at nothing.

It was that blank stare that did her in. Suddenly it was hard to breathe, the slight hurt so badly.

Damali let her gaze roam past her all-white-clad team, soaking in their regal beauty. They looked like a wedding party. She wanted to weep, but refused to do so. Rider made her smile, as he looked miserable in the skullcap and kept fussing under his breath about not having anywhere to stash a weapon.

So she forced her mind to cling to the mundane, the inane, anything but the fact that the person she wanted to wrap his arms around her and lie and tell her it would be all right, wasn't all right. Carlos was gone. When he'd return, she couldn't tell. All she could hope was he would soon.

And in that small sliver of grief that she allowed herself, she felt gypped, truly cheated by fate. The Light had brought him back, but hadn't brought him back whole. She wondered if other women had ever felt like she did now, hoping and sending up prayers that their man would safely come home from wherever . . . prison, the service, some job far, far away, only to get back his body but a very different mind. She knew the answer as soon as it had slid into her consciousness. Unfortunately, she was not alone. She just felt alone.

There was nothing to do now but wait. Wait to get on the flight to Manila. Wait to get from Manila to Addis Ababa, wait to travel from there to Dubai, and wait for the interminable flight from there to Khartoum, and from there, more waiting to skip through Cairo, Paris Orly, then Algiers, to wait some more. Then they would have to wait for time to be alone to talk, time to readjust to being in the same space, they'd have to wait for her body to heal before they could be as one, and wait to see if that was even possible any longer.

As she waited in the cool hangar, Damali studied the seed pearls and intricate white beadwork on the front of the new gown Marlene had given her. She fingered the small cowry shells that rimmed her flowing bell sleeves. She'd only briefly glimpsed herself in the mirror as Marlene had rewrapped her hair in a clean, new, starched white cotton fabric. It had been too painful to watch Marlene's attention to her, as though she were a bride getting ready for her big day. She'd never have a big day, and not with the one she'd always hoped to. It felt so impossible now, and there had been so much they'd both taken for granted. Now that was all gone.

Damali pushed herself up from the soft lounge chair and walked over to Father Patrick and his weary band of clerics. Without saying a word, she gave them each a long hug, even Monk Lin and Imam Asula, who technically weren't supposed to accept one from her. But as an adopted daughter, they seemed to make the allowance, returning her hug warmly, with deep affection embedded within the embrace.

"Thank you guys so much," she said to them quietly, "for arranging all of this, even down to the clothes, shower, and food."

Father Patrick held her more closely and stroked her back as he spoke. "The churches, mosques, synagogues, and temples are wealthy beyond your comprehension, daughter. If we couldn't provide for the one who has been sent to help us save the world, then what are we doing this for?" He held her back and smiled tenderly. "You've given up a lot and deserve much. That has always been my prayer."

The other clerics nodded as the eldest in the group released her. "And you have lost much . . . the rabbi, the ninjas, the—"

Father Patrick held up his hand and placed two fingers against her lips. "They have simply transitioned to the new place of peace. We will not mourn the dead and gnash our teeth over the fallen, not while we have been gifted with life and have still much work to do."

Damali kissed his cheek and slipped away from their small circle, knowing that his words had a hidden message within it for her to heed. She soaked in his wisdom as she found her teammates sprawled on the lush furniture. "You guys ready to roll?"

He thought he had adequately braced himself for this new surreal journey, the reentry into human civilian life. But nothing could have made him ready to deal with Damali's regal presence. Only twenty-four hours ago she'd worn a white sheath for him at the vampire's Master's Cup ball. Now she was standing in a full beam of sunlight that washed her golden bronze, the light catching in pearls, creating a dazzling display of light work against her. She'd gone from vampress to Madonna in one shower change. Street urchin to light bearer. A queen of light.

She'd been his wife, too, for a very short and unsanctioned time, when he had been a master of the night. Now, she wasn't that. Just like he wasn't what he'd been. She had more important titles to bear than that of Councilman Rivera's wife. She was the Neteru. He simply had to get with that.

He couldn't look at her in all-white. Not now. The wound was still too fresh and bleeding inside erratically, irrationally, hemorrhaging him to the core. And the fact that she and her team carried enough VIP weight to have the Vatican send a jumbo jet, outfitted like Air Force One, was creating a deeper conflict within him than he cared to address.

So, he took his time climbing up the steep incline of steps behind Shabazz, Rider, and Big Mike, with Father Patrick at his back. He was cargo, potentially dangerous cargo, in their minds. Or, perhaps, it was just in his weary brain that he was any of those things. He wondered if they viewed him as a HAZMAT that might turn, or combust, or whatever. Nothing could be certain except that he wasn't a real member of their team, just their ward to be handled with care.

"Oh, my God!" Berkfield yelled, hopping off the gurney and brushing past the cardinal and doctors. "You, my friend, are a sight for sore eyes!"

Berkfield rushed Carlos and hugged him so hard that all Carlos could do was chuckle. Tears were streaming down Berkfield's face and he pulled Carlos in a circle, his gaze darting between Carlos and Damali.

"In broad freakin' daylight! Look at you! You kids made it!" Berkfield laughed and did a little jig, and then ran down the wide aisle slapping the whole team high-five.

"Yeah, in broad freaking daylight, it's good to see you, too, man," Rider said, laughing. "You cool?"

"Just get me to my wife and kids, then I'll be perfection," Berkfield said, still giddy. He shook his head, smoothing his palm over the skullcap that clung to his semibald scalp. "I hope they have a fully stocked bar on this contraption, because a man could surely use a shot of something serious after all this bullshit."

All the clerics on board blanched, but reserved comment.

"Word," Shabazz said, smiling and pounding Big Mike's fist.

"You check out the digs?" Rider said, glancing around. "Wood grains rich enough to make your eyes squint, leather seats that could accommodate an NBA player. I know they have liquor on board. I can smell it. The bar is thataway."

The members of the Guardian team laughed, releasing pent-up tension until there was not a dry eye on the plane. Finally Father Patrick corralled the group and brought order.

"We must first thank the Almighty that we are all here and whole," he said. "We must thank Cardinal Muldavey for his intercession to Rome to get us the supplies and transportation we required. We must thank the good doctors that have stood by Richard's side, and who will attend to Damali's needs . . . may their hands be steady, their minds keen. And we must pray for safe journeys, that our missions be accomplished without further tragedy or loss. We will pray for those who have fallen, may their souls rest in peace. And we will ask forgiveness for our own trespasses, and for the Almighty to allow these teams to rest securely, to eat well, and restore their fatigued souls. Amen."

A resounding amen rippled through the group. Rider glanced at the bar, and Shabazz and Big Mike tucked away smiles.

"I will not be on this flight, as I am stationed here. But I do understand there's been some concern about safety and the lack of weapons," the cardinal said cautiously, gripping the silver medical case he carried tighter.

"I'll be honest," Damali said, her voice filled with appreciation, but also worry. "There's a lot of heat in the system right now, and during the night while we're in the air, we need something beside the Isis to protect ourselves if we're attacked."

The cardinal nodded. "That's why we put you on this. There's a full video conference room that the pontiff uses for media relations just up that spiral staircase in the center of the plane, a dining room, full cabin staff, doctors . . . and this aircraft can be refueled in midair, should it be impossible to touch down until dawn. She also carries missiles and a machine-gun turret, as a precaution. The pilots, although clergy, are sharpshooters and armed—but we didn't want an accidental firefight to break out on board where a stray bullet or shoulder-propelled rocket might accidentally open a hole in the side of the aircraft and depressurize the flight at thirty thousand feet. You're carrying precious cargo, and the pontiff only had two of these in his fleet. We'd hate to lose one, and your team has a bit of a reputation for property damage."

"Well why the heck didn't you say so?" Rider said with a sigh. "*Now* I feel better, and am *definitely* ready for that drink."

Jose smiled, noting how Rider had intentionally checked his language for the cardinal. "I'm glad you think we're precious cargo, sir. If this is the pope's plane, then I guess we're cool."

The cardinal smiled tensely. "It is Mr. Berkfield who is our deep concern and we need to be sure he is guarded at your maximum capacity. He was insistent that he wanted to join the group, and frankly, Rome is worried. But, er, uh, we accept his decision with grace." The cardinal bowed and stood, his eyes on Richard Berkfield as the rest of the group gaped.

"Not the Neteru?" Marlene stammered.

"Not until we know that she is still the Neteru," the cardinal said carefully.

Silence filled the interior of the plane. The captain's voice over the intercom was the only thing that broke it.

"Your Excellency, we have been given permission by the tower to begin taxiing into position. I have to ask all crew members to begin preparing for takeoff, sir."

The cardinal nodded and an attendant near a stern intercom relayed the message that the senior cleric had heard the captain's warning. There were no long speeches, no explanations. The cardinal simply held out his ring for Father Patrick and Father Lopez to kiss, nodded, bid the teams a safe journey, and strode off the plane clutching the case.

Dumbfounded, the teams slowly found their seats and watched the crew engage the stair motor, seal the hatch, and prepare everyone for takeoff.

Damali heard the crew explain the emergency procedures. But she heard it with numb ears. What rang in her head were the cardinal's words, ". . . if she is still the Neteru." She felt a crew member check her seat belt. But she still felt the words cut to her core. "If she is still the Neteru." She felt the plane gain speed, its massive turbines whirring, then felt the huge aircraft lift off the ground, but she strangely felt like she was falling.

The moment the captain turned off the seat belt sign and told them they were free to move about the cabin, Rider was out of his chair like a shot. Big Mike was right behind him, quickly followed by Shabazz.

"Fucking-A. Team meeting," Rider said, holding up a new

bottle of Jack Daniel's and four rocks glasses upside down on his fingers.

"You heard the man," Shabazz said, brandishing a bottle of Courvoisier. "This is some way serious shit."

Big Mike edged down the aisles with two armloads of glasses. "They got a conference room, let's conference."

"You're damned right," Father Patrick said, his tone strident. "Would you gentlemen happen to have found a bottle of Irish whiskey in there reserved for diplomats? If so, point me toward it. This is insane."

The team filed down the aisle, their disgruntled murmurs wafting through the cabin, and then snaked their way up the spiral staircase to the large conference room. Rider flipped on the light switch, shook his head at the opulent leather seats and highly polished oval table, while J.L. noted the communications technology with a gentle touch as he passed the elaborate, walnut-encased boards. Shabazz set the bottle he was carrying down hard, and scored the seal as the large group took their seats. Carlos touched the wood, remembering the boardroom table that had once been on his yacht.

"Okay, roll call the situation," Rider said, throwing back a shot of Jack Daniel's and making a grimace as it slid down his throat.

"Like I told y'all when we got on the small jet, Rome ain't taking no chances," Shabazz said, and handed off several glasses of dark brown liquor. "Right now, everybody seems cool and is standing in sunlight. But they don't know whether or not somebody will die in their sleep and wake up a problem. So, they're obviously sending us on this zigzag flight pattern for three days and nights as insurance. Feel me?"

Marlene took a neat sip from her glass and rolled the crystal between her palms. "Damali needs to be downstairs with the doctors. Let's keep our priorities in focus. Screw what they think. We know the deal."

"Thanks, Mar, and I'll go down there in a minute," Damali said, her tone patient as she glanced at Marlene. "But this is also a priority. What do they mean, if I'm still the Neteru?"

Father Patrick sighed. Shame and throttled rage turned his cheeks a light crimson color. He waited until Rider poured him a drink, then he took a quick jolt from his glass and set it down hard. "Berkfield has had the Blood of Christ in his veins, and I'm sure is impervious to a bite. The experience has changed him, and I'm sure they are interested in what powers he may now possess that can hold sway the battle we all wage."

"So, what's that got to do with D?" Big Mike asked, leaning forward as he polished off his drink and Rider poured him a second shot.

Father Lopez looked at Carlos. "They don't know if you'll turn." He sighed and raked his fingers through his hair. "They're not sure if you're a daywalker or not, and given your relationship to Damali, they know you'll take her and she'll ultimately go to Hell and back with you."

"If you haven't noticed," Carlos said evenly, anger roiling within him, "I haven't dropped fang since I got blasted by the damned Light."

"True dat," Shabazz said, no judgment in his tone, "but you haven't made it through the night, either, my brother. Daywalkers can eat regular food, right?"

Carlos nodded. The team was so still they seemed like they'd been frozen in marble.

"They can deal with the sun, right?" Shabazz pressed on. But his gaze slid to Damali as he delivered the balance of what he had to say. "And they can obviously sire with a fertile, willing, Neteru, correct?"

When Carlos didn't answer Shabazz, he nodded. "My point exactly. *They don't know.*" Shabazz rubbed his jaw and sipped his drink slowly, then made a face, and let his breath out hard. "Right now, all they can detect is that she's bleeding. Until she has a D&C, the clerical doctors won't know if they got it all, and I'm sure they're as concerned about that as we all are." He looked at Damali, his eyes filled with so much sadness that they glittered. "I hate to have to have said that in this room, like this, baby, but we have to just put it out there and deal."

Damali wrapped her arms around herself and pushed a tumbler to the center of the table. "Pour me a little Jack, huh, Rider? Something to take the edge off."

Rider nodded and complied. For a moment, silence again shrouded the team.

"You know, we've all been set up, right?" Carlos said, his tone calm, as he pushed his glass toward Shabazz to be filled.

Shabazz refilled Carlos's glass and the team watched him sip it. "You got knowledge, drop it."

"Shabazz is right. If anyone on this team were bitten, given the length of these flights and the crazy route they've put us on, we'll be in the air near turn time. If there's a female Neteru carrying a daywalker, and if I'm still one, the bet is I'll cancel a new male vamp's ass out. If Marlene turns, she's toast, because she'll instinctively rush my Neteru." He glanced at Berkfield. "The only one they're really worried about is you, *hombre*. But since you've had the sacred in you, you won't get bitten. They just wanna be sure the plane doesn't go down hard. Feel me?"

Carlos took a very slow sip of liquor, shook it off, and smiled. "Not bad, but still tastes weird without a little color."

"That's not funny, man," Rider said, pouring himself a new drink.

"If we've been sacrificed to a contained, suicide air battle," Imam Asula said, glancing at Monk Lin and then standing to reach for a glass at the center of the table, "then what harm is a drink?"

"So, you are sitting here calmly telling us that the entire clerical community expects this plane to have a last vampire outbreak on it? For Carlos to wipe out whichever of us drops fang, and then what?" J.L. shook his head and rubbed his face with both palms.

"I cannot go to Tibet now," Monk Lin said. "Not even to warn the others. I could poison the brotherhood if I am unclean."

"We sit here, as members of the Covenant, and can do nothing but wait for a fight to break out on this aircraft?" Father Lopez's voice held as much quiet rage as disbelief. "They, *our church,* would do that to us?"

"Yes," Father Patrick said flatly, and raised his glass. "For the cause. Haven't you attended your religious history classes, Padre?" The older man looked at Carlos and saluted him before downing his drink.

"And, in the battle, Guardians that may be slow to turn from a nick would try to separate me from her," Carlos said, not looking at Damali. "If I'm still what they think I am, without weapons on board, there is no chance in Hell any of you'd make it out alive. No weapons would fire; therefore, this plane would stay airborne while the carnage takes place. It would only be me and Damali and the pilots left standing—and Berkfield, if he didn't get in the way. Which he wouldn't. He isn't a Guardian and doesn't have that kill-vampires-or-die-trying instinct. But for me, after the crew, he might be a food source until I could find a safe place to put down a lair. I wouldn't do the pilots unless I was starving and out of fuel— unlikely given how many of you are on board. They know I wouldn't risk nicking Berkfield to fry my insides with the sacred blood that runs through his veins, no matter how hungry I was, and he'd be a good hostage, if I found myself surrounded by the Light. Besides, they must know that me getting her pregnant before council's schedule set off a civil war between me and council, so I wouldn't be anxious to jettison her in a tornado . . . which I'm not even sure vampires can do this high up. Never tried it."

"Sonofabitch!" Berkfield shouted and stood. "They've got my wife and kids behind the walls of the Vatican."

"Ironic, ain't it?" Carlos said without emotion. "But that's also the safest place for them."

Berkfield walked in a circle. Big Mike grabbed Rider's bottle and poured another drink.

"Logical. Chilling. With all the intrigue of old Rome," Rider said with disgust as his gaze went toward the windows. "The powerful all function the same." He looked at Carlos hard, but his tone held an air of acceptance and friendship. "Thanks for the heads-up. So, if we ain't gonna break out into a round of prayer, judging by the current mental condition of our clerical leaders here, then I vote for going out snot-slinging drunk."

"Much obliged, *hombre*." Carlos tipped his drink in Rider's direction. "I have to admit that that's why I'm always a little skeptical about things that are too good to be true." He glanced around the sumptuous environs and sighed. "Sometimes ignorance really is bliss."

"Up until this moment," Rider said, studying his glass in the light, "I was a pretty ignorant and happy bastard."

"How much you wanna bet that the pilots are sealed behind a reinforced steel door?" Carlos added. "To further blow your bliss, think about this. Why would I make this plane drop by killing the pilots with my woman and child on board? Therefore, their real cargo, Berkfield, wouldn't die, either. But, then again," Carlos said with a sigh as he sipped his drink, "they've already extracted the sacred from Berkfield. One SOS transmission, and they could shoot this bitch out of the sky." He rubbed his jaw. "I don't know if I'm still a vampire or not, but I do know how people with a lot at stake think. Men of power who plan on winning would have war-gamed multiple options."

"We should be having this conversation in our own compound, back home, in our own war room," Shabazz said through his teeth. "Brotherman is too on-target, and what he's saying makes too much sense. I know they had to take precautions, but I hate being cannon fodder."

Father Patrick nodded and his angry gaze locked with Imam Asula, Monk Lin, and Father Lopez. "I hate that we're so expendable in this grand war game. Every time I lose one of my men, I ask myself, how high the cost . . . at what price?" He stood and began pacing. "I could take dying in the full heat of battle, getting attacked by the other side. But to know that our own set us up as cheap insurance . . . to know that they'd sent us down into the mines like canaries, and if we came out alive, there was no gas leak, or if we didn't, then the mine was polluted and they wouldn't drill for the natural resource Berkfield has in his veins. This is an outrage!"

Damali stood, her gaze steady on Marlene. "I'm going downstairs, so we can all be sure and then get a few hours sleep."

Carlos looked up at her but didn't move. "I wish you wouldn't go down there to let them hack on you. What if they accidentally—"

"Then nobody will die," she said bluntly. "This isn't your decision, or your body. It's mine." She looked at Shabazz. "Carlos stays in the conference room. You and Big Mike cover him. Take shifts. I'm not sacrificing the teams on a maybe. Get my Isis, use it if he drops fang."

She pushed her chair out of her way so hard that the mount in the floor creaked and the chair spun, slamming the back of it against the table. No one intervened. Marlene kept her gaze straight ahead as both women left the room. For a long time no one in the conference room spoke. No one picked up a glass, but each man stared into his drink lost in his own private thoughts.

"It wasn't supposed to go down like this," Jose finally said, his voice quiet as he looked toward the invisible wake Damali had left.

"Tell me about it," Carlos muttered.

CHAPTER SEVEN

NO ONE said a word as Shabazz slowly left the room with Father Patrick. They returned with the two Isis blades and a Bible. Both men slid their weapons toward the center of the large conference table, one shoving blades, one shoving the Word across the gleaming expanse.

"We all stay in the room together," Big Mike said. "We fought together as brothers, we go down together as brothers."

Jose nodded as he looked around the room. "If anybody turns, it'll probably be me and Lopez first." He let his breath out in resignation, his tone calm and yet still not defeated. "I coulda gotten nicked by one of the harpies in the storm while me and D was riding. I already have vamp in my DNA from way back, so hey. Whatcha gonna do?"

Padre Lopez agreed, his eyes blazing with determination. "Do what you have to do, okay? I already know that if Carlos turns, I'll stand with him."

Carlos cocked his head and studied the young priest. "Man, now is not the time to be abandoning your faith or casting idle threats—as much as I appreciate the loyalty. These old boys are seasoned vets, and they will do you if there's any question. *Comprendo?*"

"Yeah," Father Lopez shot back. "I do understand. But do you?"

For the first time since he'd met the young priest, he really didn't understand. His facial expression must have shown it because Padre Lopez simply shook his head.

"School me, then," Carlos said, "since we have time."

"You're one of us," Father Patrick said in a tone so quiet and so deadly that every man at the table stood slowly and took a position of safety in the room. "I have already been down this road and I'm not going down it again."

"Steady, Father," Rider said, his voice filled with worry. "That's Irish whiskey talking, and not a good thing right through here." Rider glanced at the teams.

"Irish whiskey doesn't eclipse the truth, and you know what they say, a drunk man tells the truth, says what's really on his mind." Father Patrick stalked away, circling the room, his eyes slowly becoming wild with confusion. "The Covenant is made up of every major religion on the planet, and we have all done our share of harm." He pointed at Imam Asula. "Our so-called holy wars and jihads of the past and present have killed the innocent, am I wrong? If the rabbi were here, or the others from our team that have fallen, they would also have to hide their eyes in shame for what we all, men of faith, have done. Native people slaughtered for what they believed . . . men, women, and children. Tribe against tribe, nation against nation, monk against monk, army against army, since the beginning. Tell me I'm a liar."

Imam Asula lowered his eyes. "There has been much carnage worldwide in the name of the Almighty."

"Monks in Tibet have been slaughtered, just as others have," Monk Lin said in a quiet, firm voice. "Our brother speaks truth. There is no unblemished soil. The earth has been desecrated by man."

"And that was not to be!" Father Patrick bellowed. "Do you think that pleases Him, or makes Him sick enough to weep?" He snatched the Bible off the table and flipped through it, his finger landing on a passage. "How am I supposed to kill one of our brethren? If we are in the last days, and I know that we are, go to whatever book, but in this one, Revelations, chapter three, verses one through twenty-two, it says that John was instructed by the thing that had the seven spirits of God and the seven stars, it told him to write unto the angel of the church in Sardis, *'I know thy works, thou hast a name that thou livest, and art dead. Be watchful and strengthen the things which remain, that are ready to die.'*" Father Patrick looked up at the group. "It says it here! *'He that overcometh, the same shall be clothed in white raiment, and I will not blot out his name out of the book of life.'* There were few in Sardis who have not defiled their garments and they shall walk with Him in white." He looked up. "You need to read this and sit with it a while before you pick up a blade or weapon against another living soul."

Father Patrick began walking again, his gaze upon the team members as he spoke. "The Almighty has found egregious works within *all* the churches, interpreted as *all* faiths, except the one of Philadelphia. Read it and weep! We have not been on our jobs. We have all built monuments, temples, created wars, killed, and colonized." He glanced around the immaculate, expensive room. "This plane cost how much? Should it not be cargoing food, supplies, refugees, the common man and woman . . . and what have we all done to women in the name of the Most High?"

Members of the Covenant fanned out as though bracing themselves to body slam Father Patrick if his passion escalated into a nervous breakdown. Their strategic stances made the tension in the room nearly crackle with airborne static current.

"Father," Padre Lopez said, his voice soothing and psychiatric, "please sit down. You've been under tremendous strain, as we all have. But as our group seer, your nervous system may have been impacted the most." The young cleric held out his hand. "I will pray with you, if you will just sit down and rest."

"Please summon calm and rest," Monk Lin said, his eyes sad as his voice echoed Father Lopez's plea.

"Rest! Rest? There is no rest as long as weapons to kill are before me! I can no more put a blade in the center of that young man's chest, or behead him, than I could my own son," Father Patrick said, his voice fracturing. "I have watched my own wife and son die already. I swore never again."

"You had a son, man?" Shabazz said, slowly nearing the cleric, attempting to help Father Lopez calm Father Patrick. "But you're a priest."

"I was a *man,* first." Father Patrick spat, going to the table and pouring another drink. He looked at Berkfield hard. "We're all men, flesh and blood, *first.* We all make mistakes, we all sin. That is what we have to understand and have compassion about. No one down here is God. Kiss a cardinal's ring? Dogma! If he were a man of true faith, he'd be on this plane. But he left us, taking blood that's worth gold in a silver case with him!"

"You said you had a wife and son," Berkfield said, his voice steady as his line of vision went around the group, receiving nods of quiet support as he attempted to intervene. "What happened, Father?"

Father Patrick sighed, the tears that had risen in his eyes now streaming down his cheeks in a disillusioned cascade. "My boy, probably like yours does, listened to loud music to drown out the images and voices in his head. Then he went to marijuana, then pills, then anything he could to drown out the noise until heroin killed him. The young people can see what we are blind to, hear what we refuse to listen to, know what we refuse to acknowledge," he said, pointing a finger at his temple. "They *know* something is wrong and broken within all these systems. They sense the corruption. But we're losing them daily because we have given no direction . . . we've lost our own way, but they know enough not to follow us, yet the darkness swallows them whole. How can I kill a young man who lost his way, but found it?"

Father Patrick briefly closed his eyes as he tore at his hair with a clenched fist. "So talk to your son, before the other side does. An overdose of Valium and booze took my grieving wife. End of story."

"Whoa . . ." Berkfield said slowly. "Voices? You have to explain." He glanced around the room, gaining nods to keep the priest talking, lest the cleric trip over the edge of sanity.

"What is there to say?" Father Patrick said too calmly, tossing back a jigger of whiskey. "I was gifted, and it passed to my son. But I didn't know what it was and was afraid of it myself. So I hid in the military and jobs and ignored it, and I didn't spend the time with my child. Now he's gone. He was like Mike, an audiovoyant. That's why the music calmed him, spoke to him, made sense to him. My boy got the wrong vibrations, heard the wrong messages as he turned up his speakers. Michael here was lucky. He listened to music from an era that had not yet been lost and was led, not consumed."

Big Mike crossed the room and he gently placed a hand on the cleric's shoulder. "None of us knew what this was about, man. You've gotta let it go."

Father Patrick shrugged away and crossed the room again, making all eyes follow him. "My church has just sacrificed an entire crew of their best warriors! I fought for them, bled for them, lost family and men for them, and I am now expendable? And you say I have to let it go?" His hot gaze landed on Carlos. "And this young man who I have come to love as my own was brought back from the ashes, literally, before my very eyes, and now, because of some unknown twist of fate, I'm supposed to take his head off with the Isis? After overcoming the fact that he was a drug dealer—the same sort that put my own son in the ground from an overdose? I have to forget all that, have to now do the unthinkable after I already passed the test to love my enemy—a drug-dealing vampire, like a son?" He laughed. The sound of it was filled with a shrill hysteria. "Never happen. Not because *the system* says I should. I will only do that," he exclaimed, pointing a shaky finger upward, "if He tells me to. Not because men *think* Carlos might be a threat. Never again."

Father Patrick smoothed the front of his robes, and looked down at the crest on his medallion. "It is time for the commoners to band together, to take direct instruction from On High, not middlemen strutting around in robes or professions of power. The final battle will be waged by those with nothing except faith to protect them. The meek shall inherit the earth. Our religions have been twisted by dogma, rhetoric, politics, greed, you name it." A bitter sob choked off Father Patrick's words. "I trusted them," he whispered, his eyes frantic as he looked up, holding Imam Asula's gaze. "You and I go way back, my dear brother, just like me and Lin. The triumvirate. We are the eldest living members of the Covenant, and have been friends for so long, so you know what pain is in my heart. Our religious orders have abandoned us, and have become numb to the principles of love and compassion. I cannot go on carrying their banner this way."

"We have not been abandoned," Imam Asula said, trying to restore reason to his fracturing Covenant brother. "This is simply a test. We should pray, now, I believe." He paused and began walking toward Father Patrick slowly.

"In stillness we find clarity. In friendship we find the threads of faith. My dear brother and loyal friend, please do not lose your hope," Monk Lin murmured, bowing toward Father Patrick.

"Don't kill that boy," Father Patrick whispered through a sob. "Not on my watch."

"Come my friend," Imam Asula said, opening his arms to offer an embrace as he walked toward Father Patrick. "There are times when the burden is too massive for one set of shoulders. Let me and Lin share your load. We will not raise arms unless absolutely necessary, but praying now is a must. Hold the mustard seed of faith, my friend. Come."

"That sounds like a good idea, dude," Rider said, making all eyes turn toward him as Imam Asula gathered Father Patrick in his arms and held him close. "With this turbulence kicking up, and all of us losing it, who knows what forces are at work making the teams wig. We *all* need to pray."

Carlos watched the Isis blades vibrate on the table and worry wrapped itself around his spinal cord, strangling each disc in his back. Damali's was on a hospital table downstairs, and the doctors had to work with unsteady hands. That reality fought for dominance over the scene that was unfolding within the conference room.

Father Patrick's pain and disillusionment hurt him to his soul. He could identify with the old man's sense of being robbed. He'd known that violation all his life. He wanted to shore his mentor and friend up, give him something to cling to, and yet, what could he say at this moment? At the same time, turbulence was rocking the plane, making Damali's situation on the table precarious. If he didn't exist and could just die peacefully without struggle, to his way of thinking no one else would have to suffer.

"Listen," Carlos said after a long pause, his tone careful and measured. "If Damali is on the table downstairs and they are scraping the insides of her uterus out, one bad bump, one false move, and one of those doctors could puncture her womb. My baby girl could bleed to death trying to save the group from a midair nightmare. And it is fucking me up. So everybody chill, get focused, and if you know how to pray, pray for the doctor to have a steady hand."

Carlos raked his hands through his hair and began pacing. He was glad that no one drew away from him as though he had the plague. If he was still a vampire, it sure didn't feel like it. His power was gone; most of all what was missing in his arsenal was the power to make sure Damali was safe or to take away Father Patrick's anguish.

"Tell you what," Carlos said after a moment. "What if you just do me now, get her off the table, then when you touch down in Manila you can have her seen by doctors on steady ground and can incinerate my body. Fuck it. There's no more fight left in me, and in this condition of weakness, I don't want to live anyway. But more than anything, I don't want her bleeding to death up here and I don't want her made sterile for the rest of her life because of some bullshit I did to her."

Carlos snatched the short Isis blade from the table before Father Lopez could reach it, and slashed his palm. "See, red blood. It's not black. But I still don't care. I can't help you all. I don't have any special powers! I'm not a Guardian, not a vampire, not *anything* anymore. So it doesn't matter if you do me—I'm only slowing down the team, creating a variable that's weakening your faiths— and you're gonna need that to fight what's chasing you. So be men and just do it, and get your shit together and keep my woman safe from this till the end of time!"

Red blood bubbled from Carlos's clenched fist and splattered on the table, creating a crimson puddle. The teams looked at the growing pool, mesmerized by the strange iridescence it contained.

Berkfield went to Carlos's side, snatching off his skullcap.

"Everybody relax," Berkfield said. "We're all at the brink and need to just calm down." He took Carlos's wrist and held it firmly not allowing him to snatch it away.

"Aren't you afraid that I'll bite you?" Carlos said, his gaze hard as he stared at Berkfield.

"Cut the crap and the theatrics, Rivera," Berkfield said, wrapping the deep gash with the crocheted cap and applying pressure to it. "They said I'm immune. Who knows and who cares at this point? All I know is that if we're gonna survive, we have to all pull together. So, whatever beef we've got with the powers-that-be, we have to settle that later. We've got a young woman on the table who needs a steady hand and no turbulence." His gaze went to the seat-belt signs posted in the room, making the others note that the yellow caution lights had flicked on.

"My point, exactly," Carlos said, wincing as Berkfield squeezed the cut harder. It felt like his hand was on fire as Berkfield applied greater pressure. He could feel beads of sweat begin to form on his brow, and with his uninjured hand he wiped it, suddenly feeling so weak that he almost slumped against the man at his side.

"Steady, holmes," Jose said, hurrying to Carlos's other side and catching his weight to help him into a chair.

"He must have lost a lot of blood before," Berkfield said, huffing suddenly, his breaths coming in short pants as his face flushed and Father Patrick caught him before he went down.

"Oh, shit," Rider said, helping to sprawl both men in their chairs. "We just had a blood transfer up here, no Marlene to—"

"Look at his wound," Father Patrick said, turning Berkfield's hand over as his palm split, bubbled with blood, and then slowly sealed.

Carlos stared at his hand and removed the soaked skullcap from it, his gaze darting between his hand and Berkfield's. "I didn't do that. It came from him. I felt the current pass into my hand, not out of it."

"He's a healer," Imam Asula said in awe. "The sacred blood he carries heals."

"I don't understand," Berkfield croaked out and leaned forward as the entire group gathered around them.

Father Patrick took the Isis dagger and flipped the blade to the clean side that Carlos hadn't used. He made a small cut on the back of his hand. "Cover it," he commanded Berkfield, his gaze never leaving the oozing gash.

"Yo, hold up," Jose said. "Wash his hands first. Don't be crazy and mix Rivera's blood from the first healing with yours, Father. I ain't trying to be funny, but if you're up here experimenting, then you need to do it right and with precautions. Vampires heal themselves, too. We need to be sure that Berkfield did it, not Rivera."

Berkfield and Carlos nodded.

"No lie," Shabazz said, moving so Berkfield could stand. "Hurry up though."

With Big Mike at his side for assistance, Berkfield rushed to the bathroom and soaped and rinsed his hands, quickly returning to the conference room with Big Mike holding him up. All eyes were on Berkfield as he took Father Patrick's hand within his, closed his eyes, and waited. Soon a peaceful heat entered his palms and covered the old priest's wound.

They all watched Berkfield's hand open in a small cut just under the knuckles. The gash dripped in a slow line of blood onto the table, and then sealed. When he removed his hands from the cleric's, Father Patrick's wound also sealed.

"Well I'll just be damned," Rider whispered, staring at Berkfield. "Marlene's healings work differently . . . I can't explain it, but yours is . . . I don't know."

"Marlene's is internal, spiritual, she seals breaks in the aura and soul. Berkfield has the touch to seal broken flesh," Shabazz said, his eyes riveted to the healed wounds. "All I know is, we need this gift on our team if we're going into the Armageddon, brother. Coulda used you when we got our asses kicked in Hell, too."

"Word," Jose murmured, his line of vision going to Father Patrick.

"Like I said," Carlos murmured, still staring at his hand, "I'm no threat. I can't even heal myself or regenerate from a simple cut. Killing me oughta be easy at this point."

Father Lopez peered at the table, motioning to the pool of shimmering crimson blood that Carlos's wound had left. He poked at it with the tip of the long Isis and then set the short blade down slowly. All of them watched silently as Carlos's blood beaded up and formed small clusters of a reddish, mercury-like substance on the table.

"Then tell us why you have silver running through your veins," Father Lopez said in a reverent tone. "We don't know what your gift is yet, *hombre,* but you've obviously got one."

The walk through the cabin toward the sick bay felt like a death march. Each time the plane shifted from the turbulence, Damali could feel her pulse quicken. She could also feel Marlene's worried gaze boring into her back, trying to reach her, make her stop walking, and silently begging her to give up her mission to be done with it all.

"I'm not going to have a buncha drama kick off on this plane," Damali said without turning to address Marlene. "We both know this tension is about to blow, and innocent people could get hurt. There's only one way to handle this—just do the damned thing."

Although Marlene didn't verbally answer her, she knew her words had been accepted with silent, begrudging resignation. The palpable energy seal between her and Marlene receded as the older woman dropped her resistance and it became easier to move forward.

"Thank you," Damali said quietly as her hand touched the sick-bay door.

"I don't agree, but I respect your decision," Marlene said as they entered the state-of-the-art medical room. Marlene stared at the doctors. "Be very careful. She's also precious cargo, if to no one else, she is to me."

The two doctors nodded and handed Damali a white hospital gown, then pulled the drape.

"Please put this on," one doctor said. "Open in the back, put the tissue sheet across your lap and place your feet in the stirrups, and then we'll begin."

"Don't worry, Ms. Stone," the lead doctor assured Marlene. "We have state-of-the-art heart equipment on board. Our pontiff and many of his ambassadors are elderly and suffer from chronic health conditions. Therefore, our medical room is well equipped to handle any emergency that should arise."

Damali and Marlene shared a glance as both women nodded, unconvinced, but prepared to do what was necessary. She stared at the head doctor. He hadn't even told her his name. His eyes were cold blue. He seemed near sixty, if a day, and the fact that he couldn't look her in the eye didn't inspire her confidence. The younger one at his side looked like an older version of Dan, and seemed just as skittish. Heaven make this quick. She already didn't like who was going to do the medical job.

"I would feel better," Marlene said with a weary sigh, "if there wasn't so much turbulence."

"We'll strap her to the table," the assisting doctor assured Marlene. "Once we apply a local anesthesia, she shouldn't experience too much discomfort."

Damali handed her clothes to Marlene and continued to talk to the doctors who'd given her privacy on the other side of the drape. She didn't care who they were or what they thought, so long as they hurried up and did what needed to be done. "I took a couple of shots of Jack Daniels, though."

Both women stopped moving as the doctors never replied.

Damali pulled the drape open and slowly pushed herself to the edge of the table, noting the sharp instruments on the tray beyond her head. Her gaze went to what appeared to be a large plastic sump pump with a clear hose attached to it, and she studied the masked men who had scrubbed their hands and covered them with a sheath of latex.

"We're hesitant to give you anesthesia with liquor in your system," the head doctor said, glancing at Marlene as his assistant secured the table harness over Damali's arms, torso, and opened thighs. He took great care to wrap her calves and ankles in nylon fabric belts to keep her legs from jerking during the procedure.

"I don't need it," Damali said, her throat suddenly dry as she continued to stare at the pump container.

"Baby, when they start working just stare at the ceiling. Don't concentrate on the sound," Marlene murmured as she stroked Damali's hair.

Tears filled her eyes and she focused on the ceiling. "Just do it."

The doctors nodded and turned on the pump.

"Oh, great Isis have mercy," Marlene whispered, turning her face away as a doctor neared Damali. "Don't let them do this to you, baby." Marlene squeezed Damali's hand. "You can change your mind—"

Damali and Marlene froze as a gun barrel suddenly dug into Marlene's temple, the distinctive click of a hammer being cocked drowning out the sound of the pump.

"We have express orders to remove the daywalker and destroy it. Please, good woman, do not interfere with the business at hand."

The gun was pressed against Marlene's temple so hard that she dared not turn.

"Put the gun away," Damali whispered. "If turbulence hits, it could accidentally go off, killing her for no reason. She won't resist. We know we have to do this."

The head doctor eased the gun away from Marlene's head, and put the safety back on. He placed it on the side counter and sighed. "I'm sorry that I had to do that. But you have to understand that we cannot allow sentiment to overshadow reason." The doctor's eyes briefly searched Marlene's for forgiveness, and then he looked down at Damali. "Maybe this would be easier for all of us if she were to wait outside?"

Damali shook her head no, tears slipping from the corners of her eyes, down the sides of her face, and into her hair as she continued to stare at the bright light in the ceiling. "If you make her leave, I won't be able to go through this . . . and if I start screaming, I have no idea what the father will do."

Damali looked to Marlene for reassurance and to let her know it would be all right, but Marlene's gaze was fixated on the equipment, not on her or the gun, where it should have logically been. She could feel Marlene silently dry heave as panic glittered in the older woman's eyes. The fatigue, her condition, everything must have interfered with her second sight. Damali's grip on Marlene's hand tightened as a threat slowly registered within her.

Without letting go of Damali's hand, Marlene's eyes narrowed on the doctors. "It's so clear now. You don't intend to just clean her out, you intend to render her sterile so she can never—"

A sharp slap cut off Marlene's words, making her fall backward. Damali tried to rise off the table, but the harnesses held her tight.

"Tranquilize the mother-seer now," the head doctor shouted, "before the demon comes in here and stops what must be!"

"No!" Damali yelled, but became instantly quiet when Marlene held up her hands.

"I call the goddesses of Kemet! The justice of Ma'at. The ancient ones enshrined in the purple light of protection! I call the ancestral warriors, the ones who guard the Neteru. Take your child and shelter her now from these beasts posing as men!" Before the doctors could reach her or the gun, Marlene clapped three times, and an arc of purple electricity covered Damali at the same time the plane was slammed by heavy turbulence.

The two doctors were knocked off their feet, but Marlene remained steadfast, leaning against the wall as her hands crackled and arced with blue-white current, her fingertips singeing the ceiling with the purple bolts of divine energies she summoned. As the fallen men struggled to stand, Marlene lowered one flat palm, sending a purple charge that rendered them immobile as she spoke. She closed her eyes, outstretched her other hand in Damali's direction, her concentration so focused that the invisible third eye in the center of her forehead glowed violet.

"I have never called you to open the door. This one urgent request as taught in the *Temt Tchass* I have guarded; please heed. From the pyramids of Menkaure, Khafre, and Khufu at Giza, to the banks of the Nile in Nubia open the portal, pave the path to the table of Eve, to the place of Light where Khepre, Re, and Amen cycle, oh great Queen Aset, mother of Kemet, take your daughter through the door!"

"Stop the witch!" the head doctor yelled, as Damali's straps broke and another thunderous crash hit the plane.

As quickly as possible Damali sat up, electricity covering her, molding to her body and making the entire surface of her skin shimmer in a wash of blue-violet light. The purple and white light in the ceiling became blinding and pulled at her, forcing her arms to open and then yield upward.

"Flee, child, to the place beyond the drinking gourd!" Marlene yelled, and clapped three times, and shouted, "Ashe!"

In an arc of light that wobbled and then opened to a wide, steady beam at the top of her head, Damali was gone.

The conference-room discussion ground to a halt as an eerie violet charge crept over the edges of the polished table, covered both Isis blades, broadened to a wide arc of light around the sword and dagger, and folded the weapons away into nothingness.

Carlos yelled Damali's name.

CHAPTER EIGHT

"YOU PICK up a signal yet, baby?" Yonnie murmured, daring to stroke Tara's arm as he lay beside her.

"No," she said quietly, her eyes wide open in the darkness of the lair.

"Thanks for the feed and the save."

"Don't mention it," she said, her tone far off. "You can't pick up anything, either?"

"No. That's what worries me." He stood and stretched, even though he knew it was still daylight beyond the cement walls that surrounded them. The heat was oppressive and the hallowed-earth encasement around the basement vault made it difficult to breathe. "How much stock do we have?"

"Enough to last about a week. Then we'll have to hunt."

He walked over to the small refrigerator. "I don't think I can do a week trapped down here drinking cold deer blood."

For a moment neither of them spoke.

"I could ingest it and offer a vein transfer," Tara said quietly.

"From the jugular?"

"Be serious. From my wrist."

He smiled. The thought, either way, was appealing. "You're not afraid I'll get greedy and flat-line you?"

"Then how would you get out of here, since only I know how to get past the barriers?"

He chuckled. "True, but when we go hunting, maybe—"

"No humans," she said firmly, now standing to cross the room. "Do that, and neither you nor I will be able to get back into this lair. That's how it works."

"That's some real fucked-up rules, baby."

"I didn't make them, but for the last twenty or so years, that's how it's been."

"So, tell me, for real, you've never broken a human vein? Never made a live kill?"

She didn't immediately answer. "I've taken a vein, but never one that had after-a-hunt adrenaline coursing through it."

"Then you've never—"

"Shut up," she snapped. "I don't want to hear about it, think about it, or even consider—"

"Why? Because you might start fantasizing about it?"

"No, because it's cruel." She paced to the far side of the room. "I know you're a master, but I will not stay in here listening to your seduction crap. Either shut the hell up or get out and make it on your own."

"Okay, okay. Chill," he said, chuckling, coming nearer to her. "My bad."

"Yes. Your bad," she said, trying to ignore his hands as they gently caressed her arms.

"Since you were made, you never got with one of our kind again?"

She shook her head. "I have someone. I've told you that."

"But he's human."

"Yes, he's human and a man with a good heart."

"But he's human."

"And I love him."

Yonnie brushed her ear with the tip of his nose. "But . . . he's human."

"Yes."

"And, I'm a master."

"Yes."

He stroked the side of her cheek, and ran the pad of his thumb over her mouth, thoroughly pleased when her lowered fang nicked his flesh. "Damn, whoever made you made you righteous, baby."

"Shut up."

"A master ever call you to his lair before . . . just you, a fourth-generation female, for a one-on-one?"

"No, and it doesn't matter."

His hands trailed down her arms, again creating a slight shudder within her. "You sure?"

"Completely."

He molded his body against her rigid back. "Just a sip, one nick. What could it hurt? He'll never know. He's human and can't see the marker."

"But I'll know," she said, swallowing hard. "I wouldn't be able to live with that."

"But could you exist with that?" he murmured and waited, feeling her resistance dissolving under his hold. "Twenty-something years and never going all the way? We're vampires?" he said softly. "Masters need it every night and once you go there, you'll understand."

"I can't miss what I've never experienced." She shrugged out of his hold and crossed the room, wrapping her arms around herself. She looked at him hard, her eyes blazing in the darkness. "I will not desecrate his house! He built it for me. This is our home. So stop it."

"Your eyes are glowing red," Yonnie whispered, his voice like silk. "You really haven't ever been with a master, have you?"

She looked away, not able to stare at the glowing red orbs that confronted her.

"One deep plunge in the throat, and I guarantee you won't care whose house this is."

"I said stop it, or get out."

"You're trembling where you stand, girl. Why are you fighting your nature like this?"

She didn't answer. She simply went to the refrigerator.

"I thought we were supposed to be rationing." He chuckled and watched her open a bottle and slam the refrigerator door. "That is so cold." He smiled as he saw her take a shaky sip and close her eyes. He crossed the room and gently took the bottle from her hand. "Let me warm that up for you," he whispered, taking a generous swig from the bottle and opening the top button of his shirt to expose his throat. "Just lose the silver collar first."

For a moment, she stared at his jugular, then at the crimson dampness on his full, lush mouth, then looked away. "No, thank you. We'd better rest and regenerate."

"How old is he now? Almost forty-five, fifty human years?"

She nodded and walked away, leaving Yonnie the bottle. "Yes."

"And we may very well be the last of our kind in this territory, no other masters on the planet so far . . . and Carlos missing."

"What's your point?"

Yonnie polished off the bottle and cast it to the floor, shattering it. "He's almost fifty, I just ate, you've never been where I can take you—"

"Please stop," she said quietly, the request coming out as a plea. "You know what happened to me, and how I was made."

He nodded and went to the bed, circling her once, but finally lying down. He put an arm over his forehead and stared at the ceiling. "Yeah, I do," he said quietly. "You didn't deserve that." He felt her telepathically probe him for answers, and opened up to allow her to see how he was made.

"You didn't deserve that, either," she said. "But I'm glad Carlos tried to make it as right as he could."

"Yeah. I owe him and therefore his posse, big time, I suppose." It hadn't helped that he could sense that she had tears in her eyes. The fact that she cared was not in his original plan. "It's safe to lie down and rest," he said. "I ain't gonna bother you."

When she didn't move, he turned his head to stare at her. "For real. I'm cool. I'm not gonna keep messing with you. I know it's in my nature, but even I have—"

Her eyes had gone to a deep crimson, stopping his words.

"I should have never locked into your thoughts. I've never locked with a master before. Give me a minute."

She turned away and he could hear her stop breathing for a moment as she fingered her silver necklace.

"When's the last time you visited him?" Yonnie pushed himself up to lean on his elbow as he studied her.

"A year ago."

For a long while, neither spoke.

"I love him. So don't do that again. Please."

Yonnie reclined slowly and nodded, closing his eyes, trying to get her lavender scent out of his mind. "It works both ways, you know. And finding out how genuine you are wasn't something I expected, either. Not from a female vamp. Shit."

"I'm sorry."

"Let it go. We'll lay low until the blood runs out and the territory cools off, then we'll find Carlos and his human squad."

"Thank you," she said, but still didn't rejoin him in bed. "The burn will dissipate in a little while, right?"

He couldn't immediately answer her. "No," he finally murmured. "It'll get worse before it gets better."

"I'm not going to be unfaithful. Not after all these years."

"I'm not going to attack you, if that's what you're worried about." Yonnie let his breath out hard, summoning a master's discipline.

"That's not what I'm worried about," she said quietly, edging toward the bed.

"Baby, lie down and go to sleep. We do this one hour at a time."

She nodded and sat on the edge of the bed and stared at him.

"A week in here like this will be a long time." He looked at her and stroked her arm.

For a while she didn't answer. "Yes. I know."

CHAPTER NINE

DAMALI FELT like she was flying, the images whirled by her so fast. Her skin crackled with electricity, and she gasped as she landed on her feet with a thud. She crouched down, instantly on guard, and glanced around herself. She patted her side. Shit. Her blade was back on the plane.

The question was, where was she and how did she get here?

It was clearly an industrial area with a river to the south. In front of her was a wide street, but no traffic. It was dark. Not a good thing without a blade. Damali glanced down at herself. At least she was dressed for the occasion. Black leather pants, black halter top, and steel-toe black boots. Perfect for kicking vamp or demon ass. Did Marlene do all of that, too? Deep.

She walked forward slowly and cautiously, staying low. Had to be the point in the night when the clubs closed and sidewalks rolled up and partygoers went home. It was the hunting hour.

Restaurant lights behind her on the long stretch of riverfront were dim. Massive buildings were black, nary a light in a window. A bridge loomed in the distance; its architecture seeming like an eerie blue dinosaur skeleton. The hair stood up on her arms. No, Marlene wouldn't have sent her *here* to hide.

A neon club marquis read CLUB EGYPT. Damali stopped walking and folded her arms over her chest. She stared at the sign, noticing the hieroglyphics that had been spray-painted on the sand-colored exterior of the building.

She slowly unfolded her arms. She saw movement in the doorway of the club, and she forced her body to stay loose and ready. She narrowed her eyes. She scanned the area again quickly and noticed a street sign that read DELAWARE AVENUE. She was in Philly then.

"Fuck it," she muttered, crossing the wide boulevard and walking toward the club with purpose. Standing on a corner wringing her hands wasn't going to get her any answers.

When she got to the door, a huge bouncer stopped her. "ID?"

Damali looked him up and down. He was a big burly brother who looked like he was straight out of the motherland. His gleaming blue-black complexion blended almost seamlessly into his black muscle shirt and jeans.

Damali put a hand on his broad chest. "Now you know you need to stop playing." Then she smiled.

He stared down at her, his face blank, his eyes icy. Damali gave him a slow smile and then licked her lips. The ice cracked. He moved his mountainous girth out of the doorway and offered her a wink laced with appreciation. Damali blew him a kiss as she hurried past him.

Once inside, she squinted through the purple, hazy clouds of smoke. Such as it was, the interior seemed fairly normal. She glanced around. The place was half filled. The music was thumping. The DJ was all right. People were free-styling on the wide, polished wood dance floor. The bars were loaded. People were seated at round tables scattered throughout or lounging stylishly on purple and black minisofas. She couldn't sense anything pretenatural.

Damali carefully made her way to the bar. She slid onto a tall brass-and-leather stool as she continued to scan the club. When the female bartender came toward her, she remembered she was broke. Damali smiled. There were plenty enough brothers sipping at the rail to make that a nonissue. But if they were offering drinks with a shot of color, she wouldn't be drinking anyway.

Damali studied the tall, older woman as she walked over to her. Girlfriend looked good. She had on a metallic gold bustier that presented her double-Ds like trophies. A gold-filigreed waist chain that moved ever so slightly above her tight, gold lame pants as she walked accentuated her flat belly. Her complexion was of burnt cinnamon, but her eyes were a smoldering dark brown, matching the color of her shoulder-length braids. A gold serpent arm bracelet circled her sleekly muscular upper arm. She looked like she was in her early thirties. Her walk was so smooth, she almost looked like she was moving in slow motion Damali had to shake her head to break the hypnotic rhythm. Had to be vamp.

"What you having tonight?" the bartender asked with a smile.

Damali studied her. "What are you serving that's top shelf?"

The bartender's smile widened. "Sis, I don't roll like that. I've got a man."

Damali sat back. "Well, shit, so do I."

"Don't we all?" a deep, sexy female voice close to her ear said. Damali quickly pivoted on the stool, ready to do battle. "But if you're angling for a free drink, just name your poison."

"First you need to back up off me," Damali said slowly, watching the very tall Native American–looking woman slide onto the barstool next to her. She tossed her long French braid over her shoulder and sighed. Damali didn't like the odds, and they were getting worse. She could feel the females moving in on her quickly and quietly as the men slid away, making room for them.

One by one the chairs filled in around her. She glanced at the bartender, then the tall, older woman who was a fly-ass fifty, serving royal blue peacock and black stilettos.

"Pour this child a Jack Daniels," the woman beside her said. "My tab."

"This ain't no bargain," Damali said, accepting the drink with her eyes and not touching it. Another older sister had slid into a chair on her right. Her dark face seemed vaguely familiar, and her intense black eyes had that same knowing quality the others possessed.

She flipped her hand to dismiss Damali's open assessment. Sister was rockin' so much ice that the diamonds were practically blinding. Pure confidence radiated from her, almost like a heat wave. She was serving red stilettos that bordered on being "come fuck me" pumps. The red pants suit, killer. Everything about her aura demanded respect, even if she might have to kill her.

Damali raised her glass to them. Her gaze surveyed what she quickly counted as six or seven women. All older. All of varying hues and dressed to the nines, so confident and cocky that they hadn't even worn good battle shoes. . . . All of them, obviously, professional assassins who could be patient and wait to do their hits. "Well, I have to hand it to you, ladies. You sure know how to try to take a sister out in style."

The one in red chuckled and sipped her martini slowly. "Too dramatic." She looked down the bar at the others. "See what man trouble will do? Make you simple."

Tension coiled around Damali's spine. Fury ate at her tender insides. She picked up her glass and poured it slowly into the woman's lap. "Yeah. It'll do that. So, let's get this party started."

She'd expected the instant lunge, and had mentally placed her reach to the bottles and barstools. She'd expected the cool sister to jump up. At least one of her girls should have flinched. But instead she just looked down at the stain and the liquor running down her shapely leg, and dabbed it with a finger, tasted it, made a face, and shook her head.

"See, that's youth," she said in an even tone. "You don't do that tacky mess in public. You take it to the ladies' room."

Damali was off her stool. "Any time."

"Now would be good," the bartender said, clearing it with one lithe move to stand before Damali with a sly smile. "Shall we?"

"It's your house," Damali said through her teeth. "You lead the way."

Martini glasses, champagne flutes, and rock glasses were set down calmly in unison as the women flanking the leader stood.

"Baby girl, do you have any idea who you're up against?"

Damali stepped back farther, one hand on her hip, the other pointing out her complaint. "No, bitch, do you?"

It was the first time she saw a flicker of rage cross their faces. The woman in red cocked her head to the side. "What did you call me?"

Damali wasn't sure if it was the tone of her voice or the level of shock held within it, but something very strange gave her pause. Within seconds the tall, older sister was up in her face.

"Take your ass to the bathroom before I embarrass you out here in public."

What? Damali looked at her like she was crazy. The dance floor had cleared. Several bouncers had come into the open area, but didn't move. The woman snapped her arm out and pointed hard in the direction of the back of the club. Damali balled up her fist, preparing to sucker-punch her. But then the woman did something Damali never expected. She simply turned on her heels and strutted forward, her head high with her shoulders back.

Curiosity was jacking with Damali's senses. Had all the female vampires just calmly walked to the ladies' room, or was she hallucinating? There was a silent dignity about them that didn't fit. Not to mention, they should have all been throwing down, right through here. Not marching toward the bathroom like offended church ladies. If they hadn't attacked, that meant one thing—they needed information. But what?

As she cautiously followed their regal promenade, Damali worked the puzzle in her head. Carlos had to be part of this. Maybe they were really worried about where their esteemed councilman had gone. Yeah . . . that had to be it.

The sister in red swung open the heavy door, almost yanking it from its hinges and making it slam against the wall. Bright fluorescent light greeted them, Damali entering the tight confines last. She made a quick assessment. No windows. All-white metal stalls and tile with pink accent borders. The pink was disorienting. In a vamp joint? Then she stopped as they stood before a huge mirror and cast a reflection, just like she did.

She opened her mouth and slowly closed it.

"That's right, damn it!" the woman in red said. "You'd better get a grip and know who you're talking to. I'll have you know I've run empires before you were even thought of, sister!"

"*Chica,* this is bad," another said, shaking her head. "We gonna have to kick your ass now, for real."

"Aw, ladies," another tall beauty said. "You know that's not why we brought her here."

The bartender stepped forward and offered her a fist pound. "We've got bigger problems."

"All right, Eve," the sister in red said, giving Damali a hard glare.

"This is your territory. School her fast before I snatch a bone out of her narrow behind."

Damali's attention went from one woman to the next. Did one of them call the sister serving drinks Eve?

"Yeah, yeah, yeah. Long story, baby. But hey, you know how this goes. You find Mr. Right, fall in love, get your head twisted around by some other fine bastard, then have issues. Feel me?"

Damali couldn't stop gaping. Then she realized one by one, that each woman was marked by a symbol she hadn't noticed before. Their tattoos were made of silvery light, and she couldn't take her eyes off of them.

"Take a walk with us," the one pointed out as Eve said, moving toward the mirror. "You game for some insight?"

From some strange place in her soul, Damali found her head nodding in the affirmative. She came nearer to the woman than was probably advisable, as Eve's hands touched the mirror and melted into it like it was water. "We had to strip your blade from you, hon, until you could learn to use it right, because what's coming for you—you can't fight like you just did out there. The Sankofa burned off for the same reason."

The others nodded.

"You will get your ass beat down if you go after her like you just did, hear?" the woman in red said, obviously still salty about her dress. "Lilith will fuck you up good, if you don't watch your back, and no man is worth all that."

Damali's eyes were so wide that she couldn't blink. Then someone behind her pushed her and she was alone in a vast, stone enclosure.

Angry as a wet hen, she fell forward into a place that had sepia-hued marble walls. The color surrounded her and she was on the landing of a massive staircase. Towering oblong windows allowed in the breaking dawn, and an infant's coo made her look up to the top of the next landing.

Instinct propelled her forward. Bounding up the wide, slippery steps, she took them two at a time, and then stopped as she neared the child and saw the crosscut on its finger. Immediate panic tore through her as she recognized the tiny brown infant that had big, frightened eyes. It was the baby from the Australian master's castle.

Damali began backing up as the baby slowly grew, aged, and became a weathered old man with snow-white hair. He smiled a black, toothless grin, his leathery face dotted with white paint, making her remember the circle of Aborigines. He pointed to his chest to keep her from running away, showing her the markings of the sixth seal that he guarded. The white matrix of paint on his bare chest glowed golden for a moment, and then he flung a sash of white cloth from his waist over it, making it return to normal, and a walking stick appeared in his hand.

He nodded and then bowed, motioning to her with his stick to follow him. Although he didn't wait as he proceeded, occasionally he glanced over his shoulder still smiling, almost mocking Damali for being wary and keeping her distance.

Once she reached the top of the stairs he pointed with the stick to a wide hallway. A glasslike wash of violet light spilled across the marble. Impatient, he clicked the stick on the ground three times and stomped his rusty bare feet hard, waving her forward, and then disappeared.

She keened all her senses, straining to use her third eye, to feel vibrations, to hear, all to no avail. Where were they?

She began walking forward, feeling amazingly light as each footfall lifted her slightly off the floor. Soon the glasslike purple rays covered her as she entered its full beam, and instantly the mere intent of moving forward rushed her to an open atrium filled with swirling golden-white light and women's voices.

Damali squinted as a large opalescent oval table came into view, and seated before her were the seven women. Four were sitting on one side, three on the other of an empty, high, Kemetian throne carved in alabaster, with a falcon-winged sun disc bearing the Ankh symbol of fertility within it. She recognized Nzinga instantly this time. The red siren's getup had completely thrown her off. Then she saw the Amazon sitting to her right, and dropped to one knee. She'd failed the ultimate test. Oh, dear God.

She'd been summoned to the council of Neterus! Queens of old, beyond the chamber of spirits called the holy of holies within the pyramids. Maybe she was dead and this was judgment day.

"Queen mothers," Damali murmured, without looking up. "You have summoned me? I, uh, didn't recognize you, at first, and—"

"You must approach all sisters with respect. It would have avoided any confusion. That's the problem today. Always carry yourself in a dignified manner, no matter the circumstances. No one has respect." The elder queen whom Damali had offended folded her arms over her ample breasts and thrust her chin up.

"Queen daughter, arise. Your mother-seer summoned us. We had a need to intervene," the Amazon said more calmly.

Damali slowly stood, awed at the majestic women before her. Each wore a brilliant, shimmering hue of the chakra system, from the deepest jewel ruby to striking amethyst. The Amazon, the newest addition to the council, was swathed in glowing novice white, and like the others, she bore a living, silvery Adinkra symbol on her body. Hers was an Akoben, a war horn, placed on her individualized power center—her forearm; her blade arm.

Damali was speechless as she looked at the flawless beauty of the eldest woman whom she now instantly knew to be Eve. Her hair was a tangle of thick African braids scooped up in a complex cone, her headdress a crown of woven lotus blossoms. Her dress was a glasslike sheath of glistening rubies, her dark almond-shaped eyes smoldered with patience and wisdom and truth. She turned slowly to walk around the table and be seated, allowing Damali to glimpse the backless gown so she'd understand that she was also anointed with a Sankofa tattoo, one placed just at the base of her spine like Damali's. However, Eve's mark was a scrolling heart variation of the same symbol. She offered Damali a discreet wink. Her high cheekbones and lush mouth seemed to barely conceal a wry smile as she cocked her head and folded her hands before her at the table.

"I have walked a mile in your footfalls, dear one," Eve said calmly. "But you must—"

"Not be foolish!" Nzinga said, cutting Eve off, the sleeves of her royal violet gown shimmering as her arms swept before her. "She was my protégé, a warrior. This is unacceptable!" Nzinga thrust her chin upward, her proud neck stretching as the light from the wide windows behind the table glinted off her unblemished ebony skin. "We don't have time for this."

Pure panic riddled Damali as her gaze swept the powerful females before her. Their silvery symbols painted new realities in her mind; Eve had a heart Sankofa anointed over her base, primal energy chakra; it's meaning clear—you can always undo your mistakes; the Amazon had a war horn, symbolizing a call to arms. At the base of Nzinga's neck, just before her spine began, was what appeared to be a double-bladed battleaxe; *Akoko nan tiaba na enkum ba* . . . the hen treads upon its chicks but does not kill them. Damali took heart in the symbol. Maybe she'd get beat down today, but not officially killed.

"Girl, listen," Eve finally said, breaking into current vernacular to try to ease Damali's humiliation. "You know how this thing goes. She's supposed to cuss out and beat down anything that comes for her or her family. The chile is supposed to go down swinging. Now, I personally give her points for courage, because she came in that joint buck-wild and ready to just do the damned thing."

"See, that's just the thing, Eve. You always liked living on the edge." Nzinga gave her a testy smile.

Eve stroked her snake armband. "It has had its merits as well as its drawbacks, but please don't act like you can't go there,'Zinga."

"Don't get in my business," Nzinga warned with a smile. "We can turn this table over up in here, if you start."

Eve chuckled. "I know. Your secrets are safe with me, sister."

"She fought to reclaim me," the Amazon said, attempting to come to Damali's defense and defuse the brewing quarrel amongst the queens.

"Loyalty is an asset," Nefertiti contended. "I will forgive the dress fiasco. But do understand if it happens again, I will cut out your heart, little sis. That was Egyptian linen. 'Zinga didn't deserve that." But her smile toward Damali was kind, and her gorgeous eyes contained so much mirth that no threat seemed imminent. She straightened her bronze midriff-baring gown and held Damali in a tender stare as her silvery symbol gleamed around her navel. "And you were ready to fight, while in so much physical and emotional pain. You've passed my test, baby. We just want you to be shrewd, is all."

Both women nodded, and Damali could almost hear her symbol whisper into her womb; *Ntesie matemasie;* I have heard it and kept it—the symbol of wisdom and knowledge linked them for a moment.

"She is young, like I was," a stunning blonde said, and her brilliant yellow gown swished as she stood. Her blue eyes held compassion as she peered at Damali. "My own people burned me at the stake for the visions I had, yet I never had the chance to live, to love, to learn to care so deeply. To love. That cannot be a crime."

Damali could only stare at the four hearts that made a floral pattern in the center of Joan's forehead where her third eye was. It all made so much sense that Damali wanted to weep. She could clearly see each of their symbols now. Yes, *Nyame nwu na mawu;* if God dies, then I may die, thus perpetual existence.

"Her heart is of ours," a tall Native American queen said, her jewel-green headdress sparkling as she spoke. The eagle feathers in it swayed hypnotically as Damali watched the silvery *Aya* tattoo on the muscled part of her shoulder pulse. It was the symbol of the fern, but also the mark of defiance—simply stated, I am not afraid of you. "I remember trying to blend two worlds, standing as a bridge between conquerors and my people for the sake of peace . . . and for the sake of love. We shall not judge her harshly at this council. I, too, stand with our Amazon sister on this measure."

"But Nzinga is wise and has governed this council well," a queen with an elaborate Asian headdress said, the deep tangerine of her dress a startling contrast to the soft eloquence her voice held. "Before all things, she is a Neteru, and must always have the discipline as her foremost concern."

She bore the interlocking loops of two halves joined to make one, a symbol of hope, just over her heart, her symbol sending a chime resonance to Damali's ears—*Birbi wo soro. Nyame birbi wo soro na ma embeka mensa;* God there is something in the heavens, let it reach me. Damali almost covered her mouth to hold back a pending sob . . . the disrespect she'd shown, not to mention the craziness she'd gone through, and her own Sankofa had peeled away in Marlene's white bath when she'd temporarily turned into a vamp. Shame forced her to study the floor.

"Let her speak," a lean Aztec beauty said, her silver and turquoise presence so stunning that Damali almost looked away. Now Damali understood the royal peacock blue. The Aztec queen smoothed the thick rope of black braid over her shoulder. It was wrapped in a studded length of what appeared to be liquid silver and highly polished stones.

"You rule the throat chakra," Nzinga said with a smile. "Of course that would be your choice of action."

"I have led armies of men to defend my people, but never found myself . . ." The Asian queen's voice trailed off as she shook her head. "So compromised."

"And if you had met Ghengis Khan, in your era?" the Amazon said with a chuckle. "Ruthless bastard, but I heard very interesting rumors—"

"Enough!" Nzinga said, making a tent before her mouth with her hands. "We shall remain focused. My concern is that my protégé, the one who says her prayers to me for guidance, and who leads men into battle at this tenuous hour, has not lost her way." She stood and walked behind the table, her long glowing robes cascading from the high throne adding color to the moving white opalescent light on the table. "My child. You carried his seed. A vampire . . . a . . . a . . . I cannot even say it. Willingly allowed yourself to take a vampiric bite. No fight, no battle—"

"Wait," Eve said, standing quickly. "I must interject on her behalf, my queen sister. As the eldest at this table, I can assure you taking his bite was from no simple lapse in judgment or discipline. Trust me when I say, I know the dilemma she faced, and if he was half as convincing as the one I dealt with, then we should allow this daughter to tell her side of it." Eve sat slowly and smiled as Nzinga begrudgingly returned to her seat. "Dear queen sister, they are very, very seductive. May you never find yourself tangling with a six-foot serpent between your legs."

"Complete truth," the Amazon said, her gaze locking with Damali's. "My mother-seer met the one that befell our daughter. Oh, man . . . he came as a panther. What can I say? Magnificent specimen." She glanced at Eve with a sly smile. "From what she showed me, I would have lost my sword, too, if he'd been willing."

Both women laughed and the others swallowed away knowing smiles. But all mirth dissipated as a purple haze rolled across the floor and a triangular window eclipsed the brightness of the rising sun within the other panes. Two massive white lions strolled out of the lit expansion, roared, and sat beside the empty throne. Each member of the council of Neterus glanced at Damali briefly with a solemn warning, then stood, turned to face the open pyramid, and bowed. Damali followed their lead as a stunning entity stepped across the threshold of the Light.

"Nuk ast au neheh ertai-nef tetta. Nuk pu Aset, Isis." The regal entity looked at Damali and translated. "Behold, I am the heir of eternity, everlastingness has been given to me. I am Aset, Isis." As she spoke, the *Mmra krado* symbol, the seal of the law of supreme authority, on her throat flared deep purple. She waited until the council queens stood erect, her wise, almond-shaped eyes unreadable. On her forehead blazed a silvery sun marking of *Nsoroma,* a child of the heavens, the translation clear: A child of the Supreme Being, I do not depend on myself. My illumination is a reflection of The I Am. "I have been summoned, so I have come. Be seated."

"Behold, Queen Mother Aset, also known as Isis, first queen of Kemet, that had become known as Egypt. Our newest daughter has come before us with great challenges that threaten all we protect."

Aset nodded toward Nzinga and sat down, casting the Isis dagger and long blade on the table before her. Nzinga's eyes filled with alarm as she glanced at Damali and then Aset.

But the queen before her was so completely mesmerizing that for a moment, Damali forgot just how serious her predicament was. Aset's marble-smooth skin was the deepest ebony with red and copper tones beneath it, giving her skin the appearance of black porcelain fired to perfection. Her eyes literally drank Damali in. Their beauty contained so much knowledge that Damali wanted to look away, but could not. Her height was striking, yet her bone structure was as delicate as an Ibis bird's. Her hair was a glistening profusion of onyx-colored, perfectly symmetrical shoulder-length braids woven with what seemed to be living gold bands. Her throat was adorned with a wide golden collar that had an opening to allow her marking to be seen. Precious stones matching the chakra system were set in the collar, and hieroglyphics of the battles of the Neteru were etched across it. Long, kundalini golden snake bracelets covered her forearms with precious stones denoting the power points and meridians within the body energy system. Her gown was of sheer gold, showing her voluptuous nude form in relief beneath the shimmering fabric. Damali's voice became trapped in her throat.

"Queen daughter," Aset said. "I am distressed."

"Queen mother," Damali said, hoarsely. "I am so sorry." She bowed and wrapped her arms around herself. "There's so much that happened in such a short period of time. I never meant to shame you . . . or my mentor, Nzinga."

"You have not shamed us. You have shamed yourself." Aset let out a weary breath. "A possible daywalker?"

"Queen mother, Carlos and I . . . what happened was—"

"I know what happened," Aset said and closed her eyes. Every woman at the table stopped breathing. "If you had only waited until he was brought forth from Darkness into the Light. Only a few months until his resurrection. How many of the forty-two laws of Ma'at have been violated as a result of your actions? Did your mother-seer not warn you?"

"Yes," Damali said quietly. "Please don't blame Marlene. It wasn't her fault."

"We cast no blame on a mother-seer who advises an adult Neteru who chooses not to listen. Our hearts encircle the mother, for she has sleepless nights, and gnashes her teeth and wrings her hands over the headstrong nature of the daughter she's charged to instruct!"

Aset stood, making the lions on both sides also stand, circle, grumble, and then lie back down at a simple look from her. She pointed at Nzinga. "My warrior sister has not rested since you willingly offered your throat." Aset clasped Nzinga's head as she bowed it. "Do you know how many times she flew to your aid, intervened, sat with Marlene to instruct your battle strategies, and finally was the one who had to sully herself to go into the earth to bring you through the violet door—*at Marlene's request?*" Aset swept away from her throne and stood behind Nzinga's. "You should be prostrate on this floor before my dear queen sister with thanks that she came to retrieve you! I may not have done the same."

Damali hit the floor and covered her head, not sure what the women before her might do. Deep remorse filled her as she withstood the tongue-lashing. Still, something quietly defiant lingered within her.

"Please, Aset," Nzinga said, her voice becoming tender. "Let our daughter face you and speak. I, too, was beyond rage at this travesty. But there are many elements that we must consider."

"Call Ma'at," Aset said, her tone threatening. "If her story is lighter than the feather of our sister keeper of justice, which will weight the scales with the truth, then, and only then, will I return her sword."

"You know, Ma'at is blind, dear queen, and can be very harsh in her pronouncements. Maybe—"

"She loved him with her whole heart and soul, great queen," the Amazon said, cutting off Nzinga in her haste to help Damali's cause. "He also, even as a vampire, loved her that way."

"This is truth?" Aset asked, staring at the Amazon. "Your warriors were with them in the nether realms."

"My mother-seer and my Guardians were, and she communicated all to me."

Aset slowly walked back to her throne. She cast an even glare at Damali. "Stand. Speak. Explain yourself to this council."

Damali got up slowly, not sure where she would begin her explanation. "Queen council mother," Damali said softly, her tone reverent and paced. "I open my third eye to you to see all that has transpired. I share it freely with the entire council, as I have nothing to hide. I cannot force myself to be ashamed for loving him, even while he was steeped in Darkness. Yes, I went to Hell and back with him until he was brought back by the Light." Damali swallowed hard. "But through that experience, we also wiped out all topside-dwelling master vampires, bumped off two council-level vamps—Carlos's empty throne means they only have three seats filled now—and we were able to pull a man's soul from multiple levels of Darkness into the Light to fight for our side. Believe me, they have got to be feeling that loss." She glanced around when the faces before her remained impassive. "Did I mention we kept the biblical key that opens the sixth biblical seal from them, too?"

"I will admit that your record, for your age, is impressive—which is the only reason you are able to lean so heavily on my tolerance," Aset said, and then pushed back in her throne, her powerful gaze raking Damali.

Damali watched as the queens before her closed their eyes and the centers of their foreheads soon glowed violet in the shape of an Egyptian eye. Her forehead felt like a hot poker was being rammed into it, the intensity of their probe so comprehensive that she could barely stand.

After several minutes the heat receded, as the queens one by one opened their eyes and looked at her squarely, and then glanced at Aset.

To Damali's surprise, Aset had tears of compassion in her eyes. Aset shook her head and let her breath out slowly.

"What can I say to what I have just witnessed? It so reminds me of my husband, the first king of Kemet, Ausar. That is why I am so angry, so frustrated with you, daughter."

Multiple emotions clawed at Damali's mind, her gaze steady on Aset before it raked the group of seated queens.

"Aset's history is the foundation of your teachings, child. Tell me you have not forgotten it?" Nzinga's eyes searched Damali's with quiet panic. "Tell her, *now*. Recite it for her, lest she waver in her mercy."

"How could I forget?" Damali said quickly. "Ausar was the first great king, knowledgeable and righteous. He took Aset as a wife, but before they could consummate their marriage, his brother, Set, killed him." Damali held the ancient queens' line of vision. "I am so sorry, queen mother. It was horrible."

"Yes," Aset said, her gaze sliding toward the horizon. "They hacked him up into fourteen pieces, and I scavenged the land for seventy days to find each part, and bound him in fine linen to bury him as only a king should be buried. There was only one piece I could not find."

Damali nodded as the queen's eyes filled and dignity burned the sudden tears away. "But the obelisk you had carved to include with his mummy replaced—"

"You can never replace *that* once severed and lost," Aset said with a sad smile. "I was a virgin when I conceived our son, Heru, to avenge Ausar's death . . . but my husband could only come to me that once in spirit before he was entombed, no matter how many tekhen, which the Greeks called obelisks, have been erected." She sighed a weary sigh and closed her eyes. "That is why I was so outraged," Aset said quietly. "Around this table you have women who have lost much, loved hard, but none of us forgot our primary cause. To fight evil. If you had only waited . . ."

"Dear Queen Aset, after seeing what we have seen, and knowing what we know, our queen daughter could no more have waited without being sure that there would be an endpoint to their need to quench their love, than any of us could—if we are honest with ourselves." Nzinga lowered her eyes. "I am sorry to have to have spoken so bluntly, my queen, but it is the truth."

"*Nuk uab-k uab ka-k uab ba-k uab sekem;* my mind has pure thoughts, so my soul and life forces are pure. Is that not from our teachings, Queen Sister Nzinga?"

"Her love for him was pure," Nzinga said with a cautious smile. "Although the rest of it, I cannot vouch for." The Amazon chuckled and quickly swallowed it upon Aset's hot glare.

"They were to represent the number three, the divine energies of Netcher—when a male and female Light energy blends and sires a child of Light. Together they would produce a light bender, not a daywalker, if he had not been in Darkness when she conceived. Now that Darkness has clawed possible life from her womb." Aset's eyes filled with angry tears that fell without censure. "She was to do as I did, collect her beloved's scattered parts—his ashes in this case—and bring him back in spirit through her connection to the Light. She would show him his gift to draw upon the Netcher power within to fell the empire that murdered him and warred against his beloved. Their child was to fulfill a prophecy before the Great One comes."

Aset stood as each woman followed her with their gaze, Damali coming so close to the table that she could almost touch the edges of it, but its awesome power wafted from it and kept her back. The loss was now more than pain, or even heartbreak. It was something so profound that she could barely sip in air.

"Oh, daughter," Aset said, her voice breaking as it hitched in her throat. "We did not begrudge you loving him, it was the timing. You no longer carry, and we will heal your womb. But they have drawn a part of what you carried down into the chambers of Darkness because his blood was still black when he made a son!"

Tears streamed down Damali's cheeks. It would have been a boy . . .

The ancient queen rounded the council table and yanked Damali toward her by both arms. The snatch happened so quickly that all Damali could do was gasp and sway as her knees buckled and Aset held her, eyes blazing violet with a fusion of emotions that Damali didn't dare consider. The current running through Aset's hands into Damali's arms felt like lightning had struck her.

All queens stood quickly, but released their collective breaths as one of Aset's hands slid from Damali's upper arms, and covered her lower belly. Near faint, Damali's head dropped forward as Aset's hand glowed hot for a moment and a golden orb of light covered where Aset's palm laid against her. Damali could feel pinpricks of energy contract her womb and sear into her lower back.

"We burned everything," Damali shrieked, unable to keep up

the façade of warrior calm before the council of queens. "Everything, not a drop was—"

"Listen to me carefully," Aset said, her tone soothing as she held
Damali firmly. "When the cramping started, it was because a dark
force began the siphon. Ask Carlos what was spilled onto the floor
in the place we do not name. He was bound to a wall, impaled by
stakes, and he cried out to Heaven for mercy, which is the only way
we know."

The ancient queen dropped Damali's arm and focused both
hands over her lower belly, allowing Nzinga to go to her side to
keep Damali from falling. "A daywalker is the least of our concerns
if that bitch, Lilith, comes up. She used to be able to breed a hundred demons a day before she married Set and ultimately betrayed
him." Aset removed her hands slowly from Damali's abdomen,
leaving a gentle, healing warmth in their wake. "It is done."

Shocked by Aset's language, and the miracle the elder queen had
just performed, Damali touched the now-calm surface of her belly,
marveling at the soothing sensation that filled her. She somehow
knew the ancient queen had not harmed her, but had healed the
part of her that had sustained injury. But her soul was still
wounded.

She stared behind Aset as she made her way back to her throne.
Oh, yeah, something really bad was about to go down if the queen
mother had cursed. "Lilith?" Damali murmured. "I've never heard
of her." It was the truth. One of the other queens had mentioned
the name in the club, but she couldn't figure out what this new
threat meant.

"We do not speak of her, for she defames our gender," Aset said
without turning. "Tell her, Eve."

"Yes," Eve said, looking at Damali with gentleness. "My husband's first wife. After she disgraced Adam, she ran off to a cave
near the Red Sea and began birthing demon seed a hundred a day."

Damali couldn't contain herself. "Adam's first wife? But you
were the first—"

Eve waved her hand, stopping Damali's words. "She shames us

because it was the way she did it." Eve let out a hard sigh. "We all agreed, by rights, Lilith was made simultaneously with Adam. She was a copartner, a coruler, and should have never had to submit to him. When he tried to force the issue, she should have taken her complaint On High, and had it resolved legally in the divine courts. But then she took matters into her own hands; rage made her crazy. She turned against the Light. Unacceptable. Then in jealousy, she even turned against all women by stealing children, killing the innocent as they grew in our wombs. That bitch *has* to be stopped."

Nzinga nodded. "Fact. This female knows no bounds, and has no compassion for her sisters. A woman like that who goes against all of us cannot be considered one of us. She's your kill, baby. Do her and finish it. We've been searching for her for years, but she's crafty. You may be the only one who can get to her, because now you share something in common."

Joan leaned forward. "Damali, she's coming for you, honey. Eve's transgression was nothing in comparison to what she did, and our sister Eve took the weight of most of it. Many distortions have been made in the biblical texts about Eve." She glanced at Eve with a firm but tender gaze. "That was wrong, and Lilith gave them the wherewithal to cast all blame at her feet for biting the apple. Now, from some convoluted, distorted logic, all women are blamed for the transgression of one—and they have even blamed the wrong sister! The whole world became paternalistic, and they stripped our contributions from the holy books, stopped giving women their due, and stopped seeing the importance of our energy, after that."

"I went to the tree for knowledge. *That's it,*" Eve said with pride. "True, I wasn't supposed to, but I had to know about Lilith and what had made my husband go into this 'the man must be in charge all the time' thing. He was never the same, after her. That much I've gathered," she added in a sad voice. "No one wanted me to know his shortcomings, and the fact that I stumbled upon an additional situation while gaining insight . . . well that, as they say, is old history."

For a moment, all queens remained quiet as Damali and Eve

stared at each other. A deep abiding compassion bound them. Damali could feel the elder queen's pain from where she stood. "They need to let that snake thing rest," Damali said with care. "If there was something going on with my husband, I'd want to know, too."

Eve nodded and the Amazon reached across the table and held her hand.

"She knows what you've been through," the Amazon said quietly. "In Brazil she had to learn it and even feel it, just like you did."

Eve looked away. "That's why this one is so special to me, Aset," she said, addressing the queen mother without looking at her. "I don't want Damali to suffer like I did. It's a new era, a new millennium, and she's from a new generation of queens."

"I agree . . . reluctantly," Aset said. "Explain to her, then, what's she's up against."

"They sent three warrior angels after Lilith to find her and return her to Paradise for a serious discussion, but couldn't locate her," Eve said, her voice worn with emotion. "That's when the first big war began . . . Archangel Michael came down and began slaying her progeny, but he couldn't get them all. Her ability to spawn at will was revoked, and many of her offspring slaughtered, but not all of them. A fragile truce was enacted and she was forced underground. That is the only reason she submitted to marry the Dark One, for an alliance against the angels. We have been told that even *he* has difficulties with her."

Damali looked from one queen to the next. "Where did she go? How do we stop her?"

"Babylon, first, then subterranean," Eve said. "She rules over miscarriages, stillbirths, crib deaths—among other things—but you won't find her up here. She's gone into deep hiding since those times, and sleeps with the one we do not name, making demons and creating havoc when she has a chance." Unspent fury hardened Eve's gaze. "But she's sneaky, can slide into men's dreams, can come as a succubus. She breaks the treaty to remain below all the time, but no one can catch her in the act to bring her to justice."

Damali covered her mouth.

"Yes, daughter. That's why we have been so appalled," Aset said in a weary tone. She looked at Eve. "You know the Vampire Council's chairman. Well, am I wrong?"

Eve glanced away. "That was a long time ago, Aset. Do *not* go there."

Damali's gaze darted between the queens who were now locked in a silent standoff. *The serpent in the garden was the chairman? Oh, shit . . .*

"For this daughter's own good. Tell me. Do you think he was enraged enough to have destroyed whatever he drew from her womb?"

"I cannot be certain," Eve said, her tone cautious and thought-ful. "He was always extremely passionate . . . and always jealous of his father. His ambitions might have allowed him to be shrewd, with the Armageddon so near."

"A potential coup within the dark realms may be our only hope. His father would not stand for a challenger created by the Vampire Council, but Lilith could be a variable. She has always played all sides of men at war, and even started many on her own," Nzinga said, releasing Damali as she slowly returned to her throne with the others.

"Each one of us has had a turn at this same theme," Aset said. "Ausar and I created Heru who conquered Set the first time. Eve before me was with Adam, and knows the pain of two warring sons."

"Cain was implanted during my transgression and came forward as a twin when Abel was conceived. The deepest heartbreak of my existence." Eve swallowed hard and sat down. "We chastise you not from anger, but from love. We have been down that long and dusty path, and we weep for you. That is why, even above the Isis blades, your womb is sacrosanct." Eve's gaze became steady as it bored into Damali. "They have the embryo. Its light did not flicker out, but remains dormant. Lilith has to be beheaded before she can implant it and figure out how to spark it to life. Her womb is the only one down there capable of bearing what will become an atrocity against nature."

"Say it plain, Eve!" Aset shouted, holding a stunned Damali in her gaze as she addressed Eve. "The embryo is a time bomb. It's ticking as we speak. Your transgression with the chairman so many years ago was only a problem because you and Adam had joined." She spun on Damali. "You and Carlos are the only Neteru pair to grace the planet since our dear sister and her husband. That combination produces a level of energy carried in the blood that the dark realms cannot synthesize. When she had a run-in with the serpent and got bitten, it allowed her to be impregnated with something dark while she carried something from the Light. This *cannot* happen to you, and you cannot sleep with Carlos again until you destroy Lilith. If Lilith gives birth, your child will be born the Anti-Christ. She and the embryo must be destroyed. She *cannot* surrogate for you and turn what came from you to the Darkness." Aset flattened her hands against the table. She stared at Damali, her gaze narrowing. "I have given you back your Sankofa. Use it wisely to keep yourself from implantation, henceforth. That can only occur with your intent. In the future, if you lie with a male, make it burn bright. Control your births; this is your right as a woman."

Feeling as though her legs would give out, Damali stumbled forward. But a slow, smoldering rage held her up and sent a snap of straight fury through her spine to keep her erect. "She has *my* child? The fruit of *my* womb? *Our* baby?" Damali's voice was a hard whisper. "I need to know."

"A fertilized egg," Aset said as gently as she could.

"It's not yours any longer," Eve said, her voice distant. "You'd never recognize it now that they've snatched it and—"

"My baby!"

"The potential Anti-Christ," Nzinga said cautiously as two queens rounded the table to keep Damali from leaping over it, "now that we're sure of who the intended surrogate will be. You must find her and destroy her quickly. If it embeds in her womb—you have to cut that out and torch it. The chairman may or may not be involved, given Lilith's treachery. But rest assured, he's the only one that can lead you to her, unless you can bait her out of hiding in search of the catalyst."

"My egg?" Damali shrieked, struggling against the hold of the Amazon and Joan. "Oh, I will find that whore, don't worry. I will never allow her to carry what's mine and Carlos's! Ever! I will go into council chambers myself and turn thrones over, looking for that bitch. Know that!" Damali yelled, pointing at Aset as the other queens let her go. She raked her fingers through her locks and began to pace, feeling trapped, caged, and in need of weapons. Tears of rage stung her nostrils, and she sucked in hard, refusing to allow them to fall. "Get me out of here. I've got work to do. Transport me back. Give me my blade. This conversation is over."

"It is the never knowing when or if this past transgression, one that is out of our hands, will rear its ugly head to confront you both. Your beloved is now a child of the Light, as are you, so you must learn to use your Light power a different way than merely by the sword."

"But I'm not still pregnant, am I? Tell me I wasn't carrying twins." Damali's voice had escalated beyond her ability to control it. She looked at Eve dead-on for an answer. She didn't want to hear this yang about patience and strategy. It was time to kick some ass.

"No," Aset said, sitting down heavily. "You will be bound up and healed. It is what fragments of life we were not able to collect back to the Sun that concerns us."

"Where do I go, what do I do?" Damali asked, willing herself not to shriek. "How do I get down there to smoke this bitch?"

"The Isis blades remain ours until you learn to find the power of Netcher within living things and to draw the essence of Light out of them . . . to bend the Light."

"How?" Damali cried, tears now streaming down her face as Queen Aset stood. "You can't take the Isis blades at a time like this, please. Give me another chance!"

"Do you understand how important it is for you to remain concealed? They cannot know where either of you are. The blades are a beacon. They can taste the sacred metals in the air when they hit the earth's surface. They're not even sure that Carlos is the male Neteru, and they haven't pinpointed him yet. He's vulnerable now, and until he reaches his Neteru apex, the kings of old must shield him. No. You must learn to fight with other skills and other tools," Aset said. Without waiting for Damali to answer, she held up her hand to stop Damali from speaking. "Ask Eve. We understand your pain, but you cannot go into this battle with your heart, only your intellect can prevail over this matter. *Tell her, Eve.* Explain how you held Cain to your breasts, even while knowing what he was. Tell her, so she can understand and accept the ruling."

Eve hung her head and spoke in a low, calm voice. "Dear queen daughter, by rights, I am the first Neteru, the eldest of the council, the mother of all . . . but, due to the problem in Paradise, which I would not like to revisit, Aset rules. Her judgment and discipline were more profound, therefore, my title was stripped, albeit not my place in history or among the governing queens." She looked at Damali, her gaze unwavering as she spoke and her voice dropped to a near whisper. "This is very serious. We are so close to the Armageddon, and you two were supposed to be the new Neterus— one male, one female—to sway the balance."

"Tell her!" Aset shouted, making the lights within the table swirl across the top in small tornado-like eddies. "Did we not strip Cleopatra for taking her own life with an asp, when she could have sealed a deal and stemmed the invasion of Egypt by Rome? Suicide sent her to the Darkness, and we lost an important warrior. She allowed her intellect to be eclipsed by her heart. For what? A man? Damali cannot face Lilith like that!"

Damali opened and closed her mouth. Words failed her.

"You will travel to all the lands that your destiny requires; there is a shaman at each place that will find you," Aset said, her tone annoyed and brittle. "Thirteen places to bind yourself up, to collect the fragments of Carlos's scattered Light force. If we didn't have this problem, the process of readying the male Neteru would progress over seventy days, as it has always been. But you have perhaps seven days, at best, to do what must be done."

"Handle your business, baby," Nzinga said, wiping her hands down her face with fatigue. "Stay strong, and stay in the Light."

"Exactly," Aset said with a nod. "Once the male Neteru is

gathered and his power has returned on the side of Light, your healing will also be complete. Until he heals, you cannot fully heal. Until he wields the power, you cannot wield the Isis blades. You *married* him while he was a vampire, and now your power is one." Aset leaned across the table. "You allowed him to take you as a *wife,* child. That is how they were able to claw away what they should have *never* even seen or known existed. Some things are beyond our control. What about this do you not understand?"

"There was no ceremony," Damali sputtered, her gaze going from Aset to the others for support. "We never did a dark ritual, we never—"

"In the desert of Australia, on hallowed ground—'flesh of my flesh,' he said, as you willingly allowed him to take your throat, shared his blood, and deconstructed into nothingness with his cells fusing with yours at the vampire vanishing point!"

Aset slammed the table so hard that light sparks flew from it. "After you gave him a heartbeat from your own heart within my Amazon sister's territory! After you loved him without censure in a priest's compound. The keepers of the seal—the Aboriginal shaman—said you loved him with the intent of drawing his life force and seed into you on twenty-thousand-year-old prayer lines!" Aset picked up the small Isis dagger and rammed it into the table. "You had his ring, a blue-ice section of his heart, a white gown, shaman priests all around in spirit as witnesses, and the stars aghast. Oh, yes, there were priests there. It is done. You are his wife in spirit! The rest is an earthly formality, at this point."

Damali covered her mouth, her eyes so wide that she felt the sides burn as though they'd split. "Oh, my God . . ."

"Correct," Aset said, snatching the blade from the table and flinging it toward Nzinga. "And she wonders why I am beyond words."

"Therefore," Aset said, her voice returning to its previous even calm, "for your own safety, you will not bear the marker, Neteru, until you have restored your own power by your own hand. You will be hidden in plain sight. This way you will also learn from experience to never give it away to anyone, will know its true value, and will guard it the way it should always be guarded. Because he is crippled, you are also crippled, by your untimely decision. It is out of my hands." She looked at Damali with a mixture of pity and annoyance. "You bore fangs for him, my daughter. Even that I cannot make excuses for."

"I bore them, too, for a while," Eve murmured, looking at Damali with pity. "When I came back from the tree . . ." Eve's voice trailed off with a sad smile. "At least you have the Neteru council as your buffer. I had to stand before a husband and the Most High. That was in the Old Testament days, before the time of mercy. The conversation went very differently, I assure you—so take heart. This is not as bad as it could have been."

Nzinga nodded. "They have not taken this well in the Upper Realms . . . it will be the second time before a pivotal war, and the only thing that may redeem you is that unlike Eve, when she temporarily lost her mind," Nzinga said, casting a compassionate glance toward the elder queen, "you have a number of good demon kills to your honor. Significant ones, so cling to that as your hope and shield. He also has this as his shield, as well as his protection of many good men and women—like you also have. We will lobby hard, my queen daughter . . . but in the interim, you must help your own case."

"It is not my goal to punish her," Aset said, now seeming so tired that she could barely speak. "It is my goal to teach her and it is my fervent prayer that we can at some point return her title and blades. But she must do this on her own."

Shame burned Damali's cheeks, and she could not answer the charges as Aset stood and moved away from the table. Instead she focused on acceptance and whatever she had to do to regain favor. "I will make this right. But what lands, where am I to battle what? And there were fourteen missing parts of Ausar, not thirteen. Oh, Queen Mother Aset, please do not walk away with riddles that could take a lifetime to figure out!"

"Only you can find and heal the missing life force within the fourteenth section of him, which can only be healed once his mind is healed and his spirit is healed, and your body is healed and your focus is as pure as a beam of light. If you ever want to conceive with him again while he's flesh and blood, you must incorporate patience and gentleness . . . wisdom and strength, or you can suffer my fate and simply have an obelisk carved in his memory."

With that Aset turned and began walking and vanished into the violet pyramid that opened, her lions crossing behind her in a lazy, but guarded retreat.

"I will be near," Nzinga said, "as will the others. Call upon us, and we will send markers and signs to guide you."

"Beware the screech owl of the desert. That is one of the shapes Lilith assumes," Eve warned. "Remember in the last days, only the churches of one land had no sins in the eyes of the Most High. Seek that land as your final destination. But you must first collect the scattered Netcher before you do so." She sighed. "I will lobby your cause about the fang issue. I remember those days, but your case is slightly different. Carlos came back, and it was his destiny to be a Guardian . . . so, perhaps once emotions settle . . . Take heart. Look toward Philadelphia." Eve left her with a sad smile, shaking her head as she walked into the Light.

"But there are probably twenty cities in the world by that name." Damali tried to rush forward but an energy barrier held her and kept her from rounding the table.

The others had disappeared through the triangle of violet light, only the Amazon hung back, collecting the Isis blades with sadness in her eyes. "Then find the most powerful one. Start there, queen daughter. I will watch your flank."

Suddenly the room transformed into a restaurant. Dazed, Damali glanced at the white linen tablecloths and marble floor, then at the winding river beyond the tall windows. She was up high in a building in some country or city she couldn't place. She could hear movement in the hall beyond, and she glanced at a wall clock, and then ducked behind a table as a security guard passed by.

Unarmed, in a white Ethiopian gown and sandals, if she were discovered in an establishment this early in the morning, she knew she'd go to jail as a nut case for sure. She listened to the footfalls get farther away and made a run for the main hall, hugging the walls, tiptoeing like a thief, and saying a quiet prayer that she wouldn't be discovered. How was she going to get back to the plane in Manila or let the group know she was alive?

Spotting the main staircase she slipped down it, ducked low as she saw another guard cross the expansive marble entrance. She also had to keep an eye out for any surveillance cameras.

Staying out of sight, she peeped around the huge column that ended at the bottom of the first landing of the staircase and saw the shadows on the floor made from what looked like large temple pillars. From the angle where she crouched she could also see what seemed like a city-block-wide cascade of hundreds of white steps that ended with a wide circular boulevard and a mammoth fountain across the street. If she could just get outside.

A stick on her shoulder almost made her jump out of her skin. She looked up quickly expecting to see a guard shoving her with a billy club. Instead it was the old shaman, one of the keepers of the seal. He smiled a toothless grin and placed a finger to his lips, signaling her to remain quiet. He stooped down low and offered her his walking stick, prodding her to hold one end of it. The moment Damali's hand touched it a warm balm of purple light covered her hand and traveled up her arm, slowly coating and eventually rimming her body in violet light. He let go of the stick and clapped and laughed and bent over with mirth, the spectacle seemed to please him so.

Damali had to smile. It was his pure glee as he danced about and waved his arms, creating a ruckus that she was sure would draw the guards. No sooner than that reality accosted her, a guard ran down the steps, brandishing a club.

"Hey, old man! You can't come in here! No homeless on the premises! Now beat it, before we call the cops!"

Another guard hurried onto the scene. "How'd that old bum get in here? You'd better get him out before we get in trouble because the night shift guys overlooked him. I'm not losing my job over this bull."

Damali had made herself very small on the steps, practically hugging the oversized railing, but it became suddenly apparent that the two guards couldn't see her. She was being shielded.

The half-naked shaman laughed harder, his mirth becoming a wild hysteria as he danced away from the security guards and rushed down the steps. Damali stood, stared at the stick, and then the guard. They really couldn't see her . . . deep.

"Open the front doors for him and get him out of here," one guard shouted, huffing as he chased behind the nimble old man and almost slipping on the highly polished floors as he pursued him.

Clenching the stick, Damali stood and raced in the direction of the door. The first guard that had reached the huge, bolted entrances flipped a series of switches behind a control panel, swearing the entire time about the alarm systems, locks, writing the catastrophe up on the logs, his pension, and why couldn't the homeless just stay out of the place. The shaman danced, wagged a finger at the men, and evaded their pursuit until one of the doors had been opened. Then he gnashed his teeth and pulled at his wiry white hair as though insane.

"Man, he might have AIDS! Don't touch him, just shoo his dirty ass out the door!"

The shaman walked in a wide circle, motioning for Damali to go through the exit, drooling and spitting, making the men back away with disgust. Then he clapped his hands and dashed out the door and down the steps. Damali didn't have to be told twice, she was out.

Brilliant sun hit her face, and the crisp fall air brought tears to her eyes. She didn't know exactly where she was, but it was a cold climate. She glanced around for the old shaman. "Thank you," she yelled into the nothingness, and brought the stick to her chest.

They had taken her Isis blades, stripped her womb, brought her man back fractured and broken, separated her from her team, and only left her with a purple magic stick. Silent tears slipped down her cheeks as she stood on the grounds of the most spectacular temple she'd seen within a city. She stared down the broad white steps toward the grand parkway, trying to place the monuments, trying to get her bearings as her embattled brain struggled to absorb all that had just happened. She glanced back at the eight Roman columns and brass fountains that had tarnished green with age, noting how the entire relief was near a river and waterfall as though a replica of the great temples by the Nile. No wonder the queens had brought her here. But they'd also temporarily stripped her of her title, had taken her blades.

What had she done? Lord, what had she done?

CHAPTER TEN

RESIGNED TO her fate, there was nothing to do but move forward. Damali glanced around, already knowing that the old shaman wasn't coming back. She walked down the white steps, watching the few cars that passed as she reached the curb, straining to read the license plates but was too far away to recognize the state they were from. At just after dawn, most cities were quiet—except New York. She checked that one off as she gazed at the skyline. Definitely not New York. But it had to be on the East Coast. An art museum, but where?

Before her stretched a large boulevard lined with very old trees robed in hues of orange, gold, red, fading green, and withered brown. As she crossed the four-lane circular street, she came to the huge, dry fountain, staring at the larger-than-life bronze figurines and trying to see an inscription. She looked over her shoulder to the building she'd just left, and gaped up at the huge templelike structure that bore no inscription, but on her right a warrior on a horse fought a lion with his javelin drawn in battle. The monument offered no immediate clue. But it made her pause. Armed only with a wooden stick a warrior went against a lion. Damali gripped the stick she held more tightly and walked forward. Answers were all around her; she could feel them just beyond her immediate reach.

For a moment she just stood in front of the fountain, her eyes roving past the life-sized bronze woman entwined with a serpent. She sighed and thought of Eve, and then her own circumstances. "We messed up big time, didn't we, girlfriend?" Damali muttered as she trudged up the massive stone steps, past two huge bronze deer. At the four cardinal points, there were figures seemingly guarded by things of nature. That fleeting awareness also gave her pause. Two deer guarded the woman and serpent . . . Damali walked to the next cardinal point and saw an elaborately sculpted moose adjacent to a fierce bear guarding a woman with a net. As she rounded the structure there was a pair of moose, and before she could look farther she saw a Native American chief in repose, also guarded by two bison—things of nature.

Damali glanced up to the mounted general on a horse, her eyes scouring the dim inscription . . . she was in Pennsylvania! Excitement swept through her. A piece of the puzzle was found. At least she knew where she was now. But as suddenly as elation had hit her, so did a sense of impending doom.

If she was in Pennsylvania, then her team was God knew how many miles and a whole day away from her, enroute to Manila. How in the heck was she going to get from here to there, with no money on her, no means of transportation to an airport, no freaking identification, and no coat? She wrapped her arms around herself, instantly feeling the cold.

Soul weary, she leaned against the reclining Indian chief and willed herself not to cry. "This is beyond jacked up," she murmured. The icy metal set her teeth on edge, and she pushed off it with both hands. But the slight movements of the bronze structure before her made her freeze.

A light crackling purple haze crept along the structure, making the reclining figure slowly turn its head, stare at her with vacant eyes, and with the slightest tilt of his chin, a direction was offered.

Damali backed up until her spine collided with the adjacent figure, making her jump away from it, lest it come alive, too. The section of statue that had moved returned to its original pose and became still again. Not waiting to see what would happen next, Damali dashed down the wide steps in a flat-out run, across a small patch of grass, and down the center lane of an empty parking lot. Breathless, she quickly crossed the street and turned back to the giant fountain to see if it was pursuing her. But all was still except the erratic thuds of her heart.

She sucked in huge breaths and looked in the direction the statue had indicated. Benjamin Franklin Parkway? Something vaguely familiar stretched within her mind, but with all that had happened, the context left her wanting. Her eyes darted around, trying to figure out the message. Frustrated, she looked up and shouted, "What?"

No answer came as she slumped against a post and lowered the stick to the ground and leaned on it. She briefly closed her eyes and tried to regain her composure. "I'm sorry, okay? But I can't walk from here to Manila!"

Turning her face to the sky, she raised the stick and shook it. "I need answers! I'll do what you want, will travel and go to whatever lands, but I've gotta know where!"

Then she noticed the flags. The parkway she stood on had every flag of every nation represented down a long, tree-lined boulevard. She glanced down at the stick, and then up at the flags, then toward the trees. Nature. Art had inspired the direction, perhaps nature held the power? It was worth a try.

She touched her hand against a very old oak and pointed the stick toward the flags. "Talk to me," she whispered, her voice calmer.

Again the purple light crept from the end of the stick, but instead of crawling up her arm, it arced and then disappeared. To her total amazement, fourteen flags that blew in the fall breeze lit one by one. Her mind seized upon the order: Ethiopia, Sudan, Egypt, Italy, Algeria, Spain, France, Hungary, Austria, Poland, Germany, Belgium, the Netherlands, and the United Kingdom. Then oddly, the U.S. flag went neon violet, and as suddenly as they had lit, the purple light around each flag faded to a purplish tinge and then normalized.

Damali didn't take her eyes off the flags for a long time. She said the countries over and over, memorizing them like an elementary school rhyme in her head to make the information stick. It was too bizarre that it was nearly the same as their flight pattern with only a modest variation. But how could that be? The people funding their flight and travel had double-crossed them, yet it seemed as though by doing the double-cross and not allowing them direct entry to the main places of worship, they might have been unwittingly aiding the destined path. The circuitous route was possibly the path that she and the teams were supposed to be on without even realizing it.

The strange confluence of events made her banish the possibility of coincidence. Marlene had told her about there being no such thing as coincidence, and even with all that she'd seen to date, it was still a hard thing to fathom. But sure as rain, the Asian nations' flags hadn't lit, nor had world hot spots like India and Pakistan, or the roiling Middle East. Central America, South America, and Canada hadn't fired violet, just like none of the Caribbean or island nations had.

But fourteen countries did show up glowing, with the fifteenth, her own, glowing hottest. Why? What did it all mean? She knew one thing for sure, if she had to gather fourteen scattered pieces of her and Carlos's power, then so be it, she'd go to the ends of the earth to get that back.

She began walking with purpose now, not sure where she was going, but her footfalls landed with more confidence. Then she stopped. The pain was gone, the cramping was gone, and she didn't feel a thick wad of padding between her legs or the horrible warm wetness of blood oozing from her body.

This time when she glanced up at the sky, it wasn't with frustration or rage. "Thank you," she murmured, her eyes scanning the horizon for a sign, which instantly reflected back to her in a flash of gold. Damali squinted, and stared toward the flash that glistened and peeked through the treetops upon a breeze, and then disappeared in the dense autumn foliage. A dome briefly appeared over the multicolored treetops as a breeze again gently moved the leaves, and standing in the full rays of the rose-orange new sunlight was a cross.

She was so close to hallowed ground that she almost ran to it. Judging from the size of the dome that she'd glimpsed, she couldn't have been more than a few blocks away. Crossing the wide street and grassy divides, she walked quickly toward the place that offered sure sanctuary.

Halfway down the double-long block, a whippoorwill's lonely call made her stop. No longer ready to ignore the subtleties around her, she looked about hoping the old shaman might be there to explain how to use the stick to rejoin her team. Instead, her gaze encountered another statue in blackened bronze. His expression was deeply contemplative as he seemingly worked a problem in his mind that was just beyond his reach, one hand under his chin.

She looked at the historical marker on the street and on the façade of the building. "Philly! The Rodin Museum's *Thinker*— Carlos, oh my God!" It was all now so clear. She remembered Philly, but had been at the other end of town in the Olde City section, battling on the cobblestoned streets and alleys within the darkness. Everything had come full circle. This was a place of dichotomies, just like her and Carlos's life was. Philadelphia was where freedom was founded, the Liberty Bell once rang, yet where slave ships unloaded terrible cargo to be sold in a public square. The Native American guiding her now made perfect sense. His people had warred to protect their land, hers had been incarcerated within it, and it took bloodshed and marches to restore them with the right to be considered whole, versus three-fifths of a human being.

Damali nodded. She'd found a place where the highest of ideals tried to coexist with the most base of human nature.

She smiled at the discovery, becoming relieved that the pieces of the giant cosmic puzzle were beginning to fall into place, and she rushed up to the huge, sulking figure and tried to reach up to run her hand over his metallic jaw. However, he was too high up on a pedestal to touch. Tears filled her eyes as she remembered what Carlos's steel-packed jaw felt like against her throat. Damali laughed sadly at herself. "That's just how you look, baby, when you're scheming, trying to work your way out of a jam. I miss you so," she whispered, allowing her hand to fall away as she admired the bulging biceps and graceful, thick, sinew-sculpted thigh from afar. "I know you miss the power of who you were. Now I understand."

But as her gaze took in the structure and façade of the building behind the statue, she again became extremely still. Beyond the exterior walls she could see a courtyard with a low fountain pool. The water drew her as she entered the path, her eyes affixed to its glassy surface. But deeply disturbing presences also made the hairs on the back of her neck stand up.

Two sets of stairs led from the pool up toward the columned entrance of the building, and her feet moved up the stone on their own volition, a need to understand propelling her forward. That's when she saw it and began to back away. In relief before the entrance to the museum was an eerie bronze cast scene entitled, *The Gates of Hell.* For a moment, she couldn't move. Fiendish, twisted figures almost seemed like they were fighting their way out of the metallic encasement from within the building toward her. The irony stabbed into her awareness as her gaze swept to and took in both the statue and what he sat in front of. Yes . . . it made so much sense. Carlos thinking his way beyond the gates of Hell.

She hurried away from the disturbing art and touched the base of the statue with her newly acquired stick and stood back a bit, waiting, just testing, wondering what all her shaman's wooden gift could do. But nothing had happened.

She sighed and turned. As she began to walk away, water hit her shoulder, making her whirl back around. A single tear rolled down the iron face and splattered on the ground. Fear didn't enter her spirit this time, only a deep sadness. She cupped the place on her shoulder where the tear had landed. The cold, hard face didn't move. She stroked her shoulder once then turned and walked away, determined to find the nearby church. Water. That was the key. The fountains, the tear, the river beside the temple where the Neteru council had just convened. So she would not ignore it.

Her stride was much slower, more measured, as she passed the few blocks of Greek and Roman architecture–inspired buildings and fountains and thought of all the things that had to be going through the minds of those she loved. She was missing, AWOL, and she knew every member of her family on the Manila-bound plane was in a panic. She also knew how deeply conflicted Carlos had to be, not unlike herself.

To be stripped naked of one's power, thrust into an untenable position of weakness, journeying to lands unknown with no way to fight the unthinkable, with Hell on one's heels, was not insignificant. An image of a slave ship flitted through her mind. To learn from the seat of original power followed the thought. Of course her journey had to go through Africa, through what had been the Nubian empire, and then to Europe. Damali nodded as she walked, nearly thinking out loud. She and Carlos had many nations within their DNA . . . Indian, African, European, many she might never know for sure . . . Just as her team represented them all.

As above, so below, especially in the end of days. But to love someone more than life itself, and not be able to provide for them, protect them . . . Carlos had told her once that it was a different thing for a man, their wiring was so different—their perspective, albeit somewhat irrational in her mind, required being able to do those things in order to feel like a man. In that moment as she slowly crossed another street, she realized that the fourteenth scattered piece of him would never be right until his power was right. How could it be?

He'd only loved her as a master of the universe. Now he was busted, penniless, no special abilities that had come to the fore, and was being protected by her squad when he was once the protector . . . the defender . . . the alpha and the omega with territory as vast as a king's. He didn't even have his nightclub from before he'd turned, let alone anything else, not that it mattered to her—the point was *it mattered to him.*

"Oh, baby . . . you tried to tell me that before," she whispered and shut her eyes tightly.

The visceral truth drummed in her ears and echoed through her soul. Possibly the worst of it for him—and she knew he'd never take her word for it that it was okay with her—he'd been able to make love to her in a way she knew no man could. There would be no words that could mollify him about that. There wouldn't be enough gentle, "It's okay baby," to smooth over the fact that brotherman couldn't drop fang, whisk her away to the vanishing point in a blaze of sensual glory, to make him ever be able to deal. Carlos's pride wouldn't allow for it, and his anger would block him to even trying to suffer that level of humiliation. Anger would also block his learning to fight like a Guardian, find his gifts or any new center of power that he owned. How in the world would they make it as one?

Damali swallowed hard as she stopped before the cathedral, read the sign, and then pushed herself up the steps of St. Peter's Basilica. "Please be open," she murmured, trying the door and finding it locked. She leaned against the large, blue-and-ivory blocks that stood between her and sanctuary and closed her eyes. Why was everything so hard?

He'd been crippled, hobbled, just thoroughly torn apart, and was now on a plane with very nervous Guardians and half a band of warriors from the Covenant. One false move and the plane could erupt into total mayhem.

She slid down the huge double doors until she was a small huddle of humanity on the top step, cradling the stick, and hoping she was still invisible. But as soon as she hit the concrete, she tumbled backward through the entrance, slid, and hid another set of heavy oak doors as though the seemingly impenetrable structures were a fabric drape.

Jumping up quickly, Damali patted her body and then touched the solid wooden doors she'd just passed through. Her heart was racing so hard it made her ears ring. She backed away from the doors and glanced around the darkened, majestic cathedral. She'd fallen past the foyer and was in the middle of the sanctuary itself, the polished floors beneath her sandal-clad feet. Mercy had let her in.

Her gaze went to the high, arched, frescoed ceiling, and then toward the gilded altar surrounded by angelic figures, but her search was for the font of holy water. She crossed herself and found it near the back of the church, and watched with awe as the dry stone bowl bubbled and gurgled, creating an eerie echo as it filled. She waited until only silence reverberated off the walls and the pool became still. Damali touched her fingers to the glassy surface and brought them to her forehead.

"Forgive me, Father, for I have sinned . . . not because I loved, not because I cared, but because I forgot about the pain of those around me as I learned and lacked patience to wait for Your sign. Help me to do better, and not to hurt the people who love me most. I want to go home to be with them, wherever they are." She stood quietly for a long while, simply gazing into the font and trying to calm her spirit. The slight lingering smell of incense was soothing and soon she was able to move away, having made her peace with her circumstances.

Now the issue was how to get out of the church and be reunited with her family. She stared at the rows of votive candles and didn't move as one lit for her on its own.

"You heard me," she whispered, tears of relief washing her cheeks. Her attention went to the heavy doors that creaked open ever so slightly, and within moments she was through them and back out on the top step facing the wide street in bright sunlight.

Surveying the landscape for a direction, she walked down the steps with care and stood by the curb, wondering what sign would light the way next. Oddly, all resistance and defiance had seeped out of her, along with the fear. She was simply bone-weary. It felt as though the defensive, angry energy had collected in her feet and was now dripping from the soles of her sandals with every heavy step she took. It made her footfalls labored, and she walked like she had ten-pound weights on each foot. She could barely move.

With disinterest, she watched a cab drive by. But it stopped, backed up, and a young African man who looked to be in his early twenties, wearing a red, black, and green crocheted skullcap, dressed in a beat-up Army jacket, ragged yellow T-shirt, and dingy brown corduroy pants with black flip-flops on smiled and rolled down his window, hailing her.

"You need a ride, queen?"

Damali shook her head and closed her eyes. She was no longer invisible. What next? "Thanks, brother," she said in a tired voice. "My ends are short, got no cash. Thanks anyway."

"You've got money," he said, his fluorescent-white smile lighting up his dark, handsome face. "I take silver for a sister as fine as you. Come let me give you a ride and talk to me. It's lonely in the morning, yes?"

"Silver?" Damali chuckled. Men were such a trip, and she

couldn't deal with some brother from around the way hitting on her right now. "Naw, I'm cool."

"Wit all dat silver in your ears, and gold in your hair, you can't part wit one little earring for a ride to Broad Street? It's only a few blocks."

She became very, very still, and then her hand gently touched her earlobes. When she'd been on the plane, she hadn't had earrings on. She looked at her wrists and almost gasped. Thick kundalini snakes with gleaming precious stones were wrapped around her wrists. She unfastened an earring, and she stared at the sterling Ankh in her palm. She glanced down at her feet and heavy silver ankle bracelets with hieroglyphics etched upon them were weighing down her legs. A large silver toe ring covered her right middle toe. Her gaze went back to the cabbie as she gently patted her head wrap feeling it bulge with hard objects within her hair. Plus, she'd never mentioned where she was headed. Even she didn't know the answer to that. "Broad Street?"

"Yes. That is where you are going, true?"

Damali warily eyed him and shrugged. "How do you know I'm going to Broad Street?"

"What is eleven and five?" he asked, raising an eyebrow with a sly grin.

"Sixteen," she said, coming closer to the cab, curious.

"And one and six?" he asked, chuckling.

"Seven," she whispered.

"And your man's birthday is November fifth, correct?"

She simply stared at the man.

"He is twenty-four, which would make it six. Six plus seven is what? Thirteen," he said with a smile. "And the year of his birth would be nineteen eighty, which is one, plus nine, equals ten, reduces to one, add the eight, makes it nine. And nine is three threes, a triple trinity, a very powerful number. If you want to go home, you have to go to Egypt in Philadelphia, and stand on an axis of the pyramid the Masons built—*mass* with *son,* mason, meaning child of Light. His birthday is not far away . . . you ready for the full lunar eclipse that will last his number—three hours and thirty-three minutes? Nine."

This man's strange babble made her brain feel like oatmeal. The numbers and dates were coming too fast, and he knew things he shouldn't have. She remembered what she'd been promised by the queens, though. Guides and shamans would come.

"What's today's date?" Tension had made her body so rigid that she could barely talk.

"October thirtieth. A three day," he said with flourish. "The month ten reduces to the number one, which represents the Creator as symbolized by the sun. Three is the trinity, forms a triangle, and is the offspring of the union of two. Add it to get four," he said with a wink, "and you have the number four, balance."

Damali thrust her hand into the cab window and offered the earring without a word. The cabbie nodded and chuckled and popped the automatic lock so she could climb into the back of his vehicle. His jabber made her head spin, but his references totally freaked her out. Regardless of all his mystical talk, all she knew was one basic fact: If today was October thirtieth, her team was flying into the night a day ahead of her on Halloween. She closed the door to the cab without protest.

"We go to One Broad Street. That is one axis, north, a point of power. City Hall is the other, south. Invasions from the north have conquered the south, but the greatest power is in the east where Khepre is reborn each morning. What used to be called the John Wanamaker Building is the other side of the triangle. If you look at it from above and draw the invisible lines, you can see the connection." He spoke without turning and then took a small stick out of his jacket pocket and began chewing on it like it were a cigar. "This city, like Washington, D.C., was founded by Masons. All the founding fathers were Masons, and have replicated everything found in the original seat of power. Now that is hidden in plain sight within the seat of authority in the most powerful nation. Open your eyes and go through the door, just like you did at the church, and find Egypt."

"Where are you from?" Damali whispered, her voice hoarse from shock.

"Ethiopia, where else?" he said, chuckling as he drove the short distance. He turned in his seat and handed her a card. "My grandfather is waiting for you. Find him and he will give you back your earring."

The cab had stopped in front of a massive structure that looked as much like a cathedral as it did a strange museum. "Thank you," Damali said quietly, taking the card and carefully studying it before she shoved it into her robe pocket.

The man smiled, lowered his eyes, and bowed slightly in his seat. "It was my honor to courier the Neteru back to her destiny."

"You think they're gonna be cool?" Shabazz asked Father Patrick, as the teams filed down the plane's spiral staircase to the cabin's main level. He used his chin to motion toward the closed conference room that held the stunned crew.

"Who can tell?" Father Patrick said, rubbing his face with his hands while each person found an empty seat and flopped into it. "They were told, they now know, and it's up to them to believe us."

"I think the doctors are still going to be a problem," Rider said with an exhausted sigh. "Those boys were on a mission, and they saw Marlene do her thing, which in their minds is probably black magic. They could be thinking that some supernatural dark forces snatched her to save the daywalker."

"As long as they're up there, and we're down here in the cabin, and I don't have to look at those bastards for the moment, I don't care," Carlos said, his eyes on the horizon. "She's been gone a long time. We need to find out where she is."

"Yeah, man," Jose countered, "but it's not like we can just hijack this jawn. We just need to chill and hope that they believed the brothers from the Covenant."

"And if they don't?" Carlos said, looking at Jose for answers. "If they drag us into some kind of military lockup, or worse, then what? How will she find us or we find her?"

"I say we be cool, stay the course, and ride this out. All we can do is hope that the fresh pilots and crew don't trip when we refuel on the ground. If the first crew is happy to be off here with us, and feel like they got potentially set up, human nature being what it is, they are not trying to find themselves in a contamination contain-ment situation. They are going to let the new crew get on, sign on for the leg of the journey they'd agreed to do, and their con-sciences won't allow them to have us dragged off by nonclerical civilians to possibly infect them." Shabazz's tone was firm, but there was a quality of trying to bring logic within it that made Carlos temporarily relax.

"I think Shabazz is right," Berkfield said. "The looks on their faces when Father Pat told 'em what was up said it all. They want off this plane, they want us on here until they know what any of us are." He settled back in his seat and closed his eyes. "Try to get some rest. We've got a long way to go, still."

The younger Guardians and Covenant team slowly nodded their agreement, seeming too weary to further debate the possible vari-ables. One by one, each person began to slowly find a comfortable position in their seats and grudgingly dozed off. They fought sleep as though it were a sign they didn't care, which was far from the case, but the constant adrenaline rushes coupled with a long battle, cuts, bruises, and emotion had begun to wear down even the most battle-seasoned warrior.

Marlene sat with her head in her hands, resisting sleep as she continued her vigil.

"Baby, you have got to relax and rest for a little while. We all prayed as a unit, Father Patrick and his squad anointed where she left, sent up intercession, even had Carlos in the mix . . . it's time to turn it over." Shabazz stroked her damp brow. "You always tell me, sometimes you have to let go and let God, right?"

Marlene nodded, but didn't look up. She kept her eyes closed and her low murmur blended in with the drone of the plane's engine.

"I'll pick up where you leave off, Mar," Carlos said, making her look up for the first time. "You get a few hours shut-eye like

Shabazz said. I promise you, I can't sleep, and if you tell me what to say . . ."

"Just say what's in your heart," Marlene said, reaching past Shabazz to clasp Carlos's hand when he came near their seats. "Just ask that she come back whole and all right, and that all of us are able to be back as one family, with no one hurt." She looked up at Carlos, a silent understanding passing between them.

"I've been doing that since I've known her," he said in a quiet voice.

"Remember this," Marlene said, squeezing his hand tighter. "The Light doesn't rob. There are things we don't understand, but the tragedies don't come from that side—you've been to where they come from and should know that by now." She held his hand firmly, and looked deeply into his eyes as she spoke, boring her meaning into his understanding. "Do not be angry with our side, it will only slow your learning and new powers . . . I know you have something latent but very powerful within you—and it isn't evil. If you can set aside the rage, maybe you can bring it forth. We need whatever juice you've got right about through here, brother. Seriously. And so does she."

Carlos nodded as Marlene's hand fell away. "You had a vision, or is it wishful thinking?" he asked, forcing a strained smile.

She saw the fragile hope his bravado contained and stood so they could look eye to eye. She placed one hand on Shabazz's shoulder, the other on Carlos's. "Both," she said after a moment. "It has always been both. I have seen the best in you and wished the best up out of you."

Her comment seemed to satisfy him for the moment and he nodded and then looked away. "You can count on me, Mar. I'm not going to stop praying for her until you wake up and take over. I gotchure back, got hers, too."

Shabazz offered Carlos his fist, and they exchanged a pound. "You family now, bro. Marlene don't turn over a prayer vigil to just any ole body, and she passed four ironclad clerics to give it over to you. That means something real." Shabazz paused as he looked up at Carlos, both men holding respect in their lines of vision. "Thank you for spelling my woman so she doesn't collapse from exhaustion. And thank you for all those times you had our backs. I'm with Father Pat. Fuck it. If you drop fang, you're still one of us, we just have to figure out how to feed your ass so we can all stay cool."

Carlos smiled and withdrew from Marlene's hold. It was the first time since he'd been on the plane that a sense of peace and camaraderie had actually filled him. The feeling was disorienting, and was so strange at a time like this, a time when his worst nightmares were possibly being realized—losing Damali.

He looked at Shabazz and then Marlene. "Get some rest," he said, wondering when this new family had claimed and included him.

CHAPTER ELEVEN

NERVOUS TENSION riddled the teams as they watched the crew and pilots hurry off the plane. All eyes stared beyond the windows, waiting, watching as a small refueling vehicle hooked the nozzle up to the huge jumbo jet in Manila. They sat silently watching the new crew come on board and begin to prep the plane for takeoff. New food and drink inventory was loaded by oblivious airport workers, who also added a fresh stash of blankets and pillows. An airport official walked through the aisle, his expression grim as he checked all passports and identification and then stopped.

"My manifest says there's a Damali Richards on board." He waited.

The team waited.

"She's had a lot of bleeding and is in the ladies' room," Marlene lied. "I have her identification, though." Marlene produced Damali's passport and visa from her bag.

The official looked at it and then toward Father Patrick.

"She should go with us," Father Patrick said, his tone calm but filled with authority. "Unless you want to be responsible for her? I can phone the Vatican—"

"That won't be necessary," the official said, and backed down the aisle.

"Thank you," Father Patrick said, feigning submission. "It is our goal to get her to sanctuary as soon as possible."

No one relaxed until the exterior door of the plane was locked and the aircraft began to turn on the runway and move into a new taxiing position. Silent glances containing hope passed between the seated groups of exhausted warriors. When the crew came out to review safety instructions, shoulders dropped two inches in relief.

They listened to the instructions and the captain's announcements with deaf ears, each knowing that the eight-hour flight to Dubai would take them hurtling into the night. As soon as the suction of taking off pushed them back into their seats, the chilling reality spread like a silent threat that connected people on the plane. Carlos could almost feel the tension in his hands like a static charge, but tried to stay focused on whatever unanswered connection he had to Damali.

The moment the plane stabilized, the cabin crew nervously stood, made weak excuses, and then went up the spiral staircase and barricaded themselves within the conference room.

"You think they're nervous?" Big Mike said without a smile.

"Ya think?" Rider shot back, closing his eyes and leaning back in his seat.

"Whatever," Carlos grumbled, and then looked at Marlene. "We need a strategy to brace for nightfall."

"Why? You feelin' funny?" Shabazz asked. His tone wasn't glib. His expression was stone serious.

"No," Carlos muttered. "I just know that where I came from, they don't do variables. A search party is likely."

Shabazz nodded. "Cool."

"You went to ash and have the coverage of the Light," Father Patrick said, trying to keep panic at bay on the plane.

"Indeed," Imam Asula said. "This aircraft is anointed and covered, as is its crew."

"If you say so," Carlos said, sounding unconvinced. "I just don't like leaving anything to chance."

"Neither do I," Shabazz warned. "With no weapons on board, I ain't feeling right."

"They've got water on board," J.L. offered. "We could dump out the liquor and the clerics could bless it."

"Perish the thought," Rider said quickly. "Use the pop bottles and water bottles, son. Let's not get crazy in here."

"So be it," Imam Asula said. "We can create holy-water flasks so that each one of us has several at his or her disposal."

"Now you're thinking," Carlos said and stood. "We need to rig up *something.*" He walked down the aisle making everyone's eyes follow him. "In the conference room, the arms of the chairs are wood. Stakes. In the medical room, we've got scalpels that could be tied together with medical tape, if it comes down to hand-to-hand." He glanced at Marlene. "You've still got your walking stick, and need to keep that in reach."

"The man is on point," J.L. said, standing. "I bet they have alcohol, which I can rig a wick on using medical gauze, not to mention vodka, if I need to rig Molotov cocktails up in this tip."

"Two bottles of holy water on the ends of a long tether, like Ace bandage, would give me and Big Mike something to hurl . . . and with Ace bandage, I might be able to rig a slingshot—add a few hypodermics loaded with holy water and dead aim—see where I'm going?" Dan asked as he stood.

"That's exactly what I'm talking about," Carlos said. "I ain't trying to wait for nightfall to deal with anything that might try to breach this vessel. We need to be strapped enough to deal with an onslaught."

"Hold up," Berkfield said. "I agree and everything, and I'm all for a state of readiness, but what exactly are you laying for? What do you think is coming?"

"I don't know," Carlos said, his gaze drifting toward the window. "That's my issue. I just don't know, but I'm jittery as shit. We'll be flying over the damned Indian Ocean all night long, up in a tin can with a few prayers around it, and I know who definitely wants to be sure I didn't come back. Not to mention, with Damali gone, my greatest worry is they haven't already found her. Because if they have, they'll hold her hostage for the next six years until she goes into phase again. There'll be no negotiation, and girlfriend left outta here without her blades on her, feel me?"

"Yeah, I feel you," Shabazz said.

"Just when I thought we might be able to get some real shuteye," Rider said, standing to come into the aisle. "But good looking out."

Berkfield held out his arm. "According to Father Patrick, I'm packing a lethal weapon."

The group stared at him.

"You've got needles in the back," he said, motioning to the medical room. "Take some blood out of my arm and lace the edges of blades and whatever projectiles you design with it. If you go hand-to-hand with a demon, a simple scalpel will make 'em laugh at you and rip your throat out, right?"

"No lie," Carlos said with a tense smile. "A scalpel cut ain't nothin' but a love nick."

"Shit," Rider said, running his palms over his jaw. "I vote for long-distance designs, J.L. You got that?"

"Yeah, I got it," J.L. said.

"And what if homeboy has a problem when the sun goes down?" Big Mike said, looking at Carlos. "Not trying to play, just being real."

"No offense taken," Carlos said. "Truth be told, I'm half hoping that I do get back to my old self. That way, at least, I could get off this potential death trap and find Damali."

"Let's cross that bridge when we come to it," Shabazz said in a tired voice. "Like we all know, any of us mighta gotten nicked and the signs just haven't shown yet. With crossing international date-lines and whatnot, I don't even know what day it is or how many nights have really passed. Do you?" When no one answered, Shabazz nodded. "The virus could jump out of any one of us once the sun goes down, so we all need to be real clear about that, and keep a personal set of artillery in reach."

"We work while we have light, then," Jose said. "Me and Monk Lin can probably break down a few of these seats to yield some long metal. Everything can't be plastic."

"Once we compile our arsenal, we should take shifts. The fatigue will rob us of strength. It will not be wise to have the entire team in that condition," Monk Lin said with a slight bow.

"Smart man," Carlos said, moving down the aisle toward the medical area. "Jose, break these stirrups off the table. There's metal rods in the gurney, too. In fact, pillage this room first."

Juanita knelt by Mrs. Rivera on the ground, her face streaked with tears as the house burned. Neighbors had gathered a block from the home, and good Samaritans tried to comfort the older woman who clutched at Juanita with shaky fingers. Ambulances could be heard in the distance and fire trucks screamed into the street along with news vans.

"El Diablo," Mrs. Rivera cried. "Momma! Oh, Momma!"

"We couldn't get to her," a neighbor said, his clean-cut hair smoldering as ash and debris clung to his jogging suit. "Lady, I tried," he said weeping. "God knows I tried, but the flames."

"It was a gas explosion," another neighbor yelled, pointing at Mrs. Rivera as an ambulance careened to the scene. "Help her! She was blown through the front window. But the grandmother . . ." The woman turned her face away and sobbed. "They were such a nice family. Thank God in Heaven their daughter was on her way home from work and not home, too."

"Listen to me, child," Mrs. Rivera said, her eyes glassy and disoriented as she pushed away the ambulance paramedics. "You cannot run from the devil. I tried to tell you that you must stand and fight him. Find my son, Carlos. He will make this right and will take care of you." She slapped at the helping hands that tried to roll her onto a gurney. "I saw my son! He is not dead! No, *por favor,* listen! My child is alive and he has come back to help us."

Juanita brushed the bloodied, thick strands of hair away from Mrs. Rivera's face. Her voice broke with sobs of anguish. "Be still and fight to live, Momma Rivera. Please. All your children are gone, but I will never leave you. Go to the hospital now and don't fight these men."

The older woman closed her eyes, and clutched Juanita's sleeve so tightly that the emergency medical team couldn't pry her fingers loose. "I have a number to give you. All that I owned, all that he left me and Momma go to you—but you must see that my son gets all but ten percent back. He will take care of you, don't rob him." She made Juanita lean in close and she spoke a number in her ear. "Write it down in your hand. Give her a pen. If she does this, then I will go."

"Get her a pen," one of the paramedics said with annoyance.

The panic of the situation and chaos of firefighters battling the blaze beyond them seemed to make the paramedic's nerves fray and snap under the duress of an old woman's unreasonable request. "Miss, do as she asks. Her pressure is dropping and she's going into shock."

Quietly, Mrs. Rivera spoke the numbers to Juanita with slow care. She watched the young woman scribble them in her palm and smiled, finally releasing her hold. "I love you, sweet one. Call the priest. Do not come to the hospital. Sleep in a church tonight. Then go to the bank—Swiss Bank, *comprendo*?"

"C'mon, man. We've gotta get this lady into the ambulance. She's lost a lot of blood and is delirious." The ambulance team looked at Juanita as they covered Mrs. Rivera's face with a mask. "You can ride with us, but make a decision quick."

Juanita clasped Mrs. Rivera's hand, her eyes going from the injured elderly woman to the burning house a block away as she ran with the team beside the gurney. There was no way in the world she would abandon Carlos's mother. Not while she was on her deathbed, not when everything and everyone dear to her had been lost.

Stricken, Juanita made herself very small as the team checked Mrs. Rivera's vital signs and worked on her, everything moving in slow motion and at the same time a blur.

"Momma, please hold on, Momma Rivera," she murmured as the older woman's eyes rolled back under her lids and her jaw went slack.

"We're losing her!" a paramedic shouted. "Bring out the paddles. Gimme room to work, folks."

Juanita scrunched her body against the wall, and looked away as electric-shock paddles touched Mrs. Rivera's skin. Her body arched and lifted off the gurney, and then dropped, but the line on the monitors never moved. From the corner of her eye Juanita saw a strange glow within the eyes of the paramedic standing behind the one working on Mrs. Rivera. It was only a fraction of a second, like a quick flash of yellow lightning. Something was also wrong with his mouth. She watched a mist come up from the center of Mrs. Rivera's chest and hover over her lifeless body. A scream froze in Juanita's throat as she eased toward the door during the commotion. She watched the men work on the woman who should have been her mother-in-law. Her eyes went between the eerie, mesmerizing mist and the chilling flashes she glimpsed in the profile of the men's irises.

"He is not dead," a light female voice whispered so close to her ear that she almost passed out. "He is not dead. Run!"

Instantly, both paramedics looked at her. Their eyes narrowed and elongated fangs ripped through their gums. "One more, and that cleans up his territory," one said.

"You wanna do her before we do her?" the other asked, moving toward Juanita as a scream broke free from her throat and the sound bounced off the metal within the ambulance.

She was on her feet in an instant, and in two steps the beasts were on her. The ambulance swerved and hit a tree. The back door opened, jettisoning Juanita in a roll onto a church lawn.

"What the fuck!" one beast snarled.

"Run!" the ambulance driver shouted. Her voice was shrill as she materialized outside the vehicle and a large male materialized by her side.

Juanita ran and huddled against the locked doors. Her mind couldn't comprehend what her eyes were seeing. A young African-American male with massive body strength drew one of her attackers toward him, ripped out his heart, and allowed the body to combust just inches from him. The woman who had been driving the ambulance pulled out a sawed-off shotgun from someplace she couldn't see, leveled it at the other paramedic, and pulled the trigger, scattering burning embers and ash everywhere.

"I told you Carlos's territory was under siege," the female ambulance driver said, cocking back the barrel. "Those were territory sweepers."

"Yeah, baby, I know," the bulked male said, his focus now on Juanita. "Okay, you've made your point. But she has the digits to get in touch with Carlos. You heard what his momma said. Brother ain't dead."

Juanita covered her head and began screaming as the two things she couldn't describe walked toward her, but stopped just short of the lawn.

"We didn't come to harm you," the woman said, her mouth filled with long, white teeth. "But we do need information."

Papers and pens from the ambulance swirled and flew at Juanita.

"Stop screaming!" the male ordered. "Write the digits down before you sweat that shit away."

Trembling, Juanita looked at them and grabbed the papers and a pen that had landed at her feet. She'd do anything to live. "Please don't kill me," she whispered, her eyes darting between the man and woman, a new scream forming as she watched them normalize into what would appear to be an ordinary man and woman.

"Write and we won't," the woman said in a gentle voice. "Stay inside the church tonight, or at least on the steps if it's locked."

Juanita nodded and quickly complied. "Is he really still alive?" she asked, flinging the paper at them but staying affixed to the door.

"You can see spirits," the male said. "The one that was going toward the Light, we couldn't see her because of that. What did she say?"

Juanita swallowed hard, willing herself not to pass out. "Momma Rivera said, 'He is not dead.' She told me to run."

The male nodded. "My boy, yeah . . . You go!" He began walking away into the night, chuckling.

"Tell no one about this," the woman warned. "Get in touch with him and seek his shelter. He needs his resources. When you do find him by day, tell him two of his own that were supposed to be Guardians are on the run in his zones." She began walking into the nothingness of the night in the direction the disappearing male had come from. "You're one, too, *chica*. If you can see Light spirits, they need you. Time to wake up and face your destiny."

It was just too quiet. Carlos fidgeted in his seat, unable to sleep. Two men on full guard for two hours, then the shift would change. Whatever. He wasn't about to go to sleep. The most he would allow himself was to close his eyes so the burning itch would stop. It felt like sandpaper was scoring the insides of his lids each time he blinked. He *hated* being human. The night was supposed to be his, not drug him making him sleepy and possibly sloppy if Hell came to call.

He watched Jose fighting it, too, twitching and turning in what seemed near agony, trying to stay awake but unable to. Dan's head was bobbing up and down so hard that Carlos was sure the young gun would ultimately snap his own neck if the plane hit a turbulence bump. Big Mike was sprawled out, head back, snoring so hard he almost drowned out the plane engines. But he liked how Marlene slept, just like Monk Lin—like cats. Their third eyes open, the other two closed in a light but steady doze. He knew in an instant those two would be on their feet. Rider was also good, slept like a soldier, practically standing up. All he needed was a ten-gallon cowboy hat to put over his eyes.

Carlos nearly smiled as he looked over at Shabazz. His Guardian brother had made a tent with his fingers, his breaths slow and controlled, asleep but not really. Of them all, he slept most like a vampire—always ready. Marlene slept like that, too. Quiet repose, almost as though she was dead. But he knew sister could bring lightning in an instant. Serene ambush. Very cool, very wise. Unshakable. All of it gave him a new level of respect for Damali's squad and those that had schooled her. If these were her teachers, then his woman was more awesome than he'd come to know.

Lopez's sleep was fitful, just like Jose's, though. That concerned him. Both those guys had a thin line of vamp in their DNA, and their not being able to rest truly made Carlos worry. Asula was stretched out, like Big Mike, but Father Patrick's breathing would hitch, stop as though impacted by sleep apnea, and then resume, making Carlos wonder if the old man's heart would give out one night from it all.

His gaze intermittently roved the cabin, every now and then connecting to J.L.'s bleary-eyed expression, then they'd nod and acknowledge the clean sweep, and start the process all over again. It would have been so much easier if he could just read minds, sense things again, and could get a lock on his baby girl. Carlos gave up the foolish wish. It was what it was. He settled back in his seat and stared out at the gorgeous full moon. She was flossing tonight, strutting herself over the wide Indian Ocean, and had things been different, he might have gone out to dance under her on the wind.

His gaze went to Jose as he arched in his chair. Something was wrong. Carlos trained his eyes on his fellow Guardian brother and listened intently. Jose's breathing wasn't right; it was coming in short, uneven pants. When Jose groaned, Carlos relaxed and shook his head. *You thinkin' about that, at a time like this, hombre?* he thought, becoming annoyed and not sure why. But when Jose murmured Damali's name, he froze. His fingers gripped the arms of his chair as he fought not to rush Jose and start beating the shit out of him.

True, a man couldn't be held accountable for his dreams, but if they were going to be teammates, some shit was just unacceptable— even in one's sleep. Carlos forced his gaze back out the window. But what could he expect? He'd actually told Jose to step in for him, to be with Damali, should anything happen to him. And Jose had had his back, with Lopez, had collected his ashes and had joined in prayer with Damali for his return. Plus, something *had* happened to him. He wasn't right. Without his powers he was crippled. He and Jose were now equals. But if homeboy didn't stop dry humping the arm of the chair with his woman's name in his throat, he was fairly certain that he could still rip out his heart.

In all his life he never thought she'd come to him like this. It had been a dream, a fantasy, but now that she was so close, Jose held his hand out to Damali. Her eyes were sad as she dabbed at his mouth with a damp finger.

"You've got some sauce from dinner on your chin," she said with a smile.

He leaned against his bike and glanced out the garage door toward the waning sunlight. "You wanna get out of the compound go down to the beach?"

She nodded and kissed the offending stain off his chin, licking it as she drew away, but she stayed so close that he could smell the sweetness of her deepening breaths. "Or, we can go to your room?"

"You sure?" he asked, his hands trailing down her arms and back up again. He watched her nod, her nipples hardening beneath her favorite peach tank top as his hands gently caressed her arms.

"He's been gone a long time, and it's time for me to move on. I miss him, but . . ."

"I miss him, too," Jose said. "But I don't want you to wake up tomorrow and regret it. I care about you too much, if—"

"Shush," she said, placing her fingers over his lips. "We've both wanted this for a long time."

She covered his mouth with her own, deepening the kiss, her tongue finding his, stroking it until he groaned. She pulled back, and he moved with her until he was crushing his mouth against hers. His hands slid down her back to cup her behind.

She pulled away again. "Tell me you don't want this," she murmured thickly in his ear. "We can always stop."

"No," Jose hissed into her ear. "You know how long I've wanted you."

"Then don't stop," she murmured against his throat, licking a trail down it, then nipping her way back up. Her body moved against him, causing his hips to match the same rhythm as hers. "Let's go to your room."

"Okay," he said, unable to breathe. "We shouldn't let the house see us, though, you think?"

"Why do I care? You're my man, aren't you?"

He stared at her, tears filling his eyes. "I don't know. Am I?"

"Yes, ever since you saved me. Jose, you risked your life for me, went against harpies. How could you not be?"

He kissed her so hard he thought he'd chip one of her teeth. His bedroom was so far away that he wasn't sure if he could walk the distance—desire weighed on him so heavily. The garage was just fine. . . . But he wanted all night with her, no interruptions. Wanted it to be right, so she'd never say no again.

Her palm flattened against his hard length, making him shudder.

"I can't wait, either," she whispered. "I want you now." She looked at him hard and pulled her top over her head, allowing her bare breasts to fill his hands. "Take off your pants."

He couldn't stop touching her even to unzip his pants. "You sure?" he panted, nipping her throat, working at the fastening, stroking her hair, kissing her as he tried to strip the jeans from his body, and cried out when she melted against him like hot wax.

He'd only imagined what she'd feel like against him, but the sensation sent a hard shiver through his body down to his bones. The sudden burn of skin against skin brought tears of pleasure to his eyes. "Take off your pants, baby," he rasped against her throat, his face damp as her skin seared him.

"Remember when Carlos died?" she said, opening her zipper slowly.

He nodded and swallowed hard, she felt so good it was ridiculous. He couldn't even speak. His focus was singular; she had to get her pants down.

"What did the Guardian team ever do with his ashes?"

Jose blinked. She knew what they had done with his ashes. Something wasn't right. He watched her slide down his body to kneel on the cement floor.

"Tell me, baby," she murmured. Then she drew him into her mouth slowly, his eyes rolled back in his head, and everything began to feel right again. "Jose, you know, don't you?"

When she drew her mouth away, his stomach clenched. He looked at her lush mouth, the cold air kissing his ass and his wet, throbbing member. He knew he had to be out of his mind. But something was telling him she wasn't herself. She didn't really want this as much as he did. It took everything in him to reach down and hold her by both arms. She smiled as he held her, staring into her beautiful hypnotic eyes, breathing hard, wanting to cum inside her in that moment more than he wanted to live.

"All you have to do is tell me," she said, her hot breath flowing over his hard shaft.

"Damali, baby, I love you, you know that . . . but you're scaring me." He sucked in a long, shaky breath, and caressed the side of her face. "I don't want to talk about that right now while I'm loving you. Let's go back to my room and—"

"No," she said, standing suddenly. Her gaze narrowed on him as she folded her arms over her bare breasts. "I'm going to my room. If you decide you want to communicate with me, then knock on my door. You have ten minutes. Otherwise, you can forget it."

He watched her walk away, his pants down around his ankles. Conflict tore at his conscience. How many nights had he been so hot for her that he'd used his hand to relieve the ache? How many nights had he awakened alone in his bedroom just down the hall from her, twisted in his sheets, sweating and dying for her? Now she had come to him, stripped him down, offered her mouth, her body, *everything,* if he'd just talk about a situation they both knew.

Jose pulled up his jeans with a wince. He was only human . . . then he remembered, yeah, but girlfriend had also once dropped fangs. What if she had gone dark again? What if that's why she could no longer sense where Carlos was, now that he wasn't a vamp? Then it hit him. *They were supposed to be on a plane.* Carlos hadn't died. He was alive and sitting a few rows behind him when he'd fallen asleep!

Sudden terror jolted him awake. Jose glanced around hoping he hadn't given himself or his dream away. The erection was killing him. What had been on his mind? Dreaming about Damali, like that, now? All he could do was take deep breaths and try to will the tremors away. He glanced at Carlos, who turned slowly, his eyes glowing silver. Jose froze, the sweat on his brow chilling beneath that gaze.

"We need to talk, man," Jose said quietly.

Carlos nodded. "Yeah, motherfucker. We do."

CHAPTER TWELVE

"THIS IS one of only three like it in the world," the cabbie said as he left Damali on the curb.

Damali marched up the stone steps and peered at the wide, wooden door. She touched it with her hand and glanced around. Nothing happened. Becoming more confident she touched the door again, this time with both her hand and the stick simultaneously. She closed her eyes and walked forward the moment her hands began to tingle, thoroughly expecting to bump her nose.

Giddiness entered her as she realized she'd done it again. Her mind continued to hammer away at the possibilities while her eyes swept the interior. Everything was land-of-the-giants scale. A huge oak reception desk protected the Mason Temple guard that greeted her. The fact that he was calmly sitting behind the desk gave her a start. He smiled as though expecting her, which she definitely wasn't ready for.

He was a merry little man, with a kind, round face, pudgy build, and unkempt fawn-brown hair that was thinning in spots. His gray eyes twinkled as though he knew a secret. Behind him, on the wall, was a massive lithograph of the architectural layout for King Solomon's Temple. Damali stared at the wall and then at the man, so many questions running through her mind that she didn't know where to begin.

"You're very early for the eleven-o'clock tour," he said in the tone of a very well-mannered gentleman. He stood and hitched the pants of his blue uniform over his round belly as she approached the desk. "Or, are you just here for the museum and library?"

They both stared at each other. The outer door was locked; she'd just walked through it like it had been wide open. This guy had to have seen her do it, but he acted as if walking through doors was a normal occurrence. Her heart beat a little faster.

"Just the tour," Damali responded pleasantly, "and perhaps a peek at the library later."

Motioning for her to follow him, he rounded the desk and smiled. Damali's line of vision swept every facet of the rooms they passed. She could feel electric excitement pass through her.

"I'm Druid, you know."

She smiled politely, not sure how to respond. "That's very nice. I'm just in from L.A."

He laughed, his voice creating a joyful echo within the large room. "We go way back, and have suffered much, too. We've heard you've taken one of our own in under your wing." He stopped and gave her a little bow. "So, for that kindness, you receive the *grand* tour."

Damali smiled and nodded, while her mind scrambled to figure out which team member he was talking about. They'd had a lot of additions. Dan? Berkfield? She hurried behind him, amazed at how fast the chubby little man could walk.

"Did you know that George Washington was a Mason, as well as most, if not all of the founding fathers of this country?" The guide winked at her as he whispered the information like a schoolboy telling a secret. "They have his Masonic apron right here in the museum."

"Yeah, the guy in the cab was telling me," Damali murmured, her eyes darting around the glass cases that lined the room. What else could she say? Each case held emblems, shields, swords, rings, coins, and other artifacts that seemed to go as far back as the Middle Ages. Okay, so who was this guide and how did this building get her to Egypt?

Scanning the room, she noted the fine woods and Italian marbles that supported what appeared to her to be fifty-foot ceilings. Nothing Egyptian leapt out at her and the exterior of the building looked like hand-sculpted granite from Westminster Abbey.

"Right you are." The tour guide chimed in with a proud smile in response to her thoughts, "Actually, fashioned after St. Mark's Cathedral in Venice."

Damali didn't say a word. This old guy had read her mind, something only Marlene and Carlos had ever been able to do. It was unnerving.

Her guide nodded and smiled. "Correct again. It would appear that you are now ready for the real tour, now that you've loosened up a bit."

A hundred questions tripped over themselves in her brain as she followed the blue-uniformed gent into the next room and waited. Her mind was on fire, trying to make critical links between the spectacular show of power and wealth that surrounded her, and her own paltry existence as a disinherited Neteru with a magic stick. The fact that her guide reminded her of a leprechaun made her smirk. Now she *knew* she had to be losing her mind.

"Ah, I am not one of the wee folks," he said merrily. "Actually it was a coven back then— a good one," he added quickly. "People get semantics all confused and get weird about it, so I detest the word. We learned most of the mystical arts from the Egyptians. They were the true masters." He smiled broadly and clasped his hands. "I cannot tell you how thrilled I am to have a master in my midst, dear young queen. Oh, let us resume the tour!"

She almost ran in the other direction. In her mind, coven was synonymous with witches and black magic. He was right; the word coven had nearly stopped her heart. She planned to ask Marlene about this later, if she could ever get to her. For now, Damali held her peace and just allowed the man to babble on as she followed behind him at an appreciable distance.

"Each of the presently alive grand masters are represented in the life-sized portraits of this room," the guide said with a sweep of his hand, "and behind these two-ton brass doors, you will find portraits of our past, and now deceased, grand masters. These eighty-foot, vaulted ceilings have been lowered to fifty-two feet to accommodate the advent of electricity, but later during the tour, we'll see how the original structure was kept intact, and its grandeur preserved by the skillful use of skylighting. These ceiling frescos are gilded in actual twenty-three-karat gold leaf," he added, motioning for her to pass through the doors to stand before an impressive rear staircase.

"These doors have been hung with such exactness, that they open with the push of a finger, and haven't been rehung since they were originally installed well over a hundred years ago." He leaned in toward her. "Did I tell you how impressive the mathematics were that came from Egypt?" He laughed at his own gushing. "Oh, but I don't have to tell you what you already know in your bones."

Losing patience, Damali edged near the strange tour guide. "Really awesome, but I don't see the point. I was told that if I came here—"

"Patience," he said calmly. "Remember these points. If I take you through sections too quickly you'll experience vertigo."

"Vertigo?"

"Yes," he said, his voice becoming mildly strained with annoyance. "Now pay attention. The lights can interrupt one's depth perception."

"I'm sorry," Damali said. "Thank you for taking your time with me. I've just been very worried about my family."

He smiled and bowed slightly. "We understand, and are not offended."

Damali glanced around to see who the *we* he was referring to might be. But the vast hall appeared empty except for the two of them.

"May I go on?" he asked in a recovered, eloquent tone.

"Yes, thank you. I'd be honored," Damali said, feeling very much like Alice through the looking glass. She was almost sure that she saw a glimpse of something in her peripheral vision. A strange white blur, and then it was gone.

"There are seven lodge halls within this temple that we will see during the tour. We are now going to enter the Oriental Room." Her guide motioned for her to follow him through a wide door and he waved his arms as he made a slow circle, pride clear in his expression. "This room is an exact replica of the many impressive rooms within the Moorish empire's architectural palatial achievement known as the Alhambra."

Damali's line of vision fastened to the magnificent hand-cut mosaics and thick burgundy velvets that covered luxurious ornamental benches. "I'm home. And, I remember when it all fell . . . Granada, Cordoba, Seville . . . This was the Hall of Dames, and, parts from the Hall of the Ambassadors . . ."

"Yes," the tour guide remarked with obvious delight, "I see that we have a historian in our midst."

Damali was speechless as her mind drank in the splendor. It was as though she knew this place from firsthand knowledge and the impact of the rushing impressions made her have to sit down on a long, polished bench. She didn't need the guide to explain that each layer of mosaic work had been reproduced from various sections of the palace and brought together into one spectacular fusion of riches. *She knew it.*

"See," he said triumphantly, "the vertigo happens when it hits you quickly. Memory is one thing, accessing the Akashic Records for the history of empires is quite another."

"Much respect," Damali said, swaying slightly and then stabilizing herself with the stick.

"The first time you pull down the knowledge can literally be mind blowing."

She nodded and tried to stand.

"Patience," he warned with a warm smile, "we have time. Wait until you see the knights of Templar and the Scottish Room . . . we have each section of the known world to cover before we go to the most impressive one of all."

Damali shook her head and this time when she attempted to stand, her legs held her weight. "No, sir, I really don't have as much time as you think. I have to go home. Soon." But the Templars . . . yeah. Maybe there was something here she needed to see.

He sighed and bid her to follow him with a simple wave of his hand. As they approached the enormous staircase again, she was forced to hold on to the rail. Her grip seemed precarious, at best, as the tour guide happily went on about how the forty-ton, five-story, spiral monolith was actually welded together in the building. Her vision blurred again, and that white glimpse haunted her. It floated lazily between the spirals. But it didn't frighten her. A place this old would be replete with ghosts.

"If you look down at the blue rug at the bottom of this impressive masterpiece," the guide lilted, causing her to peer over the rim of the railings despite her better judgment, "you will feel like you are spiraling into the Nile River. The Bailey statue at the bottom of the first landing guards the foyer. She is a masterpiece, and represents the virtue of silence—worth between three to five million," the tour guide added with obvious pride.

"And, the Bohemian stained-glass window, which has a depiction of Moses approaching the Burning Bush, also represents the four cardinal virtues of temperance, fortitude, prudence, and justice, at the bottom. We have other statues of near value, angels, carved by William Rush—brother of the famous Mount Rushmore sculptor, and all the murals that we've passed have been created by Herzog.

"It'll pass, soon," she heard the guide murmur as a thin sheen of cool perspiration beaded on her brow. "Don't look down," he advised.

"I'll be fine," she wheezed while images and information from thousands of years of history poured into her brain. Snapshots like freeze-frame still video flitted in her mind's eye, giving her understanding, making her know why certain wars had been fought, what was at stake, and the battle strategies employed to shift power, realign empires, and redistribute wealth. "I just need to go home."

"Since you are so impatient and determined to push yourself to the limit, if you will follow me, next we shall enter one of our most impressive rooms, the Egyptian Room." He stopped and sighed. "It's a shame you won't let me take the time to show you the other rooms, but I guess you'll see what you must along the way."

The guide paced ahead of her and then waited as she slowly followed, a throbbing headache strumming in her temples. The floating white mist was back, wafting near her. The hair on her arms and neck was standing up. What did this presence want? She could detect curiosity in it. But also deep sadness.

"This room is so architecturally and historically accurate, that Egyptologists can even transcribe the hieroglyphics on these walls," he said, smiling broadly now as he ushered her through the door. "It is so perfect in replication that scholars from around the world come here to study the mystic symbols and designs. It took three years of Mason-brethren study to do the research abroad, followed by twelve years to build and complete the room. Each segment of the hand-carved pieces of furniture is of the highest-quality ebony wood, with twenty-three-karat gold leaf."

Immediately she felt like the only proper thing to do would be to go down on one knee, not due to the involuntary effect of the vertigo, but as a salute or gesture of respect. However, the guide's presence seemed to prevent her from doing that just yet. That was something she needed to do in private. She knew it, although wasn't exactly sure why, but she was prone to follow her gut at this point.

Growing deeply concerned as his gaze fixed just above the Lesser of Three Lights Altar toward the ceiling, she was overcome by a nuance in the odd sensations she was experiencing.

A distant buzzing in her ears began to increase in tempo and volume, making her dizzy. As the tour guide spoke, she half-collapsed, half-sat down on one of the side benches to regain her bearings.

"This is Hathor, above the main grand master's throne. She was considered goddess of wisdom and fertility, often represented with a cow's head and a woman's body. Note the ceiling fresco of twenty-three-karat gold rays emanating from the sun and holding the sacred Ankh fertility symbol out before her. Here she has been depicted—as in only one of the main Egyptian temples—with a woman's face, but cow ears to represent her considerable ability to hear that which is not being said—a foundation trait of wisdom."

It was like looking in a time-distorted mirror. The rounded, heart-shaped face, skin coloring, eyes . . . coiled hair. Damali's vision momentarily blurred from tears of distant recognition. Indecipherable memories began to slam into her brain in spontaneous flashes, and soon the buzzing sounds evolved into what she per-

ceived to be the low resonance of old men's voices chanting. Unnerved, she stood and slipped outside of the room away from the
vibrations, unable to listen to the tour guide and the voices in her
head at the same time.

"You should see it all, and then come back to this room," the
guide said, offering her his elbow.

She was slow to touch his arm, not sure why, but she wasn't
too sure of a lot of things. He seemed to understand her hesitation, however, and took it in gracious stride as they walked in silence. What she'd just experienced defied words or explanation.
Yet, she had no vocabulary to quickly pose a question. Too much
was running through her mind just now. The silence suited her
better.

When they approached the grand foyer, the tour guide described
the architectural feat of the skylighting eighty-feet above them, and
she watched with tears in her eyes as the man shut off the power to
let the sun filter through. Tiny stars in the man-made constellation
had been cut into the granite surface, which allowed one to walk
among the stars on a Carrara marble floor.

"Concluding our tour," her guide quipped enthusiastically, "is
our main entrance, which remains closed by day to the general
public. Between five o'clock and five-thirty P.M., we open the
doors to Mason brethren and their guests only, and throw the main
power switch to ignite approximately fifty-one-hundred lights."

Something in Damali's brain also ignited with the mention of
the lights, and she glanced in the guide's direction and made eye
contact. His expression seemed to say, *not now, but later.*

"The interior of the main doors are guarded by two hand-cast,
brass Sphinxes, and as you will look up to the center arch, there are
symbols of the zodiac, and symbols from all major world religions.
But," her guide continued, "we want to draw your attention to the
cornerstone of the building, which was laid around the same time
as that of City Hall's, and the old John Wanamaker Building, forming a powerful architectural triangulation of spectacular construc-
tion. In addition, the cornerstone in this building seals off our
Masonic time capsule, buried in a vault under this structure. Un-

fortunately, some years ago the original one was cracked and damaged when the subway lines were installed under Broad Street."

"And the seal was broken. They put a thirty-one-foot concrete wall in front of it, for the subway, but the original cornerstone seal was broken," Damali murmured, finishing the man's sentence and drawing his undivided attention.

"Absolutely correct!" the blue uniformed man shouted merrily, his voice echoing in the vast marble halls. "In that day, they tried to use X-ray technology to avoid hitting our cornerstone, but, alas, there's nothing like those old artisans. I must implore you to visit our library one day, and most assuredly, our museum—if you have not already availed yourself. Did you know that there are more Masonic symbols hidden within the alcoves of City Hall, than even in this building? After all, the seat of this city was the unparalleled seat of world power for the burgeoning New World—and Philadelphia was the founding city of the newest, soon to be most powerful, nation on the globe, that also hosted the wealthiest, most influential families of the day. It was the new Rome, so to speak. Oh, you must try out our library and see for yourself."

"Thank you, I will try to come back here with my family," Damali said quietly, looking at the refurbished stone and shaking her head. "That was a crime. A true shame what happened. The seal wasn't supposed to be broken, especially not underground near the vents."

"Indeed," her guide quipped, concluding their tour with a glance at his watch. "We invite anyone with interest to visit, tour as many times as you'd like, and to stop by our gift shop on the way out."

"May I just walk through the Egyptian Room one more time?" she asked quietly. She gazed at him with a plea in her expression. "Alone?"

"It's not policy," he said, but smiled and glanced at his watch. "But if you are quick and absorb much before the dayshift changes, I can see no harm."

He motioned for her to follow him, and she had to almost run to keep pace with him. The moment he opened the door for her, he bowed, and then quickly shut it behind her. She didn't look back as she advanced to the highly polished ebony throne, knowing that he was already gone. During the long walk across the room, she stopped at the Lesser of Three Lights Altar and went down on one knee, then pointed the stick in each cardinal direction.

A lonely, disembodied female voice whispered in the room as a cool breeze washed across her shoulder. "I want to go home," it moaned. "Please. Help me."

Damali's head jerked up and she scanned the room as she stood quickly, stopped, and listened. "Who are you?"

"Oh . . . take me home," the voice wailed. "The portals are open. She'll never trust me."

Damali stood very still, allowing time to catch up to her mind. Everything the guide had shown her was connected. The broken subway seal was a metaphor for the broken portals. Each room, one of the thirteen flags. The Templars were involved, so were the Druids. Now this eerie, ghostly voice that was almost childlike was begging for her help. "How can I help you? What do you want?"

"I want to go into the Light," the voice said, and the wafting white mist that had been following Damali moved across the floor like morning fog. "I'm trapped."

Damali shook her head. She wasn't about to help some unknown entity by releasing it from wherever it was, especially if it wasn't already in the Light. "Can't help you, sis," she said firmly. "Not my job. Got things to do. Don't even know your name."

"If I help you," it whispered, "will you help me?"

Damali tilted her head. She'd taken a short walk on the dark side and knew a negotiation ploy when she heard one. Everything she'd ever experienced in that realm might also be to her benefit. She forced a chuckle. "Maybe," she hedged. "About the only thing I want now is the chairman's head on a silver platter."

"That can be arranged," the mist said, gaining in energy and swirling up to the ceiling. "But he never leaves council chambers."

Damali froze. Okay, this was a ghost, but how did it have intimate knowledge of the vamp empire? Something wasn't right. Her gaze followed the floating vapors. "Then, get me down there to blow the fucking hinges off his doors."

She watched as the vapor formed into a tight ball and ricocheted around the room.

"I don't know the way," the voice murmured, sounding agitated. "Only masters know. You used to be one, you should know." Then it let out a long, lonely moan and the sound of sobs echoed through the large room. "Oh, you're like the others and won't help me!"

Feeling an opportunity about to slip from her grasp, Damali peered up at the ball that was now in the corner of the ceiling. "I've fluxed back to my old self," Damali said, trying to keep contact with the dissolving vapor. "I have basic info, but not the route. I was never taken to chambers."

"Ask Carlos!"

The voice became angry and aggressive. Damali stared at the mist that was growing dark like a gray storm cloud, covering frescos and almost sucking the light out of the room. "Councilman Rivera torched in the sun."

The vapor lightened to a pale gray. "Oh . . . nooooo . . . then how can you help me?" More sobs echoed through the chamber. "The only one left hides where I can't go!"

Damali tilted her head. "There's one left?" Terror raced through her veins, making her do a quick calculation. They'd made another one that quickly?

"Yes . . ."

"Where is he?"

"I can't. . . . I'm no longer a vampire since our fight. I'm just a disembodied—"

For a second Damali was speechless, but she worked with her gut hunch. This was either Dee Dee or Raven.

"I can't help you, if you won't help me." Damali put one hand on her hip. "You're a ghost! Can't you invade his dreams; suck his mind dry? You used to be one of the hottest female vamps in L.A. Find out how to get down to the Vampire Council, and I'll gladly send your pathetic, wailing ass into the Light."

The moment she'd leveled the challenge, the vapors rushed

down from the ceiling and began taking shape in the far corner of the room. A svelte, gaseous female body began to form. Damali took a fighter's stance and held the stick in readiness for attack. But she blinked twice as the facial features of the transparent entity filled in. "Raven?"

Raven covered her face. "I want to go home. They opened the portals. I never knew what I was getting into." She looked up at Damali, tears streaming down her face. "Help our mother, Marlene. She was right."

It took Damali a moment to answer. There were no words.

"I messed up my life," Raven wailed, becoming vapors again, her voice reverberating off the walls. "I made hers a living Hell. I cannot rest. I am so tired. There is chaos. They don't know I'm missing, because the leaders are hunting for you."

The voice moved around the room so quickly that Damali almost fell as she moved in a circle, keeping it in front of her.

"What's coming will kill my mother. She'll die trying to protect you. I want to be in the Light when she comes. Tell her I am so sorry!"

"Okay, okay," Damali said quickly as the voice began to fade. "I have to get to Marlene first. But you and I could work together to get what we both want—Marlene alive, you in the Light, and me down at Vamp Chambers to go one-on-one with the chairman."

Raven immediately materialized, but stood back from Damali. "You would do that?"

"I want him, bad, girl." Damali stared at her. "I want Mar safe at all costs."

Raven nodded. Then she glimpsed the slow filter of light streaming through the window. "I cannot come to you on hallowed ground. But I'll lure the master from hiding and dredge his mind." She smiled. "He's new. I was Fallon's best lair companion. I'll know what he likes . . . what he needs." She gave Damali a wistful glance. "You've been one. You know what they like. Just don't renege on me, or I'll haunt you forever."

"You keep Marlene safe, and get me in front of the chairman, sis, and my word is good."

Raven nodded. "It always was. For what it's worth, I respected that . . . envied it. I've got a little Amanthra in me, too . . . but more succubae." She slowly dissolved, leaving Damali rattled. "Go home and wait for me to bring you information soon. I must work while he regenerates."

Raven vanished. Damali held on to the stick so tightly she felt like her hands would bleed. Several emotions crowded into her mind at once. When this was all over, she was moving out. It was settled. Marlene had served her time, had mothered so long till it didn't make sense. It was time for her to be given some peace, and not because death claimed her. The rest of the fellas needed that, too. The young bucks needed to have a life and experience—what she and Carlos once had, the full spectrum of love. Her man needed his powers back and some space to get his head together. Shit, she needed that, too. It was time for a change. Big change. To her way of thinking, the only way any of them would have a life is if she handled her business and addressed a very old debt. The chairman was going down. Lilith's head would roll. Then she was gonna chill. It didn't get any simpler than that. Win or die trying.

Damali let out a hard breath, stretched out her arms, and closed her eyes as she lifted her chin toward the ceiling, resolute. "Aset, I want to go home and to know where I am to be in this world. I open myself as a positive vessel to be used for the good, and only that. Please help me."

"Come child," she heard a female voice say. "Sit and learn."

When she opened her eyes, the face of Hathor was speaking.

Fear rose gooseflesh on her arms, but she advanced up the carpeted steps and sat down on the throne that was modeled after the ones that had once held great queens. The buzzing returned to her ears and the stick in her hand became a scepter that stretched into a golden rod. The head of it became a cobra that swayed to life as purple light enveloped her hand.

A sudden power rush filled her, making her arch her back and perspiration roll down her spine. It was so swift-moving and intense that she cried out, almost unable to bear the sweet heat. In dagger-sharp images she was connected to what Carlos had seen on his throne, a mirror opposite of hers. Worlds collided, armies warred, math and science and technology stretched her mind, languages bombarded her, and chunks of history flooded into her consciousness while scrolls of secrets wrapped in papyrus swam against the spiral of truths. She saw portals opened beneath the ground, lights in major cities going out, leaving a blackened landscape. The moon was eclipsed, a man with silver glowing eyes stretched out his hand toward her, his body rimmed in pulsing silver-lit energy. She called out his name and he came to her with opened arms. Then she was in a subway, running with her team, vermin squeaking and fleeing, tumbling over her feet to escape something horrible. A child wailed, and so did she. Then it all became so still in the bright tunnel.

Two entities approached her, the light behind them so bright that she couldn't make out their faces.

"Daughter," a soft female voice said. "I should have never left you, and won't now."

"My baby girl," a deep, familiar male voice said, holding out his hand. "We watch over you day and night. The Cradle of Humanity awaits you."

The moment they embraced her, she knew who they were. "Mom . . . Dad?"

"Yes," they said in unison. "Let us take you home. You have learned what you need to know. Let the guides help you make sense of it along the path."

Warmth radiated around her, lifting her closer to the light that cloaked them. A violet pyramid opened just beyond her reach, and her parents let her go. She could feel her body being sucked into the triangular vortex as they dropped their hold on her.

"No! Mommy! Daddy!"

But it was too late. They were gone.

Damali landed hard and cracked her head against a stone step. The thick emotion of parental loss still covered her and hurt as much as, if not more than, bumping her head. The dusty streets, colorful and chaotic, surrounded her and made her head spin. She tried using her stick to help her stand, but it was gone. She peered up at the brilliant blue sky and the dazzling sunlight made her squint. The warm temperature didn't stave off the chills that wracked her body. She shaded her eyes and tried to read the marker on the building, but could not. Yet she knew the language was Amharic. "Addis Ababa." The capital of Ethiopia.

Father Patrick nestled deeper into his seat as a fitful sleep claimed him. It had been so long since he'd seen his wife's smiling face, that when she came to him and hugged him, he openly wept.

He touched her soft cheek, remembering how much joy they once shared. Her large hazel eyes drank him in, and he filled his hands with her beautiful auburn hair, lifting it off her shoulders, the silken strands falling between his fingers. He stared at her heart-shaped face, remembering her mouth, the gentle swell of her breasts, and the curves of her petite frame. He knew he had to be dreaming as she kissed his lips gently and her body molded to his, still as svelte as she'd been when they'd first met. She had been so pretty . . .

"I have missed you so," he whispered against her cheek.

"It has been so horrible here without you."

He stroked her hair, watching the shimmering highlights in it while still allowing his fingers to luxuriate in the silken texture of it. "It cannot be so terrible in Heaven, my angel. I always prayed that you'd go there, no matter how you died. Our son, how is he?"

"Fine," she murmured, and kissed his neck. "But you seem to have been doing well for yourself," she said, pulling back with a gentle smile. "You have a new young man to care after. He's kept you busy."

He nodded and chuckled, kissing her forehead. "Yes, my wayward one, Carlos. He does keep me busy."

She gently brushed his mouth with a kiss, making his body stir in a way it hadn't in years. "Tell me about him. How did you bring him back?"

He sighed. "I didn't," he murmured. "Have you come to finally take me home, darling? Tell me my days are over, and that I can be with you and our son again."

Tears filled his eyes, making her form blur.

She stroked his face. "I'll take you into the Light. But first, tell me, whatever became of Carlos?"

He paused and held her back. "What? I didn't think death was conditional." The hair raised on the back of his neck. "Who are you?" he demanded. "What are you?"

In that instant she was gone, but he could not wake up.

Father Lopez stirred at the muffled cries he heard coming from Father Patrick, but a deep, paralyzing sleep kept him from fully rousing. A young woman ran toward him, naked and dripping wet, her eyes wild and beautiful as she opened her arms.

"Save me," she said.

Juanita's warm, young nakedness filled his arms. How could he forget her? Carlos had used her as a taunt, but he could never forget the sensation of lying with her. She was the only woman he'd ever known, even if it had been a vision, an illusion. She peered up at him.

"The vampires have surrounded my home and I cannot go back. Please let me spend the night with you."

She began crying and he held her more closely, trying to calm her as he stroked her bare back.

"I won't let them harm you. Where are your clothes?"

"I escaped through the bathroom window when I heard them enter the house. I have nothing but you . . . I am so ashamed." She looked up, tears brimming in her eyes. "The other clerics are all asleep. They won't know that I'm in your bed."

He glanced away. "But . . . I shouldn't. You can take the bed and I'll guard the door."

Her hand traveled down his chest. "But we've already been lovers."

He stared at her.

"Carlos gave me to you as a gift. I felt it that night and have wanted to be with you ever since. That's why I ran to you. But if you don't want me . . ." Her wide brown eyes searched his face and tears spilled down her cheeks. "Tell me you don't want me and I'll leave," she whispered, bringing her mouth close to his.

It was against everything he stood for, every vow he'd taken, and everything he'd been trained to do, but he was still a man. His mouth found hers, and the sweetness of her tongue twining with his produced near-delirium. "Don't leave," he murmured against her hair as she pulled away. "I'll protect you with my very life."

She removed his collar. "Did you feel it when he joined us?"

He swallowed hard and nodded.

"It was your first time?"

He nodded again and closed his eyes as her hand slid down his belly.

"I can show you more," she whispered.

"I really . . . I shouldn't, not here, not in the safe house with my brethren."

"We can go down into Carlos's old lair and be quiet as mice."

He looked around the safe-house living room at his sleeping Covenant brothers.

"Just like they went down there. Do you want me?"

"Yes," he said, closing his eyes as her touch produced a shudder.

"You are so much like Carlos . . . I loved him once. He was good to me, to us," she whispered. "He never really wanted me, and always loved Damali . . . so he gave me away to you that night in the illusion. It was a taunt, but also a gift for both of us."

"It was a gift," he said, stroking her cheek. He stared into her eyes, hypnotized by the urgency he saw within them. Just staring into them made him burn. Then every sensation he'd felt that night concentrated in his groin. He couldn't breathe.

"You have a little vampire in you, true?"

He nodded and took her mouth hard, rewarded by her hard rake down his back.

"Since he did so much for you, tell me, what did you do for him? Did you save him?"

"Oh, God . . ." he murmured as her hand slid beneath his pants and held him tight.

She stiffened, but relaxed when his head dropped to her shoulder. "Tell me, did you save him?"

He was breathing so hard he couldn't get out the words. "No . . . we . . . weren't . . ."

Suddenly a hard shake snapped Father Lopez awake. Men bearing weapons surrounded him.

A huge screech owl exited Father Lopez's chest in an eerie black mist and then materialized and careened across the room, as everyone ducked for cover.

"What did you tell her, man?" Carlos said, his eyes gleaming as he took aim at the creature.

Father Patrick slapped Padre Lopez's face. "Wake up, man. Talk to us! She's visited every man in here who has fallen asleep!"

Marlene brandished her stick as the owl dove at her, deadly talons extended. Shabazz hurled a holy-water bottle at it and sent shards of glass and water spraying against the far side of the cabin. Jose ducked as the owl screamed and flew up the spiral staircase. Dan and Big Mike rushed to the foot of the stairs and took aim with homemade slingshots, missed, and then were forced to take cover behind seats as the angry creature turned on them.

Berkfield threw a blood-tipped scalpel toward Jose, who caught it and flung it at the creature. His aim nicked the edge of the creature's wing, and billowing sulfuric smoke poured out of the wound as the owl dropped to the floor and began to elongate, a knotty spine sending feathers flying. Its beak became a razor's edge, talons lengthened, and a swishing, leathery, spaded tail stretched out of where its tail feathers had been. The creature now sported a six-foot wingspan within the cabin, its tail an instrument of death, and massive hooked talons strong enough to open a man's chest.

Rider hurled a holy-water bottle that splashed the wing, creating more smoke. "She can't fly in here—her wings are too big to get airborne," he hollered. "Open fire!"

Shabazz sent water bombs toward the beast two at a time as it snapped and screeched. Marlene and Berkfield kept its tail busy, stabbing it, drawing black blood, and dueling with the prehensile limb. Dan and Big Mike backed it up toward Rider, Jose, J.L., and Carlos, while the Covenant assaulted the beast from both flanks as it screeched in the wide center aisle from atop seats.

But its measures seemed defensive, not offensive, as though it were looking for something. Its gaze met Carlos's, raked him, then it let out an eerie scream that dropped Big Mike to his knees. Its blazing green eyes swept the airplane cabin again as if still searching for someone.

"She's not here!" Marlene yelled. "He's not here! You killed them!"

As soon as Marlene said that, the twisted creature flapped its wings, and rushed headlong into a row of windows along the wall, and vanished through them. The plane rocked, and then righted itself. The captain was yelling for everyone to take their seats. The terrified crew never came down the steps, but remained locked behind the conference-room doors.

"Sonofabitch!" Rider shouted. He looked at the clerics with disdain. "I thought you said this plane was sealed shut and impervious to a breach?"

The Covenant members shared stricken and confused expressions.

"I don't know how it got in here," Father Patrick said, his gaze sweeping the group. "It was strong enough to withstand a holy water assault."

"Well, a succubus got in here," Shabazz said flatly. "She messed with everybody, fishing for info."

Carlos nodded. "They go for your vulnerable spot, and every man has one." He looked at Jose, no longer furious at him. "She came to you as Damali." When Jose looked away, Carlos looked at Berkfield. "You saw your wife, didn't you?"

Berkfield nodded. "Sure as shit I was sitting in my living room, back home, my kids safe and sound in the house. Yeah, she got me good, but I didn't tell her nothin' because when she started asking about you, I know my wife well enough to know, that's the last thing Marj would wanna know about. But this thing showed me my deepest desire—to be home like none of this ever happened."

"That's exactly how I knew, too," Father Patrick said. "My wife is dead, and while I miss her dearly, I knew she wouldn't condition my entrance into the Light. She wanted me to tell her about Carlos."

"Right, like I'd tell some stray vamp tail from New Orleans about my brother here," Big Mike scoffed. "Never happen."

Rider began picking up weapons.

"Yo, man, every one of us who was asleep has to give it up to the group to be sure there were no leaks," J.L. said, his voice easy as he looked at Rider. "She got me with the images from Brazil."

"Me, too," Dan said. "But I didn't know her well enough to tell her team secrets."

"She came as Tara, all right," Rider said, his tone brittle. "She threatened to leave me for some punk vampire named Yonnie who's supposedly a master vamp sleeping in *my damned house* and . . ." Rider kicked a chair as he passed it. "I know it was all an illusion, but that shit still vibrates so real I'm pissed off. Can you believe it? Tara has some vampire in my house? Wait till we get fucking home."

The team stared at Rider.

"Thought that was twenty years ago, brother," Shabazz said evenly. "You need to grip up and get your head right."

Big Mike looked out the window. "If you're telling us something we need to know as a team, man, you know that's some dangerous shit. Even I only did Mardi Gras *once*—and it ain't nothing to wrap a love jones around. That's a sure way to get fucked up."

Carlos watched the team dynamics in the aircraft unravel. Stunned clerics took a very cautious position, and he could almost feel their muscles go to readiness. But Rider had had his back on the cliffs. His secret wasn't a dangerous one, to his way of thinking. He knew for a fact that Rider hadn't been nicked in a year. This was his boy, and it was time to cover his man and take the weight.

"He's cool," Carlos assured the team. "Every man has a woman he can't forget. Tara was his, so squash it."

"I don't want to fucking discuss it," Rider snapped. "Obviously, what we had was history. All she was talking about was Yonnie and Carlos! Who the hell is Yonnie?"

Marlene studied Rider, her gaze gentle, but her voice was firm. "No judgment. We all have some dark corners in our minds that we don't want anyone, even God, to know about. That's what makes us human. All I'ma say is, you need to let *me* know if you need something out of my black bag, on any given night."

Carlos just stared at Rider's back. *Yonnie* . . .

Jose went to Rider and placed a hand on his shoulder. "Yo, man, it was a succubus. They're supposed to jack with your mind. What did you tell her, man?"

"Nothing," Rider said, shrugging Jose's hand off him as the group continued to stare. "Why do you think I'm so pissed off?"

Shabazz swallowed away a smile. "Yeah, you cool."

"Yonnie made it?" Carlos said carefully, staying out of Rider's swing range. "I really need to understand what she showed you, man."

Both men stared at each other for a moment.

"Who the fuck is Yonnie?" Rider said, slowly approaching Carlos.

"A good brother. He had my back when I was in the empire. I gave him master status while me and Damali had to do the thing in Australia so he could keep my territory cool."

"What?"

Before Carlos could react, Rider hauled off and hit Carlos, knocking spit and blood from his mouth. Carlos went down hard in a seat. Rider was coming over the seat before him with four team members pulling him back.

"You made a master, and let that sonofabitch run loose in my backyard with my woman out there? She's a fourth! You fucking know that, Rivera! I thought we were cool and had an understanding. If he finds her and calls her, she has to go to him! If your territory is disintegrating out there and there are no vamp females left but mine, what the fuck do you think is going to happen?" Veins were standing up in Rider's throat as his team brothers tried to restrain him. He pulled back and shrugged off his stunned Guardian team's hold. "For more than twenty goddamned years I've kept her from whatever master was running the Los Angeles yard. That house is a fucking shrine to that woman—and a succubus waltzes onto a supposedly prayer-guarded plane and throws that bullshit in my face?" He walked away from the team. "I'm done."

"Oh, shit . . ." Shabazz walked in a circle, raking his locks as his eyes scanned the group.

Stunned expressions stared back at him. Marlene closed her eyes and took in a deep breath.

"Over twenty years?" Big Mike said, shaking his head. He looked at Imam Asula who was about to move on Rider. "He's my brother, man. I got him, if there's a problem. Chill."

Father Patrick nodded, and the clerics stood down. Jose, Dan, and J.L. sat down slowly, frozen in shock.

Carlos rubbed his jaw as he stood slowly, amazed when he tasted his own blood. He'd never even seen the punch coming.

"Clearly, he's no longer vamp," Big Mike said, glancing at Carlos and then Shabazz.

"No. Not at all," Shabazz said, shaking his head. "Okay, one problem solved."

Carlos watched the team from a remote place in his mind. Rider, a forty-five-year-old guy had caught him blind and tagged him. Shit. He wasn't sure if he was stunned more from the fact that Rider actually laid hands on him, or from the punch itself.

"Next problem," Shabazz said, looking at Rider, "is how long have you had a relationship with this female vampire?"

Father Patrick cast a nervous glance at his brothers. "Maybe we should all calm down before we try to dissect—"

"To answer your accusation, Rider, if the Covenant hadn't been double-crossed," Carlos said, spitting blood, "there wouldn't have been a breach in the prayer line."

"Tell me about Yonnie," Rider said, breathing hard. "He exists?"

"He does," Carlos said. "But that also means so does Tara. If they're the only two left standing from my old territory, then they're also on the run. But if they're holed up in your safe house, and your lines around the safe house are solid, they can't be gotten to."

"That is *not* a safe house for vamps! It is a sanctuary for my lady!"

"Let's get back to the part about you seeing her repeatedly over the years—"

"Her grandmother is a shaman and took care of Rider's cleansings," Marlene said with a weary tone. "It's only once a year, anyway. Let it rest. This is a fresh wound and we don't need this in here. If Rider hasn't dropped fang in all these years, then he won't."

Shabazz stared at her in shock. "You know her grandmother? Baby how long you been—"

"Not now, Shabazz!" Marlene stormed past him and went to Rider. "Have faith. Tara needs a master to help her fight against something that we've just experienced. He needs her to get to a lair that hasn't been compromised. He won't violate her. He needs her."

After long, tension-filled seconds, Rider finally nodded.

Marlene kissed Rider's cheek. "If Yonnie was made by Carlos, then he had to have something going on that was cool." She glanced over at Carlos.

"The man is like a brother to me. He got played, like me, back in the day. The other territory masters dogged him. I gave him a chance and a little juice. He knows the teams and anybody that's attached to them are off limits. Vamps do have a code, you know."

Carlos skulked away and flopped down on a nearby seat.

After a while, Shabazz sat down, too. "Bottom line is, the succubus came in here looking for Councilman Rivera and didn't find him—or Damali."

"No, she didn't," Carlos said flatly. "She saw a guy that had similar energy, but then passed me over. I could feel the probe, but she was confused because I'm not a vampire. Not even a fucking second-gen." He looked out the window.

"The question is, how do we kill it, though?" Shabazz said. "We used up a lotta ammo on one invasion."

"You can either set up barriers and prayer circles under where you sleep to keep them out as a defensive measure, or on offense, you have to wait for them to manifest and then behead them. On the astral plane where they suck out your dreams, they're too strong," Marlene said in a weary voice. "The double-cross from the people who anointed this vessel allowed foul intent to make the lines weak. *That's* why we got breached."

"I hear you, Mar," Shabazz said in a sullen tone. "But fact is, it did materialize, and we did hit it with everything we had, and the bitch walked."

"Didn't behead it," Marlene said quietly. "Every entity has a weakness. Succubae mess with the mind, that's why you have to take their heads."

The group nodded, but Big Mike seemed unsure. "But what's a succuba doing looking for Rivera? I thought the realms didn't deal with each other? And why Rivera?" He glanced at Carlos. "What if it was a strong vamp coming for him, like the Brazilian job? With almost all topside masters gone but one, maybe one of 'em is doing a power grab?"

Carlos nodded. "Mike's got a point. The realms don't mingle. A regular succubus wouldn't have the audacity to try to take a vamp territory, and couldn't hold it if she did. Could've been topside sweepers from level six using the power of female persuasion to locate me for council, just to be sure I was ash," Carlos said, half wishing the creature would have killed him. "They're going through my zones, apparently, trashing everything I had my seal on before rebuilding clean. When I can get to Yonnie, I'll know more. I need to find out what's—"

"That was a whole different lifetime ago," Father Patrick said carefully.

"That might have been a different lifetime ago to you, but my mother and grandmother, and my boy's sister, Juanita, were also under my seal, just like Berkfield was. Don't tell me not to worry or not to talk to my boy, Yonnie. Hell yeah, I hope his ass is strong as shit and remembers who made him!"

The cabin went still at the mention of the other innocent humans dear to Carlos.

"We'll get to Yonnie, man," Shabazz said. "And Tara." He looked at Rider. "Right now, we could use help from several quarters, as long as they've got good hearts."

Big Mike nodded. "Yo, brother, we gonna check on your

momma and grandmom as soon as we can figure out how to get back. Any way you can call your boy, like you used to, when we get on the ground at night?"

Carlos shook his head. "I ran North America, South America, and the Caribbean. I'm way out of my old zones. They've probably got a communications block on my transmissions, if I could, and if I were able to open a channel in a hostile zone, we'd all get jacked. I need to get back to L.A., man." He looked at Shabazz, Big Mike, and then Rider. "I need to find Damali, first."

Shabazz let out a breath hard. "It's a messed-up situation, but right now, we have three serious problems that we have to deal with. One, we need to find our Neteru. Two, our plane has been breached, and we could be attacked again. Three, it was a succubus that attacked us, in all likelihood. I heard what Carlos said, but I didn't feel vamp. It took on demon form to fight us, instead of coming as a strong female vamp. But, check it out—succubae can't just materialize as demons, they come in the form of the human body they've inhabited." He glanced at Marlene, who nodded.

Carlos closed his eyes. His worst fears had been realized, and Shabazz had picked up on it. He hadn't wanted to go there with the team to create additional panic, but the cat was out of the bag. "It wasn't sweepers."

Father Patrick nodded and glanced around the silent group. "We just got a visit from level seven."

CHAPTER THIRTEEN

TARA'S BREATH stopped as she stood motionless at the edge of the cabin. It was not from fear, but pure awe, as she watched the majestic creature lope toward her from between the trees. Trees Rider had planted. She lowered her weapon as her pulse quickened. He moved in long, fluid strides toward her.

Of course she recognized him instantly and it was the most spectacular transformation she'd ever witnessed. He'd used his power to take from the realms above theirs to transform into something that he knew would mesmerize her. His form was the wolf. Standing three feet at the shoulders, his coat shimmered pitch-black in the moonlight. His eyes were such a deep dark gold that they were almost bronze. Thick ropes of muscles moved beneath his coat as he silently came closer. He looked at her with longing, threw his head back, and howled.

The sound of his call swept through her as the night sounds around them went still. In a slow, sultry shape-shift, he gave up his wolf form and stood before her. He motioned with his chin toward a fallen elk strewn in the brush nearby.

"I had to eat after the fight," he murmured, coming closer to her and unbuttoning the top onyx stud in his crimson silk shirt. "You should, too, baby."

She stared at him, willing herself not to drool.

"You did good tonight. Fought like a second," he said with appreciation in his voice.

"Thanks, Yonnie," she said, finding it hard to speak. His body was still damp beneath his shirt, making the lightweight fabric cling to his broad chest and every well-defined ripple in his abdomen. His black leather pants clung to his narrow hips and long, lean legs. She looked away. "I was afraid, though," she admitted. "If we had only gotten there sooner."

"We did what we could," Yonnie said, his tone comforting. "I wish we could have gotten there sooner, too. But we did what we could."

He studied her solemn expression under the Halloween moon. She was absolutely gorgeous. She looked like she'd been made from the fabric of the universe to roam free and wild as a huntress of the night. Her hair shone like stardust was in it, her motions were liquid and effortless, as though she were a stream. Even dead, the color of her skin looked like the sun had kissed it. Her voice a mere murmur, like the whispering night breeze. But her eyes definitely rivaled the moon. Everything about her seemed more natural than supernatural; then again, the fact that she was one of his kind suited him just fine.

He'd chosen to wear the wolfen form for her, knowing how much her people held the creature in esteem. He was glad that his choice had pleased her, because her courage in battle had more than pleased him. He allowed his gaze to scan her again. He loved the way her fawn-colored pants and skin-toned tank gave the illusion that she was nude. She should have been naked right now, her dark eyes smoldering, her thick velvety hair flowing over his pillow. "You smoked that second like a pro," he finally said, wanting her to know how much respect he had for her.

"It was sloppy," she countered, not taking her eyes off him.

"No," he murmured, coming closer and caressing her jaw with the pad of his thumb. "We got there late. The old woman was already dead. Your maneuver saved at least one of Carlos's marks. I sent the ambulance with his mother's body in it to the hospital, convinced the medics she died from smoke inhalation. I couldn't do much about the grandmother. But at least she died instantly and didn't suffer. It was better that way. They could have tortured them for information instead."

She stared up at him, her eyes searching his, and he could feel himself teetering on the edge of control. He shouldn't have touched her.

She was practically trembling where she stood. She'd never taken down another vampire in her life. A second? It had been exhilarating and she'd done it with a master at her side, worked in tandem with him, following his lead in an invisible dance. She'd been in hiding, spent most of her immortal life avoiding all confrontation. Her only encounter with another vampire had been when she'd been turned. But Yonnie had shown her another side of her life.

She drew away. "I must feed," she said.

"I know," he murmured, and unbuttoned another onyx stud on his shirt. "After the hunt . . . the things one's body needs after a battle—"

"Please," she whispered, and tried to back away, but couldn't seem to force herself to do it. "I've never—"

"Felt like this," he whispered. He trapped her gaze with his. "Take off the silver collar."

She shook her head no.

"Take off the collar." He made a small cut in his neck with the edge of his thumbnail, and watched her stare at the thin line of blood that trickled down his throat and pooled in his collarbone. When her fangs lowered, he closed his eyes.

"I'm not going to make love with you tonight, no matter what," she told him.

He nodded, keeping his eyes closed. He heard her unfasten the collar. How odd that she called what he wanted to do making love. He had always thought of it as fucking. "You don't trust me?"

She hesitated so long that he opened his eyes and looked at her. "I don't trust myself."

"I won't make you do anything you don't want to," he said. "But after a battle, you need to feed." He stepped closer. "Please, let me feed you, Tara."

She took the paper that Juanita had given her from her pocket and held it out to Yonnie. "We should get in touch with Carlos."

Yonnie nodded, but his gaze was locked on her throat. "Yeah, we should," he murmured. "As soon as you feed so you'll be strong enough to do it." He hesitated. "We need our combined energy to reach him undetected, since he's obviously out of our zone. You send. I'll mask your call. But you have to feed first."

Against her better judgment, Tara stepped closer to him. She half expected him to snatch her to him, but he didn't. Instead he folded her in and she crumpled the piece of paper in her fist. She held her other fist away from him so that the heavy silver collar wouldn't touch him. Then she leaned in tentatively and gently licked the trickle of blood, crossing his collarbone with her tongue, following the delicious trail up his throat, until she was standing on her tiptoes to reach the open wound.

He drew a sharp hiss of air through his teeth as she lapped at his flesh, and she felt the erotic connection to him quake her torso the moment the sound carried on the wind. She'd never been with a master, never dreamed that one would offer her, a fourth-gen, his throat. And this one was not just handsome and kind, but also had a deep sense of honor. He'd gone on a risky mission to save three humans. He had put aside his own personal safety, to protect Carlos's people—just because it was right. There had been a debt of friendship acknowledged that went deeper than his first lieutenant rank.

Tara stared up into a pair of warm brown eyes, her gaze accepting his rugged cinnamon beauty. Her hands ached to touch his thick, springy twists of hair and she wondered what the kinky texture would feel like, wondered what the fullness of his mouth would feel like against hers. His earthy male scent filled her nostrils. It clung to his glistening, dark skin and wrapped itself around her.

"Take it," he said quietly, no force in his tone. "What I've got will make you stronger."

She nestled in against him. He shuddered when her pelvis slid against the hard length of him. She studied his vein with care, needing just a sip to satisfy her. He leaned down to give her full access to his throat.

Before she could change her mind, his hands slid around her back and yanked her to his body in a tight seal. She was lost. She seized upon his throat, breaking the vein in one swift strike.

He moaned and it made her pull harder. Her skin was on fire, her body throbbing to the rhythm of each hard suckle, forcing her hips to match until they both shivered.

He cupped the back of her head, holding her against his throat, luxuriating in the feel of her thick tresses. No female had ever scored him, taken his jugular like this. His hands spread over her delicate back, holding her closer, wanting to pull her inside him. The paper she held torched in cold, blue flames. She dropped the amulet to the ground as their minds touched.

"You should be a second," he said on a ragged breath, when she lifted her head. "If it's just you and I left to rebuild, you *have* to know certain things."

"Carlos, the numbers—"

"I've got 'em." Ash fell from her unburned hand. He took her hand and kissed the center of it. "You never commit important things to paper. They can be discovered," he said. "His mother didn't have much to leave him after the government did their thing. Besides, I have an account number." He tapped his temple with one finger.

"He wouldn't want you to steal from—"

"What? Other drug dealers, Mafia, the government?" He dragged his fang along the edge of her shoulder and swept it up her throat. "Let me show you how it's done."

His arms encircled her, one palm flattening against her back, the other against the swell of her buttocks. The strike was so swift that it made colors dance beneath her lids. Knowledge, power, and desire filled her, arching her back, her nails digging into his shoulders.

Her cry fractured the night, and instinct clawed its way up and out of her. She bit him so hard they both stumbled backward. It was all building inside her, almost a painful, overwhelming tide. All she had to do was release her resistance and say yes.

"Be mine," he whispered. "Share my strength, fight with me, side by side as a mate."

Conflict tore at her. She couldn't answer him, nor could she pull away.

"Baby, all you have to do is stop fighting the inevitable."

A slow shudder started in the pit of her womb, and it climbed up her abdomen, ripped through her torso, and entered her lungs. He siphoned it up through her veins, into her throat until tears wet her eyes, the shudder becoming his name in her mind as the orgasm crested. "Yolando!"

His knees buckled and he caught her and took them both to the ground. She'd called him by name. The sound of her voice reverberated through him, a dark echo. He held her in a firm grip, her legs wrapped around him, his hand cupped beneath her head, keeping it from touching the ground. Her long, dark hair spilled across the grass and into a section of the white prayer line. Light danced along the strands of her hair, making it glow. Heat rose and warmed his face. But it wasn't comparable to the heat she'd stoked in him.

She began to cry. He could literally feel the depth of love that she had for the man who'd built her this sanctuary. It flowed through her veins, poisoned her tears with the agony of her decision. Her commitment was so deep for this human that he could almost feel it connected to her soul, actually giving her one of those, its pure essence oozing through her skin into his and coating him with a desire beyond raw lust that he'd never known.

The conflict broke through the steel cage of his conscience; as much as he wanted her at the moment, he didn't want her like this. Vampiric instinct compelled him to simply take her throat; willing or not, she had no defense. Everything vampire within him knew that the pleasure he could give her, even while she wept for the human, would be incomparable to anything she'd ever experienced before. But he also knew that she'd never forgive him . . . eternity was a long time. With Tara he could do forever, as long as she was his in her heart. Right now, she wasn't. She didn't want this to happen, even though her body did.

Yonnie forced himself up, bracing his weight on his arm as he stared down at her. He'd vowed that he'd never violate a woman against her will; he'd seen his own mother raped and destroyed by men as she tried to hold onto her dignity while her pride was stripped naked on a plantation-barn floor.

"Has he been faithful to you?" Yonnie asked her, the frustration making his arm around Tara's waist tremble. *Please, baby, I know what he's done to you. Carlos transferred everything in our line to me! Every tear you've cried, I know of, because you're in my line—we share the connection. Talk to me.*

When she only sobbed harder, he pulled out of the intoxicating mind lock with her. She had to say it, tell him it was all right to love her like they both needed it now. The words had to come out of her own mouth. No illusions, no games, no trickery involved. He wanted her straight. Her heart his. No forgery to accept at this point. He kissed her temple. "While he's on the road, rolling with the band, moving country to country, has he ever taken another knowing he had you . . . an incredible, gorgeous woman waiting for him?" He kissed her throat, scored it, and drew his mouth away, pure fury lacerating him as she clutched her misplaced loyalty. "When he was in Brazil, didn't he take another woman to bed who looked like you?"

The desire to violate her and satisfy himself battled with his urge to just drop her on the grass and leave her. This human, the Guardian named Rider, didn't deserve her. How could a man simply walk away from a woman like this? "Why didn't you just turn him? Make him like you, so you could be with him forever, since you can't seem to leave him? I don't understand. Then you allow him to dog you . . . why? You don't have to exist like this."

His questions only made her cry a new torrent of tears. His voice was hoarse as he nuzzled her temple. "Baby, why do you allow him to do that to you? Hold his ass accountable," Yonnie said, his voice tender but firm. He kissed her temple hard, unable to draw himself away. "I'll take care of you, baby . . . I'll give you whatever you want, whatever you need. Just be with me."

"He's done so much for me," she whispered. "I can't leave Rider."

Yonnie dropped her and stood.

"Has he?" Yonnie stared at the cabin. "A house is the least you deserved. Has he sacrificed for you, the way you have for him?" He stared at her hard. She sat up, wiped her face, avoiding his gaze.

"But you sacrificed for him." Yonnie waited. "Too much, I think. Even human blood."

"That's different," she said, still not looking at him.

"How? He's even made you close yourself off from real pleasure. Has you living like a nun." Yonnie spat out the remnants of her blood on the ground and wiped his mouth with the back of his hand. "You've even accepted not cuming. He can't take a bite or deliver one to release you—and you died in your damned prime!" He rubbed his palms down his face, so thoroughly outraged at the concept that he could barely stabilize his breathing. "You're emotionally and physically starved," he said, his glare becoming tender as tears ran down her cheeks. "And you make excuses for him because he's human . . . yet, whenever the urge hits him, he can go for a drink, watch the girls dance the poles, jack off if he has to or take one of them to bed. And you choose to live like that?"

"He's human, and it's different—"

"How? In what way? Don't you have needs? Only his matters because of a cabin? When you met him, you saved his life as much as he saved yours. Fair exchange. Your debt was paid. What do you owe him now, Tara? You think you're not worthy of loving on your own merit alone? Ask yourself: Did he give up his friends, interacting with his own kind, screwing his own kind, anything that makes his life easier to live?"

When she didn't answer him he stared at her until their eyes met. "You gave up everything for him. *Everything.* After more than twenty years of existing like this, don't you deserve to do more than survive?"

She only swallowed hard and turned her face away from his. Humiliation and defeat caused her shoulders to hunch. Yonnie came to her, knelt, and touched her face. He wanted to claim her. Not as a trophy but as a part of him. He'd never experienced the kind of love she had for this Rider, and if she could ever give a fraction of that to him, his lonely existence would be worth it. Her struggle to remain faithful to a human who hadn't plundered him.

"I envy him," Yonnie whispered. "You tell that bastard that if he ever messes up, you've got someone waiting to give you the world.

I can wait. I've got time on my side." Yonnie drew his hand away from her face. "Make sure you also tell him that the only thin thread standing between you and me is your decision, and the fact that my boy Carlos doesn't need dissention in his ranks while he's rebuilding right now."

He stood, turned, and began to walk away.

She scrambled to her feet. A mild current of panic washed through her. "Where are you going?"

He stopped but didn't turn around. He couldn't bear to be alone with her another minute, any more than he had it in him to tell her about the coven brothel that was his destination. It was Halloween, and there were willing witches that he could use to purge her from his mind—for the night, at least. He glanced at Tara over his shoulder.

"I'm going to see what the witches can divine for me," he muttered, walking farther away from her. Why he'd felt it necessary to cover his whereabouts truly disturbed him.

"Where?"

"Don't worry about it."

"But if you get trapped out there, alone," she said quickly, the urgency in her voice making him shudder and know she cared.

"Go in the house!" he yelled, pointing at the front door without looking at her. The sweet sound of her voice was making him crazy. The melody of it laced with concern rippled through him. "Don't argue with me. You've made your decision and I'll take care of me."

She didn't move, and he turned to look at her, eyes blazing solid red.

"I said," he repeated, more gently, "go in the house. I'll be back before dawn."

"Be careful," she murmured, backing into the barrier light.

There was nothing to discuss. The team gathered up the remaining weapons. Carlos took up a position by himself in the rear of the cabin, while others fanned out strategically in seats throughout. That suited him just fine. He needed space to think and to nurse his wounded jaw and pride.

They had been rerouted just before midnight, so their flight never touched down in Dubai as originally planned. He thought about the attack and knew he was missing something. Numbers kept jumping into his mind for some reason. So did locations. Strategy and figuring out connections had always been his strong suit, living or dead. He toyed with the logistics, knowing there was a clue within them, becoming agitated that his loss of additional insight and powers of discernment that he would have had if he were still a vampire, blinded him to the root cause of the attack. Daybreak couldn't come fast enough for him, especially now that they were over land. Once they'd neared the Red Sea, all Hell had broken loose on their thirteen-hour flight. There was a connection; thirteen had to be a bad number; he could feel it in his bones.

He glanced up and saw Rider stand up and noted the time. Four A.M. In an hour they'd touch down. It would be dawn. If they could just get to the ground in Addis Ababa without any more drama, that would be enough for him. He leaned his head back and closed his eyes. He was too exhausted to fight.

All of a sudden, he felt a presence standing over him and he opened his eyes.

"Can we talk?" Rider said, looking down at Carlos.

Carlos shrugged. "Yeah, whatever."

Rider sat down next to him. "I'm sorry about the jaw."

"It's cool," Carlos said, and stared out the window.

Rider held out his hand to Carlos.

Carlos turned his head, looked at Rider, then at his outstretched hand. After a few long seconds, he accepted the handshake. His pride still stung. A forty-five-year-old guy had flattened him.

"Listen," Rider said carefully, when he went back to talking to Carlos's profile. "We're all a little touchy right now. Everybody's senses are off, except maybe Marlene's. So we may not be making the best decisions." He rubbed his jaw. "I know while you were a vamp, you had to do what you had to do to survive," Rider finally said through a weary sigh.

"Yeah, I did," Carlos muttered. "You have no idea what kinda

shit I had to contend with, man. Having people who could watch
my back was imperative."

Rider nodded. "Your boy, Yonnie, is cool . . . he'll honor your
marks?"

"Yeah. He's cool, man," Carlos said, looking at Rider for the
first time.

He saw real fear in Rider's eyes.

"Look, man," Rider said. "I've done a lot of shit that I'm sure
she knows about, and, by rights, she could . . ." He glanced away,
finding that same vacant space on the horizon that Carlos had been
staring at. "We've been together a long time, dude, and she means
the world to me."

Carlos nodded. "He won't hurt her. I never rolled like that and
neither does he."

Rider looked Carlos in the eyes. "That's not what I was worried
about, dude."

For a moment, neither man said a word.

"I'm forty-five, and I'm the only one she's even . . . you know
what I'm saying?"

Carlos nodded, this time understanding fully. Wasn't he plagued
by the same fear? That Damali might stay with him because she just
didn't know what else the world had to offer her yet. The word
"yet" burned in his mind.

The older Guardian drew a shaky breath and let it out slowly.

"If you made him, dude, he's strong," Rider said quietly. "But
him being a good guy is what could get under her skin." Rider's
voice became distant as he spoke, telling Carlos what haunted his
soul in halting sentences. "And he's in my house with my woman
who I see maybe once a year." Rider shook his head. "My baby's
never taken a throat nick from a master, done a mind lock, or . . ."
His voice trailed off. "I'm human. I'm getting older. I'm not what
I used to be when we met."

"She loves you, man. She'll be cool," Carlos said quietly, becoming lost in his own thoughts. His statement was as much for his
Guardian brother as it was for himself.

"The two of them together, on the run," Rider said softly. "Relying on each other to survive, under siege. You know what kind of bond that forms." He chuckled sadly and closed his eyes, leaning back in the seat. "Been there. That's how I met her."

Carlos glanced down at his knees. "Yeah."

"But it's even more than that. They're both vampires, first. I'm just a human on the outside looking in."

Carlos rubbed his face with both palms. What else was there to say? That Rider was wrong? That there was nothing to worry about? That Tara wouldn't leave him? He'd been there, too. Teetering on the edge, the not knowing how it would all work out kicking his ass. He had met Damali the same way, while she was on the run so many years ago, and what they had even death couldn't stop.

Compassion filled him. The irony was severe.

Carlos closed his eyes and mind against the painful possibilities. "I know, man. I know."

For what felt like a long time, Carlos and Rider sat quietly side-by-side in the aft section of the plane, unable to sleep, unable to turn the worry off in their minds, exhaustion and defeat a blanket over them.

But the entire team looked up as a nervous crew member crept down the steps, brandishing a large silver cross.

"There's a call from the Vatican for you, Father Patrick," the thin, frightened man said, his blond hair plastered to his scalp as he leaned over the rail and called out.

"The Vatican?" Father Patrick said, standing quickly and hurrying to the steps that led to the conference room. "At this hour?"

"Please, Father," the clerical crewman said, his voice filled with fear. "It's urgent."

All eyes were on the priest as he rushed up the spiral staircase and entered the conference room. A thud followed him, as did the certain click of the door being safely latched behind him by the crew.

Within moments Father Patrick was at the top of the stairs. "Carlos," he said, his voice anxious. "It's for you. Bring Rider."

Both men stood and ran down the wide cabin aisle, the teams tensing for another possible incident.

Carlos entered the conference room and grabbed the phone. Before he put it to his ear, he asked Father Patrick, "Who is it?"

"A woman, but she won't identify herself," Father Patrick said. He glanced at Rider. "I thought that it might be Juanita, but there was something in her voice that troubled me."

Carlos put the phone to his ear. "Yeah. Talk to me."

"Councilman," the unidentified woman said with a rush of relief. "So much has happened. Open a secure lock so I can transfer quickly."

He instantly remembered Tara's voice. It made him aware that he hadn't forgotten everything he'd learned and every imprint he'd carried from his old line. He nearly stared at the phone, but for Rider's sake, didn't. He also didn't repeat the name. "I don't go by that title any longer," he said, hesitating. "And I can't lock with you."

"Tara," Rider whispered, instantly knowing a female vampire was on the line based on Carlos's response and the fact that Father Patrick had said there was a woman on the phone. He also knew it could only be one that he'd trust with Father Patrick's number. "How did she get through Vatican phones? I need to talk to her."

"She didn't," Father Patrick said quickly. "My safe-house number was routed to another safe house that's tracking us, and the Covenant must have put it through using their code to link. Time is short. If she's in L.A., she's ten hours behind us. But once the sun rises here, we will lose the link."

"Are you somewhere safe? It's six P.M. here, but I sense dawn near you . . . have you fed?" Tara hesitated. Her voice held true concern and honest compassion.

"I'm fine," Carlos said, ignoring all her references to his old way of life. "Where's Yonnie?"

Rider stared at Carlos.

"Safe. Trying to get some answers. I don't have much time, and I can't hold the link much longer. I'm supposed to give you a number. I'm sending it now."

"No," Carlos said, knowing she was trying to send it telepathically. He looked at Father Patrick. "I need to write it down." But the fact that she was now strong enough to send an airborne transmission this far had to mean one thing. Yonnie had elevated her from a fourth-gen to second lieutenant. Elevating a vampire was a very sensual act. Carlos couldn't look at Rider as guilt stabbed at him.

The elder cleric quickly provided the instruments Carlos needed, and he heard Tara's instant gasp. Her horror rattled his skeleton. A councilman needed paper and pen. She swallowed hard, as though crying inside.

"Watch the numbers as you write them. Yonnie did this for you and still stands with you, as do I."

Carlos nodded and jotted down the ten-digit alphanumeric code, then watched several of the numbers reverse and transform on the paper. The nines became sixes. The threes became eights. The sevens melted into fives. He then wrote down the new code, too. The numbers didn't change.

"Ten thousand," she said. "From the account established by Berkfield."

He wrote it down and stared at it.

"That's all they left you."

He stared at the number in disbelief. But then he watched the zeros continually affix themselves behind zeros until a hundred million dollars graced the legal pad.

Carlos let his breath out slowly. He closed his eyes and sat down with a wobbly thud and shoved the paper into the side pocket of his African robe.

"Your family will not forsake you as long as we exist. We love you, and you need resources," she said, her voice filled with panic. "Carlos, *it's all gone.* The demon wolfen clans overran the L.A. club. Council sweepers have compromised all the lairs. All lower gens have been assassinated. Blood Music had its ownership transferred to council-compromised humans in a hostile takeover on Wall Street, just to keep you from receiving the monies from it. From Yonnie's sensing, all of North America, South America, and your Caribbean lairs and holdings have either been destroyed, transferred to council loyalists, or pillaged by roaming were-demon clans and lower gens from other zones not on the Vampire Council's hit list. But even those have fractured into feudal law. Even the Guardian compound burned to the ground."

Carlos had known that the chairman would go to extreme lengths to blot him and everything he'd built from the face of the earth, but he was still stunned. He was glad he was still sitting down. "Everything, even the Guardian compound?" he asked numbly.

"The compound?" Father Patrick held onto the edge of the table for support.

"What?" Rider said, stepping closer to him.

But Carlos waved him away and listened intently.

"Mr. Councilman, vampires couldn't have acted alone," Tara said, answering Carlos's unspoken question. "Power to breach protection lines had to come from level seven," she said, terror evident in her voice.

Carlos nodded, unable to speak. It had been confirmed. No further guesswork needed. If level seven was on his ass, and could get through compound barriers, then what fucking chance did Damali have out there on her own without even her blade? As soon as he thought it, his mother and grandmother's faces flashed in his mind.

"My mother and—"

"I'm sorry, sir," Tara said, a sob breaking her voice. "We got there only in time to save the girl."

"How?" he said, his voice a low rumble filled with rage.

"A gas line exploded beneath the house."

"Tell me," he said, hot tears stinging his eyes and choking his voice.

"It was fast. Mercifully so, sir."

Carlos nodded and drew in a ragged breath. "Tell Yonnie I said thank you," he whispered. "I'll let you know where to send resource transfers. For this, I need an army."

"Done," she said, the sound of her voice weakening as the gray filter of near-dawn began to peek over the horizon. "We stand ready for your orders."

Carlos reached out to hang up the phone, but Rider grabbed his wrist.

"I need to talk to her."

Carlos thrust the receiver at him and turned away to walk out the door. But a sudden crash against the side of the plane sent the phone sliding across the table, and all men standing to the floor.

"Mayday, Mayday," the captain's voice shouted over the intercom. "We're under attack! Brace for an aerial assault!"

The lights went out, the emergency lights on the floor of the aircraft summarily lit and then went black. The engine sputtered as the plane rocked again. Guardians and Covenant team voices shouted in the cabin mayhem below. Machine-gun fire from the aircraft's turrets echoed within the plane as Rider, Carlos, and Father Patrick struggled to get to their feet and down the spiral steps.

The whoosh of a missile leaving its housing sent the plane into a dangerous list. Battering sounds clamored at the skin of the aircraft generating high-pitched scrabbling screeches like claws going down a blackboard. The sky lit with multiple red and orange target strikes, splattering green and black gook against the windows as the pilots maneuvered the plane into a hard semiroll. The team clung to seats as they were thrown side-to-side, and thrashed to right themselves while futilely grabbing at weapons as the air battle commenced.

Carlos looked on in horror as the swirling black cloud of harpies approached again, passed the bank of side windows, and dove beneath the plane's belly. Their impact slammed into the hull, taking out the landing gear. Their feral grimaces mocked the living inside the plane as their faces pressed to every window, bearing fangs. Smoke was billowing from a fractured wing. Flames had erupted in the other. Something tore at the skin of the plane, opening a vacuum suction through the conference-room wall.

Before anyone could draw a breath, weapons, debris, food carts, and furniture were instantly sucked up through the rip, hurling human-crew bodies into the void as oxygen masks dropped. Guardians linked arms and weighted themselves to teammates and seats that were straining against their anchors, making the Covenant a part of their lifting human chain.

Flashes of light immediately entered the cabin, and suddenly

three large entities unfurled massive white wings, staying the suction and sealing the rip with light. The light emanating from them
was so bright that the teams could not stare at them. Only Carlos
could lift his head to see his reflection in their raised golden shields
and glowing, polished broadswords, his eyes blazing silver against
the metallic surfaces.

"Fear not," one entity said.

"We guard the dawn," another said.

"An army will be raised," the third said, as the plane began a
dangerous spiral to the ground.

The light snapped back, receding like the passing sun and swallowing away the entities that had stepped out of it. But the seal on
the aircraft's torn exterior held.

"We're going down!" the captain shouted, his voice laden with
hysteria as his words broke up over the intercom and the engines
went dead.

CHAPTER FOURTEEN

DAMALI STOOD and brushed herself off and looked around. The emotional pain of seeing and being separated so abruptly from her parents still lingered, but she had to do what she had to do and just suck it up. She'd fallen against the steps of what seemed to be a beautiful wooden house, but upon further inspection of the multilingual signage, she learned it was the Addis Ababa Museum.

Unsure of which way to go, she tried to get her bearings and organize the jumble of experiences in her battered brain. Museums kept popping up—there was a reason. As soon as she thought it, an inner knowing replied: Old history. Draw power from it. Lilith was old history, too.

Feeling steadier, she began walking away from the building, using her senses to guide her.

Unlike the other structures, nothing in this one particularly called out to her or jettisoned her through its doors. She stopped walking. Her sensory awareness was slowly coming back. The sensation that washed through her created as much joy as recognizing an old friend. It gave her energy, made her want to laugh, and she continued along an unknown street with a satisfied smile on her face. Perhaps something was starting to go right in her life. She could only hope that her team had stayed the course and would be on their way to Ethiopia soon.

A certain confidence filled her, even though her stick was gone. If she could manage to barter using the silver in her ears and whatever gold was tucked in her hair under the fabric wrap to eat and hang out at the local holy shrines, she'd last through a few nights until she could search for her team. Meanwhile, if she could only get to a phone. . . . Then it dawned upon her—none of them had a cell phone on them since they'd been in the battle at Sydney. Very strange.

It was as though all normal means of communication and resources had been cut off. But she took heart in the fact that she knew there had to be a reason. She stopped walking. The gifts and the number thirteen slammed into her brain. Yeah. She rattled the abilities off in her mind like a laundry list, taking none of what she'd originally been given for granted.

Five senses. As a Neteru, she had heightened awareness in all areas, and that had been severely damaged. If it was coming back now, the added bonuses might also. All Neterus had bodies designed to take a blow, plus preternatural endurance. They had the ability to withstand a bite in battle and not turn. Immunity. Visions, extrasensory awareness. Excellent battle tactics, gleaned from the Akashic Records of all generals before them. Ability to be a healer . . . yes, she remembered how she'd helped Marlene in Brazil. And how could she forget the twelfth gift that had almost been her ruination—the ability to lure master vampires to a state of frenzy from her scent.

The Isis blade was a tool, not a gift, when put in context with all the others. She was clear about that now, and knew the queens wouldn't have taken it away if it were. Not with what she was facing. Although she sure wished she still had it on her, regardless. But what was the thirteenth gift she was supposed to be looking for? If she couldn't figure it out as a more seasoned Neteru, then how was she going to help Carlos find it? She was missing a critical piece of the puzzle.

Damali shrugged away her doubt as she began to aimlessly walk down the streets. She refused to allow the question to lacerate her. She tried to get a sense of time and date. Was it October thirty-first, November first? Going through the purple light left her unsure. But one thing she did know for a fact, all this went down and had started seven days before Carlos's birthday—something she hadn't even entered into the equation until the strange cabbie had approached her in the streets of Philly.

There was a link. Dates, numbers, locations all had meaning. She knew that like she knew her name. So what was the deal with being thrust into Ethiopia? Questions swirled in her mind as she walked, and she took pleasure in what she now could tell was the early morning beginnings of a sprawling, dusty city of vibrant colors coming to life. The air was cool, temperate, for what she'd believed Africa to be. As she continued onward the huge market she'd stumbled upon awed her. She people-watched and enjoyed the early vendors creating a clamor of chaotic activity as she strolled past their stands while they set up for business.

The hubbub of activity was fascinating. Incense and vegetables, meats and jewelry, everything was there that one could imagine. She stopped at several jewelry stands, marveling at how the earrings she wore so resembled what many of the shopkeepers offered. Once again, it gave her pause. The old queens had adorned her to be able to barter in a place without cash. Damali smiled.

A table with a tent and an elaborate array of finely carved walking sticks made her stop and gape. One cane reminded her of Marlene's, and in the row of beautiful ebony woods, she saw a very plain stick gnarled in the same spots as the one she'd lost. She reached out to touch it, and a man came from behind his truck bearing boxes, which made her draw back her hand.

"Tenanastellen. Dehna Neh?" he said with a wide smile that broadened the one on Damali's face.

She shook her head and gave him a shy shrug to try to tell him that she didn't understand a word he'd said. She stared at his dark, long, handsome face, judging him to be near forty. He wore a plain, dingy, khaki pants, woven straw sandals, but a brilliant turquoise African-cut shirt with elaborate satin embroidery of the same hue that added magnificent color accents and intensity to his chiseled features. His shoulders were held back straight, his carriage impeccable, and his head held high and proud, but there was a very accessible warmth about his attitude as he came nearer to her.

"Hello, how are you?" he said, restating his greeting. "You are not from here, I can tell."

Damali chuckled. "No, and thank you so much for speaking to me in English. I wish I knew your language, though."

"To say thank you, in Amharic, it is, *amesegenallo*." He offered a slight bow and then rounded the table. "So beautiful and no one to escort you?"

Damali laughed harder and shook her head no. African men were such a trip, persistent. In an oddly sentimental way, although she was not sure why, he reminded her of the African master when he took her hand, swept the back of it with a respectful kiss, and glanced up.

Maybe it was the regal flourish in which he did it, or the ever-present magnetic sexuality that seemed to just ooze from men from the region. There was an "it" factor that they seemed to possess, and she studied him as he looked up and smiled, asking a mischievous question about her availability with his eyes. She wondered if she'd become so accustomed to battling dark forces that she'd lost her ability to see the basic nature within regular people. Given what she'd experienced, the vendor's slight gesture and his resemblance to something she'd just fought should have sent off alarm bells within her. But she knew this man wasn't anything to fear. It was simply his way, and it tickled her no end to realize that the refinement of approaching females hadn't changed in several thousand years.

"It would take many, *many* years to teach you our languages," he said with pride. "There are as many as the people, and the script of Ge'ez, the one used in the churches, has two hundred and thirty-one letters. But many of us have learned English in school." He gave her a wink and waved his hand before his table of wares. "So, you have seen something here you like?"

Damali nodded and affixed her gaze to his table as she considered what he'd said. She did the math, the language used in churches . . . with as many peoples as the languages . . . and he was fluent in hers, thus they could communicate. But he was also letting her know he'd received some formal education, a point of pride. Damali offered his comment a gracious nod that seemed to please him. She also knew why she'd instantly recognized his language to be Amharic. It was used in the old liturgical services. Yeah . . . Marlene had told her that.

"I noticed you had a plain one on the table," Damali said, her thoughts leap-frogging as she stared down. "Why is this one so plain, when all the others have designs on them?"

He laughed. "It is often the plain that are the most powerful."

Now she looked at him.

He smiled and nodded. "Thank you for returning it."

She didn't move.

He reached into his pocket and made a fist, chuckling as he slowly withdrew it and opened his hand. She stared down at her silver earring as he held it out to her.

"Now, I have returned what you loaned me." He walked away and began unloading items from his small Toyota pickup truck.

Damali was on his heels. "We need to talk, and I have to ask you a *lot* of questions."

He wagged his finger at her. "No, you must ask my father. Did my son not give you his address?"

Instant memory snapped back as Damali shoved her hand into the pocket of her robe. "Yes," she said, pleased. "But how do I find him?"

"He is a long way away, in Askum," the man said. "But I have people who can get us there. This is why I must unload my truck so we can go to the north."

"I'll help you," Damali offered, wanting to hurry and get the show on the road.

"No," he said with a deep chuckle. "Be still, then we will go and eat some *injera, alicha wat,* and *shiro,* with *ambo.* No meat in what we eat now, for we are on a pilgrimage, yes. So look about and learn to have patience. Enjoy this place that is called Thirteen Months of Sunshine."

That number associated with the sun as a country slogan made her simply stare at him.

Carlos managed to drag himself into a seat, as had all the others, bracing for the sure impact. There was no way to survive a crash from this altitude as mountains whirled by; it was futile. They all knew it. Perhaps that's why no one, except the pilots, was screaming. An eerie calm had befallen the cabin. Everyone's head was tucked down to their knees with their seat belts secured. What was the point, though? Oxygen masks dangled, but no one had reached for them to cover their faces. Whatever the entities had done, breathing within the compromised aircraft was possible. The Light had a very strange sense of putting things right. Let them breathe, then let them crash. Carlos wasn't sure if he was more angry or afraid; perhaps it was a mixture of both.

The sound of rapid descent was creating a horrible whine of impending doom. Then a gunshot made Carlos lift his head and simply look out the window. He could see it in his mind just as clear as day. One of the pilots had opted out of the anxiety of watching oneself crash and burn. The other was already dead—skull cracked from being flung against hard metal during the battle. The copilot's brains added to the gore against the windows. Now was a fine time for his inner vision to be coming back. But what had triggered it? Sure death?

Carlos affixed his gaze to the layers of thick white clouds set within a flawless blue sky. The ground was becoming larger, its green carpet and small dots of buildings now becoming recognizable. But peace filled him. It would soon be over. It just hurt him to know that people he'd come to know and love like family were going to perish, all because they'd tried to cheat fate.

He looked at the teams, each man and one woman, bravely bracing themselves for the end. No one cried out, no one screamed. Marlene's low murmur of prayers had blended in with those of the Covenant. Their faith and acceptance of what was to come was truly amazing to him. Humbling, is what it was. Because all along they had been right. There was another side. A dark side and a light side in dimensions he could have never fathomed while he was simply alive. And he wondered where they would all go; if he'd ever meet up with them again. He wondered if the Light would have mercy on them for trying so desperately to spare his lowly soul and smuggle his resurrected body to a safe haven.

"Whatever you do," Carlos murmured, as he stared at the team, "don't blame them, and especially, don't blame her."

Empathy dulled the fear even more. He'd been tortured already, knew what it felt like to be broken, gutted, his insides twisted, skin shredded, bones shattered, body parts amputated, and to be burned alive. But these people were human, had never experienced the twisted knife of pain to that degree. All he could hope for would be that the plane would explode on impact, that his family wouldn't be left half alive, semiconscious, and torn to butchered bits. "Make it fast," he whispered. "That's the least you can do."

His prayer became more urgent as the treetops came into view.

Carlos stared at the bent backs before him as a wing collided with a cliff side and was shorn off. His head slammed into the seat in front of him and bounced off it, nearly snapping his neck—but he refused to cover his head or his face. He'd stared death down before in the dark, and in the brightness of dawn would do no less.

The horrible turbine sound against the wind seemed to become muted as his hands clutched the arms of his seat. Flickers of fast-moving light darted between the aisles and swirled around each of the people he watched. Maybe he had snapped his neck? All the better. Maybe the strike against his head had him seeing stars and had deafened him? Mercy was measured in increments and during moments when time seemed to have slowed down, it was indeed a blessing.

He watched the dancing white lights, dazed and fascinated, despite his pending death. He had to be hallucinating, that was the only rational answer that came to him as he watched the oblique forms become people he knew but should have never known.

Parents had come to their children. Aged spirits touched faces gently, put loving arms around each passenger, and made their peace. He could hear them all at once as well as individually as they hugged their deathborne children to them.

He saw Marlene become encircled first by what seemed to be a tribe of elderly people that he instantly knew were from the Gullah Islands. Why he knew that, he wasn't sure, but he watched her mother and father gently touch her face, tell her she'd done her job, it was good, she had struggled long and it was time to come home. Rider and Father Patrick, Jose . . . Big Mike—each of them were touched until every Guardian and member of the Covenant was attended by Light beings that placed their silvery orbs around each person, leaving no space between the seats, the windows . . . like padded clouds they wrapped around them.

Dan wept and held his grandfather's hand. Jose was sobbing and hugging his grandmother to him tightly. Berkfield laid his head in his mother's lap. Father Patrick stroked his wife's hair as his son hugged his back. Monk Lin was encircled by a bastion of Tibetan brothers, and Imam Asula had elders around him that were so old and wise that Carlos could not make out their faces.

A sense of lonely abandonment made him weep. No one had come for him in the last moments, and he simply covered his face with his hands. Had he been so bad that even his own brother . . . or his mother . . . or his grandmom wouldn't come to say good-bye? He hadn't been able to say good-bye, that's all he'd wanted, if he couldn't protect them! And where was his father? Where had he ever been? A gentle breeze blew against his face as the plane jolted again.

Carlos looked up as a male hand touched his hair. "Papi?" He couldn't breathe as he saw his father standing tall and strong and whole beside his mother. She looked so young and was smiling; his grandmother was beside them both.

"I was wrong . . . I'm proud of you and love you," his father said. "You have suffered so much, now come home. *Por favor,* Carlos . . . my most troublesome, but favorite, son."

His father embraced him and a sob tore up and out of his throat as the plane hit the ground hard, bounced, and the tail section broke away.

"We love you," Alejandro said, holding his head firm as another devastating smack waffled the plane's underbelly.

Smoke had begun filling the cabin and the stench of gasoline filled the air as the aircraft skipped against the ground like a pebble skeeting across the surface of a pond. Carlos squinted, refusing to allow the thick black plumes to eclipse the faces he'd loved and missed so dearly. Hands touched him, held him, caressed him, his sister, his cousins, his boys, they had all come. "I want to go home," he croaked, clutching his mother's hand so tightly that her silvery essence oozed between his fingers. "I'm so sorry . . ."

Water lapped at his feet, a hard rocking collision threw his body forward, and something soft braced his neck and spine as the slam lifted him and set him back down hard, jarring his teeth to near chipping. Then everything went silent and black within the cabin.

He could hear people coughing; the aircraft wasn't moving. He heard someone vomit, someone was sobbing. Carlos quickly felt his torso, his neck, and his legs with his hands. He seemed to be in one piece. His seat belt was mysteriously unfastened. He instantly stood, and covered his nose and mouth against the smoke.

It was blinding, but he could somehow see through it. Gasoline fumes made him bend and hurl as he moved forward, ignoring the chunks of vomit that now covered his sandaled feet. They'd made it. Some of them had. He began calling out names as he blindly rushed forward. Then his sight became like laser, cutting through the smoke in a silver wash. He picked Dan up and flung him over his shoulder, then yanked at Big Mike's uninjured arm, shoving at Shabazz and Rider as he went for the door. "We have to get out of here before she explodes!"

Damali looked down at the food with disinterest and tried to summon grace. Her stomach was in jumpy knots. But in order to proceed she'd have to feign patience for her gracious host. Something was so wrong she could barely sit in her seat. She could feel it as her newfound friend prattled on about his homeland.

"You eat it like this," he said, tearing off a piece of the spongy, foam rubber–like bread from the common bowl they shared. "The bread is called *injera,* and you dip it this way to get the *alicha wat* up and into your mouth." He extended his hand for her to take a small taste, his eyes holding expected excitement.

Damali leaned forward and took in the mildly spiced concoction of vegetables and forced a smile. Under different circumstances, she would have enjoyed the tasty dish, even though she wasn't ready for the Ethiopian way of sharing a communal bowl. The custom was just a tad too familiar for her liking, and not using utensils to share the dish was somewhat disturbing—she had no idea where this man's hands had been, but at least she'd blessed the food first. Besides, for all her powers, she couldn't tell if this was just an Ethiopian patience endurance test, or if this man was stalling because he was subtlety hitting on her.

She took a swig of sparkling bottled water, which she'd learned was called *ambo*. "This is very good," she said, truly meaning it, but needing to get going more than she needed to eat. However, she was quickly learning that in African culture, if you wanted to get anything done, one had to employ patience—eat with people, break bread, and pass a quiet vibe test—*then* you could handle business.

"But you cannot eat like a bird," the man said laughing. "Have some *shiro*. You must be strong for the journey."

Her nerves were about to snap, but she leaned forward and accepted a taste of the spicy lentil and chickpea mush with a smile. It slowly dawned upon her that the sooner she just ate the dag-gone food without picking at it with resistance in her soul, the quicker they'd be on their way. Damali took a deep breath and sighed, and then tore off a large section of bread to begin scarfing down the communal meal.

"That's more like it," he said, clapping his hands in triumph. "Try the *messer*—it's black lentils, and *ye som megeb*—that's a medley of vegetable dishes we traditionally serve during fasting."

Damali nodded, mumbling her assent to try whatever, as long as they got going soon. "Tell me about this area, Askum," she said through a gooey mouthful of food. She had to understand what the link was here.

"Ah . . . Askum . . ." her guide said. "First, to discuss Askum, we must understand the history of this country."

Damali groaned, but when he gave her a fishy look, she passed the sound off as her enjoyment of the food.

That seemed to mollify him. He perked up, widened his smile, and leaned forward with great pride in his expression.

"Our country is known as the Cradle of Humanity. It all started *here,* they even have the bones of Lucy in the National Museum for proof. But we do not need the bones to tell us what we know," he quipped, sitting up taller in his chair. He glanced around the out-door café and waved his arm toward the diversely colorful moving throng of people that milled about. "We were the only ones, the *only* country, that was never colonized."

Just as his long, winding history lesson was about to bore her to tears, she got part of the answer she was searching for. *It all started here.* In the Cradle of Humanity. The first Eden. Lilith's origin in the garden before she banished herself. And these people had been fighting everything she'd wrought since the beginning of time.

"Tell me about Lilith," Damali said, her eyes never leaving the man's face.

He brought his attention back to Damali and stared at her with a firm gaze. "We are about the size of Texas on your country's map. But we withstood the greatest powers of the eras, and were never conquered to be made slaves. With all we had against us, we used our natural environment—the Simien Mountains, and those to the north, where they call it Eritrea now, but they are the same as us, Ethiopians. All one family, same people, but split by wars and misunderstandings too much to discuss now. However, when we were one, evil could not come down from the Red Sea and take us; we stood our ground. You follow?"

Damali stopped breathing for a second and watched this man's eyes, nodding yes slowly. Although he hadn't answered her question directly, the words, "Red Sea," echoed in her mind like a train-crossing warning. Although she didn't understand it all, she under-stood enough. She also understood his need to be cagey about delivering the information. Level seven ruled the airwaves and could pick up a message in an instant. She'd been foolish to mention Lilith's name openly and admonished herself to not do that again.

But the fact remained, a tiny country that sat like a spec within the huge continent had withstood an invading power that had ran-sacked and razed nations ten times its size, but these humble folks with no arms to speak of had never succumbed. And that was possible because for all their diversity, they had all come together to fight as one and take a stand. Yeah, she definitely got it. Her skin itched to get reunited with her team. She almost stood and dragged the man by his arm, but decided that would be rude and too rash.

She leaned forward instead. "How did you do it?" Her voice came out an awed whisper.

"We are God's people," he said with a wave of his hand. "We are part of old Kemet, which stretched to the Nubian Empire." He leaned in close over the food and peered at her. "Askum will show you. We know our ancestors back to five thousand years. Even the queen of Sheba visited King Solomon joining nations, and her son became the first emperor here, this we know for a fact. We had the Nile, water, a source of power and commerce. We predate biblical history of Christ—we were Jews, first, and then we converted . . . some became Muslims. Fifty-fifty," he said, offhandedly.

Again, the whole issue of water. The clue was said so obtusely that if she hadn't been listening carefully, she would have missed it . . . just like the Druid told her—listen.

"I got it," Damali said, looking into his eyes without blinking. "I'm home, back in the last frontier of people who were never taken." As she said it, she could feel the earth's energy beneath her feet soaking into her. "They were outgunned, outmanned, but were not conquered—and they came from a complex blend of the Nubian and Kemetian empires."

He smiled and clasped her hands like a pleased schoolteacher. "Be inspired. Have faith and hope. Famines, droughts, wars, disease . . . plagues, but we never bowed to greater powers. Remember from your teachings that the meek shall inherit the earth. But we are not meek, the word was mistranslated—we believe it is the small, the downtrodden, and *we* have the original Bible." He stopped as though allowing that last point to sink in. "The original one, the orthodox one, and our people, although small, have held their ground." He drew back and nodded. "Hold yours against that which comes against you."

"Always been my plan," Damali said, her voice strong. "I just need a good blade."

"We will travel by air," he said, dismissing her request for a weapon.

Damali let her breath out slowly. "Do we have to get on a plane?"

"No," he said in a casual tone.

"Good." She let out an audible breath and took a swig of water. Air travel had not been good to her lately.

"It will be by helicopter. My brother works at the airport."

Damali almost choked on her sparkling water.

"That is the only solution. Many of the Ethiopian Christian priests became monks and hermits in order to keep the religion alive during the ongoing attempts at invasion," he said without missing a beat. "We will pass Lake Tana, which sits as a basin beyond the thunderous Tis Isat Falls . . . we will see this from the air along the way. This is where some of the holy men held up on the many islands—some of them just small rocky places in the lake where they built monasteries." His eyes became sad. "You can only see from the air because many of the islands do not allow women."

Made sense. If they were up against Lilith, any female crossing a threshold would be suspect, and would make identifying her easier.

"That's cool," Damali finally said, hoping they could travel by rickety Jeep instead. Whatever, so long as they got moving.

"It is my apologies to you, though," he said, seeming to fret about the dilemma.

She really didn't care. A lot of monasteries had strict policies against women setting foot on their grounds. What concerned her more was getting to where they had to go in one piece. She wasn't feeling air travel at all.

"No," he said, actually cutting off her thought. "To go by Jeep is too long a journey to get there before nightfall . . . and too dangerous, as there are still many unfound land mines along the back roads and in riverbeds. Foreigners aren't even allowed to really enter Askum freely—but that is no matter, we can provide papers to say you are here as my wife . . . we shall work that out."

His sense of agitation made her wary. Why was this brother

intent on getting her into some chopper, and more specifically, why was it necessary that she go to this crazy lake that had monasteries around it? But she could definitely go with his aversion to nightfall and unseen land mines. For now, she'd let some of her questions rest. But he was so suddenly nervous that it was making her edgy, too. She followed his gaze as it traveled toward the horizon.

"You weren't supposed to be a woman," he said quietly, now picking at his discarded bread, then reaching for his water.

"Excuse me?" she said, not offended, but curious as a knot unfurled in her stomach.

"Heaven has imparted a riddle. I was told that the Neteru would first go to the monks, and then to my father in Askum." He studied her hard. "Without violating what is sacred, how can that be?"

Damali smiled, thinking of Carlos. "Have faith."

CHAPTER FIFTEEN

PANIC MADE him forget what he could no longer do. It was impossible to open the plane door alone with Dan slung over his shoulder and the junior Guardian's heavy backpack still strapped to his body creating deadweight. There was no way to judge what was beneath them—ground, a steep drop off the side of a cliff, treetops—they were blinded so badly by smoke and choking on gasoline fumes. Carlos handed off Dan's limp body to Monk Lin, and worked with Imam Asula's raw strength to force open the door. Were it not for Asula, Carlos would have tumbled out of it as the heavy metal creaked open and swung wide.

To his amazement, there was no need to scrabble at the inflatable slide. The flat surface of the ground was only a three-foot drop to safety, as the plane listed to the side, billowing clouds of noxious fumes. No discussion was necessary. Coughing and hacking the polluted air from his lungs, Carlos jumped down, turned, and accepted Dan's body as Asula lowered it to him. Marlene was still clutching her satchel and fighting stick in shock as Shabazz pushed her forward next, and in less than a minute, everyone was out and half jogging, half limping away from the potential inferno.

They all knew the deal. The plane was gonna blow. Father Patrick and the other clerics turned back once. Marlene shook her head no to signify that the pilots were already lost. The team put more than a hundred yards between them and the aircraft, scrambling over the rocky terrain around the rim of the lake, coughing, running while vomiting, trying to find shelter around the bend of a small crag. The moment they rounded the bend came the sound of thunder and the resounding shock wave that knocked them off their feet.

They hit the ground with a simultaneous thud, covered their

heads and held stiff and shuddering waiting for airplane parts and fuselage to come back to the ground with fiery conviction. No one moved, no one turned to stare, no one breathed as the sound of heavy objects returning to earth and metal colliding with rocks rang out. The sky rained fire and death for nearly five minutes, and then all became still.

Shabazz was the first to lift his head and peer around. His movements made the others slowly begin to lift their heads, but it was a long while before anyone could speak.

"We've gotta move," Shabazz finally said, his voice a raw whisper.

Father Patrick pushed himself to sit up and crossed himself. His eyes met Padre Lopez's, and then Monk Lin's, and finally settled on Imam Asula. "Heaven help them," he murmured, his gaze toward the plume of black smoke in the distance.

There was no need for him to say more as everyone bowed their heads and said a silent prayer for the crew that was lost. Slowly the teams stood, the unharmed helping the injured, every person still wobbly as they tried to get their balance.

Dan roused to semiconsciousness and rubbed the back of his head, his backpack causing added inertia. He winced as he looked around, tears streaming down his face. Berkfield stood, but then slowly plopped back down, his legs unable to hold him. Jose seemed like he was about to pass out while Big Mike steadied him with one good arm.

Rider touched Big Mike's flaccid biceps. "Can you move it?"

Big Mike shook his head no. "Broke, clean through, I think." Sweat poured off Mike's face and he was shivering.

" 'Bazz, this man's going into shock," Rider said, making Shabazz hustle to Big Mike's side just before the gentle giant went down.

They caught Mike while Carlos steadied Jose. Marlene dropped her satchel and stick and was at their side as they stretched Big Mike out on the ground while she ran her hands over the known wound then his entire body.

Marlene began to examine each team member quickly and efficiently. With the exception of Mike, injuries appeared to be surface wounds and smoke inhalation.

"I'll be all right," Mike protested, as she examined him. "It's just an arm."

"Lie your big, lurchy ass down," Rider said, "and let Mar see what she can do."

The group had gathered in a small, ragged circle. Carlos squatted down and peered at Mike.

"I ain't never been hurt before," Big Mike said. "I hate this shit."

Carlos nodded. "Let her work on it. We need your strength, man. Mar's good. That's what she does."

Marlene glanced at Carlos, thanking him with her eyes. But the team stared at Berkfield as he stood and staggered toward them.

"Maybe I can help?" Berkfield said, glancing around the team. "I worked in the conference room on Carlos's cut."

"Wait," Father Patrick warned. "I've seen the laying on of hands before." He looked at Marlene. "Many times healers take on the wounds, just like what happened on the plane. When you healed Carlos's hand, it was a minor cut. This is a major break, and the pain from it can be staggering. I've seen healers go into shock themselves, and require medical attention."

"I can try to dull the pain in Mike," Marlene said quietly, "but I don't think I can shield his psyche from it all."

"I don't need her to take the pain," Mike said, closing his eyes tightly as agony swept through him. "I'm cool."

"Yeah," Berkfield muttered. "But I do."

The comment made the group look at him. Even Big Mike opened his eyes and squinted at Berkfield.

"Listen, I don't know if this will work, or if I can even do it. But I had an idea . . . like if we work as a team, Marlene. If you can stop some of the pain so I can lay hands on him, maybe I can help the injury. Like I said, we tried an experiment up in the conference room. I sealed Carlos's cut." Berkfield studied his hands as he spoke. "But it hurt like hell. If I try to heal him and have to pull that from him, Father is right, my ticker could give out." He glanced at the group, and then down at Mike. "I'm a lot older and not as strong as your big, burly ass . . . so I'm being honest about my limitations—but I'm willing to give it a shot." When Marlene nodded, Berkfield knelt beside Mike.

"No, he don't have to do that for me," Mike said through a pant.

"Yo, man, we family," Jose said, glancing at Berkfield. "Mar took a lot of the agony out of that near-turn I went through. She pulled the poison up and out and kept me going for days until y'all could get to Nuit, right? So, at least let her try, Mike."

"That was a spirit wound, brother," Shabazz said carefully. "Only time I seen a body injury healed was when Damali covered Marlene's chest. We need a Neteru, and this one ain't ready yet."

Jose's gaze went to Carlos. "No time like the present to learn some new shit, *hombre*. Our brother here is in agony. See if you can go in with Mar and draw some of the pain, or with Berkfield in a three-way, and draw it to you. Berkfield can't hang by himself. None of the rest of us has the ability like that. Plus, from your old life, you know how to seal a body blow, right?"

"I'm down," Carlos said, stepping forward.

"Your ass is strong as shit," Jose said. "I've seen it myself, and if you can't deal with it, it ain't to be dealt with."

"I don't want Mar on this detail alone, feel me?" Shabazz said, staring at Carlos. He motioned toward Berkfield. "This man could be in jeopardy of a heart attack. If you're down . . ."

"I said I was," Carlos said evenly, stooping beside Big Mike. He looked up at the others. "Y'all wanna debate it, or do this before this man passes out?"

Marlene clasped Carlos's hand. They each covered Mike's forehead with a palm and sat quietly, her lips moving, her shut eyelids fluttering, Carlos taking deep breaths. Marlene's eyes abruptly opened as Carlos cried out and a loud snap sounded. Two Guardians were at his side.

"Don't break the connection," Shabazz said. "If you pull out now, the injury could transfer."

"Oh, shit . . ." Carlos said, panting. His head dropped forward, sweat stung his eyes, and his body flashed cold then hot. Pain shot through his arm, up his shoulder, and pierced his brain. He struggled to tuck it beneath the layers of pain he'd remembered from Hell before he blacked out. This was bad, but not the worst he'd felt.

Slowly, calmness started to enter him. He could hear people asking him if he was all right, and could feel Marlene's gentle squeeze. It was almost as though he could mentally see the pain seek him, radiating in a jagged red line toward Marlene's hand, then stop and find his. Memories of the past collided with the present. He knew the art of healing, but then it had been supernatural, not a gift. But the human body worked the same way, nonetheless. Meridians, energy fields, all he had to do was stay focused on the damaged field and draw that energy to him, away from Marlene, away from Big Mike, and trap it until Berkfield could do his thing.

Another searing pulse ran up his arm. He let go of Mike. Pain slammed him to the ground. He was shuddering so hard his teeth chattered. He tried to send his mind elsewhere, think of anything but the broken bones. But his brain worried it like the tongue hunts for a missing tooth, pushing into the soft, tender spots, making him holler.

Marlene didn't let go of his hand, her grip tightening until the grimace on Mike's face was gone. And as slowly as the agony left Mike's face, Carlos could soon feel the pain abating to a dull ache.

"How do you feel, big man?" Rider asked Mike, as Marlene withdrew her hand.

"Way better. Thanks, Ma. You always got da juice," Mike admitted as he stared up at Marlene and looked over to Carlos. "Thanks, man—you cool?"

Rider knelt beside Carlos, who had only nodded with his eyes closed. "That was some cowboy shit, brother. You okay?"

Again, Carlos only nodded and continued to breathe deeply.

"This man went down hard," Shabazz said, stooping beside Rider with concern. "He went above and beyond, and I don't think—"

"I'm holding it," Carlos whispered through his teeth. "Let Berkfield fix that break fast, 'Bazz . . . this shit hurts like a motherfucker."

Berkfield moved quickly to Mike's side, glancing back toward Carlos once.

Marlene focused on Berkfield, her eyes intense. "Give it your best shot, partner. I don't know if it'll transfer, or how long the pain block will last."

Berkfield nodded, his gaze concentrated along Mike's arm as his palms slid down it. He winced and stopped, then held the place that brought tears to his eyes. But he didn't cry out, just made a face as though uncomfortable. After a moment, they all watched as the bone in Berkfield's upper arm began to move beneath his skin, and they all turned away as a sudden hard snap made them cringe.

Panting, Berkfield kept his hold on Mike's arm; cold sweat leaked down his forehead as shivers consumed him. Then suddenly he let go and vomited. Carlos curled up in a ball and shuddered.

"Test your arm," Berkfield wheezed. "That's the best I can do. I couldn't hold on anymore."

Mike flexed his fist and slowly lifted the tender limb. "Y'all got skillz. Thank you." He sat up with assistance from Shabazz and Rider, and then glanced at Carlos and Berkfield who'd both begun to relax.

Jose looked at Dan. "A head injury ain't no joke, though."

Carlos rolled over on his back and kept his eyes closed.

Berkfield stretched out beside him. "So, what are we now," he chuckled as he slung an arm over his eyes and breathed deeply, "the team's doctors?"

"Hired," Rider said, helping Dan to lie back.

"Seems we are gonna be in the ER a lot, Dr. Berkfield and Dr. Rivera," Marlene said with a smile, though still winded. "This mangy group is always getting themselves busted up."

"This is my cousin, Dori," her guide said as they quickly greeted the man who possessed a wide, infectious smile.

Damali extended her hand and shook Dori's, totally amazed at how the two men shared such a striking likeness. Dori was a little younger than the man who'd introduced him, a head shorter, a bit leaner and browner than her guide, but the family resemblance was undeniable.

Dori assessed her from head to toe and then bowed. "You're the famous one—the singer of truths!"

Damali tried her best to smile. That was all she needed—a fan to recognize her and to alert the media hounds. For once, things needed to be easy, go smoothly, and with no added drama.

"I have all your CDs," Dori said in awe. "I am honored to be your pilot. My cousin, Telek, tells me you are quite nice and have an invitation to our family elder's home in Askum."

"But you know we must be discreet," Telek warned. "Grandfather will—"

"No, no, no. I have told no one," Dori assured him. "This mission I will take to my grave as a secret."

"Thank you for taking us, and for keeping everything cool," Damali said, simply relieved to have finally arrived at the airport. The harrowing drive through Addis Ababa was enough to make her think it was safer to be in the clouds. However, the man's comment about taking the mission to the grave worried her no end.

"My pleasure," Dori said as they began to walk along the tarmac toward the helicopters. "You heard about the terrorists?" He had spoken to his cousin and had not even turned to glimpse Damali.

"No," Telek said, making the small threesome stop progressing toward the craft. "We were at the market, and we ate, but were engrossed in conversation. What has happened now?"

A sinking feeling crept into Damali's abdomen as she listened hard.

"A rocket-propelled missile, it is rumored, hit a passenger plane over Somalia this morning at dawn. But the aircraft returned fire, so it couldn't have been a passenger plane—probably military spies versus rebel forces," Dori said with uncertain authority. "It was smoking badly, went right past the airport in a Mayday landing, swept down, and went boom!" he exclaimed, talking with both hands and waving to show the force of the explosion. "They say it crashed out by Lake Tana. No one knows for certain, but it has made it difficult to get tower clearance."

Before he'd finished his vivid description, Damali knew it was her team. She willed herself not to scream. She needed answers and information. The one thing she'd learned was that things were not always what they seemed. She bit her lips to keep from speaking.

"But I trust that your government connections . . ." his cousin said, obviously unsure if they'd be allowed to fly today.

Dori smiled. "A chopper can go," he said with flourish and began walking. "I have friends who know me well. It's just the commercial jets that must wait." He walked taller and put more emphasis in his stride. "Let us go see Grandfather."

As Damali entered the helicopter and strapped herself into a seat, the hair remained raised on her arms. Something was so terribly wrong. She'd arrived in this strange land well after dawn. Could it have been possible that she was out of time-sync with her team? Why hadn't she seen a smoking jet cross the clear blue sky? And if that were the case, why wouldn't Telek have seen it—unless he hadn't been here until she'd arrived.

She prayed with all her might that the downed plane wasn't the one that kept flashing through her mind, yanking at the fibers of hair pushing through her skin. *Please, God, not them. Please, God, not anybody, for that matter.* Damali closed her eyes.

With only an hour left before sunrise, Yonnie stared down at the witch's red hair—spread across the pillow, looking like blood—and considered his options. She was all right. Might make a decent lair queen, as lair queens went. But in truth, he just wasn't feeling her. The succubus that he'd tried first had offered so much more of a mental diversion. Crazy hoe wanted to know how to get to council chambers.

He chuckled to himself, remembering how she almost came on herself from just the mental picture of the descent through the caverns he offered while doing her. Succubae were too easy of a conquest, though. Their bites, phantom. However, he had to admit, girlfriend was awesome, knew exactly what a master liked . . . this chick was just okay. He sighed. The coven was cool, and they had plenty of playthings to sample, but they just weren't what he really wanted tonight. Tara.

He withdrew from the witch's curvaceous body, studying the two punctures in her throat that he hadn't bothered to seal, and glanced at the sated expression on her face.

"Will I turn?" she asked, her eyes filled with excitement. "We never get masters through here, only second- or third-gens." She sighed and closed her eyes. "A master's bite. My sisters will be green with envy."

"It wasn't a turn bite," Yonnie said, materializing his clothes and dressing himself. He glanced at the changing light. It was time to go, and fast.

"What!" She sat up, indignant. "You promised to—"

"I said I'd give you an evening you wouldn't forget in exchange for info on why my territory was being overrun by were-demons." Yonnie looked out the window. This bitch was truly getting on his nerves. He didn't have to explain anything to her. After being denied Tara, he was still in a truly foul mood. "And given the way you were just hollering in here, I'd say I lived up to my end of the bargain."

She stood, snatching up the sheets to cover herself. "You arrogant vampire bastards are all alike."

"Correction," Yonnie replied, bored. "There's nothing like a master—so you need to get with that."

"Why won't you turn me?" she asked, coming to stand in front of him. She thrust her chin up and narrowed her gaze.

He sighed. "I haven't been sanctioned to, that's why, and I don't know if I'd feel like it, anyway."

She folded her arms over her ample, silicon-created breasts. "If you're a master and coming here to get your rocks off, then obviously the lair queens at your disposal aren't worth a damn," she taunted, glowering at him. "And if you have to wait for permission, then some mast—"

He reached out and held her jaw between his forefinger and thumb, stopping her argument while critically studying the now-bulging vein in her neck. It would be so easy to simply rip her throat out, to tear into the paper-thin flesh that was already devoid of color from his earlier bites. "Then I'd have to listen to your bullshit all night long, sis." He let her go and prepared to make a hasty exit before he committed himself to flat-lining her just because she'd gotten on his nerves.

"I'm sorry," she murmured, looking disappointed. "Don't go. It's just that I was hoping."

"You'd have to die. What about this don't you get?" Yonnie shook his head and gazed at the prosthetic fangs in her lovely mouth. True, she'd used them like the pro she was, but damn. This chick had a death wish that wasn't healthy.

"My sisters will come in here and join us in bed, if that's why you're displeased, Master." Tears filled her green eyes and she tried to blink them away without success. "All you had to do was say you needed all of us at your disposal."

He closed his eyes. This had definitely been a bad idea, but her concept had merit. Yonnie glanced at the window. "Five of y'all, and a brother's only got an hour."

"We've got a lair in the basement—concrete, reinforced metal door, and an hour with a real master would—"

"Nah. You crazy? I don't know your asses, and you think I'd allow myself to get set up to get smoked like that? Fuck it, I'm out. The info you gave me was weak, anyway. How you gonna tell me a succubus wreaked all this havoc in my camp and try to let that bullshit stand as info? Shoulda known." He shook his head and smoothed the front of his suit. "I did one in here tonight, and trust me, she wasn't strong enough to do much more than get a good nut. Probably blew your minds and got you all confused. I'm out."

"No. Seriously. My eldest sister, Gabrielle, has been doing the divinations. Let me call her, okay?" she pleaded, hurrying toward the door. "We didn't authorize a succubus to come in here. If one got in and . . ." Her words trailed off as she stared at him. "Something's not right."

Yonnie waited, feigning disinterest, studying his manicure as a shrill female voice sliced into his senses. Her voice alone was reason enough not to want her in his lair each night, but information was information—so he waited while worry formed a small knot in his stomach. He'd just fucked a succubus, and fucked her good, but girlfriend had gotten the path to council chambers, too.

Within minutes, three of the unoccupied sisters rushed through the door, the eldest one stepping forward with appreciation in her eyes.

"I'm Gabrielle," she said on a sexy breath. "When you picked Susan over the rest of us, we cannot begin to tell you how envious we were. Tell us you're going to make amends and heal this little family riff."

Man . . . he didn't have time for this shit. Yonnie appraised the three sisters, each owning the same dazzling green eyes and waiflike figures plumped by silicon and a little black magic, but they'd hard-dyed their long hair to unnatural black, blond, and copper, which gave them each a ghostly appearance. The stark contrast of the black thong lingerie made them seem as though they might disappear right before his very eyes. They practically looked like skeletons with tits. He could count each rib bone as Gabrielle sauntered toward him, donning glistening, red, spiked heels, thigh-high black silk stockings, a thong, and push-up bra. Her hipbones jutted out at glaring angles. If he was gonna get his turn-on, he would have preferred a coupla babes with thick thighs and bootylicious behinds and a little color—but hey, he did have almost an hour to kill.

"I don't mind turning you out," he said with unfiltered disdain, "but a man needs to know what's going on in his zones before all that. Feel me?"

Gabrielle leaned against him, stroking him with one palm. "Yeah . . . I feel you, lover. It's simple. They're opening the gates."

"An unsanctioned succubus got in here, too," Susan said, glancing nervously between Yonnie and her sister.

"That concerns me," Gabrielle said evenly. "Especially since there's a disruption in the gates."

Yonnie stepped back a bit and stared at her hard. Witches had been known to lie almost as well as vampires. They both smiled. Her sisters began to tremble as he exuded a slow seduction trance.

"It's true," she pressed on, glancing at her forlorn sisters. "We're getting all sorts of traffic that we normally don't get, and our regulars from your lower gens haven't been around *at all*. Someone is obviously hunting your energy trail very hard through your linesmen, Yonnie." She offered him a triumphant smile. "And now *you're* here? You do the math."

"You do the math," he said, sweeping his nose along her jugular. "I have about forty-five minutes, and there's how many of y'all in the room?" Yonnie glanced past Gabrielle toward her sisters. "Very tacky. Not my style. I could turn one of y'all tonight, if you can tell me who sanctioned the openings. . . . but tomorrow night, I could come back to do this right."

"You've already bitten me," Susan said, coming forward quickly and yanking Gabrielle's arm. "Finish it."

"I'm the eldest—"

"Ladies. Please," Yonnie said, chuckling. "Susan did come with a good attempt," he said, moving toward the redhead and running the pad of his thumb over her mouth and fake fangs. "I guess I could give her a real pair." He watched the eldest sister move back with a scowl as the youngest one filled his arms. But he kept his eye on Gabrielle. That was the smart one, the one who had information, the one who had to live to explain what he needed to know before daylight.

"Can we at least watch you turn her?" Gabrielle whispered with a quaky voice as her hand slid down her abdomen.

Yonnie filled his fist with Susan's hair and jerked her head back to expose her throat, his eyes never leaving the eldest sister's as a moan escaped her lips. "Just talk to me while I do it," he murmured. "Nice and slow—you stop talking, I'll stop in the middle of the turn and flat-line this hoe without blinking."

The blonde and the coppertop were practically holding each other up as Gabrielle swooned against them. Susan had become a panting rag in his arms, waiting for the strike. He took mild pride in the showmanship of it all—if they talked, he'd give them pure theater. He almost laughed out loud as he allowed his fangs to drop to battle length and one of the sisters nearly fainted. Yeah . . . a brother was packing. "So," he murmured, lowering his mouth to Susan's jugular and adjusting his fangs for realistic turn length.

"Word is on the street," Gabrielle whispered, "that there's a bounty on Rivera's head." She gasped as Yonnie broke Susan's skin and began the slow siphon, their gazes locked while the youngest witch writhed within his arms. "The were-wolfen clans are making a territory grab, and I've heard the Amanthras have unleashed a few of their own to get in on the available assets, just border testers at this point . . . incubi and succubae are also trying to materialize themselves for the onslaught." She stopped, swallowed hard as her sister went limp, and whispered, "Yolando!"

He lifted his head. "Tell me something I don't know," he said, momentarily glancing at Susan as her nails dug into his arms. "I already know a council bounty is on my brother's head." But he didn't tell her that he didn't know the other legions could cash in on it. That bit of info was worth something. Council had never done a hit that involved the other levels. The chairman had to want Carlos real bad to go there. Unless . . .

"Don't stop," Susan wheezed, her gaze furtive and weakly going toward Gabrielle. "Tell him what he wants to know!"

"Appreciated," Yonnie said, lowering his mouth to her throat again, teasing her with a nick. "You all were saying?"

"We did a pentagram ritual to level seven," Gabrielle said quickly.

Yonnie bit down hard and closed his eyes, the women's gasps passing through his skeleton as he sucked hard. *Yeah . . . and the Dark Lord said what?*

Instantly, he could tell something had gone wrong. The sweet blood in his mouth became acidic, forcing him to pull out and spit. Stunned, he stared at Susan's stricken expression. Screams from her sisters surrounded him. Their screeches intensified as Susan's body temperature heated up. They covered their faces and screamed louder as her flesh began to smolder. He dropped her and stepped back.

"You murderer! Ingrate!" Gabrielle yelled, rushing to Susan's fallen body as she began to quiver and her eyes liquefied.

"What did you do to our sister?" another yelled, going to her knees and crawling beside the slowly charring remains.

Susan was making guttural sounds deep in her throat. Her skin blackened at her throat where she had been bitten and then fanned out to cover her neck, shoulders, and face, running down her arms and torso until she was totally consumed. An internal blaze could be seen through her empty eye sockets.

"No!" the third sister screamed, walking in a circle around the ghastly carnage that was taking place in the center of the floor.

"We will have your head!" Gabrielle shouted, her finger pointing at Yonnie as she sent a black electrical current toward him.

He deflected it with ease, but went to Susan's body. Shoving her sisters away from her as she instantly turned to ash, he tried to reach out to her but couldn't. "I didn't do that!" he shouted, now pacing. "What purpose would torching her serve? Think!"

The three remaining witches huddled together, sobbing.

"Use your skills," Yonnie demanded. "I was in the middle of a legitimate turn, and she flamed. What the fuck?" He wasn't sure if he was more outraged than shaken. Never in all his years had he witnessed anything so foul.

Gabrielle wiped at her eyes hard and went to the dresser on the far side of the room. Extracting a small black velvet bag, she murmured quietly as she dumped stone runes over her sister's ashes. "We'll get to the bottom of this, vampire!"

"You do that, sis. I need to know who's jacking my turns. Blocking a turn, if you've lost council favor, is one thing. Torching them is another. Level six doesn't have that power. This is bullshit!"

The other teary-eyed sisters nodded as Gabrielle looked up, her expression confused.

"But this came from your own council," she said in a barely audible voice. "You're neutered," she said, her voice holding disbelief. "Your turn bite isn't just blocked, it's lethal."

"I'm what?" Yonnie stepped toward her and held both her arms, yanking her forward. Only hours ago he'd elevated Tara, and nothing like this had happened.

"You can't turn anyone. You cannot replenish your territory."

It didn't make sense. Yes, they would assassinate him. Yes, they would keep him from making more of his own, but the torch bite? Never done on six. Maybe they hadn't been lying. Level seven was definitely involved. Panic swept through him as he began to assess all the territorial damage.

He dropped her arms and walked away from her. "I don't understand. That is not our way. Cast the runes again!" Yonnie looked at her hard and then stared at the divination on the floor. "We always replace territory, immediately. You're wrong." The sweepers made sense. Level seven didn't have to come up for a basic vamp dispute. A new master would be made to bump him off. What the fuck did Rivera do?

Gabrielle carefully gathered up the stones while everyone in the room remained silent, waiting for her to get a second opinion. Again, she flung the stones against the pile of ash. "Your own chairman did this," she said in a faraway voice. "You were made by Rivera, and he's purging the entire zone of all he made, of all that could ever be made by his line."

"I know that!" Yonnie shouted. "Tell me about level seven and this damned succubus you claim—"

"You mean Lilith?" Gabrielle said coolly, her eyes studying him as he began to pace.

"That's bullshit," Yonnie whispered. The mention of that name chilled him. He backed up, studied the sky, his focus divided between the facts before him and Tara. "I have to go," he said, sure now that the transmission cover that he'd provided Tara hadn't held.

"We are now sworn enemies of the vampire nations, and level seven," Gabrielle said, picking up each rune stone one by one and kissing away her sister's ashes as she replaced them in the velvet pouch. She clutched it in her soot-covered palm.

"Good," Yonnie said, holding her gaze, "because, now, so am I."

"She's his lover."

Yonnie stared at Gabrielle. "She's the devil's wife? Get serious. Him, you don't fuck with."

"Your chairman."

Again, Yonnie just stared at her for a moment. "Now I *know* you're crazy."

"Am I?" she asked coolly, looking him dead in the eyes.

It was so treacherous that he couldn't speak. What could Carlos have done to make the chairman risk sure extinction? There had to be more to the puzzle than blowing a shot at the Neteru. "If you're lying, I'll kill your ass. If you're right, I owe you."

Gabrielle cocked her head to the side, wrestling with the proposed alliance.

"Obviously, my chairman hasn't been able to take all my powers back—for some reason. But if he did this hit with her . . ."

Gabrielle nodded, joining hands with her remaining sisters as the fourth platinum-haired sister entered the room and covered her mouth. "You'll swear allegiance to help us avenge Susan's death?"

"If you'll swear allegiance to help me avenge my councilman, Carlos Rivera's abuse."

The four sisters spoke in unison. "Done."

"My transmission was compromised!" Tara yelled as Yonnie entered the basement lair. "Where were you?"

"You got through?" Yonnie spun on her as he sealed the door against approaching daylight.

"Yes, and—"

"Save the drama about where I might have been. Talk to me!"

She stared at him. "Yonnie, what happened?"

"They torched a turn of mine—while she was in my arms, Tara!" He walked a hot path across the concrete floor. "Sonofabitch just—"

"You were actually going to turn an innocent? Get out!" Tara shrieked. "Get out before you—"

He waved his hand and knocked the wind out of her, making her fall to the bed. "Shut up and listen!" He raked his fingers through his hair, his eyes wild. "It was a willing witch, not an innocent. A barter; so these barriers aren't compromised. The only thing keeping us alive is whatever your people laid down here." He walked over to the walls, feeling them for the approaching heat of dawn. "I don't know if they'll hold, though. The Guardian compound had to have a better seal than this hovel, and black lightning struck it and the heat from that caused the brush fire. You saw that with your own eyes."

Tara swallowed hard and stood, going to the walls, testing with Yonnie for heat. "He's so weak," she whispered. "I tried to give him the code, and he had to write it down."

Yonnie froze. "What do you mean he had to *write it down*? Stop playing, woman! I had to form an alliance with a weak-assed coven in order to watch our flanks. That's what we're dealing with, and now isn't the time to let some jealousy corrupt your logic. We have a major crisis to—"

"*It was him* and he had to use pen and paper *like a human*," she said slowly, succinctly, cutting off Yonnie's question while her even tone stoked his horror. "While you were out getting your swerve on, dawn fractured my ability to hold onto the connection." Tara locked and trapped Yonnie's line of vision within hers. "He was so weak I was ashamed for him."

Yonnie shook his head and backed away from Tara, tears rising in his eyes as he pointed at her. "You lie!"

"I wish I were," she said quietly, finding the edge of the bed before she collapsed.

"Nothing!" Lilith said, blue-black smoke billowing from beneath her gown as she walked before the council table. "No Neteru! No Rivera! I personally looked in every man's face on that plane, and not one of them even resembled him." She stared at the chairman through red glowing slits. "Do you know what this means?"

"No," he said evenly. "Tell me, darling. Your fangs are showing."

Pointed, leathery wings ripped through her shoulder blades casting a twelve-foot shadow over the table as bats above took shelter.

Her scaled, serpentine tail emerged, altering her spine and tearing through her gown to bear a spaded razor that sliced his cheek before he could pull away. As her rage mounted, her shapely legs transformed into gargoyle gray granite, the varicose veins in them thick and corded by stagnant black blood. Her once sexy spike heels became yellowed, clawed talons that now dug into the marble floor. Only her arms, torso, and head remained the sultry female she'd just been, although her lush mouth was brutally distended by a hideous set of jagged, demon fangs.

"I *personally* intercepted the transmission from his lieutenants! They put a weak Guardian on the phone, and everything he said was garbled—damn their barriers. But it wasn't Rivera." Lilith's voice rumbled in a deep, threatening baritone, her breaths a ragged gasp between each word as fury overtook her reason. "All that's left of him is two last holdout vampires that aren't worth the bother to pursue beyond troublesome Native American shaman barriers. The master Rivera made was so weak he's taken to bedding *human* witches instead of real vampire lair mates!"

"That's because there aren't any left in his territory, except one, darling. A man has to do what a man has to do, especially if he's about to be exterminated. Have a goblet and relax."

She stormed away from the chairman and pointed at him. "I was so infuriated that I torched that little redheaded bitch while he was turning her. I should have incinerated him, too, and would have, if I didn't think he might still have access to Rivera. He only lives as bait." Her eyes flickered darker. "But that did send him a very serious message to call his maker, ASAP. So we wait."

"I know," the chairman said in an amused tone to stoke her ire. He glanced around unconcerned as the torches in the chamber went out and bats screeched in fear at her thundering. "I've also blocked his turns so he can twist for a century or so without a lair mate. The female is so weak that she barely took the elevation he attempted. I'll dust her when I have time—maybe while he's on top of her, who knows? But do not waste your precious time micromanaging this minor detail; it will be excruciating for both of them when I'm done amusing myself with their panic, *that* I assure you. I'm a patient man." He smiled. "Why didn't you just abduct and torture the information out of him?"

"Because Rivera would never come out in the open then, once he heard Yolando's howls. Are you insane? You saw how Rivera resisted my harpies! Neteru information about the female was locked inside his mind like one of our best vaults! It's clear those two loser vampires don't know where he is any more than you or I do!"

He allowed Lilith to seethe. He ignored her blinding wrath and concentrated on the tiny questions nagging his mind. Why wasn't he able to torch the two lower-generation vampires, when he'd been able to ash all the others? She didn't need to know that his attempts had failed, or contemplate how two vampires had been able to hide behind a shaman's prayer line . . . why was a small cabin impervious to his black lightning strikes when the Guardian compound and the Covenant's safe house had so easily burned to the ground? They were missing something crucial. He could feel it in his skin, but he kept chuckling with haughty disdain in his countenance and avoided glancing at the small compartment hidden in the center of the table beneath the fanged crest that only he could open, allowing Lilith's ego to make her twist. *Oh, darling, I have such a prize in there.*

"Dante, I dredged every man's dreams trying to wrest out Rivera's location. Nothing!" she shouted, oblivious to the chairman's mood shift as she railed on. "They were only able to try to send *ten thousand measly dollars* to *a human* that had to write it down. That's *all* Rivera has left. My harpies ripped open the belly of that aircraft, searching in vain for his coffin, in case he was still one of us! Nothing! And if a Neteru had been on board, we would have known the moment he or she launched into battle."

She swished away, leaving the chairman to seal the deep gash in his face, his black blood splattering the front of his robe and blending into it. "The female Neteru did not come for her Guardians, even when I sent the plane to crash and burn. No male Neteru rose to the challenge to come to their rescue, either. The last remnants of the Covenant were even on that aircraft, and no Neterus came . . . no Isis blade or disc of Heru was ever raised."

Lilith shuddered and gave Dante her back to consider, knowing she was running out of options. If she didn't find the Neterus quickly, she'd have to destroy the embryo, lest it ever be discovered. Or, worse, turn it over to her husband and try to claim that in her search for the dead Neterus, she'd discovered it. Either way, she refused to concede total defeat. If there was no bounty to be won to take over all the weaker realms, she *could not* lose favor on level seven. Her mind raced for a back-door solution.

She'd blame it on Dante, if she had to give up the egg. The egg had passed through his chambers, and this had been a Vampire Council matter, originally. But that bitter black pill was something very special that she was saving for when she'd exhausted every measure. To prematurely unveil that it even existed meant potentially tipping her hand, if the Neterus were somehow still alive. Dante was holding something back from her; she could sense it. So she skillfully changed the subject and allowed herself to appear totally spent. He could never know her ultimate aim. Men were foolish. There were no friends in this game.

"Warrior angels made it necessary to back off . . . but the plane went down. There was no way anyone on board could have survived. Damnable daylight interfered, but they're history." Lilith covered her face with her hands and breathed in deeply, causing her wings, tail, and talons to recede as she regained her composure.

"Hmmm . . . are you quite sure? The same way I was so sure that Rivera had been burned alive by the sun?" The chairman shook his head. "Very sloppy—or did you say that to me not long ago?"

"I looked them *each* in the eye before we decimated their aircraft at dawn, and all I saw was frightened humans. No Neterus. The plane went down over a holy region that even I cannot penetrate without my husband's assistance. I'm officially banned from that area, except the Red Sea, by truce," she wailed, suddenly becoming so distraught that she waltzed back to the table and took a shaky sip of clotted blood from the chairman's goblet and set it down hard.

"Perhaps, if warrior angels showed up, they're masked. Did you ever consider that? It has been done before." He studied his goblet and circled the rim of it with his finger.

She stared at him without blinking.

"You seem awfully impatient, my dear. That is not like you. Maybe you should call my father to help you—"

"Don't fuck with me, Dante," she screeched, growing fangs again. "This is a catastrophe!"

"I thought our goal was to kill them, anyway?" He risked another sly smile, baiting her further as he took a slow sip from her abandoned goblet. "Calm yourself. My remaining councilmen are in stasis repose in their vaults, and we must conserve our energy for the future—"

"What future, Dante? If we don't deliver them, there is no bounty," she said flatly, leaning into him. "Our Dark Lord deals in absolutes. I will not suffer his wrath for failing!"

He stood and chuckled. "Or, if I did indeed kill them both, first, then what you mean is, I've won the challenge—and didn't fuck up so badly after all." He caught her hand before she could strike him and caressed her face with his free palm. "Come, come now, dearest Lilith," he whispered, his fangs growing to battle length as his form bulked to shadow hers. He squeezed her wrist until the bones within it snapped and she winced. "Is that any way to treat the possible ruler of the *entire* dark realm?"

CHAPTER SIXTEEN

CARLOS WATCHED with morbid detachment as each member of the team was attended back to reasonable health. The odd sensation that he and the others were not alone kept him on guard, staring out into the crystal blue water. The vast expanse was dotted by lush land, green with foliage as though Eden. No one, for all the stilted discussion, had made even passing mention of the spirits he'd seen. The angels, their parents—it was such a powerful phenomena—and yet, it hadn't come up as the basic logistics were argued.

Who cared which way they should walk, how they would get back to any modern transportation? They were alive. Didn't they see the angels? A small part of him wondered if he were still losing his mind.

Dan knelt by the edge of the lake. He was babbling something about needing water. Carlos watched dispassionately as Shabazz grasped the junior Guardian's arm and warned him about parasites. True enough, but it still didn't make sense. A jumbo jet had crashed in the mountains, but hadn't immediately exploded. Everyone on the united teams had walked away—surely a divine hand had been the cause. Parasites were the least of their problems.

The moment the thought crossed his mind Carlos squinted. It seemed as though the vaporous mist hovering just over the surface of the still lake was parting. Then out of nowhere, they were there—three old men with scruffy white beards in long white tunics and small, embroidered, flat round hats peered at him from the tiny canoe. They seemed as old, dark, and weathered as the ebony wooden canes they leaned on for support. Their canoe eerily moved forward on its own accord. Carlos waited a full thirty seconds before his teammates even saw them.

"Yo!" Rider shouted, jumping back a few steps. "We've crashed—a little assistance?"

Marlene held Rider's forearm to quiet him and the team waited. The old men's cloudy, bluish-white eyes followed the sound of Rider's voice and the rustle of Marlene's robe.

The eldest among them lifted his cane and pointed toward Carlos. "The voice is not the one we seek. The woman cannot go to the island of knowing. Only one travels with us."

"No can do, brother," Shabazz said, stepping in front of Carlos in a protective stance. "He's one of ours, and we all go down as a team. State your business."

"He must learn things before the apex that only we can show him," the second old man said, his blind eyes traveling to find Shabazz's face as he pointed his stick toward the sun.

"He must learn his true name, then he will guide you home," the third old man said, and then turned to motion toward a far-off island.

Carlos placed a hand on Shabazz's shoulder to indicate he was willing to give the strange request a shot. "It's cool, man. If these old dudes have wisdom, I'm down for whatever." He watched Shabazz rub his chin then stand aside reluctantly. "Hey, they came out during the day," Carlos said with a half smile. "Beats the courier service I used to have."

"You sure, man?" Big Mike asked, grunting as he stood with effort.

Carlos simply nodded and walked forward until the edge of the water dampened his sandaled feet.

Grit and dust stung Damali's eyes as she dismounted from the helicopter and reached for Telek's hand. She couldn't get the image of blue water and smoke out of her mind. Panic had covered her skin with a cool sheen of perspiration, and no amount of small talk and platitudes could make her shake it.

Without a word she trudged behind her overly hospitable guides, listening to nothing except the hard yellowish dust crunch beneath her feet. This land was one of contrasts, like so many others she'd seen. Gravel and dust, but also shade-producing trees. In Askum there were white stone monuments and an eerie vacancy all around, but it also gave one the feeling that eyes were everywhere.

"He is not far from here," Telek said proudly as he waved toward the litter of palace ruins and stelae bearing strange inscriptions. He smiled broadly. "You feel the ancestors watching from the many underground tombs, if you stand very still."

Damali glanced around nervously as she picked up her pace. "Yeah, I sorta had the feeling that there was some seriously old energy around here."

"Indeed. My grandfather is so near the St. Mary of Zion Church people always want him to allow them to board there while on pilgrimages. It is one of the holiest shrines, the church, and it is said that the Ark of the Covenant is hidden somewhere here, however grandfather claims that three seers have long since moved it to an island home." Telek chuckled and shrugged as he kept walking. "Who knows? But grandfather is very peculiar and particular about whom he allows in his home. Dirt from his yard, and granite pieces from the huge obelisks in Stele Field, are believed to be mystical." Her guide leaned in closer and offered Damali a jaunty wink. "Local people even swear that the water pumped into his small well actually travels beneath the ground, past the ancestors' resting places, from Queen Sheba's pool."

After a winding path, Telek stepped through a low iron gate into a circular courtyard where a small, one-story, whitewashed brick house stood surrounded by pink-and-red blossoms on prickly vines. He walked around toward the back of it, where a high wall protected it from the north, and the majestic mountains in the distance seemed to stand guard. The high iron gate on the far side of the courtyard led to what seemed to be a centuries-old church or temple that she now knew was the one Telek had mentioned earlier. But the tall, intricately carved granite obelisks that flanked it made Damali stop for a moment and stare. Telek smiled and motioned to a large, leafy tree that she could not name and bade her to sit down beneath it. Dori began to walk away, and only then did Damali summon her voice.

"Our pilot, though . . ."

"Dori is not an elder. He cannot be here. The children cannot be here. The mothers and fathers do not come to grandfather's compound unless invited." He hugged his cousin and said something to him in the language she would never fully learn, and then took his time to go to a small pump by the house to fill a flat metal pan with water. Balancing the water with care, he set it down before Damali. "I must wash your feet before you enter. We should do this near the door, and you must leave your shoes outside. Grandfather is very particular about the spirits you could walk over on his threshold."

Damali nodded. "Marlene has some of these ways, too," she said, slipping off her sandals. She allowed the earth to warm her feet as she again took Telek's hand. But an inner wave of despair hit her as soon as her soles connected with the bare earth. Tears sprung to her eyes and she shut them as images reeled against her mind and made her temporarily cling to her guide for support.

Women so weary that tears would no longer come to their eyes pressed skeletal-weight infants too weak to suckle to their flat, milk-empty breasts. War and famine, disease and drought so treacherous that it had left babies mere brown skin and loose bones. Damali covered her mouth as Nzinga's voice filled her ears. *You had to see this, queen sister. Your suffering pales by comparison. This is whom you raise your Isis for. Always remember the ancestors in your quest.*

Damali knelt, the dust and gravel of the outer yard eating into her knees as her hands skimmed it blindly. She touched the surface as though a gentle lover, revering those that had gone before her. "But you never gave up," she whispered, her tears wetting the ground.

"*No . . .*" the ground whispered back. Damali lifted her face and turned quickly toward the huge tree above her. "*All over the world,*" the tree murmured in the breeze. "*The children are dying. The earth has been desecrated.*" She picked up a small pebble that suddenly rolled toward her. "*Take me,*" it echoed, "*I was here in the beginning and can tell you much.*" A tiny beetle pushed its way between blades of rough grass. It stopped and stared up at Damali, its beady black eyes unblinking as she looked deeply into them. "*Collect seven stones,"* it murmured. *"The flat ones worn smooth by my friends, time and water. They will find you. Just open your hand."* Then it parted its hard outer metallic green casing, spread a pair of sheer tawny wings, and flew away.

Telek gazed down at her with a warm smile as she sought his gaze for confirmation. When he nodded she opened her hands and laid them palms up in the grass and waited. The tree shuddered as another breeze disturbed its branches. A small brown bird lit upon a low limb and dropped a smooth, clear quartz rock near her hand and was gone.

An elderly man appeared in the doorway of the house and grinned a full dazzling white smile. His leathery, brown skin sparkled with youth just beneath it, and he motioned to Telek to bring Damali forward. He said several long sentences, and looked at Telek, then gazed at Damali tenderly.

"My grandfather is Ephener, his name means 'to have plenty.' He says that his garden likes you. This is good. You may now wash your feet and enter his home. The rest of your stones are on the way."

Carlos walked into the water shin-deep, the lake silt making his sandals slippery against the bottom. He was unsure about how to climb into the canoe without tipping it and sending the blind old men splashing into the water, so he studied the problem for a moment until the eldest one leaned over and offered him a hand, bracing his long walking stick against the shoal.

It was amazing, the strength in the old man's grip. Carlos was certain he'd felt a mild current run through him as he clasped the gnarled hand and stepped up into the narrow craft. But it never wavered, nor did the surefooted elders budge. Then he watched with pure awe as the two on his flank each reached out into the air and grabbed at nothingness, as though the air were a blanket to be balled into their elderly fists and they were closing an invisible cloak around them.

He could see his teammates' shocked expressions, could see everything going on along the shore as they panicked and rushed about, hollering behind the slow-moving boat as though it were gone. The two men chuckled and threw open their arms, the one on the left flinging open his left arm at the same time the elder on Carlos's right flung his right arm away from him. A new shore stood before them with a small, white sand bank that gave way to lush, tall green lake grasses. Beyond it loomed a white stone monastery, weathered gray by wind and storms. Moss ate at its mortar, creating velvet down between each centuries' old stone.

The oldest man in the boat calmly stepped into the water, his walking stick guiding him as he simply waved for Carlos to follow. He bowed toward the shore, then toward each cardinal direction, but never actually stood on the shore.

"Before you enter, you must be cleansed by the waters of life," he said, "and reborn to be given a new name."

Carlos gingerly stepped out of the boat into the mystically still water, but unlike the old man, when he stepped down into it, he was waist deep. The old man came to him, bent, and dipped his hand in the water, drizzling it over Carlos's head. He handed off his long stick to one of his brethren, and placed a flat palm on Carlos's back and one on his chest. Before Carlos could protest, a pair of strong arms that belonged to a twenty-year-old man had dunked him backward.

He came up sputtering and coughing to nods and smiles of approval.

"You are *Alemayehu,*" the man who'd dunked him exclaimed. "This is also the name of an Ethiopian prince. Two words made together, just like the two halves of yourself. *Alem* means 'the world' in Amharic. You have wanted the world. *Ayehu* means 'I see.' You have also seen many worlds," he said, pointing upward and then down to the ground. He made two fists and pounded them together. "World vision, or the world I see. To balance your energy, this must be connected to the one called beautiful vision—for the world I see. Damali Alemayehu. You are one. Together means beautiful vision for the world I see." He stared at Carlos hard. "You understand, now?"

Carlos nodded even though he didn't quite comprehend. Damali's name registered in his ears, however, and if the old man had mentioned her, she wasn't dead.

Oddly, the side of his neck also burned, and he brought his hand up to cover the pain. Then, as he held his palm against the tender skin, he slowly became aware that something just under his skin was moving along the part of his throat that had sustained the original turn bite. As he brought his hand away, the old men around him smiled.

Carlos peered into his palm and a strange, silvery symbol flickered in it for a moment and then was gone. The image was box-shaped, with a line that zigzagged across his palm from right to left and back again in four distinct but connected bars, ending on a platform of four spikes. The shape eerily reminded him of the kundalini snake, but had harder angles. He stared at his opened palm and then at his newfound guides with a question in his eyes.

"*Nkyin kyin ohema nkyinkyin*—changing one's self. Playing many roles," the eldest guide murmured. "You now wear the mark of our side, which covers what had been and seals off the Darkness. During your apex, this will become permanent. It is a source of strength, also a source of choice. You can determine the next time you sire, and your intent to do so, or not, will be carried through your seed when this burns bright."

The old man nodded, appearing temporarily satisfied, and took Carlos to shore by his elbow as the others jumped down from the canoe and followed as though they were teenagers. Once they were assembled on the white sand, he turned abruptly and laid a hand on Carlos's shoulder.

"You must raise an army."

Carlos nodded. "No doubt. But our resources—"

"Are many," his elder said, cutting him off. The old man motioned for his stick and waited until it was provided by the brethren that held it. He drew large circles on the ground with Carlos inside it. "Seven days from the beginning of your end, you will go through the first ring of your power. You were born this day."

"November fifth," Carlos said quietly.

"The eleventh month plus the fifth day renders the number seven, the number of heaven—the place where the dead are resurrected, and the abode of Asuar . . . you will die to the old way completely during the eclipse." The elder rubbed his chin. "The eclipse will last three hours and thirty-three minutes. Three threes is nine, your birth year is also nine. You were born in the year 1980. Add each digit, and you have nine. Nine is a number of completion, because after it, one goes back to one, or the One. This death is not defeat, but a stripping away to give you the Light. Your apex will be rushed, because of circumstances."

Although Carlos was truly confused, he nodded. He wanted to get to the part about Damali's whereabouts, so not interrupting the old man seemed best. But the fact that numbers had been swirling in his head now made sense, as well as his fixation on them.

The elder stepped back and drew another ring around the first one, taking his time to be sure the stick bore down hard into the soft sand. "Normally, leading up to the time of a male Neteru apex, he has seventy days to build what had been stripped away. Let your woman close to you only after you mourn the losses." He sighed and pointed at Carlos's shoes. "They are hard losses, but you come from people that traveled to where the flat pyramids were built. Olmec."

"Mexico?" Carlos simply stared at the man.

He nodded. "Native to the earth, the Indians and Africans there—we were one. But you have many worlds flowing through your veins, even that of the Visigoths . . . this is why you and the beautiful vision see the world. Your teams will be one, and from all worlds. You must travel to gather your energies from each land. The time is nigh, old wars cannot be fought while preparing for the one war of all."

Although he wasn't completely clear about everything the old man was rapping about, he did know that it was impossible to mount an offensive against the gates of Hell with a splintered team. All bull had to be set aside. As soon as the thought completed, the old man smiled and began drawing another huge circle around the first two in the sand.

"You should have had seven months of preparation for battle," he said calmly. "Seven days, seven days, plus seven months—

seven, seven, seven, a trinity of sevens be upon you." The old man sighed. "Your brief detention in the dark realms, while unfortunate, did teach you much about how that enemy functions. Use it to your advantage."

"Cool," Carlos said, not moving outside of the rings that felt strangely protective. "So, I'll build an army in seven months, seventy-seven days. We lay low till we're ready, then what?"

"You don't have time. First, you must learn to conceal yourself against your enemies. We have temporarily masked you, but you must carry that energy forward yourself." The old man chuckled, made two fists and gathered the air, and closed it in around himself and disappeared. He reappeared ten yards away.

"That was profound, man . . ." Carlos said, respect and awe in his tone.

"You are a light bender," the old man said, chuckling as he disappeared again. "Do not believe in the illusion of powerlessness cast by the dark side. Grab the particles of light and magnetize them to you . . . your new eyes can see them."

The other old men laughed and pointed at Carlos's eyes.

"Silver seekers," one said.

"Spirit finders," another murmured.

"My powers will come back?"

The old men smiled. "Only if you believe you have not been left destitute by the Light."

Carlos didn't know how to answer.

The eldest in the group of three sighed, his tone impatient. "Young people, humph!" He shook his head. "Did you have visions?"

"Yeah . . . I sorta saw—"

"You see worlds and angels and spirits." He scratched his scraggly beard. "Your eyes changed first. There are more changes." He came close to Carlos, sniffing, and then looked at the others. "Not yet, but soon."

"His hands," one said, making Carlos look down at his palms. "You heal?"

"Well, not exactly, I—"

"Feel the pain of others!" the eldest shouted, making birds fly from the trees and settle down slowly.

Carlos nodded, feeling foolish for even making the old man go there.

"Your mind," he said in a tired voice, "a steel trap of logic. Negotiations. Battle tactics. Soon, you'll be impervious to the demon bite." He finally smiled. "But you have to wait till your birthday, and not slip into some of your old ways."

Carlos looked at the ground.

"We were not always old or wise, but this is critical."

"I hear you," Carlos said, duly chastised.

"Good. Then stop fretting about the endurance or strength that comes soon . . . like the five senses. For some odd reason, these are blooming last, instead of first, but you did arrive to us from a very circuitous route." He looked at the others. "We never expected our Neteru to come from the realms we do not name. So, one can only assume that his development is unique."

"You mean I'll get my night vision back, and everything else, too?"

They smiled. "A lot of it. Not all of it. But what you do get will be more than adequate."

Carlos wrestled the dangerous question that nagged him out of his mind. He wanted in the worst way to know about Damali, and if it would ever be the same between them again. But this wasn't the time nor place. There were greater concerns. That could wait. But when the old men laughed at him, he simply closed his eyes.

"Thirteen gifts," the eldest man said, chuckling. "All Neterus have these."

"I counted twelve, though . . . not being funny," Carlos said, his gaze going to the shore. "I'm not being disrespectful, but if we're going into battle—"

"Twelve?" the man said, seeming perplexed. "How did you arrive here?"

"By plane, or plane crash, to be more accurate," Carlos said, now looking at all three of them.

They sighed in unison.

"A plane did not crash on this island, son."

Carlos blinked. "Travel through . . . I don't know . . . uh . . . Y'all did some mystical thing, and we were here."

"Light displacement and dimension distortion," the eldest replied. "I know you miss your old transportation methods, but did you know Neterus can move through time and space?" He belly laughed when Carlos just stared at him. "We in the Light rings invented it. The others only imitate it!" He walked away scratching his head, seeming completely amazed. "Angels do it all the time, son. Spirits to help humanity come to rescue those in peril. Did you bump your head and lose all your senses in the crash? Who saved you, then, anyway? They showed you the thirteenth gift, *then*."

"Can I try it?" Carlos whispered in complete awe.

"Only if you're ready, and you need to be," the eldest urged, taking Carlos's hands without crossing the circles. He extended Carlos's arms. "Concentrate on the particles and grab them as you ask their permission to be held with your mind. Then pull them around you like a cloak." He smiled. "The dark ones are blind to it, even in the moonlight—but other Light benders can see you within it. We know where we are."

Excitement riddled him as he gazed first at one hand and then the other. Power . . .

"No!" the old men said in unison. "Defense!"

The eldest among them sighed. "The dark ones take from the Light without permission and abuse it for cheap tricks and to make war and chaos. You must ask permission to conceal yourself for protection, to aid those in need. Raw power is no better than lust. Go down that road, and you will never learn or have what you need!"

Duly chastised, Carlos nodded. "All right. I'm sorry. My bad. Old habits die hard."

Albeit disgruntled, the three teachers sighed and nodded.

"Light," Carlos said quietly, feeling a bit insane to be talking to nothingness, "may I have your permission to proceed?"

"Say it like you mean it," the eldest said firmly, pounding his stick on the ground. "Both in your mind and from your words. Soon you can do it without saying it out loud. But for now, practice. Again!"

Carlos took a deep breath and put emphasis in his voice. "Light," he shouted. "May I have your permission?"

The old men looked at each other.

"It's not in his heart and we are running out of time."

"He has to think of something he wants to get to badly enough to—"

"I got it, I got it," Carlos said. "I'll focus."

The threesome fell silent, but the scowls on their faces made them seem unconvinced. Carlos closed his eyes and turned his face toward the sun. He could see her eyes. That was all he needed, all that had ever penetrated his façade down to the core.

"Light, please work with me! May I have your permission?"

"Feel the energy tickle your palms and build like lightning tickles the clouds before striking," an excited elderly voice said.

It made Carlos open his eyes. Carlos stared at the eldest man before him, remembering what a lightning strike felt like and concentrated harder. Soon his palms tingled and became hot.

"Now close the cloak!"

Carlos did as he was ordered and felt so light that it was hard to keep his footing. He stumbled forward and opened his arms to hold his balance. "Did I do it? Did I disappear?" He looked around expectantly to the smiling faces that soon broke out into full laughter.

"So clumsy, but yes," one of his teachers admitted.

Another shook his head, laughing. "And this is our warrior? We have troubles."

"Indeed," the eldest said, "but he is what we have." He sighed and pointed to the ground. "The earth has energy. Neteru, a small piece of the Creator, is in all natural things. Ask for permission to be of it. The chameleon can be green, like the leaf, or brown like the tree trunk. You, too, can melt away and conceal yourself until danger passes. When you are stronger, you can conceal an army. Until then, sleep within the circles."

He would have felt better if he'd been given an offensive weapon but accepted the gift of their knowledge with an appreciative bow. "Thank you," Carlos said, truly meaning it. "I will try to learn quickly to protect the Neteru."

Puzzled glances passed between the old men.

"You are the Neteru," the eldest said, scratching his beard. "Explain."

A weird sensation coursed through Carlos, causing mild alarm within him as he tried to carefully choose his words. "She . . . Damali . . . is the Neteru."

They tilted their heads and stared at him and then huddled and began talking in hushed, animated tones in a language he couldn't fathom.

"I must understand!" the eldest one finally said, pounding his walking stick in the dirt. "We are to prepare a male Neteru for his apex, and in males it happens in his twenty-fourth year, two plus four is six, his death to life as a man and his beginning as something greater—then follows the concentric rings of trinity sevens!" Thoroughly agitated, he waved his arms about. "You have the silver vision. Your blood casts silver prisms within red, so no demon can turn you if bitten. Your hands will hold Light fire soon . . . you can walk undetected. The shield of Heru and his sword have your name on it—*Alemayehu*. No woman was sent to us. Your father-seer was on the shore."

"The Guardian female . . . the other seer," one of the teachers said, pacing. "But she was past the age of—"

"No. She is a Guardian," the third said.

"Damali is definitely the Neteru," Carlos argued, becoming more worried as they argued. "In my old life," he said carefully, "the entire sixth realm of darkness was looking for girlfriend, and I—"

"The vampires hunted her down?" the eldest man asked, cutting off Carlos's explanation. "We live a cloistered existence here. The things of the other seers are not our concern. Our mission is singular, to wait for the male Neteru!"

"Yeah," Carlos said, now stepping beyond the circle. "Fact. But the Light sent two this time, I guess?" He glanced around, confused. "You all don't talk amongst yourselves?"

The three old men stared at each other, seeming as though they were silently conferring.

"And she . . ."

"Spiked?" Carlos said, answering the eldest teacher's lingering question. "Yeah. Produced the scent that started a damned civil war underground and topside."

"We thought that was the beginning of the Armageddon." The eldest looked at the others. "We were told that a sign was to come. But, then . . ."

Carlos tilted his head and looked out toward the distance. "She fell off your radar, didn't she?"

They nodded. "We thought . . ."

Carlos rubbed his palms down his face, renewed guilt stabbing him. "Yeah. She did go dark for a moment—but fluxed back."

"Her condition was so tenuous that she was concealed, even to us?"

"Probably," Carlos said quietly, knowing within his heart that she had to be. Any strong Neteru team would have smoked his baby girl if they'd seen her. The Light had held out hope after all.

"She's not just a Guardian," one teacher whispered, his eyes wide.

"Not just his Guardian mate," the other said, leaning on his stick, stunned.

"We got one half of the whole," the eldest murmured and closed his eyes, turning his dark, lined face toward the sun. "She's cloaked. This is more than was even foretold."

"Okay, I know it's deep—but do you know where she is?"

They opened their eyes and stared at Carlos.

"Yes. Of course we do. She is learning battle formations to assist you—we thought. But, she's not your assistant; she's your equal. You're her equal. We thought we were ensuring your Guardian mate's safe passage, but a Neteru was being ferried. That is *entirely* different." They all looked around nervously as the eldest teacher spoke. "Do you understand what that implies?"

"Not totally, but—"

"Do you know why our land was never conquered?" the eldest shouted, pointing his stick at Carlos. "How people so small with so little could never be defeated?"

All Carlos could do was stare at the man.

"Touch my stick and close your eyes. This was carved from the Tree of Knowledge in the Garden." He chuckled sadly as he looked at it. "I made assumptions, and didn't use my own gifts fully." They shared a smile. "Happens to the best of us. Be gentle with yourself. You are never too old or too wise to learn."

Carlos didn't move. What this teacher implied was beyond profound. *"The Tree . . ."* he whispered. *"Hombre,* that's a lot of juice to be pointing at a newbie. Now, I'm no punk, but I know about getting fried, and—"

"Touch the stick," the elder commanded. "We were almost about to make a grave error. Something has hidden her so deeply away that even we could not see her. It has receded her power, taken her Isis to keep her hidden from evil until you are readied as one."

Reluctantly, Carlos stretched out his hand and gingerly touched the wet, sandy end of the long stick that was held before him. Instantly a bright light scored the inside of his lids, causing him to drop the end of the wood and cover his eyes. But the image held as the blinding brightness bored into his skull, carving past his normal sight, searing his brain until the hair on his head stood up with static charge. For a fleeting moment he saw it. Glistening gold, its long lid ajar, spilling forth waves of iridescent light, the sound of metal swords and the clamoring voices of eager angels made him drop to his knees. "You have the Ark of the Covenant here?" Carlos croaked. "They said it was a myth."

The elder withdrew the stick and shoved the tip of it into the sand, stopping the intense vision. "It has always been in Ethiopia, the land of Eden and the first peoples. Its Jerusalem location was a myth. Our fighting sticks, like that of the Mother-Seer; also come from here and hold the power of the Donga. The words from our land are legendary. Know this, our eyes are within the wood."

"He could see it," the second elder said. "He is Neteru."

"He is the one who is supposed to work with the sixth ring!" the eldest said, grasping Carlos's hand and yanking him to his feet. He began drawing circles to create seven layers in all.

"Look," he ordered, not even allowing Carlos to recover. "You sank to the depths of the sixth realm of darkness and must be quickly reinstated to the sixth ring above."

The old man walked back and forth, his robes kissing the sand and using his stick as a pointer. "Ring one is where the ancestors go. Spirits that guide us and help us until we are strong enough for them to leave us after they've crossed over. Ring two is where they prepare for their ascension and lessons, after they have helped others close to the edges of transition. Ring three is where those guides that inspire and impart wisdom reside to make the human existence better—art, music, science, medicine, all. Ring four are carriers of prayers—they bear up the intercessions and answer them . . . we have ancestors there, too, if we are so blessed. They keep family lines going and merge them to one worldness. Ring five are the keepers of the Akashic Records of all knowledge and they protect the keepers of the seals . . . they are also responsible for healing, nature, the things we must teach you to fight in a different way . . . but ring six are where the generals are . . . the warrior angels that fight the righteous causes and fear not the depths of Hell." He stopped speaking and closed his eyes. "My short description does not begin to explain the power of the rings. More will be revealed as your strength grows."

The old man had broken out into an impassioned sweat, beads of it rolling down his temples as he spoke. "They are strong enough to fly into Hell danger zones, extract the lost, and return them to the Most High's realm, even after death has tried to seal their fate." He stared at Carlos. "Only the sixth-ring warriors can see the Ark. After that ring, only seventh Heaven exists—where the Creator of All resides. You've seen warrior angels."

"Yes," Carlos whispered, tears brimming in his eyes.

"Only those that do not fear even Hell itself, and would walk through it for another soul's salvation can see them. You have done this."

Carlos nodded and swallowed a sob. "For her. Yes."

"You went into Hell for the female Neteru?"

Emotion caught in Carlos's throat as he nodded and tears streamed down his face. "For her and her team . . . and my brother."

The old man clapped his hands and spun around in a madman's circle. "You were demon once and did this! It is all so clear now!"

"Vampire . . . a councilman, to be exact," Carlos said, bristling at the memory.

"A dark throne-level demon, recanting power? You chose love over *that*?" the old man asked, astonished. "All for her. And you come to us with Guardians and the Covenant brethren as protection to stand in the sun on hallowed ground . . . the oldest in the world?" He threw his head back and laughed, opening his arms to the sun.

Carlos didn't know how to answer. "Something brought me back, but I burned in daylight and served my sentence." He raked his fingers through his hair. "All I know is three huge *hombres* with gold shields and blades drawn got me and lifted me up . . . the same guys that kept the plane from going down hard, I think."

"No," the eldest said. "You cannot have mere Neteru powers— not entering into the big battle with the female Neteru at your side. This hasn't been done since Eden." He shook his head and the others appeared to agree, their indecipherable mother tongue creating a cacophony of chaotic voices on the small beach. "We did not expect this and must confer," he finally said, walking away from Carlos toward the temple with the other teachers quickly following him. "We must hasten your lessons and give you offensive weaponry to address what's headed your way."

"You must go to the place where the Blue Nile meets the White Nile," Telek said, repeating his grandfather's words. "He says your power is in the coming together of the Light and the Darkness, represented in the two sides of the Nile . . . you are a child of the Nile, Kemet—and women are water. Draw from the natural energy of the water that gives life."

The old man took Damali by both hands and stood her in the

middle of the dirt floor. He waved to her right side, as though motioning for a missing person.

"Your mate stands there," Telek said, drawing a chuckle from his grandfather. "He says that he will have a new name, and his first name will become your son's last name—it is a good one to keep the family strong."

Damali smiled, but the recent miscarriage made it less than brilliant. She swallowed away her melancholy as she focused on the lesson, remembering what the land had shown her about other people's losses. Then it slowly dawned upon her, if he was forecasting, then Carlos and her whole team were definitely still out there somewhere—alive!

The old man nodded, as though reading her thoughts, and then drew a flat line along each cardinal direction, north, south, east, and west.

"In relationship to where you were born, he says put a member of the Covenant to stand at each direction as your outer ring—the Irishman to the west—as his beliefs reside there. The one from Mexico to the north, he looks to the north for guidance. The monk from Tibet, east. Imam, south, toward here, his motherland." Telek quickly walked around Damali with his grandfather, pointing to the floor etchings as his grandfather gave hasty directions.

"My family, my team—they didn't crash? Where are they?" Damali held her breath as the old man waved away her questions.

"Yes, they crashed, but are not dead," Telek said, dismissing any further details as the short, elderly man glared at them. "The work of angels just off the sacred islands within Lake Tana's mystical shores. Do not break his flow."

The grandfather nodded and grunted, seeming annoyed that he'd been interrupted.

"Between north and west, add two newest male Guardians," Telek said, without looking at Damali's seeking gaze and motioning toward the floor instead. "Between west and south, two old friends—the one who rides the motorcycles and the other one who is tall like a mighty tree."

"Rider and Big Mike?" Damali asked quietly, and was rewarded by the grandfather's avid nod as he clapped his hands with approval.

"Between south and east, your mother-seer and father figure—a couple—are to stand when you fight. Each person in the circle is placed where their strength lies . . . they are southern directed, and look east for wisdom."

"Makes sense," Damali murmured. "Shabazz is always quoting *The Art of War,* and all of Marlene's herbs and wisdom come from the southern hemisphere and the motherland, south of where we live."

"Yes!" Telek shouted in harmony with his grandfather's laughter. "You understand! Now, the young Guardian from the east should be next to the monk's line, between east and north," he said, moving around her back to the top of the circle where his grandfather began, "and the other young Guardian with the broken heart should be next to the priest who will also share the same broken heart for the same reason."

"Jose and Father Lopez?"

The men fell quiet but nodded. Slowly the grandfather entered the circle and drew a line and looked deeply into her eyes and then touched her cheek, before walking away to begin jabbering again.

"The priest must keep to the Covenant and his vows; the girl, once your enemy, will have to become your friend. She has seen much, and has done a good deed for your partner. This will be hard." Telek sighed with his grandfather. "A mother, a daughter, and a son will be added to the inner ring, with a very old friend of yours."

The grandfather shook his head, chuckled, and closed his eyes as Telek conveyed the strange riddle.

"A policeman has his wife, the young Asian will have a challenge, your tree trunk will have a small bird to make a permanent nest in his old branches and make him happy. Two young men will be left without a mate until the circle changes again, but their brotherhood will lessen the hardship. The younger of them needs a friend, the older of them needs to be looked up to. Needs respect. An old warrior will want to kill a demon in his home that is his strange ally, and a daughter spirit will come home seeking her mother so that he won't have to. She is not a Guardian, like the others, but will help you as a friend. Two will bear fangs, flanking your man—but do not worry. This is necessary . . . his old life will help him, and he will elevate them from the pit. Your new number is twenty-one, which is also three. It should take the time of three sevens to build to this number. But it will be rushed, as time is speeding up. Seven days could be seven minutes, seven months, seven days—you see? There are new variables shifting the sands of time. This is also your age now, three sevens. Twenty-one. All still balances. The universe is mathematics, and must balance."

With that the grandfather waved his hands across the floor, glimpsing up at Telek to be sure his message had been made clear.

"Twelve on the outer ring, seven on the inner ring, then you and your equal warrior. When you go into battles, you must fight this way in this formation. Seven months and seventy-seven days until you are ready, or sooner in sevens—but be at home by November fifth, bury your mate's ancestors so they may rest in peace."

The grandfather straightened his back and leaned on the old, plain walking stick that she now knew contained the awesome purple light, and sighed. He seemed to look his ninety-some years of age after his divination, as though the reading had thoroughly spent him. He mopped his moist brow with a shaky, frail hand, nodded, yawned, said a few words, and left the room.

"He is tired and says to feed you and let you rest. We will make some tea and have food, yes?"

"But my team," Damali protested gently. "If he's giving me all this information about them, then they are definitely still alive, right? And if that's the case, I need to get up with them as soon as humanly possible."

Telek smiled. "Yes. They are still alive. And they are on their way. Still so impatient, little one? Did you not learn to flow with the energies around you, yet?"

Damali had to smile. "True. Where are my manners?" Damali opened and closed her mouth, so intrigued that she could barely wait for the lesson to begin.

"In Africa time is of no consequence, as we original people invented this concept called time. But we respect it, do not rush it; she has her own schedule and seasons. There are some things I have yet to show you," Telek said with a wink. "Like how to grab the Light like a blanket to hide yourself, for starters. Then, how to create a Light wand to replace your lost Isis . . . until you can draw down the Light into the sacred blade and spew it from the tip toward a dark aggressor."

CHAPTER SEVENTEEN

"SO NOW what?" Rider sat down hard on the shoreline and stared at the water.

"We wait," Shabazz replied, finding the shade of a tree to shield him.

"Great, Confucius. But shouldn't we be going after our new Guardian brother?" Rider leaned forward with his forearms on his knees.

Shabazz shut his eyes. "We don't know where he is, man."

"Like that's ever stopped us before." Rider issued Shabazz a sideways glance when he didn't respond. "The man vanishes into thin air like a puff of mist with three old wise men like in some biblical passage, and—"

"It wasn't vampires, dude, so chill," Big Mike said, finding a spot near Shabazz to doze. "We wait. If we move out on a rescue and recovery, and he comes back here, we'll pass him."

"Especially if he is in a time-space differential," Monk Lin said quietly as he sat.

Everyone turned and looked at the aging monk.

"Time is an illusion, space is also that," the monk said in a matter-of-fact tone as though he were describing a blade of grass.

"I cannot wrap my head around that right now," Rider admitted, flopping back on the sand. "All I know is we are in a foreign land, got no water that we're particularly ready to drink without boiling it first and dropping in some purification tablets—which you may have noticed, got incinerated on the plane—cholera and yellow fever shots, notwithstanding, along with food, supplies, we got no papers—"

"We've got papers," Dan said, hosting his backpack off and letting it hit the ground with a wobbly thud. "I was scared so shitless, I never took it off."

Rider and Big Mike chuckled.

"Way to go, newbie," Rider said, offering his fist for Dan to pound.

Shabazz glanced at Marlene. "Sis got her black bag and fighting stick, too. Ma don't travel without it, even through a damned crash." He winked at Marlene as she stretched out on the sand. "But girl-friend's Ju Ju is strong, so if they had gone up in flames, whatever."

"All right, cool," Rider fussed good-naturedly. "So, I stand corrected. We've got papers. But has anyone given any thought to the fact that maybe, in a very short while, this area could be flooded by Ethiopian police that will have questions we cannot answer? They might take us in for questioning, putting us miles away from where we're supposed to be. Then what? And, does anybody know if there are lions or anything around here that we should be concerned about, given we don't have a weapon between us? Holy-water bombs ain't gonna fend off a hungry—"

"Jacob Rider," Father Patrick finally scolded. "After the miracles you have just seen, why do you *persist* in being negative?"

"It's his way," Jose said, chuckling. "You know *hombre* has to always play devil's advocate and dream up the worst possible scenario. But once he's gone through his battery, he's cool."

"Sort of like my computers," J.L. said, nudging Rider in the side as he plopped down next to him. "The old dude has to run self-check diagnostics before he completely boots up, then he's cool."

"At least someone understands me," Rider said, becoming testy. "I'm not being negative, I'm just being real."

"Words and thoughts have power," Imam Asula said quietly. "Let us focus upon our goal to be reunited with both Damali and Carlos, for now, if we can."

"Let us also not forget to continue our prayers," Father Lopez said, glancing at the others. "It has been our most effective weapon thus far."

"Yeah, yeah, yeah, I hear you," Rider said, slinging his forearm over his eyes.

Damali sat beside Telek, quietly watching the landscape as it passed them in slow-moving still frames of beauty. The open-air Jeep allowed the wind to brush her face, and the dust from the road reminded her that she was alive under an azure, cloudless sky. She'd been told much, but it was all a riddle. Some of it made sense, some of it didn't, but she knew enlightenment was something that would come in time.

She fastened her attention to the small shanty homes that they passed on the hillsides, marveling at the people working, women walking with baskets upon their heads and children strapped to their backs in bright-colored cloths within the rural community. It was as if time had actually stood still, or bypassed this part of the world. People still farmed with hand instruments, but seemed also to possess a profound sense of peace, even in a land devastated by war.

And what was time, really, she wondered. It now seemed to be a manufactured illusion of western culture designed to manipulate people into becoming worker bees trapped within tiny cells that could not appreciate the expanse of time's greatness, rather than something tangible and real. The seasons had her own time, Telek's grandfather had said . . . rainy season, the dry season, a time to plant, a time to harvest, time with family—invaluable. Time to love, endless. Birth, death, renewal; it was all a circle not judged by time, simply coordinated by it. The beginning of time lived here, as did probably the end of it.

Then, again, what was the end of time, if one considered the infinity of the other realms beyond earth?

Damali clutched the two stones she'd acquired in her palms. In her left hand she held the first one she'd seen on the ground. It was a tiny white stone, worn smooth. Perhaps it was limestone, or something more solid, but it felt like it had once been a part of the great rock formations that had serviced the building of temples, churches, and the monumental obelisks she'd seen. In her right hand she fondled the small quartzlike stone that the sparrow had dropped. What did each mean? What was each for? There were five more days until November 5, and each day a stone would come to her of its own accord, the old man had said, until she possessed seven in all.

The sky, although brightly fired by the sun, offered a warm blanket of sunshine while the breeze gave a mild, balmy fusion to its covering. Balance jumped into her mind as they silently progressed down the bumpy, unpaved road.

Seven rings above mirrored the seven levels below. It was all so well orchestrated, how could one not believe? she mused.

Below, on level one, confused and anxious spirits resided. On the outer ring above, helpful spirits and ancestors with clear purpose and love rested. On level two below, angry, fierce poltergeists screamed and howled and frightened; on ring two above, the ancestors became more focused, gained wisdom and knowledge, and assisted the living in more profound ways. On level three below, jealousy and envy lived in a slithering, vengeful, serpentine world . . . Carlos had told her that.

Yet, on the third ring of grace, collaboration took place in the arts, sciences, and all manner of creative inspiration that uplifted humankind through beauty, not twisted ugliness. On level five below, raw, primal, murderous aggression lived in the were-demon realms, but above within the fifth ring, the Akashic wisdom and knowledge protectors resided in a place that garnered temperance created from integrated understanding.

Tears made her sniff as she became overwhelmed at the depth of truth within it all. The vampires she'd hunted from the dreaded level six were the shrewdest of all, hardest to kill, fiercest combatants because they possessed all the attributes of the levels of Darkness. It was only fitting that their cosmic match would be warrior angels—huge, strong, bulked entities with glowing silver eyes, those powerful enough to withstand the furnace blasts unafraid, with the ability to manifest, carry messages, and draw a blade, if necessary, to defend a righteous cause. Oddly, both protected their territories with vigilance. The concept gave her pause until she remembered, *as above, so below.*

It all made so much sense.

"And you were saying I had no reason to worry," Rider muttered, standing slowly with the others, his hands raised above his head as Ethiopian police trudged toward them with guns readied.

The officers motioned with their guns and shouted commands that the teams could not understand.

Father Patrick and Father Lopez slowly pointed to their dirty clerical collars and the crosses they wore, producing instant understanding. Guns were lowered, and the head of the militia stepped forward.

"Foreigners are not allowed to roam freely in the North Country," the officer said, agitated. "A plane went down nearby due to terrorists, and we are still experiencing rebel skirmishes. It is dangerous in the region for unescorted missionaries." He shook his head and stepped forward. "You have papers?"

Dan nodded and motioned toward his bag. "Yes, sir. But two of our members were on board the plane that went down," he added, covering quickly as the officer snatched up his backpack. "That's the only reason we're here."

Rider and the others gave Dan an approving glance.

"You should have gone to us—the authorities. Where are you headed?"

All eyes were on Dan and the officer as his fellow officers cocked their machine guns skyward.

"Uh, Sudan?" Dan said, unsure, glancing at his teammates.

Marlene nodded, but didn't speak, knowing a woman's voice was not going to inspire positive action. Shabazz stepped forward slowly with his hands still clasped to the top of his head.

"If you check the papers, we lost a man and a woman in the crash . . . and we wanted to search for them before we crossed the border."

"Not possible," the officer snapped at Shabazz and began rummaging in Dan's sack. "Travel to Sudan is very dangerous on the roads. There are war zones, you are aware? Also armed bandits along the way, driven by starvation." He clicked his tongue with open annoyance. "Foolish Americans. Look around. Do you not watch the news? Ethiopia, Eritrea, Egypt, and the Red Sea are Sudan's borders, as is Libya, Chad, Zaire, Uganda, Kenya—fighting everywhere, armed militias beyond all major cities." He waved his arms about. "Especially along our border and Eritrea and Sudan's frontier—so we would be irresponsible to just point you to a road and say, 'Go!' No!"

"Thanks for the heads up, brother," Big Mike said, his low, confident voice soothing the agitated official. "Then, can you give us a best way to get back to a safe zone?"

"We will take you to the airport in Addis Ababa, from there you can fly to Khartoum and check back daily to see if your family's remains have been recovered. I will give you a number; however, we cannot have civilians interfering with police matters or creating a possible embassy issue—since you are Americans."

But as the officer continued his inspection of Dan's backpack, glaring at each team member to accurately match a face with a photo, when he took out Damali's passport, his gaze softened as he stared at her picture. "This was the star from the music," he said, awe covering his face and coating his tone as he rushed toward his men. "Look, look, a very important person has been lost over our land. This is tragic!"

"May Allah be with her," Imam Asula said, through the din of African voices.

The officer looked up at Imam Asula. "I am sorry for your loss, brother. I am Muslim, too, and we revere our fallen." He motioned toward his fellow officers. "Some are Christian with us, as well. We will say prayers, but it is doubtful your people have made it, given the severity of the crash." He sighed and put the safety back on his weapon, tossing Dan his backpack. He stared at Marlene. "The woman who has tears—this was your daughter?"

Marlene simply nodded and looked down.

"See the waters coming together in your mind," the old teacher said as he instructed Carlos before the rushing grandeur of the Blue Nile Falls. "Use the might of Tis Isat and close the cloak about you as though a coat over your shoulders. Imagine yourself somewhere high and safe, using the energy of a river so mighty that it flows from south to north."

Carlos gazed across the four-hundred-meter expanse of rushing water that dropped into an impressive fifty-meter chasm below. His teacher smiled and nodded. Carlos did the math—four plus five, the number nine, like his birthday came out to. The old boys wasn't no joke when it came to breaking the universe down into mathematics. He summoned courage while looking at the continuous spray of rainbow-hued water that created a mist that hovered above it like a ghost to render its name, Tis Isat, the elders had said—smoke of fire.

Still unsure, he tried to take comfort in the comparison as he readied himself for the first real challenge they'd levied. Indeed he'd been through the fire, now it was time to try illusion in the colored bands of sunlight and rise like smoke above what had once burned him. If water could cast the illusion of being a smoking fire, then he could break through the illusion of time and space and go to where the Blue and White Nile met. Yeah right. God was deep; he was just a spec of dust in comparison. Even to his own mind their logic seemed flawed, especially while watching an extreme force of nature thunder around him.

"Are you sure he should go unescorted . . . so far?" one of the younger teachers asked, glancing around the small gathering of men.

"We have conferred, yet have not taught him all that we must. He should, perhaps, stay with us for the three cycles of seven," the third teacher offered with uncertainty.

The eldest shook his head. "No. I have had a vision of him at the nexus of the rivers, *alone*. What he must learn to gain in his arsenal cannot be taught or given, but experienced, then he will own the knowing of it." He sighed. "It is the ancient site of Nubia, the genesis location of our male Neterus—from the water, he will merge his disconnected halves, and then go to the desert, six hours, to see the Al-Ahram, the ancient royal city with great pyramids of Meroe. Learn this history, the peoples of Kush, and of the independent Christian kingdoms. That land, Sudan, was also invaded by tiny countries, conquered because they fought within themselves and could not stand united against invaders . . . British, French, that spawned wars with Muslims in the name of Christ that created bloodshed and famines and genocides in the millions up to present days—but the connection to Addis Ababa was briefly forged that stopped civil war for a time."

The elder teacher opened both palms and then clasped them, symbolically bringing them into a single fist. "This Neteru must bring together many sides. Indigenous plus Christian and Muslim, Nubian and European—all as one. It starts with quenching your thirst for knowledge at the joining of the two Niles, and then you must forge the desert to seek more knowledge."

"What if I wind up drowning?" Carlos said, growing wary. "My landings haven't been exactly on-point so far . . . maybe I need to practice a few more times?"

"If you drown, you drown. So be it," the eldest said with a wide smile. "There are no accidents within the universe."

Carlos found himself sprawled out on a beach. He jumped up before he even looked around. This was *not* what the old men had told him about. This place didn't look *anything* like where he was supposed to be. He froze, and then glanced around slowly, trying not to panic as he recognized where he was.

L.A., Venice Beach. He almost wept from frustration.

"Aw, shit!" He snatched off his crocheted skullcap and threw in to the sand and then clutched his hair. How in the world was he gonna find Damali, the team, or ever sync up with her? His maiden flight in the Light, botched!

He willed himself to take deep breaths and focus. He blotted out the people that were out for a sunny afternoon stroll. Basketball-hoop games thudded in his ears. Laughter, waves, volleyball, all of it made him insane. Dogs ran with joggers; he could hear in-line skaters up on the street level. Old men talking trash and playing chess. If the world would just stop spinning for a moment, he'd get off the crazy ride and get back to where he was supposed to be!

"Luck be a lady tonight!" an old man hollered, laughing and standing as he moved a chess piece.

Carlos sighed, picked up his skullcap from the sand, and hit it against his leg before shoving it in his pocket. Beaten, he trudged through the sand. Judging from the sun, it was late afternoon. Maybe his boy, Yonnie, would be around—or most likely they'd both get slaughtered.

"But my queen is going to kick your natural, black ass!" the other contender shouted as he laughed. "Take that, you old Mo Fo. How you like me now? Ain't she purty?"

Carlos had to laugh as he passed the game. It so reminded him of home. Reminded him of his dad and uncles playing cards, before things at home got bad. Maybe that's how he'd messed up and landed on the beach, being so homesick in his heart that no matter what the Neteru teachers had said, he'd ended up here.

Another sigh pushed past his lips as he stopped and watched the game. If he was gonna die, and there were no teachers around, what else was there to do without a cent in his pocket? He had a bank account and number, but no ID on him—so how was he gonna get cash? Right now, he couldn't even bury his mother or grandmother if he wanted to and wasn't sure if he could go to the morgue to even see what the chairman had done. Besides, in what was likely to be his final hours, just listening to these old codgers talk smack gave him some semblance that part of the world was still normal, even if his wasn't. He sure wasn't gonna test his wings again, and possibly end up in Siberia, or some shit.

"See, my brother," the first man teased as a small crowd formed. "You've gotta take risks, is what I'ma show you when I whup your ass."

"You ain't whupping my ass without a fight," the other said, moving a piece and squinting his eyes. "You know me, don't ya? I'm a cat and got nine lives. But like I tol' ya, I can smoke you in seven moves."

Carlos moved in closer to the board, listening harder.

"Aw, hell naw. You ain't gonna do me like that," the first player said. "I got something for ya that you ain't seen befo'. Trust me, gots aces up my sleeve I ain't even used."

Carlos remained very still as the first man picked up his queen and studied her with a smile.

"When I put her down, here, right next to your king, I believe they call it checkmate."

The crowd clapped and passed high-fives and exchanged fist pounds before it slowly disbanded.

"Rematch," the second player demanded. "That wasn't fair!"

"I didn't cheat, just used what I had. You the one with a blind spot that can't see opportunities right before your eyes—so don't be casting no aspersions on me, brother. Besides, what about life is fair any ole way?" The first player looked up at Carlos and winked. "My buddy is a sore loser. Can't stand it when he gets his ass kicked in public." He leaned back as the other player got up from the table and skulked away. "You look like a gamblin' man, young fella . . . or don't you have time for an old man to show you a trick or two? You play the boards?"

Carlos sat down slowly. "Been known to in the past."

The old man leaned forward. "We ain't talking 'bout the past. If you stay there, I'll kick your young ass for sure."

Carlos chuckled. "Set 'em up."

The old man gathered several pieces and held out his hands. "You better on black or white?"

Carlos's smile broadened. "I used to be better on black . . . but, I think I'll try white."

"Wise move," the player said, nodding and chuckling. "So, the young buck thinks he's got skills . . . hmmmm." He blew out his breath and rubbed his hands together.

"Got a few," Carlos said, pushing a pawn forward.

"No. A man needs many," the elderly player said, summarily taking Carlos's pawn.

"Aw'ight," Carlos said, studying the old man more than the chessboard. "Then stop talking yang and school me. Show me whatchu got."

The old man smiled and laughed, then pushed a pawn forward.

This time, Carlos didn't rush his move but sat back.

"You're running out of time," the player said, setting a tiny hourglass on the side of the board. "Any day now, works for me. Unless you're scared?"

Carlos met his eyes. "No, I'm not," he said, moving a piece without looking at the board.

"Good, because I was getting worried." The old man took his knight and shook his head. "Still am, sorta kinda."

"Don't be," Carlos said, and took his bishop.

The old man laughed and scratched his head. "Okay," he said, nodding in appreciation. "So, it's like that?"

"Yeah it is," Carlos said, reaching for the hourglass and flipping it over. "Like you said. Any day."

In a bold move, the old man pushed his black queen forward and waited. "Tempting, ain't she?"

Carlos nodded and the smile left his face. "Thoroughly, but booby trapped."

"Right," the elderly player said, "and I'ma show you how." He moved a knight three hops and then a castle along a short line. "Come for her like that, and I've got your king."

"Game over," Carlos murmured.

"Soooo . . . maybe you don't go for her like that in a straight line. Pace yourself, but keep moving."

The two men stared at each other.

"The queen you need to protect can protect herself, these days. You need to worry about your king. See all the pieces she has around her?"

Carlos's gaze sought the ocean. "She doesn't need me," he said quietly.

"We talkin' 'bout chess, or a woman?" The old man made a tent in front of his mouth with his fingers.

Carlos stared at his chess partner's ruddy brown face that sprouted hard white whiskers and assessed his raggedy plaid shirt and tattered, blue uniform pants. His semibald scalp gleamed in the sun. Wisdom was coming at him so hard and so fast from so many directions it made his head spin. "Maybe both," Carlos finally said.

"Women are confusing," the old man said with a sly chuckle. "That's why you can't focus. But looky here," he added, removing Carlos's king from the board. "Take out the king, and she's wide open." He did several knock-down moves. "With the king out of position, I could come for the rook, the other knight, the remaining bishop, and march all the way through your fortified defenses to take her down hard." He quickly reset the board. "Do it the other way, and look what happens to the king. Gone in two moves. They both need each other behind the lines."

"Interesting.' Carlos rubbed his chin.

"Ain't it just."

"But the king can't move as fast as she can, ya know? Like, he can only go in these little moves, whereas, she can go lateral, vertical, horizontal, and take out everything in her path." He stared at the ocean. "He used to be able to do that, too, but . . ."

"Different skills. One holds the line; the other does the quick, surgical strikes with motion. A queen has to move fast, cut deep, and be out. The king—"

"Has to hold the shield."

His newfound mentor nodded, his snaggle-toothed grin catching sun rays. "But, uh, I thought you was in a hurry? Ain't you supposed to be somewhere?"

"Yeah," Carlos said, standing. "Thanks for the chess lesson."

"Any time," the old player said brightly. "They didn't tell you 'bout the fourteenth piece you're missing, did they, or you wouldn't be looking so glum."

Carlos sat down again, this time very slowly.

"I didn't think so. They's monks. What do they know?"

The elderly man reached into his pants pocket and then held out his hand, producing a pocketknife for Carlos to inspect. "Lotsa things seem to be one thing, then be somethin' else. But if you looking for her, then, hey, ya needs to be strapped."

Carlos sighed wearily and declined the knife with a glance.

Seeming both amused and perturbed, the old man flipped open the short blade and stared at it. "Impatience is the curse of youth," he said, turning the dull blade to the sun. "But in the right hand, one with a mark of greatness, even this small thing might be of use." He offered it to Carlos again with a sly smile and waited until Carlos finally took it from his outstretched palm.

The moment Carlos held it, the pocketknife extended into a foot-long, golden-handled claw with a three-inch diameter.

"Jesus," Carlos said, turning the clawed weapon from side to side.

"The claw of Heru, to be mo' accurate," the elderly chess player said with a wink. "Put the other hand on the bottom and pull." He sat back and waited until Carlos followed his instructions, and he laughed deeply as Carlos's left hand extended the handle until it disconnected, leaving a thick gold chain between both halves. "Claw on one side, chain in the middle that cannot be broken, and a handle on the other side. I take it you know how to use nunchucks?"

Carlos stared at the weapon, and began to swing the dangling end in a slow circle.

The old man sighed. "You'll need practice. Guess she gonna hafta show you that, too. But, when you need it, you can kick some serious booty if ya swing that sucker right, catch a throat with the chain, bust a skull open with the end, and match fangs for fangs, claws for claws with the sharp end. Like I said, though, ya needs technique and training, but that ain't my department. Alls I know is, put the end back in and put it away until you need it—like ya needs to put your Johnson away until ya need it." He laughed hard and shook his head. "Airport security won't see it, as it comes from a very special place. Just leave it in your pants, got that?"

Carlos couldn't take his eyes off the weapon as he snapped the handle back on and it again became a small, ordinary-looking pocketknife. He put it into his pocket like the old man had told him and stared at the strange individual before him. "Thanks," he said, meaning it with his whole heart. "But I have to find her and need to know about this fourteenth gift. I need to know as much as I can to be able to do what I have to do."

Carlos leaned forward, but the old man held up his hand. "Ain't my place. That's fer her to show you."

"I'm trying to find her now," Carlos said quietly. "Please, man, for real. My head is all jacked up, a lot has gone down, so if you know—"

"See, now, I ain't ask you all of that. That's your personal business. All you had to do was say, 'I'm lost, tryin' to get back on the right path,' then my job is simply to offer directions."

Carlos closed his eyes. "Sir, I'm lost and trying to get back on the right path, honest to God, I am."

"From this point, I can go no farther," Telek said, stopping the Jeep by the side of the road. "There is war along the borders."

For a moment, she just stared at him. "Then we came all this way to turn around? Why?"

"No, we came all this way for you to go to the two Niles."

Damali glanced around. "Okaaaay. But if there's war and you can't drive me . . . a chopper or—"

Telek shook his head no. "Many problems with crossing borders in unauthorized aircrafts, not wise. Not possible. So, I leave you here."

"What!"

He leaned across Damali's lap and unlatched the door with a smile.

"No way! Out here? By myself? Brother, you know that ain't right, after all the good Samaritan stuff we talked . . . I told you thank you, right? I haven't offended you, have I? We're still cool, right? Oh, Lawd, man, don't just make a sister walk through a war zone!"

"I'm not going to make you walk," Telek said, gathering her tight fists within his palms.

Damali slumped back into her seat with sudden relief. "Bless you. For real."

He gently opened her palms and his gaze at them made her stare at the stones.

"In your left hand, granite from the ancient obelisks, covered by hallowed ground from the holy shrine of St. Mary of Zion—for spiritual strength. Quartz crystal on the right, for vision and healing . . . clarity of direction. Your feet, this path, washed clean of the past by Queen Sheba's pool." Telek's voice became soft. "It is time to fly, little bird. Take one stone in each hand and make the arc of Light around you to become the sparrow."

Again, she stared at him, mouth agape. Oh, no, he was not going to go cosmic on her, out here, without real practice, and send her flying through a war zone with rocket-propelled grenades, freakin' land mines, and whatnot. Oh *hell* no. Damali withdrew her arms and folded them over her chest. He could *not* be serious.

When Carlos opened his eyes, he landed with a thud and stood quickly, his heart pounding so hard that he could barely breathe. He immediately felt the temperature shift from fairly cool to hot and dry as he glanced around the bustling modern city that owned tree-lined streets. It took a few moments to get his bearings and sort out the traffic noise from the roaring falls that still echoed in his head.

Yet he was practically giddy when he realized where he was standing—the White Nile Bridge. *He did it!* The old chess player did it. Somebody did it, but it was all good.

New confidence filled him as he walked along the pedestrian and bikers' path gazing at the water. Just like the old days . . . well, almost. But the fact was he'd concentrated on a location, folded Light in on itself, and had actually walked through space and time without a passport, even if his first attempt was a little ragged.

Savoring the moment, he leaned on the metal guardrail and stared out at a body of water that had once ferried pharaohs. Excitement made the hairs on his arms stand up with electric charge. He had no idea the guys from the Light could pull off a stunt like this. As soon as the thought entered his mind, he self-corrected it. "No stunt, my bad. But this was awesome," he murmured to no one in particular, but to anyone that might be in spiritual earshot.

A small bird shot past him with stones in its beak, and he laughed. Everybody was always in a rush, he mused, delighting in just being alive. Just like the chess player had given him something serious to ponder, there was something that he was supposed to get or learn where both rivers met, so he looked out at the massive body of water, concentrating on their nexus as hard as he possibly could. Nothing came to him but his own inner voice, which was beginning to wrestle with worry again.

A biker whizzed by and his voice floated behind. *Shari el-Nil.* Carlos stared after the man who was long gone. He repeated the words. Was it a message, or just a greeting in the land's mother tongue? Carlos sighed, knowing there was only one way to find out.

Carlos walked a bit, sidling up to nonthreatening-looking pedestrian with the intention to try out the new words. The man seemed regular enough, like he could be somebody's pop. But with all the bizarre things that had happened, one couldn't be so sure.

The man sported a pair of worn leather sandals, a green plaid shirt, rough-hewn tan cotton pants, and a small burgundy cro- cheted cap atop his partially balding head. He had an easy gait that suggested he was in no particular hurry to go wherever he was headed. If the unintelligible phrase was a curse word shot by an overly aggressive biker, then Carlos figured he could apologize in English and plead tourist ignorance. However, if it was a greeting, and the locals were friendly, then the reply would give him two new words in his arsenal within this strange land.

Carlos reached into his pocket and quickly put on his crocheted cap. No need in being culturally incorrect to create a barrier.

"Shari el-Nil," Carlos said as pleasantly as possible to the older man once they were side by side.

The man smiled and began speaking a mile a minute in sen- tences Carlos could never begin to sort out. But the fact that the man was smiling helped a lot. Obviously it wasn't a bad word.

"Wait, wait," Carlos said, laughing. "I only know Shari el-Nil."

"Oh," the man said, shaking his head. "Foreigner. I see. You look for the neem trees to stroll the Blue Nile Corniche? This is what Shari el-Nil is—a place, like a park—or what you call a park- way, maybe."

Carlos smiled. "Yeah . . . uh . . . I guess so."

The man tilted his head, seeming amused. "A friend recom- mended this, yes?"

"Well, not exactly. I heard it and was trying to pick up the language."

The man laughed and stopped walking. "There are more than one hundred languages here. Not easy to pick up. But Arabic is official, but many know English, too, and French."

"Cool. Thanks."

The older gentleman's expression remained pleasant and curious, as though he wasn't ready to end the early morning discussion. "You are new here, so just say, *salam aleikum* to greet others, or if they say it to you, you answer, *wa aleikum as-salam*."

Carlos slapped his forehead and laughed, making the man beside him also laugh harder. "Right! How could I forget something as basic as that—as many brothers from 'round the way say it all the time. Standard!"

"You are also Muslim?" the man asked, his eyes becoming more excited. "You know to tell them in the mosque, *ma-atkallam arabi*—that you do not speak Arabic, and they will still embrace you as Allah's. No problem."

"No, I . . . I'm not—"

"You go to the neem trees and think about what you already know and can remember," he said, beginning to walk away, still grinning. "You seem like a man of many languages."

Now he had Carlos's full attention.

"Yo," Carlos said, quickening his pace to catch up with the now spry old man. "Hold up, sir. Please. Why would you say that?"

"You pick up languages so well, like you wanted to go to Shari el-Nil and you listened to the sounds and said it like you were from here." The man cocked his head to the side as confusion wrinkled his brow. "At first glance, I truly couldn't tell you were not from here until I went beyond your vocabulary. Did anyone ever tell you that was a gift?"

"No," Carlos said, truly intrigued. "I'd never thought of it that way."

The older man began walking. "If you follow me, I have to go past there. You should sit, listen to the birds, and think. Maybe there are other things you can do with your life, young man."

Carlos only nodded as he walked quietly beside this newfound friend. Interesting. He was expecting some big power jolt to come surging up from the waters, and instead, this subtle but powerful message had been delivered by an old man wearing baggy pants. This was a new perspective. Nothing like what he'd expected. The Light clearly worked with subtlety, that was for sure. *Smooth.* They literally let wisdom sneak up on you, seduce you with such silk that if you were unaware, you'd miss it.

Parallels began forming new and open channels in his mind. His old side used cold-blooded power and sheer dark force to draw in prey; this new side was all pro. The Light simply let birds fly by, an old man saunter along, then knocked your head back with an epiphany that was too profound for words.

The quiet revelation almost made Carlos laugh out loud as his kindly guide prattled on about the pharaonic stone carvings and stunning Christian frescoes to be seen within the National Museum. During the easy few-mile walk, Carlos soaked in everything the old man had to say about the great exhibits to witness and the best places to get *shai bi-laban,* sweet tea with milk, or *bi-nana,* sweet mint tea, and the stewed white beans, *fasooliyya,* or *fuul,* stewed brown beans and *tabouleh* salad.

One thing Carlos knew for sure, to learn a new culture, one had to learn how the people ate. As above, apparently, so below. There were so many things he had to remember. He just wished his old grasp of languages and knowledge would snap back—that was one thing from his old council seat that would have been a serious benefit, all other issues notwithstanding. But he made his peace with the problem. It was what it was. The Light had shown him some pretty cool new abilities; this old man was making him see parallels that he'd been blind to before. Just like the chess player had reminded him of how to be strategic, but also to take risks. Now if he could just find Damali and get back to the team, many of his immediate worries would be solved.

"Before you go to Meroe, which is a good place for you to see history," Carlos's walking partner said, "be sure to go to the Omdurman Souq." He opened his arms wide and his smile also widened. "That is our largest market, and on Fridays, except during Ramadan," he pointed out with care, "the whirling dervishes dance." He bobbed and swayed and turned around. "It is a sight, if you have ever seen one. They look like great birds and stir the dust high!" The old man danced and pointed to the neem trees above. "Like birds, just like this," he added, spinning and chuckling, and then poof, he was gone.

"Oh, shit!" Carlos jumped backward and almost fell, sending a plume of sparrows airborne. He glanced around quickly and nothing else out of the ordinary was evident. But he remained very still as he double-checked the position of the birds, given that any and everything was fair game to be something other than it appeared to be.

One by one, the birds went back to their branches, flustered and fussing their complaint as they settled down. But one edged near him with its beak filled with stones. At this point, he studied everything so closely that he bordered on righteous paranoia.

"So, I suppose you've got a message for me, since you look like the same chick carrying stones across the bridge a ways back?" Carlos said to the small brown bird, laughing. Oh, yeah, he was over the top. He watched the curious little creature with an overstuffed beak cock its head from side, to side, studying him. Now it was really time to check his sanity. He was talking to birds!

He watched it hop closer toward him, as though begging for food. He laughed and squatted down. "Greedy little thing," he said quietly, amused by its boldness. "You can't eat rocks, and I'm sorry to say that I ain't got nothing but love for ya."

The bird immediately dropped a dusty white pebble and a clear smooth one the size of a lima bean. It chirped a virulent complaint and spread its wings, like it wanted to fight. Carlos burst out laughing and stretched out his palm to see if he could coax it near. "Tough little thing, huh? A bad momma . . . okay, but I don't have—" Total fascination gripped him as it jumped into his open palm and then flitted away. "Wow . . . That was so cool."

Before he could stand up, it transformed from the feet up. The surprise knocked him on his butt and he sat on the pavement, sprawled in wonder. "Damali?"

"Yeah—and where have you been?" she said, putting one hand on her hip.

Carlos was on his feet in two seconds. "Boo! Girl! It's you!"

They both laughed as he swept her up and whirled her around. The image of the old man's dance grazed his mind and made tears come to his eyes. She was back, whole, and had shape-shifted, no less! Messages and signs had been all around him. He danced a jig with her like she was a rag doll, laughing and squeezing her harder.

"Oh, my God, D—I was so worried, so much went down. The plane crashed, we all got out, angels came, old seers hijacked me to an island—girl, I have to tell you so much stuff—"

"I know, I know," she said, laughing through the tears. "The Council of Queens kicked my butt, read me hard, sent me into the streets, I was lost—you cool—everybody good? Where is everybody anyway?"

"All right, all right," he said, kissing her face and wiping his with sweaty palms. "I'll fill you in as we walk, you tell me all that happened to you and how you did that awesome bird thing in broad daylight—there's this place up the way where we can get some kebabs and *shai bi-laban* to get a grub on before we head to Meroe. Cool?"

"Wait," she said, picking up her stones and placing them in her robe pocket while laughing. "Before you even tell me about this new jawn, Meroe—you've been in Khartoum how long, and you know the restaurants and can speak Arabic?"

He threaded his arm around her waist. "Girl, you know I've got mad survival skills. Why you gonna front on me and ask me something like that?" He kissed her temple, making her giggle and shake her head, as he gave her a sly wink. "But, uh, my pockets are a little light right through here, baby. I forgot. You got any money?"

CHAPTER EIGHTEEN

"OH, MAN, what I wouldn't give to check into the Hilton."
Rider briefly closed his eyes and rubbed his neck as the teams
stood in the long customs line within Khartoum Airport's dense
throngs of wayfarers. He glanced at Father Patrick and dropped his
voice low enough so that only his teammates could hear him.
"Can't you make peace with your people and maybe pull some
strings in high places?"

"No," the elder cleric said in a testy tone. "As soon as we go
wherever we go, I'm no longer willing to bear this crest," he said,
motioning to the knights of Templar insignia on his robe. "I am
ashamed of that history. How can I not be, now that I've stood on
honest hallowed ground and felt the pulse of truth?" He swallowed
hard and looked away, angrily, at the airport crowd. "Reading
about it is one thing, feeling it through your bones is another.
There is genocide happening here, like it has so many places on so
many continents. Almost two million people. . . . But no one with
power seems to care to intervene. Again, just like always."

"Dude, I hear you," Rider said, going to the older priest to put
a steady hand on his shoulder as the other road-weary members of
their group tensed for a potential outburst. "I was just joking about
the Hilton," Rider said, making his voice low and calm to invite
Father Patrick's to do the same. "Not here, though." Rider's eyes
met Father Patrick's and the momentary silence between them
drowned out the multinational din around them. "We'll discuss all
that later."

Father Patrick reluctantly nodded and looked away as Rider
dropped his hand from his shoulder.

"If you want to do the Hilton," Dan said very calmly, "we can
do that."

THE FORBIDDEN 269

The group looked at him.

"Talk to me," Shabazz said in a quiet tone that contained hope.

"The cash is gone, courtesy of the Ethiopian authorities, for our so-called flight expenses—even though that should have only used a third of the bankroll that was in my backpack," he said with an angry sigh. "But, hey. Road taxes, I suppose."

"It's cool, though," Big Mike offered, his huge shoulders sagging from pure exhaustion. "We're alive and not detained on some bogus formality. So, let's get back to the part about the Hilton, that oasis image I have in my mind of hot water, a bed, and some basic, regulation grub."

Dan reached into the sack and unzipped a compartment, producing an array of gold and platinum credit cards like a card dealer's fan. "Good as cash," he said with triumph in his voice. "The way I see it is, we get through customs, find an AMEX counter in the airport, or whatever, do a cash advance. From here, we call the Hilton and make a reservation and get their shuttle to pick us up. That way, we go in a marked van and don't have to take our chances on the street. Then we check in, and me and J.L. can scout for team clothes—again, using credit to conserve the cash we'll need to help grease local police palms if we get into another jam. We eat, we rest, and then we all get in the same space and try to use our seers to lock in on any locations of the missing."

"You'd better *go,* boy," Shabazz said with deep appreciation in his voice. "All right." He smiled and offered Dan his fist to pound, which Dan did with admiration in his eyes. "You just stepped up."

"No doubt," Jose murmured with respect. "That was an awesome move back there with the authorities, too."

"Smooth," Big Mike said quietly. "Professional."

Dan smiled, a rosy tinge entering his cheeks. "Thanks, guys. I've been doing a lot of thinking, ya know. Like, the fact that they saw two extra passports and recognized our girl . . . maybe our man, might be working to our advantage," he added in a conspiratorial, private tone, and speaking in quasi code while the line inched forward.

Marlene nodded and smiled. "Follow your gut, baby. Finish the thought. Just let it flow."

"The media will broadcast her possible death over a holy site—which makes sense, since she was supposed to be on a religious pilgrimage."

Berkfield stepped in closer. "Our man's mug shot is very recognizable, too. It won't be long before they make a link to him and also show him missing and assumed dead."

"That's where I was going," Dan said, struggling to keep the excitement from raising the level of his voice as he began using his hands to talk. "The compound going up will be added to the news—either wildfire or speculation about our man's past. Either way, it will explain her need to find religion, as well as any explosions from our ammo."

J.L. chuckled. "And the reason we had such tight security, all the high-tech gadgets they may find in the charred rubble is because her lover had some nefarious origins." He shook his head. "You're the man."

"We work it," Berkfield whispered, gaining nods from the group. "Cover our tracks."

"The hole in the plane will suggest that most, if not all of us, got sucked out through the pressure-seal breaks. And, if you'll notice, courtesy Father Patrick's people, those two names, his and hers, are the only actual ones on the docs." He dug in his sack again and produced the visas for each person to inspect.

Dan waited until each person had looked at their documents and tucked them away into the folds of their robes, both stunned and satisfied.

"My face isn't recognizable, nor is my name," Dan added, "not like you guys who were in the band. Mar has me on the insurance paperwork as the second businessperson in command. It's a limited liability partnership that lives on even if one of the principals—our girl—goes down. So, I can settle the estate, long distance through faxes, or do it in person as the executor once we get home. The fire may be deemed an act of God, though. Therefore we might be assed out as far as a financial recovery from the loss of our compound. They may not settle the estate, either, for like a year, until the search for her has been legally concluded . . . just so you know. Which is really best, since we don't want to get caught up in any insurance-fraud backlash when girlfriend resurfaces. But for now, I can still manage the business, or draw on what we had in the banks. We have to have resources while—"

"The entire team stays undercover," Berkfield said, finishing Dan's sentence in a whisper. He glanced at the group that held the same awed expression and then looked at Dan.

"When did you notice the names weren't right?" Father Patrick whispered, making the other clerics come into a tighter huddle. "*We* didn't do that . . . our people didn't do that."

The group drew in closer and waited, their focus steady on Dan.

"It had to happen in the air," he whispered with a shrug. "It wasn't like that when we took off in Manila. That's all I know." He glanced around and allowed his line of vision to settle on Marlene. "You know how we've all been a little off . . . like how our gifts have been rusty, not working, right?"

Marlene nodded. "Yeah, baby. Talk to me."

"Ever since Rivera and Berkfield did their thing on everybody with you . . . and we sat by that lake, I've been getting my old hunches back, thinking clearer." He looked at Rider, then Jose. "How's your snozes?"

"My sinuses are killing me," Rider said, sharing a look with Jose, who nodded.

"Yeah, my point exactly," Dan said, his eyes wide with wonder. "And Mike began complaining of a headache from all the noise in the airport, the same way J.L. and Shabazz have been jumpy."

"And the way it resonated with me when Rider mentioned the Hilton," Marlene said quietly, looking off into the distance. "Our sensory gifts are slowly coming back." She looked at the four clerics who silently nodded their agreement.

"That's why I'm with Rider," Dan said, shuffling forward with the slow-moving line. "If we get to a place where we can really rest, take a load off, eat to replenish ourselves, get some clean water, maybe what we lost will come back."

"Whew," Rider whispered, letting his breath out hard. "This is deep enough to make even me consider wearing a clerical collar."

Damali reached across the small outdoor café table and covered Carlos's hand with her own. She watched him toy with a pair of her silver earrings, pushing them around with his forefinger on the rutted surface of the wood as he spoke. He'd told her so much; they had shared so much. Their gifts were so new and there was so much to celebrate. There was also a lot to dread, and her name was Lilith. But as he told her about what happened to his mother and grandmother, suddenly her lungs couldn't hold enough air.

"Baby . . . I'm so sorry. We have to figure out a way to go back immediately, and—"

"No," he said quietly, his gaze gentle. "I have time to go bury her proper. I'm making my peace with that. It's about patience."

She stared at him, not knowing what to say.

"I saw her," he murmured. "Saw all of them. They're in a better place, and this was part of the whole equation."

Damali tilted her head, not sure what he meant. Grief was stabbing her in the belly, making her breaths shallow.

"I can see them," he whispered, leaning in closer. "Oh, I will address what happened," he added, releasing her hold on his hand and sitting back in his chair. "Trust me on that. But right now, I'm cool. Like the old dudes said—seven days to get my head right and my spirit right. Seventy days to locate all my gifts and gather an army. Seven months to get those resources strong. Yeah. Always operate from a position of strength, baby. You know that. Problem is, with this axe hanging over our heads . . . with the egg. We can't let that happen on our watch." He briefly shut his eyes. "D, I'm so sorry, baby."

She nodded. "It wasn't your fault. We both didn't think . . . Next time, if there's—you know what I'm saying—we'll plan."

"Right. I know you're right." He looked at her. "You sure you feel okay, no aftereffects?"

"No," she said softly, and reached forward to clasp his hand to squeeze it tightly. "I'm good."

"Cool," he said, and then looked down at the table.

However, as she watched him glance away, unshed tears sparkling in his eyes as the muscle in his jaw pulsed, she knew he was anything but cool about any of what had gone down. She withdrew the two stones she had in her pocket and held them in her fist above the table before him. "Granite," she said, setting the small white stone down hard to draw his attention away from his pain. "Your spirit has to be impenetrable on the side of white Light. Now I know what this means." She next placed the clear quartz crystal beside it. "Your mind must be crystal clear—laser sharp." Damali paused to allow the information to sink in. "I'm to collect five more stones for a total of seven for you, and until you're healed, I'm not completely whole, either. We're partners. If you go down, I go down, and vice versa. *Comprendo?*"

He smiled, although his expression was tense as the tears in his eyes receded and burned away. "We're both in rehab. Gotta relearn the old stuff, plus a bunch of new. I've got your back, and you've got mine—always was that way, girl."

She smiled, tension easing away from her shoulders. "Yeah," she said, covering his hands when he leaned forward. "You can bend light and conceal yourself. I can shape-shift into living natural creatures. Makes me able to hide, or get into small places to hear what I've gotta hear." She paused, struggling with the decision about whether or not to tell him about Raven, and decided not to go there. If he knew she'd try to hit council chambers, they'd be in a huge argument that they didn't need to get into right now.

"We can both travel in the Light bands, just in different ways. Just like these two stones, we just picked up two gifts," she said, covering her dilemma with a tender smile. "Your thirteenth gift and mine. A celebration is in order."

He leaned in closer. "True. That's deep." Carlos sighed. "All right. But what about weapons while we're rollin'?"

Damali lowered her voice. "They said you'd get the shield of Heru and his saber. I'd get a Light wand that would leave a deadlier cut on an enemy than the Isis blades alone. Problem is, they haven't given me my blades back, yet, and you don't have a shield, yet . . . so, we cope until then with conventional stuff, is my vote."

"I know," Carlos said in a near whisper. "But when, where? How do we get those? That's what's bugging the hell out of me."

Damali shrugged. "I don't know, baby. Somewhere or sometime during this whole collection process, I suppose." She looked off in the distance, thinking. It was all so crazy, yet made perfect sense. He was changing, she was changing, the team was changing. Everything she'd known was in total flux. Food oddly made sense, too. How the old cultures used it to nurture the soul as much as it nurtured the body, this was the first gift they offered, even when they had so very little of it to share.

"Yeah, girl. I know what you mean. Food is important, the gift of offering a meal is like—"

"Carlos," she said quietly, stopping his sentence midstream. "I didn't say that out loud."

They both stared at each other. A current ran through her as he extended his hands across the table and held hers. When she looked into his eyes, she could see his dark irises rimmed with a thin thread of silver, and then it seemed like his irises had filaments of silver breaking them up. She breathed in deeply, and tilted her head. Damn . . . he smelled good.

He took in a deep breath as he watched her expression. Her hands felt like they were on fire. He had to glance down at them to be sure his weren't. But as he looked up slowly and her stare captured his, he saw a thin golden band of shimmering light just above the surface of her skin. It was as though she was glowing in the sun, and he followed the trail along the edge of her shoulder until her eyes drank him in.

We're back, she thought, gazing at him intently.

I hear you, he thought, not blinking as he continued to look into her eyes.

It's not a vamp lock. She squeezed his hands more tightly. *It's like what I used to be able to do in impressions with Marlene, but I actually hear your voice in my head.*

Carlos nodded. *We haven't been able to do that since . . .*

Yeah. She swallowed hard, fighting against the new emotion.

"When you see spirits," she whispered, "what do you see?"

He hesitated, searching for vocabulary to describe the phenomena. "Light all around them, they actually glow with it, too. They're translucent, clearish, but not. You follow?"

She nodded. "I see in rolling visions. Snap frames of impressions, not actual beings." Damali released his hands and sat back, wiping the sudden moisture from her brow. "You see the present, I see the near future and can pick up the past. I have the third eye working; your sight is coming from your actual eyes." He sat back and stared at her. "When you first came back, your eyes glowed silver. Now I better understand."

"Girl, as always, you are blowing my mind."

She smiled and it gave way to a nervous chuckle. "That's my job, ain't it?"

"I guess it is." He smiled.

"But the people we saw. They were something real, but not. Since you can see in the present, who were they?"

"Third-ring guides. Maybe even fourth-ring Akashic file protectors. Light entities that are strong enough to push through the density of earth's gray zone, manifest, and deliver a message."

Again, she stared only at him before slowly speaking. "We've reconnected our spirits, me and you," she said with reverence. "Then our heads synced up—one mind. The whole of which can see past, present, and future . . . and you can discern beings of light from the outer first ring, like your mother's spirit, all the way to warrior angels on ring six. Oh, this is wild."

"No," he murmured, clasping her hands within his again. "What's wild is, I get the info, and then you break the code on it. I can call up stuff, can tell you what I've experienced, and you analyze it so on-point that it's scary, woman. It's like I get the knowledge, then you put the wisdom to it."

"Balance," she stated flatly. "As you remember things from your old life, I can put it into context with this new path. But you have to trust me."

"No doubt," he murmured, his voice traveling toward the horizon as his gaze slid away from hers to the sun. "I may be new at this whole Neteru thing, but I know we need weapons . . . thirteen gifts, notwithstanding, D. We've gotta get strapped."

"No lie," she said, looking toward the sun.

"They told me something about pyramids in the desert and Meroe."

She smiled. "What's in Meroe?"

"I'm not sure," he admitted, and returned his gaze to hers. "It's like a three-hour trip, we could make it there and back well before it gets dark."

"By bus for a coupla bucks, right? I know we have this new set of skills, but I don't want to test it and have you wind up one place, me in another."

"I heard that," he said, removing his hands from hers to take a sip of tea. "I thought I was gonna have a heart attack when those old boys made me grab the filament edges, and then pushed me into a Light spiral. No, girl. Lemme work my thing out first before I get all fancy and mess up."

She had to laugh. "Aw, brother. C'mon. You used to whirl in on a black tornado and—"

"That was then, this is now," he muttered, growing peevish.

"My bad," she said, trying to soothe his offended feelings. She had to remember to drop references to the past. Had to remember that he was indeed all male and his pride would always goeth before a fall. And most of all, she had to remember that when he gave her a small inkling of the fact that he was a little unsure or afraid, it was not about tap dancing on that news. "I think the new way you do it is more suave, anyway. You'll perfect it, and be showing those old boys how to roll in no time."

He glimpsed up at her while sipping his tea, beginning to lose some of the surliness in his tone. "You think so? I mean, you like the new way better? For real, D . . . don't jack with me about my transport. I've gotta get it down right, and don't need you making fun of me about learning how to fly again."

"I wouldn't play with you about something that serious," she said, her voice the balm of Gilead. "I just wish I could have been there to see it." She leaned in close enough for her breath to kiss his. "I bet you were majestic . . . threw open your arms and snapped right into the middle of the bridge and began walking— no one ever saw you reenter this dimension, did they?" She could see him struggling not to smile.

"I was all right," he said, and slurped his lukewarm tea. He wasn't about to get into how he'd crash-landed by accident on Venice Beach.

"Modesty will get you everywhere," she said with a sly wink. But when he bristled again and looked away, she fought not to sigh.

"How are you feeling, for real?" he asked, changing the subject. "You said the queens healed you . . . but—"

"They did, and those old dolls *are bad*. Trust me."

He nodded, but didn't look up at her. "I think they really did take your blade, D, because they've got you deep undercover. I'm not getting a sense that it was pure punishment."

"What makes you say that?" Now she was really curious, and his statement made her place both elbows on the table as she rested her chin on her fists to listen hard.

"The Light doesn't roll with retribution," he said plainly. "If you had your blades, number one, you wouldn't have ever learned to use the stones to convert into nature."

While what he said was profound, the fact that he was analyzing her condition like he used to made her want to reach across the table and hug him and shout. But she remained very still, soaking in the newfound moment as she watched her man defragment and begin to come back to himself.

"It's the same reason the compound burned," he said quietly so that only she could hear. "Think of it this way. If you weren't there, and none of us had your Isis on them, and nothing you'd touched was giving off Neteru energy, what came on the plane couldn't track you—or me. The thing looked me dead in the face, baby, and passed. It's vibrations they must be tracking. The prayer barriers around the compound and the clerics' safe-house cabin were strong enough to hold anything back. But my hunch is the Darkness was *allowed* to think it had a temporary victory, if not a total one."

What he'd said made perfect sense, but the fact that Raven had been able to easily find her in Philly worried the hell out of her. She could only hope that what he'd said about tracking vibrations had been right. She and Marlene had connected harder than ever before on the plane. She prayed that it was Raven tracking Marlene in her aura, but hadn't seen her because of a breach in her concealment. It was hard to look at Carlos with this on her heart. She'd never kept anything from him, really.

She spoke slowly, picking at the edge of her dish. "And the plane went down with everyone on board presumed dead and burned beyond dental records, or sucked out of the side of it over the mountains."

"Correct," he said, setting his tea down very carefully. "So, we have a window of opportunity to rebuild while the other side is in the blind, while they have false confidence." Carlos picked up her earring off the table. "But I ain't trying to press my luck. The bus is a good low-key option."

Damali smiled as she watched his mind work behind his handsome brown eyes. "We got lucky with the restaurant. This little joint accepted a pair of earrings for some grub worth a tenth of that. But now, a bus ticket may be a little bit of a stretch. Besides, I'm running out of jewelry to pawn."

He gave her a teasing scowl. "Girl, you worried about me being able to negotiate transpo? A bus ticket? Just because we're in a foreign country with no papers and no cash?" He laughed deeply when she broke down and laughed at the outrageous concept. "D, pullease. You oughta know, dead or alive, I can talk anybody into anything."

True to his word, Carlos had talked them both onto a minibus, and within an hour they were on their way, bumping along the congested, dusty roads to Al-Ahram, the pyramids. She continued to stare out the window past his chest, a sense of peace petting her to

sleep against his shoulder in the sweltering confines. Body funk
from the overpacked passenger load assaulted her senses. Yet, no
matter how rugged a journey, this was Heaven.

*Thank you, Lord, he has a heartbeat and a soul. Thank you, thank
you, Jesus, this man has come back in one piece.* Her knees ached to
bend in prayer to say thank-you that her entire family had made
it out alive, as well as to offer up her deepest hurt that his mother
and grandmother had been sacrificed in the process. That's why
she had to do this thing with Raven to settle the damned problem of being hunted, once and for all. Lilith definitely had to get
smoked, but not without the chairman's head also rolling. None
of them could live like that, always looking over their shoulders.

The warmth of Carlos's arm settled into her skin, his hand gently stroking her arm the way it always had. What the old queens
said she'd lacked in wisdom, she knew she more than made up for
in faith. Yes, she had faith in this man. Yes, she trusted him with
even her life. Yes, she wanted to have his children, the luck of the
draw be damned. But did her wanting all these things take away
from her desire to meet her destiny? Not hardly.

True, she had respect for them, but they also needed to respect
her. This was a new era. Things were the same, and yet different. A
compromise was necessary. She was glad Carlos had helped her see
past her own rage and head trip about losing her powers to understand that it was a timing thing, really a gift that they'd be-
stowed . . . one that had possibly saved all their lives. Before she'd
been bold, out there, just baiting danger. Now, just like when she
was a baby, it was time to hide and conceal herself until she was
ready to resurface again even stronger. The way he'd described it
made the stripping of her blades more tolerable, if not exciting in
an odd way. She wondered what her new arsenal would look like
when she was in full bloom.

When he nuzzled her temple, she thought of family. Yes, everything was in flux. Not necessarily chaos. She'd learned that transition could be masked as chaos, but if one became still enough, a
pattern would always emerge. It was time for everyone to shift on
the wheel as the team dynamic took on a new formation. It was all

so clear as she rode in the smelly bus. Her Guardians were there to guide her, and not to do the hard rebuilding work for either her or Carlos. They had to do it without relying solely on the skills of the group. There would be time for that, later.

The cycle of life was as it had always been—balanced. There was a time for family to protect you from harm when you were a little kid, then simply guide you as an adolescent then young adult, then release you to fly on your own when fully matured . . . but the nest would always be a beacon, just as your kin would always rise to stand with you no matter how old you became, if you were lucky . . . if you were righteous, if they were, too.

Why she'd struggled so hard against the basic rhythm of life was beyond her. As she listened to a steady heartbeat that was in sync with the harmony of the seasons, she couldn't begin to figure out why she'd taken herself and her family through all those changes while growing up. She wondered if Carlos asked himself the same question. What had been the point? Yet it was indeed what made up the wisdom of whom they all were now. Family included had learned and grown from it all, even though they'd weathered much. Nothing was a waste, but so much had been squandered. The dichotomy was as unfathomable as the very universe itself.

The old man had shown her the new rings and how they would be formed. The riddles he offered still pecked at her mind like the tiny bird she'd become . . . that transition was awesome. Now she also understood Carlos's fascination with the panther form, but knew better than to go there—*ever*. To go there would be a slap in his face. The Light also demanded a subtler approach . . . show oneself as the meek and unarmed to disguise one's true power. It was a different, but very effective strategy that she was now in the right frame of mind to employ.

Carlos listened to Damali breathe, her warm exhalations coating his skin in waves of serenity. He had a little bit of Heaven in his arms. His boy had hooked him up with mad-crazy cash that he could only pray wouldn't evaporate. He'd be patient and wait for a sign that it wouldn't before he got Damali's hopes up too high. Her compound had burned, his baby girl was stressed . . . he could feel it beneath her surface calm. A lack of resources made it hard to flow and do what they all had to do.

It was time for them all to get back on their feet and reestablish a base camp. When he got his ID, and maybe over to Europe with a full team and some basic combat gear, then he'd access the Swiss accounts. One thing was for sure; he'd learned patience and how to wait for the right moment. The old men promised that he'd find weapons and new skills; he had to be patient and have faith that what he needed would come. He would try to be patient. Had to keep telling himself to do that.

Ironically, the most tangible power he knew about, cash, his boy on the dark side had provided. The dilemma was tricky. The only thing keeping him sane was the fact that he'd seen his family in the Light.

Carlos closed his eyes, remembering how serene they all looked, how complete. He knew the instant they'd appeared that it had been quick, their transition softened by the purpose of their sacrifice. He would not let their deaths be in vain.

Grace had been granted, though. Damali was whole, her breaths of life a steady rhythm that matched his pulse. The heat within the minibus fused her to him, and the old girls on the Council of Neteru Queens had healed her body . . . her mind and spirit were also intact. Their common loss, the baby, was probably for the best . . . momentary peace had him enthralled. Oh, yeah. He'd find Lilith all right and take her head. He'd deal with the chairman, too, no doubt. But torture and high drama had taught him to pace himself. Right now, Damali was back in his arms. The lumbering motion of the minibus began rocking him to sleep.

It had been so long since sunlight had warmed his face, since his woman had been next to him—normalcy within all the insanity they'd experienced—that he wasn't immediately ready to pick up arms or go chase down a mission. Revenge could wait a little while, so could everything else. They needed time to be still, time to assess not just the damage, but also the process of repair. Time had been a robber baron until now.

He opened his lids and looked at her with sleep-bleary eyes. They were actually *both* Neterus. Deep. He would have never imagined that twist of fate. His hand traced her shoulder, feeling the delicacy of her bone structure but knowing it was made of what could pass for flexible steel. The old wise men had told him he had that, too. Just like she was impervious to a demon bite, his blood carried liquid silver that would torch a predator on contact. Everything she had, he had, and they were still learning what that meant. What was in Meroe, though?

Carlos and Damali came out of their semisleep doze as their bus rumbled and sputtered to a jolting stop.

"When you get out," the driver said, using a static ridden intercom, "you walk seven hundred meters in that direction to get a close look at the pyramids." He flung open the doors, stretching the curly intercom cord. "I have water for sale, you need plenty of that, if you have not brought it. This site thrived from 592 BC until the Abyssinians overran it in 350 AD. It does not have pyramids the scale of the pyramids of Giza, but what it lacks in size, it makes up for in number and breathtaking location."

The bus driver hopped down the steps and began helping passengers off the minibus. Carlos and Damali shared a glance.

"Do the math," he murmured as she stood.

"592 BC . . . five, plus nine equals fourteen, plus two is sixteen, reduces to seven." She looked at Carlos as he stood.

"And they are seven hundred meters away."

Damali held Carlos's hand and squeezed it as they made their way off the bus. "Eight years to make it the year one, plus 350 years, is 358. Three plus five is eight, plus eight."

"Sixteen," Carlos said in a low murmur. "One plus six is your third seven."

"And the old men said watch for triple sevens because you needed to come into your own quickly," she said in an awed tone. "Okay. Look alive. It's on."

They squinted in the bright sun as the small group of passengers organized backpacks, camera equipment, and began to trudge across the dramatic backdrop of desert toward the sprawling flat pyramids that dotted the living canvas.

Carlos allowed a short, private distance to separate him and

Damali from the others as he slowed their pace. He waited until a group of waiting tourists filled the minibuses that consistently drove up, shed passengers, and collected new ones for the return trip.

"Talk to me," he said quietly, his gaze raking the horizon. "What's your vibe on this?"

Damali stood still, sweeping the landscape using internal radar. "Your shield is here," she said after a moment, and began walking.

He had to lengthen his strides to catch up to her. "What's it look like?"

She shook her head. "I'm not sure. All I'm feeling is that it's just like the blades are now. It's not actual, it's pure energy."

He didn't fully comprehend, but wasn't about to argue with the amazing woman who was pacing along at almost a trot. As he got closer to the pyramids he stopped as a current sent a shudder through him. Damali turned and looked at him and then brushed down the raised edges of his hair that crackled around his crocheted skullcap.

"Your hair is standing on end," she whispered, seeming delighted. "You feel it?"

He nodded. "Hell yeah, I feel it. What is it?"

"A power surge." She glanced around as they neared the base of an ancient structure, careful to keep their voices to a private low murmur between them. "Concentrate. Logic it out. Have you ever been here, or remember anything like this?"

"The desert," he said quietly, and suddenly leaned against her to keep from falling. The surge wafted through him in waves that stole his breath.

"He just needs some water," she said to a few nearby tourists who'd offered glances of concern. "You okay, baby?"

Carlos shook his head no and sat down hard on the sand.

"I have a bottle," a lady said, struggling with her backpack to get out a liter of water. "You kids came out here without even a camera?"

"We were just so excited to get here," Damali said. "We forgot."

"Oh, the haste of youth," the woman said, clucking her tongue like a mother hen. She thrust the water toward Carlos, and Damali accepted it for him, sensing for any danger of malice before she allowed Carlos to have it. Damali smiled as she quickly appraised the older European female who bore a slightly British accent. She seemed nice enough. Looked to be about fifty. Had on khakis and a floral print shirt that aged her and added to her robust midsection. The assessment took five seconds.

"Thanks so much," Damali said. "We didn't know better and thought the bus driver was just trying to milk us."

The kindly tourist chuckled and shook her head. "When on holiday, it is best to bring all your own supplies. It is amazing how the price of things goes up on the spot when you're unprepared. They sense it, like sharks, and hike the prices—and if you're stuck, what will you do but pay?"

Damali twisted off the bottled water cap, and thrust the container toward Carlos, trying to keep any panic from her expression. "You are so right." She watched Carlos guzzle the water and douse his neck with some of it splashing the ground. "Thanks, really," Damali said. "Out here in the desert, water is like gold."

"Yes, it is," the woman said calmly. "Enjoy. Cheerio." Then she hoisted up her backpack, rearranged the camera over her neck, and walked away toward the others.

Carlos looked up at Damali from where he was seated in the sand. "That was one of 'em."

"What?" Damali squatted down beside him. "You okay?"

"That was one of 'em," he wheezed, nodding to the woman who was now several yards away. "You heard what she said about being prepared, just like the bus driver said that what this place lacks in size, is made up for in volume—sheer numbers. Look around."

Damali did as he'd requested, but remained stooped down beside him.

"Messages. Battle strategy," Carlos said. "That's what we came here for. But I remember this place. When I got jettisoned from the big battle after the concert, they sent me to the desert."

"But that was in Mexico," Damali said, sitting down beside Carlos with care. "You didn't come up here."

"I know, I know," he said, suddenly agitated. "That's not what I mean."

"Maybe the sun is—"

"I'm not disoriented," he snapped. "I'm not as fast on the vibe thing as you, yet, but I know when I'm near something—tracking it."

"Okay. I'm sorry," she said quietly, touching his shoulder. "The desert, there's a connection."

He nodded and shut his eyes. "I was left to die in the desert. I was found in the desert by the clerics. This desert has flat pyramids. So do the deserts in my homeland. You said the shield is here. The two people who spoke to us said to essentially be prepared."

Damali began doodling in the sand with her finger, trying to think as Carlos talked, swirling the wet patches of sand left from his dousing around in little balls. "All right. We got three sevens—that message is clear that we're in the right place. You are obviously magnetized to it—your hair, the energy zap. Cool. The strategy tips all make reasonable sense. We are smaller than whatever we have to deal with, so we have to add to the team. We need more pyramids. Twenty-one, to be exact. In my mind, that's just validation of what we heard before. But why did I say the shield was here? It just popped into my mind."

"That lady was one of 'em, D. One of the Light guides, she wasn't just sweating."

"Huh?"

"I knew them, sorta when I saw them before. Like . . ." Carlos struggled for words as he began doodling in the sand with Damali. "Like I'd know who was safe to talk to or not. Now, I'm starting to see the silver outline in their sweat."

Damali looked up and stopped doodling. "You mean you actually see auras?"

"I don't know what you call it, but regular people have different colors around them, the info guides seem to have this silvery light that looks like perspiration to the average eye."

She chuckled. "Oh, that is too deep."

"I know," he said, pushing his palms against the damp sand to stand. "I can't figure this out," he added as Damali jumped to her feet. "Why did we have to come all the way out here, waste precious daylight, to remind me that I got saved in the desert the first big battle I fought? See, I can dig having to learn lessons, but some shit just isn't practical. Basic information shouldn't require all this drama. We could have saved time, girl, and hunted for our teams. You feel me?"

He was talking with his hands and she stared at his palms, then grabbed his wrists hard. "Look at your palms!" she whispered sharply.

Carlos stared down as the wet grains of sand sparkled with the iridescent shimmer of gold dust. "Oh . . . shit . . ."

"That guide agreed that water out here was like gold, and then walked away." Damali glanced around nervously, checking that no one was watching. "The shield is your hands, Carlos. Raise your shield," she ordered, placing her hands out in front of her in a martial-arts move Shabazz had taught her. Then she spread them to go into an Aikido stance. "Mirror me."

He did it without hesitation and they both watched in awe as a shimmering, translucent band of golden light emerged between his palms, blocking his body. Damali picked up a clump of rocky earth.

"Hold the energy, baby. Pyramids at your back, me, an attacker at your front. Imagine the team flanking you like the pyramids and behind raised battle shields."

He nodded and bent his knees more to withstand the blow she was about to levy against his sheer barrier. She hurled the clump of rock at him, and the dirt burned away, never penetrating it.

"Hot damn!" Carlos held the stance but looked from one hand to the next, laughing out loud. "Aw sheeit!" He stood up straight and kept clapping and opening his hands, making the Light band between them widen and contract like an accordion. "Will you look at this, D! This is da bomb."

She chuckled as she watched him play, jumping into fierce warrior poses, and beckoning her to continue to throw sand at him.

But she also kept a lookout for the milling tourists who were scouring the historic site. Paranoia throttled her enthusiasm. That's all they needed now was to be seen and rushed by gawkers, or to create some sort of scene. She was thankful that the folks on the bus were old enough to not know who she was, and glad that she wasn't on their top ten music list of recognizable celebs. It was all she could do to keep part of her focus on Carlos, the other on the oblivious tourists that were far away and engrossed enough to be temporarily a nonissue.

However, the more Carlos laughed the more she was forced to laugh with him. He was like a little kid that had found a new toy and witnessing his new discovery brought her unimagined joy.

"All right, soldier," she finally said, bringing an end to his play. "Chill before one of the tourists sees you and our cover is blown."

"Aw'ight, all right," he said, winded and laughing. "Just do it one more time, then we'll find a bus and be out."

Damali sighed, but gave in. How could she not go along with him when he was so happy? The discovery had given her comfort, too, and she was secretly reveling in his newfound gift. She clawed the earth, gathering more dirt under her nails, and groaned. "You are seriously messing up a sistah's manicure. You know that, right?"

He laughed. "Hit me with your best shot, girl. I can hang. When we get back, I'll negotiate us a room at the freakin' Hilton, if you want, and you can soak the dirt out."

"Oh, now you're lying, boy," she said, laughing as she flung sand at him. "You're good, but the Hilton? Pullease. We ain't even got bus money, last I checked."

They both watched the dirt singe away, just as it had before. But when a pebble broke through Carlos's barrier, they stared at each other. The game was summarily over.

"I'm sorry," she said, truly meaning it. "The gift is just new. Maybe you just have to get stronger, is all?"

"Yeah," he muttered, wiping his hands against his robe with disgust. "I was just fooling myself, I suppose. It'll take a long time before my shields can hold against a bullet or a grenade, or a flat-out

vamp squadron attack, if some itty-bitty little pebble got through. I
didn't have enough energy to block your miniattack for three minutes . . . how can I hold the line with shields raised if we fall under
an all-night attack? This is bullshit."

"Yeah, but, you still have to admit that it's a beginning. What
was all that yang you were telling me about being patient? C'mon,
Carlos, what we just saw was very, very cool."

"Cool, but useless." He bent and picked up the troublesome stone
and sighed, about to pitch it when Damali's shriek stopped him.

"Don't!" She rushed toward him and snatched his arm, peering
down at the small pebble in his hand.

He stared down at it with her, mesmerized by the smooth-jewel
green-and-black vein texture that shimmered in his palm like glass.

"Malachite," she whispered. "It carries the properties of peace,
wisdom, transformation, protection, general healing, cleansing, balance . . . don't you know what this is? It's the third stone in my arsenal," she said, answering her own question. "Brother, stop
tripping. I can always get through your shields unharmed, so can
anything from the Light."

"Wow . . ." he said, still staring at what he held as she pushed at
it with her finger. "I didn't—"

"All right. I'ma hafta do you like Marlene did me. First off, stop
cussing. Words have power. Secondly, stop being so negative and
impatient and blocking your own danged gifts with an I-can't
mentality. From this point forward, there is no such word as can't.
Her grandmother told her that, now I'm telling you—stop believ-
ing what you've heard, or what you think is impossible."

He smiled at her as she snatched the stone from his hand and put
it in her pocket. "I love you, but I can't promise I'll stop cussing
overnight, girl."

"Yeah, I love you, too—but you seriously get on my nerves
sometimes." She laughed and gave him a wink. "I cussed out a *major* queen and called her a bitch—that's when they hauled my ass to
the table, so I'll let an occasional bad word slide."

"Nooo!" He doubled over and hollered. "Aw, daaaamn, D!"

They both laughed hard.

"Wanna ride the bus back to town, or try something new?"

Damali stared at him. "The bus will be fine. You used a lot of energy, brother, and need to chill."

"I thought you said you were open and down for whatever, and that there was no such word as can't."

"I'm also a practical kinda girl," she said, chuckling and walking away from him. "If you can scam us into the Hilton, that would be enough for me."

He smiled and cocked his head to the side. "No problem. Remember where the bridge was?" He waited for her to nod and enjoyed her peevish expression. "There's one right down Sharia el-Nil, by the Blue Nile Riverside Restaurant we ate at. I don't have to scam our way into a hotel, though. You have money."

"Two teeny earrings left is not enough to . . ."

Carlos shook his head and motioned to her hair wrap with his chin. "Take it off."

Damali brought her fingers up to the fabric and gently felt at it blindly. "I forgot . . ."

"Gold. Resources at your disposal but not used. Hidden gifts. You've got enough stashed up there to order a limo and rent out the penthouse."

"How did you know?" she stammered, carefully sitting down to unwrap her hair over her robes. She covered her mouth to keep from shrieking as gold coins and foreign currency littered her lap in a pelting rain.

"I could see it right through the wrap now." Carlos smiled.

She glanced up at him, her gaze locked to the flicker of silver within his irises. "Your eyes . . ."

Carlos shrugged. "Wanna test out my daylight flight pattern, or you still scared, Miss No Such Word As Can't? Let's get out of the desert and into the Hilton."

CHAPTER NINETEEN

DAMALI LEANED into Carlos's embrace, her back against his stomach, his outstretched arms covering hers, his palms slowly covering her knuckles until their fingers threaded together. His body heat became a coating of energy that sent a tingling electric sensation through her, making her feel light, porous, and breathless with anticipation. Soon he released her hands to gather an invisible filament just beyond her fingertips. A thin light blue current arced for a brief glimpse, showing her the edge of the curtain he'd closed with her folded within his arms.

But there was no rushing wind, no force against nature, rather a gentle fusing with it. The bottom didn't drop out of her stomach, as though on a wild roller-coaster ride, nor did she feel the instant panic spike of adrenaline or the centrifugal force of being jettisoned against gravity. She could tell she was airborne, but also inside a brilliant bubble that was tranquil, soundless, warm, and soothing. This was so different than the transport she'd experienced with him before. When he opened the drape around them, time had stopped for a half second, and she was in the Hilton Hotel lobby.

For a moment, neither she nor Carlos moved. In that fraction of time-space differential, people seemed frozen, and then simply picked up whatever activity they'd been engaged in without even missing a beat.

"You stopped time, girl," Carlos murmured in her ear, stepping beside her as she caught her breath.

"What do you mean? I didn't do that," she whispered. "Your transport—"

"Nope. When I do that I just merge into the flow. This time when I did it, time hitched. Did you notice?"

He threaded his arm around her waist as she looked around the lobby, trying to seem like she was just a patron who had waltzed in the front door.

"I saw the hitch, but can't explain it." She glanced up at him. "Maybe it's the stones?"

"You told me to work with my gifts; I'm telling you to work with yours," he said, now standing beside her. "A fraction of a second in battle can mean the difference in dodging a bullet, or worse. Work it, baby. You're the one that moves nature's energy. My thing is a little different. I don't think what we just saw came from me."

She nodded as they surveyed the lobby, and then she froze, motioning with her chin toward the doors, drawing his focus there. "They made it."

He squeezed her hand as his arm fell away from her waist. "Go over to them easy, they'll freak and we need this reunion to go down smooth until we get somewhere private."

"I know," she said quietly, as they began to casually walk toward the group. "Try to send to Father Patrick, I'll send to Marlene. If the seers aren't startled, then the group will be on guard to be cool."

Carlos closed his eyes briefly, following Damali's lead, and then they both began walking forward. Marlene looked up first, and Father Patrick jerked his head up from his suitcase quickly. The seers touched Shabazz and Imam Asula. Word rippled around the group in a quick, private flash. Casual smiles were exchanged. Shabazz walked away from the team and embraced Damali with a quick hug, and then pounded Carlos's fist. He nodded like he'd simply been expecting to meet up with them on another flight. It all went down as smooth as silk.

Dan was at the registration desk in minutes and came back with the keys to three suites. Eager bellmen were paid, bags all centralized to the main suite, while Rider kept watch out of the peephole to be sure the bellman was gone before the chaos broke out.

That's when the celebration began in earnest. Whoops and cheers and laughter and tears and everyone began talking at once.

Finally, Rider flopped down on the sofa and closed his eyes, wiping away the stream of tears running from the corners of his eyes. "So close to a bed, but so far," he said, laughing. "I thought I was gonna get a good night's sleep and here you kids come crashing into the lobby."

"You're a sight for sore eyes, I'ma tell ya—for real, girl," Big Mike said, laughing and hugging Damali up and off her feet. "You ain't too bad to look at, either," he added, dropping Damali and hugging Carlos so hard that he was two inches off the ground.

"Yo, man," Carlos said, laughing, unable to get Mike to release his bear hug. "You have no idea."

Marlene held Damali around the neck so tightly that she had to pry herself away just to breathe. "Oh, chile, Lawd, chile . . . my chile . . . oh, girl . . ." Marlene said through sobs. She held Damali away, petted her face, and then began bawling so hard that she made Damali cry.

The love siege didn't end until everyone had had their turn passing Damali and Carlos between them; even cool Monk Lin wept and laughed.

The missing were thrust onto the adjacent sofa, and furniture was moved out of its place as chairs and coffee tables were made into seating and the youngest Guardians in the room sat on the floor.

"Begin at the beginning," Marlene said, wiping her face. "We must tell the story. Oral tradition holds. Let it be said." She looked toward the clerics. "Please open this with a prayer, and when we're all done, seal it with the same . . . let the circle be unbroken."

And they did. Each told of their recent history and what they'd learned and seen. Awe, sadness, hope, joy, and fear filled all eyes and each expression, and their gifts were multiplied by the sharing of love. They all sat mesmerized by what they'd each endured, many times becoming overwhelmed by the emotions each storyteller conveyed. They were all repeatedly moved to tears as each member of the group testified about their last thoughts, how they felt about the others, their concerns for the safety of those people whom they'd willingly die for and how they were so worried about those that were left behind.

They all sat spellbound as Damali began her saga—no one interjecting, let alone barely breathing—as she told of her meeting with
the queens. But she kept the more intimate details of the embryo
and Lilith to herself, glad that Carlos caught her drift and let it be.
Revealing that it was level seven and the chairman was enough at
this point. They needed to get weapons and get onto hallowed
ground at home before getting into all of that. It was a conversation she needed to have one-on-one with Marlene, where she
could let down her guard and just weep.

So she put on her best face for the team, like any general would.
The troops needed courage, inspiration, hope. They didn't need to
know that they were sitting on a live explosive, were surrounded,
and had few options. Not now. If they could believe, they could
beat this thing. If they lost hope before they started the battle,
they'd be doomed. Ethiopia had shown her, just like each wacky
guide had, that it was possible to slay Goliath, no matter how small
and outmatched.

As Damali dissected the science, Marlene scribbled wildly on a
small pad she'd extracted from her bag. And as Damali went further to describe her passage to Ethiopia, Marlene diagrammed the
new circle of protection that the grandfather had instructed and
inspected the stones Damali had received.

But when Carlos began explaining about the ancestral spirits
that had cushioned the crash, it was all the team could do to pull
themselves together to hear the rest of his tale. Clerics broke down
upon hearing their loved ones described in acute detail. Guardians
wailed at the memory of dear parents and grandparents who'd
come to collect them.

"The boy can see angels," Father Patrick said in a thick, mucous-
laden brogue, pointing at Carlos. "I always had my faith in that one,
him. I knew he'd come around and I'm so glad that I have lived
long enough to see it."

"My momma, she's okay, right? Nana and Pops?" Big Mike
asked, and then began sobbing all over again. "That was her favorite dress . . . the yellow one. That was her, man. I hope I did her
proud."

"You mean my father came for me?" Rider asked, his voice a hoarse whisper before he stood, walked over to the wall, and broke down. "If he went to Heaven and could care . . . there's hope."

Carlos covered his face and breathed into his hands to steady his voice as he wiped his face. He couldn't even look at Jose who was sobbing with his head in Marlene's lap while Shabazz sat with his hands over his face rocking and saying his mother's name. Clerics hugged. Dan, J.L., and Berkfield held each other in a father-with-sons triad. Damali ran from person to person, rubbing their backs and kissing damp faces, holding the Light for each person as they purged years of anguish in a total group meltdown.

"That's what I'm trying to tell you, for real," Carlos said, his voice faltering as he put distance between himself and the tears. "Ain't nobody up there still mad about anything. All is forgiven. They love you, came to help, know what mistakes they've made and what you did, too . . . but it's cool, now that they've crossed over." He stood and walked to the window to get some sunshine and to mentally breathe. "I didn't understand it, never did until I saw it. They're in a better place; only want you to be safe and happy. That's it. That's all they want."

He turned and looked at the wide-eyed, stricken family before him. Then he took his time to explain about the warriors he'd seen, the old men, and the island . . . the whirling old man, Damali becoming a sparrow, and their trip to and from the pyramids.

Marlene laughed through the sniffles and went to fetch tissues for everyone. "Keep your eye on the sparrow," she said, trying not to set off a new round of tears in the group. "They always send the most obtuse sign that is really very simple, indeed."

"Yep. I'm learning, Mar," Carlos admitted, glad that the purge was coming to a close. It had left him spent and the group ragged, but in his soul he could feel that it was all necessary and all good.

"You know what we should do?" Big Mike said, wiping his face and then reclining on the floor. He closed his eyes and folded his hands over his chest.

"You okay, Mike?" Carlos asked, coming to his brother and swatting down. "It's gonna be all right, man."

"I know," Big Mike said thickly. "That's why we should all just take a deep breath, let the past go, and order some food."

For a moment no one said a word, and then laughter erupted.

"I want me some chicken wings and ribs and anything they've got American on the menu. Order up a case of brew to go with it, and let's celebrate that we made it this far by grace." Mike sat up, smiled, and pushed himself off the floor. "Y'all down?" he asked, not waiting for an answer as he walked toward the phone and pushed the room-service button.

Increased laughter was the response as one by one folks made it to the bathroom, splashed water on their faces, blew their noses, and took deep breaths.

"Whew, man . . . I didn't know all that was in there," Shabazz said, coming from the bathroom with a wet face and a towel.

Carlos nodded. "Went there a time or two myself during all this, my brother."

Both men hugged and let each other go, but stood close.

"I know you have, man," Shabazz said, his tone gentle. "It's all good."

"Yeah," Carlos restated. "It's all good."

The late-afternoon sun poured orange and gold rays through the window by the time the feast was over. Chicken and rib bones and all manner of fare littered the tables, the pungent scents mingling with fatigue. But no one seemed ready to venture away from the huddle of humanity in the room. Instead they each showered between stories and laughter, taking their individual suitcase into the bathroom to change and get the road dirt off them, only to return to the main room and sprawl out on the floor.

"Looks like those other suites are gonna go to waste," Marlene said, sipping a beer as she gave Dan a gentle glance.

"Reminds me of old times at home," Carlos said in a distant tone and then chuckled as he picked up his beer. "We didn't have no space in Momma's old house, but everybody came there, hung out, and crashed there. Might be twenty of us up in there on any given day . . . those were some good times."

"To old times," Damali said, raising her bottle toward Carlos. "I remember being in that house with them, too. God bless your momma's and grandmother's souls. May they rest in peace."

Everyone lifted their beer and held a moment of silence as Damali went to Carlos and hugged him, quietly conveying her condolences. There were no words that could take away the loss, only this gathering . . . a wake in abstentia, love of surrounding family, and the warmth of human touch.

Carlos stroked her loose hair, swallowed hard, and sipped his beer. Her gift was a living one—family. There were no words or enough thanks to offer her for that. So instead he rubbed her back and led her to sit quietly beside him. That was all he needed right now.

"I think we should all just plan on staying together tonight," Father Patrick said, gaining nods from the others. "There's comfort in that. Thanks, Dan, for your fast thinking, though."

"Yeah, I'm just glad homeboy had the foresight to double back and suggest we get clothes and luggage in the airport so we didn't raise suspicions when we checked in," Rider said, downing his brew and grabbing another one. He glanced at Carlos. "The kid has been on-point since you left." He nodded toward Berkfield. "Medic ain't half bad, either. Everybody is coming into their own, ya know."

Carlos smiled. "Yo, Berkfield. You're in now. You know that, right? Once Rider dubs you with a nickname, that's a sign."

Berkfield raised his beer. "I'm with you, dragging a wife and kids, too."

Dan smiled. "Good. Then I don't have to be 'the kid' anymore." He gave Rider a wide grin. "I'll need a new nickname."

"I'm working on it," Rider said, rubbing his chin. "Maybe Maestro, because of the way you orchestrated that paperwork and conducted that mess in front of the authorities, I think that's deserving. Whatduya say, brothers?"

"Maestro," Shabazz said as he and Big Mike clinked beer bottles. They laughed when Dan blushed and punched the former kid in his arm.

"Done," Jose and J.L. said in unison.

"Looks like you just stepped up," Damali said, chuckling. "Boy, a lot *did* happen while we were gone." She yawned and stretched and flopped back on the rug beside Carlos. A sense of contentment eased its way into her bones. With her belly full, the effects of the beer kicking in, as long as she had her peeps around her talking and laughing, she could finally sleep.

Peace was like a tranquilizer, and soon the voices felt far away in the room as she dozed on the floor like a lazy cat in the afternoon sun. True, she and her family were not on hallowed ground, but she reasoned that they had had church, nonetheless, and were in hallowed company. She remembered that wherever two or more were gathered in His name, there also was the Father. She could feel a ring of protection around them as they healed and recovered and fellowshipped around her. She wondered if Carlos could see smiling ancestors joining in the party. And in her semi-sleep state, she also prayed for Carlos's healing and comfort, and she asked for angels to lift up the pain of losing his mother and grandmother just as he'd so gifted the group with his new sight of their loved ones.

For the first time in longer than she could remember, there was no anger, no fear, no guilt, no tension. This new elixir of serenity was like a nature-sent drug that allowed her to slip away into that floating place of calm, her family's voices a warm blanket over her as she slept.

A soft female voice roused her, but didn't wake her. She felt so sluggish that she could barely even stand in her dream.

"I brought news," the voice whispered. "Hurry."

Damali forced herself to stand and stagger to a dark corner in her mind. Raven stepped out of the shadows.

"Yonnie told me the way." Raven glanced around nervously. "But the problem is getting worse. If you're going to do this, you have to hurry. You have to make it back alive, too, to fulfill your bargain with me."

Damali nodded. "My intention. Tell me."

Raven shook her head no. "I have to show you. It's not like a street map. You have to follow dark-energy currents. I can take you down as far as the Amanthra level, but from there, you're on your own."

"What's below that?" Damali stared at her trying to sense a setup.

"Were-demon realms."

Damali laughed. "Oh, great."

"They're brutal. Don't get trapped down there. Be you male or female."

"Like the Amanthras are a picnic." Damali let out her breath hard and raked her hair.

"But if you get past the weres," Raven said, her gaze darting around like a frightened doe, "you can land in the hallway just outside chambers. Their couriers are weak and sluggish, however still dangerous. The bats are almost grounded, but those that still have energy will rush you. The passage to the door is a narrow crag, molten lava on either side to worry about. But the doors are impenetrable. You have to take a fang bite to identify your black blood to open them. If you blast your way in, you'll fall into the Sea of Perpetual Agony." Raven began to pace. "The chairman may be old, but he's not to be fucked with, Damali. He's strong, agile, and his international men—"

"I know," Damali said quickly, cutting her off. "I've seen them."

"If you take your Isis blades down there, Hell legions will swarm you. They'll smell it as you descend. Without a master to bring you there . . . and regular weapons won't work. You can't beat him in hand-to-hand combat, no matter who you are. This is suicide, then you'll be trapped down there forever like me." Tears formed in Raven's eyes. "I've told you all I know. Now, it's your turn to do what you promised."

"I said I would, and I will. But let's be honest, it's not like we used to be girls and have that type of trust between us. I'm going down there, and when I get back, you and I will settle our business."

"How?" Raven demanded in a sharp whisper, her hands going to her hips.

"Let me worry about that," Damali said. "I smoked Nuit down there, didn't I?"

"With a lot of help," Raven argued.

"You want to do this, or not?"

Raven hesitated. "You really did bring him to the other side, didn't you?"

Damali hesitated. "How come you're the only one that found us? We're masked to everyone else."

The two women stared at each other.

"Because I still love my mother," Raven whispered. "And she loves you. That tracer is never lost."

Damali nodded warily.

"I have to go," Raven said quickly, looking over her shoulder. "If you want this info, I need to mind-lock with you."

"You must be crazy," Damali said with a slow sneer. "Stop playing."

Raven's eyes narrowed. "I don't know of any other way. This is all we know."

The conundrum stood between them like a brick wall. Damali stepped forward.

"How about if I dredge you—just bring it to the surface?"

Raven let her breath out hard. "You sure you wanna see the pain I have in me? It's right under my skin." She looked away and swallowed hard. "Go ahead. Maybe then you won't hate me so much."

Warily, Damali moved toward Raven. She reached out her hand and allowed it to first rest on Raven's shoulder, amazed that on the astral plane her form was so solid. By increments, she gathered up the nerve to touch her temple. But she couldn't have prepared herself for what she saw.

Years of heartbreak flooded into her in a hard jolt. Fallon Nuit's abuse, tears for a mother that couldn't save her, turning to rage. Wailing, so much wailing that it made Damali's ears ring. She panted as the visceral images swept through her mind, and she finally got to the path to council's doors.

She snatched back her hand quickly, as though it had been burned and tried to shake the horrible images out of her mind. But as her blurred focus returned to Raven's haunted eyes, she could feel tears continue to rise and spill down her cheeks.

Raven's expression was serene. "Thank you," she whispered. "If only for a few moments, someone actually went down there with me and cared. I don't know how long the buffer will last, but if the Light is anything like that, please don't deny me."

Before Damali could stop her, Raven hugged her and began to sob. Damali didn't know what to do, the whole thing was too surreal. All she could do was pet Raven's back. Then just as suddenly, Raven pulled away and glanced around like she was being hunted, and became vapor.

"Your touch is healing," Raven's voice echoed. "No wonder they all craved it so."

Then she was gone.

The next thing Damali knew, she was standing over her own body, watching it lie prone on the hotel floor. She had an energy map carved into her mind, but a mission carved into her conscience. She owed Raven, big time, and felt for her beyond words. But more than anything she knew that she could never allow a child of hers and Carlos's to be trapped in that abyss. It was a wonder that Marlene hadn't gone mad.

She eased herself down to lie beside herself. Within her mind's eye, she saw the three stones; the last one acquired was the malachite for healing and balance and transformation, among other good things. It had lived up to its properties, and she saw all three stones on the coffee table in a small triangle formation that glowed violet and beckoned her to look within it. In her new dream her spirit left the floor, stood as ether above it and wafted over to the purple light. She peered down at the lit surface and saw a city. Then she felt a snap and was suddenly awake.

Slightly dazed, Damali stood on shaky legs and searched within the lavender-hued robe she now wore, courtesy of Marlene's faith that she would return. She found the three stones and roused Marlene with a gentle shake.

"Mar," she whispered, so not to wake the others, "I just had a dream that may be a vision. I want to check it out with you advising on what you see, too."

Marlene nodded and yawned, and quietly left Shabazz's side.

They walked to the tables by the telephone, cleared off a space, and held hands.

"Lay the stones, child," Marlene said, wiping sleep from her eyes. "You can do this yourself, now." She smiled, patted Damali's cheek, and stood aside.

Damali held the stones in her right hand and allowed pure thoughts to clear away any possible debris left over from Raven's visit. She mentally called down the white Light to guide her hands and to provide clarity about the pending message that she might receive. Then she carefully placed the stones in the triangle as she'd seen them laid in her vision and peered into the center of them until a slight violet glow connected the invisible lines between them and swallowed the center.

"Look into it and stay in the Light."

Damali did as Marlene coached and took her time, focusing on the wavering emission. They were supposed to be picking up a weapons supply in Algiers, and she definitely needed that now. "I know we were supposed to go to Algiers, but something has changed. The date, October thirty-first, and seven years comes up. It's more of a feeling, a sense, than specifics."

Marlene nodded and smiled. "Their war of independence began on October thirty-first, 1954—seven years and millions slaughtered. I know my history of the motherland, baby," she said with a wry smile, answering Damali's unspoken question.

"Okay," Damali said, smiling as she stared into Marlene's wise eyes. "But I was shown that country when the flags lit, and we were supposed to go to Algiers . . . there's all this desert, too."

Marlene chuckled. "Eighty-five percent of the country is desert, so no wonder. But Algiers is off-limits to foreign travelers, so I knew when we heard that as a destination, something would change. Therefore, now you have to put on your detective hat and look for the submeaning within the vision . . . this is the part that takes the skill—analysis. Ask yourself, child, where is the link?"

Damali smiled and offered Marlene a slight bow. "Oh, wise teacher, this is why I asked you to advise."

Both women chuckled as they moved back to the stones and peered down.

"It's like a castle, a huge palace, but it's not hallowed ground . . . not a mosque, like I'd thought we'd be going to."

"Listen quietly as you look. What are the mother tongues? What do you hear?"

Damali stared in silence for a moment. "Some I don't know." She jerked her head up. "Some Spanish?"

Marlene nodded. "There's an Islamic link from the motherland to Spain, by way of the Moors who came from North Africa across the Strait of Gibraltar, and ruled there for almost a thousand years. The last palace standing was the Alhambra, in the southern area."

"But . . . I don't get it?"

Marlene smiled wider and touched Damali's face. Her fingertips created a tingling sensation against Damali's cheek as her wise eyes remained gentle.

"Baby," she whispered, "we are preparing a second Neteru." Her hand fell away. "The queens told you that. . . . You didn't spill all the beans to the group."

They shared a knowing smile and Damali clasped Marlene's hand.

"I couldn't," Damali whispered. "Not in front of the other men in the family. They didn't need to know how destroyed Carlos had been by all of this. His dignity . . ."

Marlene nodded. "Now you are wise." She held Damali's gaze within her own. "The Moors were mighty warriors and known for their swordsmanship. They carried the best-minted blades made of Damascus steel. Before he can wield a blade as well as you can, he has to go to where it was done best—and that wasn't in the courts of England, contrary to popular belief." She sighed and folded her arms over her chest. "He's gotta pick up that energy where the old brothers rode Arabian stallions, a thousand hooves thundering the ground going into battles with fearless abandon." She winked. "Girl, don't you know that's why the queens temporarily stripped you of your blade, among the other reasons they cited?"

Damali tilted her head and questioned Marlene with her eyes.

"At that time you hadn't acquired the wisdom to let him think he was the general until he could be comfortable enough with you by his side as an equal. Call it diplomacy or détente, but the old girls know that despite women's lib, ain't nothing changed under the sun. They can't have their Neteru squad fighting and arguing, and whatnot."

Marlene wagged a finger at Damali and Damali covered her mouth with both hands to keep from laughing out loud.

"You are *better* at wielding a blade, know Aikido, and he hasn't apexed yet. Right now, you would rock his world in a one-on-one sparring match, and before you make him lose confidence, boyfriend's mojo needs to be strong . . . especially if you ever want to find his obelisk one day. I don't know *what* he's gonna do when he has to practice mirroring your fighter's stances—might get his head lopped off when you swing. Poor baby's third eye hasn't even opened all the way yet."

Damali turned away from Marlene and waved her hand for her to stop teasing. Her shoulders shook with repressed laughter as Marlene poked her in the ribs with one finger. They glanced at Carlos, who was sprawled out on the floor snoring with the other men. But as Damali stared at him, she sobered, although she couldn't allow Marlene to see the abrupt change.

How was he gonna react when she did this chambers job alone? He wasn't ready, even though it had been his old yard. That was the thing that was gonna rub his nose in it, but she didn't know any other way. *She had to get the egg back.* The old queens had said to let nothing stand in her way, not even a man. But her man was a part of the equation, the other half, and it was his child as much as it was hers. He knew the realms, but damn if she was gonna drag him back down there when he'd so recently escaped. Damali let out a sigh.

"Listen, baby, girls mature faster than boys," Marlene said with a wise chuckle. "We had that talk about the birds and the bees a while ago."

Damali forced a smile. Her connection with Marlene had changed. She couldn't openly read her. The awareness made her pulse race with new worry. She was actually going solo, for real. The cosmic apron string had been cut!

Damali swatted Marlene's arm playfully, feigning as though she had a sudden case of giddiness. She turned away as tears stung her eyes. She remembered doing that to Inez, just playing it off, laughing to keep from crying. Marlene was the last person on earth she thought she'd do that to, but it was out of love. There was no way in the world she could drape all this on Marlene without wounding her for life, and making her worry herself into apoplexy. She glimpsed Carlos. Her man had just lost his mother and grandmother and escaped a torture wall, only to be burned alive by the sun. Hell no. She had to keep this on the down low, and simply suck it up.

"Mar, it can't be that bad," Damali said, keeping her voice light. "He was able to transport. I love him, but when it's time to handle our business, I can't walk around him like his ego is glass."

Marlene just shook her head and sighed with a wide smile.

By her hinting statement, she'd tried to let Marlene know that there was something she had to do without him, and it might not be pretty. It was convoluted, though. A message within a message. Damali pressed her case, hoping that maybe one day Marlene and Carlos would understand. Rationalizing that they had kept big secrets from her in the past didn't help, nor did it make the burden feel any lighter. "If that's all the vision was about and this side trip is just. . . . Look, we have to move out an army, and—"

"Damali, be nice," Marlene warned with a smile. She arched her eyebrow and placed one finger over Damali's lips. "He needs to go get some of that *mano-y-mano* vibe from the old Islamic power centers to bolster his confidence. That's also where the fusion of cultures takes place—old world Spain, one of his root origins, plus the motherland influence . . . he's Latino, girl, by way of the motherland, and then Spain, then the conquests in Mexico. So we've gotta do the circuit with him, just like we did it with you, to allow him to come into his own. He's almost there and ain't there yet, plus he has a steep learning curve with a *baaaad* sister for a partner, and Hell bearing down on us. He's gotta get ready fast, so extreme measures had to be taken. Plus, you've both been through a lot. He just lost his mom and grandmom, and has to fight in what looks like the beginning of the Armageddon."

Marlene sucked her teeth and glanced at Shabazz. "He won't admit it, any more than the rest of them. To put it bluntly, they're all bugging out, and until you came back, the brothers were wringing their hands. Even the male clerics freaked."

Damali stood wide-eyed again, covering her mouth to contain the gasp.

"Yeah, girl," Marlene murmured. "Be gentle. Men don't have our intestinal fortitude, and that ain't changed since Eve, either. Got it?"

Damali hugged Marlene, kissed her cheek, and gathered up her stones. Marlene had told her all she needed to know. Carlos wasn't ready.

"All right. I hear you. We do Spain as soon as the team gets a good night's sleep." She sighed and put the stones back in her pocket, the whole time just shaking her head—not at him, but at herself, and over Marlene missing her point. "You don't have to say another mumblin' word."

CHAPTER TWENTY

A SEARING pain stabbed into Carlos's chest. His eyes opened wide and he yelled out as the sharp projectile tore away cartilage and bone and then lodged into the soft organ beneath it. He gasped for air in vain and scrabbled at the unseen object that had split his breastbone and pierced his heart while he was lying flat on his back in his sleep. The team was on their feet, Damali and Marlene on their knees beside him, while his body convulsed, a cold sweat covered him, and total chaos broke out in the room.

He could taste his own blood in his mouth as commands were shouted all around him. Then just as suddenly as the horrible attack had begun, the pain snapped away from his body. Carlos was on his feet in seconds, clutching his chest. When the team rushed toward him he clapped his hands, opened them wide, and surrounded himself with an impenetrable barrier of Light.

Big Mike hit the shield first and dropped as though he'd run into a brick wall.

"Back off!" Carlos shouted, his chest heaving as it took a moment to orient himself.

"It's us, man," Shabazz yelled, helping Big Mike up.

Slowly Carlos brought his hands together and made the shield recede. His body flashed hot then cold and shivers made his teeth chatter as he tried to speak through pants. "She staked me," he croaked. "Put it right through my chest!"

"Who?" Damali yelled. "Was it a flashback, or—"

"I dunno," Carlos gasped. "I couldn't see the face."

"It'll be all right," Damali said, "Go over what you saw slowly. You're a seer. It coulda been a flashback, baby, or a vision. We just have to make sure it doesn't happen. You cool?"

Carlos nodded and rubbed his chest.

Berkfield looked around the room. "After what he's been through, it mighta been a PTSD flashback. I used to get 'em after 'Nam."

Big Mike nodded as he got up from the floor slowly and went to Carlos. "Man, been there. We gotchure back." He extended his hand and waited for Carlos to accept the handshake. "You feel anything messing with you, you call Big Mike. You my boy, healed me, helped the team." Mike glanced around as all heads nodded. "Until you feel comfortable, I'll sleep with one eye open and guard you while you rest. Then when you get up, I'll go off shift. Cool?"

"Yeah, man. Thanks. But that won't be necessary," Carlos said, straightening his back. "I'm cool."

Everybody looked at each other. Damali ran her palms down her face. Her man was anything but cool. It was settled. She was going to Hell alone to squash this bullshit once and for all.

Marlene glanced at Father Patrick. "Psychic attack?"

"Or premonition, like Damali said," the priest said, studying Carlos as he approached him slowly.

"Whatever it was, we're out. Party's over, gentlemen," Damali said, snatching Dan's backpack and tossing it to him. "We're on the next flight to Spain."

Carlos shook his head and took in several huge gulps of air. "Hold up." Carlos glanced around at the shaken team. "I ain't feeling Spain. One stop, London, to get us a flight to the States. Period. I'm going home." He raked his fingers through his hair. "Whatever this bullshit was, one of my squad just bought it."

Damali and Marlene glanced at each other.

"You're still linked to Tara and the guy you elevated like that?" Rider said, moving in front of Carlos and holding him by both arms.

"Yeah," Carlos said, looking at Rider without blinking. "One of mine just went down. Problem is, I don't know which one."

Rider dropped his hands away from Carlos's biceps and walked away, picking up his overnight bag without a word and facing the door. "It's about a fifteen-hour flight to London. What difference does it make if it's day or night when we fly? This went down in broad daylight. Other problem is, and not trying to mess around here, is this—the way you woke up and freaked out, man, if you had a weapon in your hand, you coulda taken out one of the team." He looked at Damali and then his gaze went back to Carlos. "I've almost done it myself a few times. This shit ain't nothin' to jack with, and I'm not saying you'd do it intentionally, but you've been battle-freaked, and need to get with that for your own and everyone else's safety."

Damali watched Carlos's line of vision seek the window for shelter, knowing that Rider was right. She could feel her man's pride peeling away, and his confidence ebbing by the second. Nothing had prepared her for this turn of events. How did one deal with a partner who was so shook that he couldn't delineate a dream from an attack, a premonition from postbattle jitters? Whatever staked him might as well have put it in her chest, too.

"Okay," Damali said, trying to bring back calm so they could develop a logical plan. "Think about it. For just two minutes."

Rider turned around slowly and dropped his bag and folded his arms. Damali went to Carlos and touched the center of his chest, trying to sense for the origin of the attack.

"Marlene and I were just talking about Spain." Damali walked away from Carlos and he followed her to the coffee table as the group gathered around. Carefully removing the stones from her pocket, she laid them out the same way as she had just done for Marlene. "Before you were jolted awake, what were you dreaming about? What did you see?"

Carlos drew an unsteady breath. "I was in a sword fight. Couldn't see who I was fighting."

"Where were you?"

Carlos stared at Damali for a moment. "I was in a castle."

"Describe it." Her line of vision went to Marlene, then to the stones on the table, before returning to Carlos.

"It wasn't like the one in Australia," Carlos said slowly. "It was massive, spread out on gardens and grounds. High arches in stone with marble pedestals, Spanish tiles everywhere in the ceilings . . . red, everywhere . . . clay . . . the ocean." He looked up. "It felt like a mosque, but I heard Hebrew and Español with the Arabic. It doesn't make sense."

"The red castle," Imam Asula said, diverting everyone's attention. "The Alhambra, in Al-Andalus, old Moorish Spain. He is hearing the peoples of the old books—Christians, Jews, and Muslims—all had strongholds within the old empire, and until they were invaded, lived peaceably side by side. It is another nexus zone."

Marlene and Damali nodded.

"If he's already accessed it, he doesn't need to go there now," Imam Asula said. He glanced at Father Patrick, who nodded.

"I thought he had to go there, physically, to strengthen himself," Marlene said as her gaze slid toward the window in deep thought. "That was apparently just metaphor. It was the energy of the history he needed, and that transcends time and spatial relationships. I stand corrected."

Team members shared confused glances as they assembled around the coffee table to peer at the stones.

"But what about all the flags I saw lit on the parkway?" Damali said, stopping to stare down at the stones. "He has to go to thirteen countries to get—"

"No. Not necessarily," Father Patrick said quickly, interrupting her as his focus went to Marlene. "His male Neteru learning curve is ramping up so quickly that it's erratic and hard to follow. It could have meant that he has to amalgamate the histories and teachings of those sites . . . or gather the energies from there or its battle strategies." The elder cleric ran his fingers through his hair in frustration. "Son, I wish I knew . . . had we more time to bring you into the fold in the seven sequence, I would be sure." He looked up at Carlos with an apology in his eyes. "That's just it. I'm not."

"Father Pat, you've done a lot for me. My case ain't standard, so, hey. It ain't on you." Carlos looked at his mentor with respect. "If I had been where I was supposed to be, I would have had the time." He looked away, shaking his head. "I burned over a year going dark. That was when I was supposed to be marshalling forces, learning my shit, getting trained, so now I'm playing catch-up.

Guess this is what happens when you take a left turn—you miss out, and gotta do it the hard way."

No one spoke, but no one disagreed. Eyes just sought a neutral point within the room.

Carlos went to where Damali was standing and peered down at her stones. "Get back to the Alhambra for a minute," he said, addressing Imam without looking at him. "When was it invaded?"

"North Africans crossed over to the Spanish peninsula in the year 711 AD," Imam Asula said, "and that Moor Empire reigned until 1492."

"Do the math on 1492," Damali said, staring at Carlos. "One plus four is five. Five and nine is fourteen, plus two is sixteen, reduces to seven. We're still working with sevens."

"The year the currently strongest nation was supposedly discovered," Father Patrick said. He looked at his clerical colleagues. "I so wish our rabbi brother was here, because the team is unbalanced. We have to have the Hebrew element. Something is missing. Our Covenant team is lopsided. According to the divination given to Damali, each one of us is to stand at a cardinal point in the formation. The Christian, Muslim, and Buddhist elements are with us, but our Jewish brother . . ." Father Patrick ran his finger through his thicket of white hair again and began to pace.

"How did it fall?" Damali said, her voice so quiet and far away that Father Patrick stopped pacing.

Imam Asula looked up. "The king's wife betrayed him. She wanted to set her son on the throne and she entered into a secret pact with Isabella of Spain. With Spanish gunships in the harbor, and cavalry invading by land from the north, the Alhambra was taken. But Isabella had secrets and was trying to double-cross her husband, Ferdinand, the king of Spain. They took the Alhambra, exiled the Moorish queen, and the bounty from the castle actually funded Columbus's voyage to the new world . . . her lover."

"Damn," Jose whispered. "And they said Rome was treacherous."

"It's female," Carlos said, walking to the window. "It was female energy that put the stake in the center of my chest." He turned and stared at the silent team that looked at him, waiting for him to elaborate. "I was battling her forces, and she kicked my ass. That's all I know."

Damali and Carlos shared a knowing glance. Yeah, it was female. Yeah, this thing was trying to betray a very bad husband with an empire-building lover in his midst, and then put her own heir on the dark empire's throne. It would happen near a large body of water, she knew it like she knew her name. That's why water kept coming up in the equation. There had to be something this entity needed near water, or the charge being near water created, *something*. Water was the essence of life and carried an electrical charge. Females were made mostly of the element; dark or not, it was the basis of their DNA. And it was gonna go down in what was, then, the New World—the States. The East Coast. Philly.

"Spain is out," Damali finally said to the numb team, grabbing up the stones that seemed to have gone dead. "Where to?"

"Heathrow," Father Patrick said. "London. The only other location in the world that has a Masonic Lodge like the one you visited in Philadelphia. The Rosetta Stone is also in London, at the British Museum, which unlocked much of the code of old languages—"

"I don't give a rat's ass about any of this crap until one thing gets straight," Berkfield yelled. "My wife and kids are somewhere in the Vatican, last I was told." He paced from the door to the sofa, his face becoming beet red as fury roiled within his voice. Berkfield stopped pacing and stared at the teams. "My wife and children. First. We could chase around the globe for twenty years and hit every so-called hot spot in history. So what?"

Berkfield opened his arms, imploring the stunned group when no one spoke. "Take every country Damali listed. Each has a history of invasions and conquests, with monastic outposts, refugees. Dichotomies abound. Whatever. Gorgeous, scenic landscapes where horrors have occurred centuries prior, or even in this current day and age. Don't you all get it? That's the point!" He looked at Carlos and Damali hard and dropped his arms. "You two kids suck it up. Once you step foot on London's soil, draw in whatever energy crap you have to. Siphon it all and be done with it. We're running out of time, and Rider's woman might have just been smoked." Berkfield looked at Father Patrick, his gaze determined. "You call your people over there, and have my damned wife and children under heavy guard and waiting for me when I touch down. I've had enough."

There was nothing to say during the long commercial flight to London. Even the pending darkness of night hadn't made the team so much as murmur conjecture. Civilians were on board with the team and at extreme risk because of that. No one wanted to open a potential horrific can of worms with babies sleeping and families going on vacation and business junkets. This had to go down smooth.

Night came and went in a slow-dissolving consciousness. Damali's hand remained clasped firmly within Carlos's. Their shared vision was the only communication between them.

It went by the forefront of her mind in a blur. The green oasis of Hyde Park chased the dark grandeur of Victoria Station. The imperial stood beside the plebian. Winding streets cast gray and dank transitioned to the solemnity of the Houses of Parliament. Bookstores on Charring Cross Road bumped into images of Bond Street fashions. The bubonic plague left corpses in the streets and high-domed golden ceilings within St. Paul's Cathedral ushered spirits in an upward spiral. The Tower of London loomed over the Thames River with the gothic structure of the Tower Bridge eerily stretching the expanse before the river spilled into the sea. Men in red jackets with straight carriages and high black mutton-plumed hats guarded the royal palace, while beggars begged for alms in a Dickens-like world of filth beyond it. Bankers in bowler hats toting umbrellas passed punk spiked-hair rebels. Celtic and Gregorian chants made her ears ring. The gray pelt of rain made her bring one hand up to shield her shut eyes.

"The one thing I remember from my old nights," Carlos murmured. "Don't try to take it in all at once, so fast, or you'll hurt yourself."

Damali opened her eyes. He smiled. She smiled.

"You talking about the vision?"

He chuckled and nodded. "Once you've sat on a throne, you never forget an information slam." He raised an eyebrow. "Why? Were you talking about something else?"

Damali shook her head no and swallowed a further comment on the subject that couldn't be broached. "Berkfield was right, though. We're running out of time."

Carlos nodded. "Yeah, but I'm not trying to concentrate on that at forty thousand feet in the air. Been there, done that, and came down hard. No picnic, baby, trust me. You got off the plane in a much cooler way."

So she left it alone and rode with him, immersed in her own thoughts and terror.

He could feel the plane shift and begin to descend. Carlos closed his eyes more tightly, bracing, praying, promising to kiss the ground if he ever got the chance. Images slammed into his mind the way he knew it was possible to slam into the runway. Monasteries, nunneries, winding secret passageways, rolling green hills, fetal remains, and baby skeletons littered the caverns. He opened his eyes and squeezed Damali's hand, making her turn to him.

"I know why we were supposed to go to the other countries on the list," he whispered, touching her face.

"Why?" Her eyes searched his, trying to connect with whatever he'd seen.

"You don't need to see it, only I did. That's why the route was changed." He sighed and petted her hand within his. "Even the churches have secrets, bad ones. Pregnancies aborted in olden times. Babies smothered. Hidden away. Sites of holocausts as one nation overtook another in endless feudal wars. Like my old empire. I was supposed to see it, know it, and incorporate the memory so I wouldn't go there again, wouldn't seek revenge that would leave innocent bodies in the street. It's all there, strong northern invasions, cannibalizing their own . . . Hungary, Austria, Poland, Germany, Belgium, the Netherlands, and France . . . everywhere we were supposed to go. Italy and Spain, we know that history, and bypassed it. Berkfield was right. It's time to go home, gather our forces, and take a stand."

"All right," she said, stroking his cheek. "I just want to make sure you have everything you need to fight. I can't lose you again."

He kissed her forehead. "I'm not going anywhere."

She smiled, wishing he'd brushed her mouth. "You told me that before."

He brushed her mouth. "And I keep coming back, don't I?"

She chuckled and kissed him more deeply. "You're like a cat with nine lives."

"I've been a cat . . . a rather large black one," he murmured, filling his hand with her hair. "Missed you."

She smiled and snuggled against him. "You wait until we're almost about to touch down and go into battle to start some mess?"

He laughed and kissed the top of her head. "Yeah. My timing is always bad." He stroked her arm. "But . . . you're feeling okay? The queens . . . uh . . ."

"Yeah. But . . ."

"I know. Later."

She nodded and sighed and closed her eyes, claiming a small sliver of momentary peace. They were back, or at least coming back. The image of him as a huge black panther flitted across the insides of her shut lids, making her smile. But something terrible happened, making her face contort and his body tense.

"Did you see it?" she whispered harshly, jerking her body away from his as she faced him.

"Shit, yeah . . ." he murmured, dazed and stricken.

"What the hell was it?"

"Hey, D, I'm not trying to *ever* go there," he whispered harshly. "Get that out of your mind."

She looked at him, locking his gaze to hers. "Together. We do this. Stare it down and make it give up info. It knows you. The thing went from male to female."

"Not up here circling Heathrow. Uh uh."

Now," she ordered, still staring at him. "Before we lose it."

Carlos sighed and reluctantly held both her hands, leaning forward so that their foreheads touched. "You're crazy."

"*This* is crazy," she whispered, as the image joined in both their minds.

A large panther paced back and forth within a semicircle of grayish-blue-white stones in the moonlight. Dark jewel-green mountains and rocky gravel surrounded the eerie structure. Wisps of grass leaned from the attention of the wind. Black static charges emitted from tall standing stone to stone as though the creature was penned in by an electric fence.

Its massive shoulder muscles knitted in a complex coil of moving sinew beneath its blue-black velvet coat. The creature stopped and stared at Carlos. Upon seeming to recognize him, its face transformed into that of a white spotted owl, its head massive for the bird. Wings tore through its shoulders, and its front paws became the long scaly legs of an owl, leaving the creature's body half panther, half owl, like some sort of wretched Griffin.

It screeched and the wind stopped blowing. Its oversized yellow eyes blinked curiously. "She's pretty," it said, glancing at Damali. "No witch, though. Pity."

"Who are you?" Carlos asked in his mind, drawing Damali closer in a protective hold.

"No worries from me. The question is, who is she?" The creature flapped its wings and reared back on its panther haunches. "Not her. The other one. Ask the witch among you. She'll know."

"There is no witch among us," Carlos said carefully.

The thing laughed. "Your friend formed a pact. Gabrielle sent us the message. That is the only reason we will speak to you from the Celtic Stonehenge. The Brits used to burn us for less. No wonder she hides like a true Druid."

The creature turned to leave and Damali found her voice. "No, wait. Who is Gabrielle?"

"Ask the master," the thing snapped. "Or the one with one blue eye and one green." It let out a terrible screech. "She is in the white Light, has denied her heritage of the coven. But her ability remains in her blood . . . as it remains with us all."

Just as suddenly as it came, the vision evaporated. Carlos and Damali stared at each other.

"Yonnie made a pack with a coven?" Carlos sat back, too astonished to say more.

"Yeah, but, if she said to ask him, then he wasn't the one who took the stake in his chest this morning," Damali said, glancing at Rider who was staring out the window. "This is really jacked up, if there's any truth to it. I'm hoping the witch was lying."

Carlos shook his head. "They lie, that's for sure. But not when marshalling alliances. She was imparting major info. She gave up a name and also said the thing that's after us is female."

"All right. But we knew that. What we really need to know is what she looks like," Damali said, not satisfied. "But who in our group has one green eye and one blue eye? Nobody we roll with fits that description."

Airport security was a nightmare. Had they been normal travelers, the inspections and layers of bureaucracy may have provided her some comfort. But after the unceasing ordeals they'd been through, and the vision while touching down, it made her feel like she was about to leap out of her skin.

The entire team was so jumpy and nervous that it set her teeth on edge. It was as though someone or something was running fingernails down the chalkboard of her spine. When they were finally able to enter the large open waiting area, Damali scanned the airport like a sniper.

Berkfield's body tensed and then he dropped his bags and began running forward. The rest of the team didn't move. Damali watched him embrace a short blond woman flanked by two priests. A teenage girl who could double for a short Britney Spears was crying and hugging his back, a lanky teenage boy with sandy brown hair wept and hugged him, too. All Damali wanted to know was the color of the woman's eyes.

"Yeah," Carlos said, walking toward the family reunion. "Father Pat, talk to me real cool as we meet the Berkfields. What's Stonehenge?"

The cleric held Carlos's arm. "What did you say?"

The group moved with caution when Carlos stopped.

"I asked you about a place I just saw." Carlos motioned to Berkfield with his chin. "Those your boys from the Vatican?"

Father Patrick nodded at the clerics who stood beside the Berkfield family as though they were Secret Service. "Yes. They check out."

"We move as one," Damali said in a low tone, keeping her voice private. "Fall into the pattern when we get close." She eyed the team. "Covenant brothers, you're on cardinal points. If it gets messy in here, we do what we've gotta do."

Carlos nodded. "You got their tickets to the States?"

"I asked for that. They will have them," Father Patrick said. "I also asked to be replaced." He stared at Carlos. "I told you I could no longer wear the crest of the Templars. You need a rabbi to stand the point."

"We'll address that later," Carlos said, his voice dropping to a firm but tender whisper. "Man, don't pull out on us now. Your faith is strong; it's the institutions you're having a problem with. Like Damali said, we move as one."

The elderly cleric reluctantly nodded, and led the group forward. When they'd reached Berkfield, his wife was in his arms, weeping. The team casually surrounded the group as though forming a welcoming ring. Berkfield's children looked up first. The clerics beside them stepped aside and offered Father Patrick a handshake like soldiers changing shifts.

"All the papers are in order, Father," one stoic clergyman said in a thick Irish brogue.

"The Covenant is disappointed by your request, and has not decided upon it yet," the other said, his Italian accent crisp and filled with concern.

"Your team is valiant," the first cleric said as he placed a hard grip on Father Patrick's shoulder. "Be well, old friend. Your fight is not over until the battle is won."

They turned and walked away, their huge shoulders held back and heads held high, never flinching as their muscular frames cut a swath through the crowded airport. If it were not for their clerical black robes and white collars, they could have passed for Marines.

"I don't care, I don't care," Berkfield's wife repeatedly whispered against his chest. "We're not leaving you or getting separated again." She looked up at him, ignoring the others. "We were so worried, Richard. We love you and thought you'd been killed."

Berkfield pressed her tear-streaked face to his shoulder and shushed her as he stroked her hair. "Honey, I'm all right," he said as tears coursed down his face. "I'm just glad you and the kids made it out in time."

The young girl glanced up and then turned in a circle to gape at each member of the team. "Dad . . . they're with you, right? They came to help?"

Berkfield nodded as his daughter went to him and replaced her mother within the embrace. "That there is my good buddy, Carlos," he said, and squeezed Marjorie's hand when she blanched.

His son walked up to Carlos. "My name's Rob. My sister is Kristin. Saw your picture in the papers," he added, and withdrew his hand. His eyes held hot contempt, and although he was several inches shorter than Carlos, the youth bristled and puffed up his chest. "Are you the reason my mom is crying and my sister is freaked out?"

Carlos watched the kid ball up his fist just as Berkfield landed a hand on his shoulder.

"Stand down, Bobby," Berkfield warned. "He's on our side, always has been, and he saved my life. *Capisce?*"

Carlos watched confusion soften the kid's deadly gaze. "Don't believe everything you read in the papers." He offered Berkfield a lopsided smile. "The kid's got spunk, man. A chip off the old block."

The teen slowly smiled and relaxed. But the group was still tensely watching Damali as she stared at Marjorie.

"You ever notice that you have one blue eye and one green one?" Damali said bluntly, as she stepped back from her.

Marjorie's face flushed as Berkfield stepped between his wife and Damali.

"What's your problem?" Berkfield said. "You walk up to my traumatized wife in the middle of a foreign airport, not even say hello and—"

"Because we don't have time, like you just told us to get our asses on a fifteen-plus-hour flight," Damali snapped. "School her quick, as well as the kids. Make the friggin' formal introductions over a cup of coffee." Damali looked at the airport monitors. "Three hours till we're in the air again headed for the States, and by the time we touch down, they'll need to know what time it is."

"I don't care what you say, I am not a witch," Marjorie whispered, her eyes nearly catatonic as she stared beyond her tea, past her husband, at the moving crowd.

"Honey, listen—"

"No, you listen, Richard," Marjorie said so evenly and so quietly that Carlos backed up in his chair. "I do not believe in witches or warlocks, vampires, or were-wolves, the boogie man or ghosts. I believe in the Mafia. I know drug dealers and bad people exist. *That* I will listen to. But this *Twilight Zone* episode you all are trying to draw me into—no." She sipped her tea like her formal reality still existed and the debate were about regional politics at a Sunday-afternoon brunch. "No," she said, smiling. "No," she repeated in a lighter, airy voice that had the sound of a woman coming unglued.

"Honey, it's a lot to take all at—"

Marjorie slapped Berkfield's face so hard and fast that his head jerked back and his paper cup of coffee toppled over. "Don't say this to me ever again. Tell me the truth!"

"That's why I backed up," Carlos said. "Knew *that* was coming."

"Mom, don't," Kristin wailed, holding her mother's arm. "Stop it. Please. Daddy's not lying."

Marjorie looked at her daughter, hot tears of anguish rising again in her eyes as she narrowed her gaze on her husband. "Look at what you've done," she said in a low, hissing whisper. "My children are delusional—they want you to be right so badly that . . . oh, my God, Richard. What have you done to our family?"

"Aunt Gabrielle is a witch," Kristin said, making her mother's attention jerk toward her. "She's been trying to recruit me for years."

"Aw, man, Krissy," her brother moaned. "I told you to never tell Mom that crap. Look at her, she's already freaked out—why'd ya—"

"What?" Marjorie said, snatching her daughter's arm.

"Your aunt Gabby asked you to do what?" Berkfield said, standing as he continued to wipe the coffee off his pants leg. "That bitch, I'll kill her, I always hated your mother's family. When did she do that? Huh? Answer me!"

"Since I was thirteen and got my period, she's been trying to recruit me to come study with her in Boston and then move to L.A."

Carlos caught Berkfield under the elbow. "Sit down, man. Your own uncle gave away the key, so give your wife a break. She obviously didn't know. The name and link is all that's important now. One more puzzle piece just fell into place."

All four clerics shook their heads, their expressions filled with compassion as they looked at Marjorie and Richard. He slowly sat, and Damali sighed and threw her locks over her shoulder.

Shabazz wiped his palms down his face. "Family secrets," he muttered in a weary tone. "Gets you every time."

Marjorie's son shrugged when she opened her mouth, closed it, and looked toward him for support that was not forthcoming. In a slow motion she released her daughter's arm. Her bottom lip trembled. Her face began to draw together in tight lines.

"Hold on to her, man," Shabazz warned. "She's cracking. First-time reality is just setting in."

"Lady, don't scream," Rider said. "Mar, you got a Valium in that black bag of yours?"

"Girlfriend has to get her head together," Marlene snapped. "Period. I don't carry western pharmaceuticals, just herbs."

Berkfield pulled Marjorie into a hard, fast embrace and stroked her hair. "Not here, not now, honey. It's dangerous if you melt down on us. Think of the children."

"My children," she wailed. "Oh, God in Heaven . . . my children!"

"Mrs. B, you've gotta chill," Damali said, her nerves shredded beyond tender patience. "Right now, people aren't staring because it looks like family coming together for a funeral with all these clerics around. But if you don't keep your voice down—"

"Marj, please." Berkfield looked at his teenagers and continued to rock his wife. "They're strong, they'll be all right. As long as we stick together. Okay? Honey, you understand? We'll figure out how to homeschool them, will work it all out, sweetie. Okay?"

Marjorie pushed him away and stared at him and then allowed her gaze to rake the group. "No. It's not okay. None of this is *okay*. I want my house, *our* home back, and *our lives* the way they were." Her gaze went to Father Patrick and futilely sought it for help. "You're supposed to be a man of the cloth! Say a prayer, take us home, and make this nightmare go away."

"Were it in my power to do so, I would," he said quietly. "You have no idea how much I wish I could do that."

"So, we're gonna all live with you?' Robert said, gazing at Rider with admiration. "I mean, you guys are *the Warriors of Light*, dude. You play the axe like a—"

"Get this kid away from me," Rider snarled, pointing toward Dan. He stood up and began walking toward the counter to buy more coffee, muttering. "You take him under your wing and find out his specialty. I'm not training another newbie, ya hear? Home-school my ass."

Dan slung an arm over Robert's dejected shoulders. "He'll ease up. He did me like that, too. But he's cool. Just a little rough around the edges."

J.L. smiled and gave Kristin a sideline glance. "You're good on computers, your dad said."

"Yeah, and she's *seventeen,*" Berkfield muttered. "Her father's also a cop."

Jose shook his head. "*Hombre,* have you lost your mind?"

"She's gifted," J.L. said, opening his arms. "Her dad said he was scared she'd hack into the White House one day, if he didn't watch her. Man, what's your problem? I'm the only one who can teach her to bust a file like a pro. Shit."

"I didn't sign up for all of this," Carlos said, leaving the table. "Damn, this is sloppy."

"Young bucks," Big Mike said, shaking his head and studying his brew. "Y'all make me tired."

Shabazz stood up. "Anybody want any more coffee?"

"Yeah," Marlene said, standing with effort. "Three newbies in one fell swoop? I'm getting too old for this."

CHAPTER TWENTY-ONE

HER HEAD felt like it was about to explode. While it all made sense, the situation was still ludicrous. Just like the old grandfather in Ethiopia had foretold, the inner ring was being built quickly, only two missing human elements were still a big question. It was clear what J.L.'s dilemma was going to be—not getting shot by Kristin's father. Damali almost groaned. Intrasquad drama. "Oh, Marlene, Marlene, it does come back on you," she whispered to herself. Marlene nodded without even opening her eyes.

What were the two parts; who was missing still? She briefly opened her eyes and glanced around at the team that was scattered about the wide-body plane cabin. Big Mike was definitely the tree trunk, and a cleric was going to have his heart broken, but stay true to his vows? She glanced at Father Patrick who was deep in prayer. The old man was definitely on the edge of his faith. His heart was broken by disillusionment, no doubt. But what additional member of the team was going to come in to break it? Plus, how did this coven led by Gabrielle fit in? It was all so insane that Damali wanted to shriek.

During the entire plane ride, Berkfield continually petted his weeping wife, whispering God-knows-what to her until she either fell asleep or passed out from sheer mental exhaustion. His kids were amazingly cool, though, Damali had to admit. Kristin was funny, definitely had some Ju Ju in her DNA, and was as rebellious as she remembered once being. Her poor older brother was just dumbstruck—but not as scary as Dan had been. He seemed to be enjoying the whole adventure of life on the run, not going to school, and rolling with eclectic celebrities. Damali sighed sadly. The poor kid would learn better one day, or more likely one night.

The most important issue now was how to keep them all safe

while they trained, and while she no longer had a blade or even a compound. The prospect of having a teammate's children to care for gave her hives. It would be bad enough if one of the Guardians went down, but if Berkfield's kids . . . She shuddered and banished the thought.

She glanced at Robert who was engrossed in Dan's whispering monologue, then over to Kristin who'd taken a seat next to J.L., her face alight with awe.

"Oh, Jesus . . ." Damali slung an arm across her eyes.

"It's all very cool, now," Carlos muttered. "Wait till they all see their first pair of fangs. The young boy will piss his pants, guaranteed."

"I know. That's why the others have just given up and gone back to sleep, because when we get where we're going, who knows when we'll get any shut-eye."

Carlos settled back in his chair. "Conserve your energy, D. Stop thinking so hard."

"God bless America," Rider said, standing with a stretch. "Somebody remind me to kiss the sidewalk when we get outside of JKF airport, would ya?"

"With pleasure, my brother," Big Mike said, unfurling his huge body from the cramped seating, and wincing with pain as he stretched his limbs. "One more flight to L.A.—then I'll get on my knees right next to you and kiss the ground, for real."

They were so used to the slow shuffle forward between narrow aisles that they didn't even crane their necks or get annoyed when people in front of them slowed down the exit process by yanking down luggage from the overhead bins. They just wanted off.

Berkfield's family had found some semblance of peace. If not peace, then it was stunned acceptance. Whatever it was, it was better than Marjorie Berkfield's previous hysteria. Now that they were home, that could be particularly dangerous.

They trudged along, moving with the crowd, intermittently glancing out of the long windows, taking in the night.

"Don't say it, Rider," Marlene said, holding up her hand as they kept walking.

"Just wondering if anyone but me had noticed that it was dark outside."

Carlos stopped and stared out the windows for a moment, making the group come to an uneasy halt. "Incoming," he said quietly. "Everybody stay very cool."

"Incoming?" J.L. said, glancing at Carlos who'd begun walking forward.

Damali's hand went to her hip, reaching by instinct for the part of her that was no longer there. "Oh . . . shit . . ."

"My point being," Rider said as he watched Carlos's back.

Damali hustled forward to catch up to Carlos who was now twenty-feet away. "Yo, hold up," she said. "If you see something, we do this together."

Carlos chuckled and opened his arms, not looking at her. The dark-energy outline of an invisible body moved rapidly toward him. "Yo . . . *Ese!*"

"*Que pasa, hombre!*" Yonnie materialized and hugged Carlos hard. "Damn, I was worried about you!"

"It's all good," Carlos said, slapping Yonnie's back. "You done bulked up and shit. You look good, man."

Damali started, but Yonnie winked at her.

"I'm smooth, baby. Ain't nobody see me." Yonnie nodded toward her as he laughed with Carlos and straightened the front of his black Armani suit. "Nice, man. She's sweet. No less than a councilman deserves."

"C'mon, man. Where you been?" Carlos punched Yonnie's arm and laughed.

Damali looked at the team and gave them the signal to halt and not come forward. All she needed was for Berkfield's wife and kids to meet a master vamp their first time out at night . . . or for Rider to put two and two together. Yonnie was still standing. Tara was not.

"Maybe we should go somewhere and talk, man," Carlos said,

his voice growing tense. "I've got some people with me, and with Damali being so recognizable, here in New York we could get swamped by media, and whatnot."

"I've got her shielded from recognition for a few. Did that when y'all touched down, just in case—and got you covered, too. Figured you'd have an illusion up, but there's a lot of heat in the system right now, and a double layer couldn't hurt," Yonnie said. "But we do need to talk, man. A lot has gone down."

"So, I've heard," Carlos said, now scanning the environment.

"Where's Tara?" Damali asked, stepping closer. "Yonnie, for real, my Guardian brother is gonna lose it up in here if something happened to her. You've gotta let me break it to him easy. Cool?"

Yonnie frowned. "You pick up something I didn't?"

"Maybe, man," Carlos said quietly. "A lot has changed . . . but you look good. Like you're doing all right for yourself. I'm glad."

Yonnie stared at Carlos and then raked him up and down with an assessing gaze. "Tara said you were injured. You cool now? Let's get out of here, go eat, then I'll fill you in."

"Look at me hard, man," Carlos said quietly. "Can't you tell?"

"What, that you were injured? No. Man, if you had something missing it regen . . ." Yonnie's voice trailed off and he touched Carlos's cheek with two shaky fingers. "Oh, man, shit. Don't play. Not like that. It ain't funny." He dropped his hand and looked away. "You ain't crippled, *hombre.* Just need to feed right. We'll get you in lair . . . we'll . . ." Yonnie hung his head and took in a slow breath. "We'll get you right, man. Just stay strong for now. Cool?"

"I'm not a vampire anymore," Carlos said quietly and placed a hand on Yonnie's shoulder.

Yonnie looked up and made the tears burn away from his eyes. He glanced at Damali. "Can I have a minute with my brother, here?"

For a moment, she hesitated, but then withdrew from Carlos's side. "I'll go talk to the team. They're getting nervous."

Both men waited to speak until Damali was out of earshot, and then began talking at once.

"You have to keep trying to drop 'em, man. Just because they've retracted from the injury—"

"Yonnie, listen to me—"

"Naw, man. I ain't giving up on you, even if you've given up on yourself. In battle, you could drop ten—took out a whole—"

"They're gone. Not even in the gum line, brother. It's—"

"Shut up! You're scaring me," Yonnie said, covering his ears. "I'm not listening to this bullshit."

"Look at my aura." Carlos waited, pure humiliation burning him.

"Yeah. So what? Looks human—but that's because you're the baddest motherfucker in the valley. Makes sense, you've got skillz. If council is hunting you, that to me, makes sense." Yonnie dropped his hands away from his ears. "I told you, it's not funny. You know how sick to death with worry we were? Do you?" He pointed at Carlos. "This ain't no way to treat your boy—I'm *family*, man. Inner circle."

"You really can't tell, can you?" Carlos stared at Yonnie, a slow awareness entering him.

Yonnie looked him up and down. "Stop testing me," he grumbled. "Your night vision is working, you've got the capacity for flight. You're strong as an ox. Can walk through dimensions. A bite won't turn you because—"

Carlos held out his wrist, stopping Yonnie's words. "Smell the blood. Your nose didn't pick that up?"

Yonnie leaned down cautiously and drew back quickly.

"I just flew round the clock from Africa to London, and from London to NYC in a regular passenger seat and changed time zones so many times I've lost count. You do the math. At some point I had to go through broad daylight."

"Oh . . . shit . . ." Yonnie rubbed his jaw. "You've got liquid silver in your veins." He stared at Carlos. "Daywalker?" He went down on one knee. "You did it? The witches broke the code—that's why you've got one with you?" He peered up at Carlos. His voice became an amazed whisper as tears streamed down his face. He glanced at the Covenant team. "You got to them? Made them do it? Tell me, man. With their Neteru? That's why council is on your ass." He laughed and grabbed Carlos's hand. "Oh, shit . . . my boy is awesome."

"I don't like it," Rider said, standing in a small huddle with Damali and only the eldest Guardians. "Where's Tara?"

"Rider, there's a lot of complex shit going down right now," Damali said quickly, her line of vision holding his as her mind screamed to Shabazz and Big Mike to help avert a catastrophe. "Let's just stay cool, allow Carlos to do this thing with his contact, and we wait for good info." She glanced at Marlene who nodded her agreement.

"What's going on?" Berkfield said, coming up to the small cluster of seasoned Guardians. "Why did we stop moving, and who's the big guy with Rivera?"

"A master fucking vampire," Rider shot back in a tense whisper. "So, if I were you, I'd go back and keep my wife and kids between the four priests and our young bucks, and stay put until we get the order to move out."

Yonnie stood slowly. "Your Eminence," he said, not looking Carlos in the eyes. "I thought . . . I know we were boys when you made me, and I'm sorry I got familiar, and—"

"Man, stop that shit. We *are* family," Carlos said, becoming so upset by Yonnie's lack of understanding that he wanted to yell. He looked into Yonnie's eyes. "I trust you, crazy though that may sound." He reached out, grabbed Yonnie's wrist, and pressed his palm to his temple. "If you can go in, suck it bone dry so you can understand. We ain't got time."

"I can't," Yonnie said, his voice faltering as his hand came away smoldering. "You're too strong, man."

Carlos stared at his friend without blinking for a moment. "You can't go in?"

Yonnie shook his head. "Let me try to show you what's been going down." He looked at Carlos, seeming almost afraid to stare into his eyes, then turned away and yelled, covering his face as the information jettisoned between them. "My eyes!"

Pain made fangs rip through Yonnie's gums, and he covered his mouth with his forearm and stumbled away blindly. Carlos reached for him and held his friend up.

"Man, what happened? I'm sorry. What happened?"

"Silver. Your eyes went silver. My retinas are shot. I've gotta eat to regen. I'm blind, man. I can't lock with a daywalker, or whatever you are."

Carlos held his friend up and they walked forward to put more distance between them and the team. He'd siphoned Yonnie's mind, but the two-way transmission was too intense. He'd learned much, but had never wanted the knowledge at his friend's expense. "Call her now. Don't do one of these people in the airport. Let her feed you."

"I don't know if she's in range. You've gotta hold off her man, though. He'll wig, and I can't see him."

"I've got Rider," Carlos said, trying not to panic. "Just be smooth, when you feed. I'ma sit you down over here," he said, walking forward with Yonnie slowly. "You call her, eat, and then we're all outta here."

"It's not permanent, is it?" Yonnie followed the sound of Carlos's voice.

"I don't know, man. Just call her and sit tight. I'll be right over there holding back a disaster."

Carlos walked quickly toward the teams. They didn't understand. How could they? It was written all over their expressions—fear, worry, mistrust, bottled rage. But they hadn't been what he had been, known this particular friendship and loyalty like he'd known it, nor would they ever have any concept of what he'd given up to be a part of what they were now.

"My man is injured," Carlos said flatly, looking at Rider. "He has to feed."

Damali yanked Carlos's wrists and flipped them over, checking for wounds. "You didn't! You cannot go back to the old life, ever!"

Carlos jerked away. "Oh, and you trust me?" He turned his attention to Rider. "Not from me, but he has to feed, *now.*"

"In an airport?" Rider shouted, gathering the team into a tight circle. "Are you crazy? We're supposed to just hang back while he takes a bod—"

The members of the Covenant and the entire Guardian squad looked up as a shapely woman with long, dark hair gracefully walked out of nowhere toward Carlos's friend and slid into a seat next to him. She flung her hair over her shoulder, caressed his face, peered into his eyes, cringed, turned away, and then hugged him.

It happened so fast but also in slow motion. Rider had broken away from Carlos's block, leaving a portion of his torn T-shirt in Carlos's hand as he raced toward the seated couple, hurdled a bank of chairs with Carlos and Damali on his heels, and dove at the woman's body.

Tara sprawled out flat on the floor, hissed, and rolled away to stand upright just in time to yank Rider out of the way of a black bolt of energy that left a smoking hole in the airport floor.

Passengers screamed, security scrambled, Guardians and the Covenant rushed forward, Carlos and Damali got between them and Yonnie. Blood dripped from Yonnie's battle-length fanged mouth in an oozing string of saliva. Robert stood frozen like a deer in headlights, a wet spot forming down his jeans leg. Kristin caught her mother before she fell when her legs gave out. Berkfield was in front of his wife, brandishing luggage. The Covenant and other Guardians had Yonnie surrounded, but not a soul had a weapon.

Cops were coming from everywhere. People where shouting and running. "Freeze!" Damali shouted, and everything beyond their small ring went still.

Rider pushed Tara away from him. "From the throat? From the throat in my face!"

"He was injured too badly," Tara said, covering the wound with her palm. "There was no other way."

Yonnie's fangs slowly retracted as his eyes flickered an intermittent red glow, then held gold with patches missing in the orbs, until they finally came back brown. He breathed out hard, wiped his mouth on his sleeve, and stood up straight. "Thanks, baby," he said, still out of breath. He looked at Carlos. "Burned through to the sockets, man."

"Thanks, 'baby'?" Rider said, moving an ill-advised step forward.

Carlos was immediately between Yonnie and Rider.

"Hey, hey, hey," Carlos said. "It wasn't nothing but a regen feed—"

"Fuck that!" Rider shouted, not looking at Carlos. "So help me, God, I will find some wood up in this airport and put a hole in his chest!"

"You'd better be cool, old man," Yonnie said, snarling and circling with Rider. "I'm only letting you keep your throat because she asked me to—but every man has a limit."

"What! *You* have a limit? You come into *my* house, wall up in there with *my* woman, feed from her throat in *my* face and think you're not going to ash tonight?"

"Stop it!" Tara shouted. "Enough, already!"

"Oh, yeah, I've had damned enough," Rider said and spit on the floor. "You and I will have a long conversation later, but—"

"He kept me alive, Rider," Tara said quickly, ignoring the ping-pong glances that shot between members of the team.

"You don't have to step up for me, baby," Yonnie said, unbuttoning his jacket and walking forward until he was chest to chest with Carlos. "If this sonofabitch has a death wish tonight so be it."

"She ain't your baby!" Rider said, pointing over Big Mike's shoulder as the huge Guardian attempted to hold him back. He spun on Tara. "Oh, and I *bet* he kept you alive while I was gone. Like I didn't do that shit for the last twenty-plus years!"

"What did you say to me?" Tara whispered, making Big Mike move away from Rider's side.

Carlos dropped Yonnie's jacket lapels. All Guardians fanned out. Damali stood in front of the newest members of the team as Tara circled Rider.

"He insulted you," Yonnie shouted. "That's what the fuck he did. Hurt her—swing at her, and your arm is mine."

"Shut up," Tara said, pointing at Yonnie. "This is between me and my husband."

Yonnie looked so shocked that he backed up a step, but lifted his chin higher as he glowered at Rider.

Tara tilted her head and stared at Rider, a millimeter of fangs showing. Marjorie Berkfield covered her mouth and shut her eyes tightly.

"Don't kill him," Marjorie squeaked. "Not in front of my children."

Tara advanced on Rider so quickly and slapped him so hard that for a second, the team reached out to catch his body, thinking she'd snapped his neck. When Rider only rubbed his jaw, Big Mike and Shabazz sat down hard. Marlene wiped her brow and Robert upchucked.

"After all these years," Tara screamed, pointing at Rider as she paced away from him. "You had no right to even question my whereabouts. Ever!"

"Baby," Rider said, trying to slowly walk toward her. "It just looked—"

"Like what?" Tara whirled around, her mouth filled with razor-sharp battle-length teeth, her eyes glowing red.

"Honey, you've never gotten so . . . like this around me, and—"

"Her ass is fine, and if you can't handle it, I will," Yonnie said with honest appreciation. "Damn, man, if you don't want her . . . make up your mind, tonight."

Nuts and bolts holding the chairs to the floor began unscrewing and a tear scorched the carpet around them.

"Both of you—stop!" Tara shouted. "You," she said, pointing to Yonnie. "The reason I never allowed you to consummate after the elevation bite was because you were in *my husband's house*."

"You didn't have to put that out there like that, girl," Yonnie muttered and began walking away. He looked over his shoulder. "That was between me and you and personal."

"Don't you walk away from me and try to serve me mist," Tara said. "You disrespected him, after I asked you not to rub a throat exchange in his face!"

Rider nodded and stood up a little taller until she whirled on him and resumed her tirade.

"And, you—oh, I'm done until the end of time."

"Wait, baby, now, I may have been hasty and——"

Tears streamed down Tara's face. "You may not have been able to give me a master vampire's castle, but I was willing to live there in the cabin with you until you died." She started crying bitter sobs and when Rider went to her she pushed him away. "You don't think I know how much love you put into every piece of wood, every window you hung by hand, every fiber in there?" She snatched away from Rider as he tried to embrace her. "I can feel all that through *my skin. That's* what keeps me going when you're away. *That's* what I hang on to when you're on the road." She slapped him again, but not hard enough to break his jaw this time. "And *that's* what keeps me sane when I hear you with those damned pole dancers—so if I was really the vicious type, I would have done him in our room!"

She walked away and went to Carlos, who absently opened his arms for her, not sure what to do.

"Make them stop it," Tara said, sobbing. "You stand between their worlds. Our old one is dying, and we don't have time for this nonsense."

Carlos looked up at Rider and rubbed Tara's back to try to get her to calm down. "Handle your business and treat your wife right." He petted her back and scowled at Yonnie. "And you're my boy, and all, but stay out of Rider's territory—some shit just ain't done, especially for a master, man. C'mon. If we was 'round the way, your ass would be shot by now, messin' with *hombre's* wife, or trying to. Peace in the family."

Carlos looked at Rider hard and repeated his statement as Tara calmed down and sniffed. "Peace in the family."

"Yeah, all right," Rider said, coming to collect Tara from Carlos. "Peace in the family." He looked at her. "Baby I'm so sorry." He held her tightly as she slid from Carlos's hug into his.

Carlos nodded, but kept his eye on Yonnie, who still had his back turned to the group. "Peace in the family, man?"

"Yeah, yeah . . . peace in the family—whack-assed combination that it is."

Carlos chuckled and walked over to Yonnie and placed a firm hand on his shoulder. "It is that, but it's all we got right now."

Damali went to Berkfield's son and slung her arm over the stricken teenager's shoulder. "Welcome to the family," she said with a weary sigh. She glanced at Marjorie. "Now you believe in vampires?"

Carlos shook his head and he patted Yonnie's shoulder. "It's all good. You up for a little nighttime transport? You still da man, a Master." He waited until he could sense Yonnie smile even though his back was still toward him.

"I got this little place over in Manhattan, if you're game. It's a coven safe house, but, uh, your boys are gonna hafta spend the night at the religious joint around the corner with the chick that's scared of her own shadow," Yonnie said, glimpsing the clerics with a grin. "Even I can't push my luck with the ladies that far."

"Sho' you right," Carlos said, raking his hair. "Travel logistics with a team this big—"

"Is a bitch," Shabazz muttered. "We've been doing it for years, so suck it up."

Yonnie considered the Berkfields for a moment and nodded toward Marjorie. "She might be able to get them in on a family blood pass, and your boys are no problem—as long as they bring cash. You've got a councilman's standing VIP suite in reserve, but they'll be disappointed that you're bringing your own woman, unless you're ready to share. They gave Tara the blues." He neared Robert and chuckled when the kid backed up. "They'll love him, though. Will turn his ass out—he won't come out of there a virgin, that's for sure."

"My son is going to the church with the clergymen, thank you very much," Marjorie snapped, quickly body shielding her boy. "In fact, that might not be a bad idea period, Mr. Yonnie, I heard them call you . . . so, if you would be so kind as to drop us off at a nearby cathedral, we would so deeply appreciate that."

"Oh, *my* goodness," Marlene sighed. She looked up at Big Mike. "And you're staying in whatever room me and Shabazz get put in tonight—no more mess."

"After all of this," Mike said in a weary tone, "even I'm re-formed."

"I just want some weapons," Damali said. "The hair is still standing up on my neck."

"Once we get on hallowed ground, done," Father Patrick said in an exhausted tone. "We'll all get artillery resupplied."

"Cool." Shabazz nodded. "I've been feeling naked lately."

Carlos smiled and glanced around at the motley team of unlikely characters, wondering if fate actually did have a wicked sense of humor. "Everybody, peace?" He waited until everyone shifted and nodded in weary agreement, and then turned his attention back to Damali. "D, release time and let our boy blow us out of this joint."

CHAPTER TWENTY-TWO

YONNIE'S TRANSPORT cloud touched down in a whirlwind of rocks and twigs, scattering dirt and debris in the middle of Central Park West. Guardians and Covenant members wobbled and fell against each other as the tornado-like funnel cloud slowed to a gentle breeze.

Damali saw the streetlights glint off the gun barrel first. "Get down!" she shouted as she slammed Berkfield's teenage son to the ground.

A thunderous shotgun report echoed. Her team hit the dirt. Yonnie and Tara dematerialized and fanned out. Another shot rang through the foliage. Bodies rolled behind park benches and took shelter behind trees. Carlos was covering Krissy, his body a shield over the young girl.

Damali's line of vision keened upon the two vampires who were stalking prey. The young boy beneath her was shivering. "If it's civilian fire, don't kill the shooter!" Damali ordered.

A shotgun whizzed by them broken in two. Damali scrambled to her feet. Carlos was on his in seconds. The team got up slowly.

"I'm an old man!" a crotchety voice said. "I'm not afraid to die!"

Damali and Carlos took the lead, following the elderly voice bearing a Yiddish accent. When they rounded the path they didn't know what to make of what they saw.

An old man stood there with defiance blazing in his eyes, pointing at Yonnie and Tara. He was so hunched over he looked like an elderly gnome as he stamped his feet and slapped his chest, squinting through thick wire-rimmed glasses. His black hat and coat were dirty and speckled with twigs and dried grass. The black-and-white stole about his collar was rumpled as though he'd been in a struggle. Sticks and dust clung to his long white beard as he lobbed his complaint, shaking an angry, bony finger at Yonnie.

"They killed my only living relative—my brother! He was a great scientist! I will have my revenge, demons all of you!" As the team gathered near, he squinted and slapped his chest with opened palms. "So you gang up a whole army of demons on one little old man—but I have something for you! Come on! Come on! Tonight is a good time to die!"

Yonnie and Tara snarled. Damali and Carlos rushed forward with Father Patrick.

"Sir, no one's going to hurt you," Damali said as calmly as possible.

He spat on the ground. "A pox upon you! No, you won't kill me, but make me the living dead! But I've outsmarted you, ha! I'm already dying of cancer—how do you like that?"

"Yo, mister. Chill. You'll give yourself a heart attack if you don't calm down," Carlos said, trying not to smile.

"Heart attack, smart-attack—who cares! But I will not be taken hostage!"

"Rabbi, I implore you," Father Patrick said, walking forward slowly. "We are not the undead and we have children with us, too. Please, no heroics or violence."

"Children? Children! Oh . . . no . . ." The old man covered his face and wept, then he began beating his chest, looking up to the sky. "Oh, abominations, they know no bounds!"

"We're all human," Damali said, going to the old man. She glanced at Yonnie and Tara. "Cover your ears and stand back, we have to do something." She nodded for the team to surround the old man and gave the nod. "Dose him with something from the Old Testament—I don't know, pick a prayer from the old books that Imam Asula can get with, too. Anybody got a Bible on them?"

The mention of the Old Testament stemmed the man's momentary complaint. He peered around nervously as Yonnie and Tara loped off to stand in the distance. Marlene dug into her bag and brandished the book she always carried and tossed it to Damali.

"Here, Father," she said to Father Patrick. "Maybe the Book of Job might help, who knows."

The old man waved his hand and sighed. "If you touched it, then fine. I stand corrected and I know Job's story well, just as I know the book of Abraham." He adjusted the smudged glasses on his nose. "But you saw them, two at least, that came in the cloud?"

Damali smiled. "Yes, sir, we did. We hunt them. That's our job. But the two that came with us . . . well . . . there's an alliance, they work with us to help us get on the inside of the main nests."

"Hmmm . . . double agents . . . I don't know," he said in a peevish tone. "My brother thought you could negotiate with that sort, too—but the enemy has a silver tongue."

Carlos thrust the two Berkfield teens forward. "We're trying to keep these kids safe, mister." He nodded toward Berkfield, who stepped forward. "Their dad is a cop, undercover. He was recently assisted by your brother, or maybe his people—then abducted. We had to go to extreme lengths to get him back unbitten and alive."

"Oh . . . so young," the rabbi said, shaking his head and peering up at Krissy and Robert. "You sure they weren't bitten? Sometimes the demons pose as the weak and vulnerable, they trick you and can even become images of your own family. Their mother . . ."

"Right here," Marjorie Berkfield said, going to stand between her children. "Sir, I know this is a terrible strain on one's nerves, believe me. In the last few hours I have seen things that will probably make my hair go white—but everyone in our small group has undergone every clerical test you can imagine, and we've passed." She came near and held his withered hands.

Dan stepped forward and pulled his Star of David from beneath his shirt. "Rabbi," he said, taking off the jewelry and placing it in the old man's palm. "Shalom."

The rabbi clutched the necklace in his fist and hugged Dan, and began to sob. He banged on Dan's back with his fist as emotion consumed him. "They said I was old, getting dementia, because I had no more family. They didn't believe what I had seen! They didn't believe!"

Dan stroked the elderly man's back. "We believe. We've seen it. We know. We stand with you. We won't leave you."

Slowly the old man lifted his head, his glasses askew on the bridge of his nose. He wiped his face and took several breaths as Dan helped him to a park bench.

"You're not a hallucination, then?"

Dan smiled. "No, Rabbi. We're here to help."

He glanced around at the team and his eyes settled on the clerics. "You, too? All of you have seen this . . . men of many faiths?"

Father Patrick nodded. "We have. We must band together and fight."

He smiled and adjusted his lopsided hat. "And fight we shall! We will never give up!"

Sirens in the distance made everyone become still.

"Not to break up this party, but there's a few housekeeping details that we need to decide, pronto, given that we're out here in a deserted area at night," Rider said with emphasis. "Like, first of all, we need to get away from the scene of the crime, namely a round of shotgun fire on the ritzy side of town, unless Yonnie masked it."

"No lie," Shabazz said, staring at the old man. "Plus, before real predators show up, hallowed ground might be advisable."

The rabbi nodded and stood up, all resistance gone. "We need more ammunition, too. I have access to some things we'll need. Artillery."

"Artillery?" Damali shared glances of concern with the team.

"Of course artillery," he scoffed, walking quickly. "In Brooklyn. My brother was worried and knew something bad was coming. He made provisions." He winked and nodded, chuckling as though he knew a secret the others did not. "My brother had such a mind. He shipped things to me by a very circuitous route and told me that if anything ever happened to him, to be prepared. I am."

The group followed the rabbi to the other side of the park, but Rider hung back.

"Yo, Rider!" Damali yelled. "C'mon."

Rider shook his head. "She can't go to a synagogue."

The group halted motion.

"Neither can my boy," Carlos said, standing caught between Rider and the rest of the group.

"Oh, Lord . . ." Marlene sighed. "Now what?"

"We have to split up," Damali said, going to stand near Carlos.

"Oh, no," Big Mike said, advancing toward her. "We just went through that and we're not—"

"Take the Berkfields to higher ground, Mike. That's an order!" Damali said more firmly than she'd wanted. "Listen—me and Carlos are the only ones who can withstand a bite and take hard blows, if we get into a firefight. I'm a half-decent healer, if we get into a skirmish, but Rider can't be out here alone, and you *know* he's not leaving his woman. Berkfield is a medic and can tolerate a bite, too—so he goes with you to where it's safe with his wife and kids. You guys fill in the rabbi and gather weapons. Seers, contact me and Carlos via telepathy as soon as day breaks and we'll figure out where to rendezvous. From there, we'll figure out where our new base of operations will be. The compound is gone, Rider's cabin is most likely compromised by now, and we still don't know exactly what we're up against."

"You have two choices," Yonnie said, his eyes scanning the street. "Gabrielle has this nice little brownstone on the Upper East Side, steel VIP vaults in the basement for clients that need to stay past dawn . . . or there's this bangin' joint up on Lennox and One-hundred-twenty-third. Voodoo sisters, fine as shit—"

"What's the closest and safest joint, man?" Carlos said, his nerves fried. "Where can Rider go and stay overnight and not asphyxiate in a cheap vault or worry about getting jacked once Tara has to regen?"

Yonnie chuckled. "I feel you. Well, Gabrielle's would check out, we have an alliance."

"So I've heard," Carlos muttered. "Is she gonna be cool with Damali, or will I have to ice your partner?"

"Oh, no, man. She ain't like that," Yonnie assured him. "Besides, Marjorie is her sister—even though they have issues, family is family. Plus, I know she ain't crazy enough to go after a council-man's wife in her own house."

Carlos and Damali stared at him.

"I'd feel better with a weapon," Damali said, as the group began walking up West 154th Street. "Rider needs one, too."

"I can't materialize silver or hallowed-earth-packed shells." Yonnie gave Damali a wry smile with a hint of fang glistening in the moonlight. "Damn you're fine, girl. No offense, Rivera, only a compliment."

"I'll settle for a Glock nine, or a handheld machine gun," Damali said, ignoring Yonnie's flirtation and Carlos's frown.

"That works for me," Rider said, putting his arm over Tara's shoulders.

"Hold up," Yonnie said, and stopped walking. "It's bad enough that Mrs. B was ordering a transport to the door of a church like she was ordering a cab. And I don't mind accommodating my boy's woman. If Damali wants heavy artillery to snuff a coupla witches that might get out of pocket, cool. But your ass doesn't ask me for shit. Got that?" Yonnie began walking and muttering. "Bad enough you're probably gonna fuck her under the same roof with me tonight; don't push me."

"What?" Rider removed his arm from Tara's shoulders. "Come again."

"Stop it. Both of you," Tara said, stepping in front of Rider.

Damali and Carlos had also come between them.

"Listen," Damali said, fatigue making her eyes blurry. "We can-not go into a witches' coven unless we're united."

"Squash the bullshit," Carlos said, glancing at Rider and Yonnie. He settled his focus on Yonnie. "You're the master, so act like it. There's probably five or six of them in there that will be happy you stopped by . . . which, in all honesty, will keep them occupied enough to keep us alive for the night."

Yonnie offered Carlos a grudging chuckle. "I can do that, keep 'em off your back and not thinking about spell-casting or spirit possessions until they pass out."

"That's my boy," Carlos said, banging his fist against Yonnie's. "Do 'em right, give us a few hours to get a plan together, then we'll jet in the morning and you and Tara can catch up to us next sunset."

Damali climbed the wide cement steps that led to the posh Manhattan brownstone. Hookers and witches, business mavens and gentleman's whores, politicians and landed wealth—what did it matter, they all owned primo real estate.

From the exterior of the well-kept properties, who could tell? She watched Yonnie lift the brass knocker on the heavy oak door that had tasteful panels of leaded, beveled glass, and announce his arrival by dropping it once, and then waiting for the door to eerily creak open on its own.

They crossed the great foyer that had huge inlaid blocks of black-and-white marble, the décor refined and held in stasis from the Art Deco era. Tall black-and-white candles lit the entrance, and Damali peered at the bloodred long-stemmed roses that stood aloof on a central white marble pedestal before a grand, sweeping staircase.

Pure curiosity tugged at her as a black cat slinked by, looked Carlos, Yonnie, and Rider up and down, and then turned up its nose at her and Tara and pranced away.

"Bitch," Tara muttered.

The cat hissed and fled up the stairs.

"Friend of yours?" Carlos asked with a smile.

"I know her," Tara said offhandedly. "Gabby's familiar, and she's as old as dirt."

"Be cool," Yonnie warned. "Show some respect." He turned his attention toward the stairs as a tall, angular woman appeared. He smiled and loped forward, his motions fluid.

In Damali's estimation, she was ghastly white and skinny. But she tucked away the appraisal. When leaning on hospitality one's best manners were in order.

"Hey, baby," Yonnie said, his voice dropping a purposeful octave. "No weres in the house?"

"You said you were coming," she purred. "You know I don't service that sort of clientele up here. Only in L.A. If you really want a walk on the wild side, I can make accommodations in our New Orleans establishment?"

Yonnie kissed her slowly, making her draw a breath when he pulled away. "I have a few friends that just need a safe room. New York is best, though. Their lairs have been compromised. That's cool, right?"

She smiled and left his arms to greet Yonnie's party. She narrowed her gaze on Tara and Rider, but softened it to professional disdain. "You're not planning on spending the evening with her are you?"

Yonnie shook his head no. "Nah . . . she's only a second-gen. My boy got that covered. I was hoping you'd be free?"

"Maybe," she said, moving to Carlos's side and giving him a purposeful look. "This cannot be who I think it is?"

Carlos smiled and swept her hand with a kiss. "Pleased to meet you," he murmured.

She withdrew her hand slowly and covered her heart with her palm. "*The* Carlos Rivera?" She wobbled a bit and a rush of color came to her face. "Councilman, it is an honor. Your reputation precedes you, and you have a standing vault in my establishment— no matter what may be going on with that nasty civil war. We take an apolitical stance, much like Switzerland, and our barriers are well fortified. So do enjoy your stay for as many evenings as you require." She took several deep breaths and closed her eyes as though steadying herself. "Your exploits while living and . . . transitioned . . . are legendary." She glanced at Damali with outright disdain. "I'm Gabrielle. If you need *anything* during your stay, you have but to summon me."

"Hello," Damali said, not extending her hand. "*We* thank you for the hospitality."

Carlos looked away and smiled.

"Put it on my tab," Yonnie said, gathering Gabrielle into his arms before rage reduced her façade to a catfight. "I'm sure you understand why the councilman needs to keep the Neteru close to him and under heavy guard."

"Yes," Gabrielle snapped, but then gentled her gaze as she looked away from Damali to Carlos. "But, sir, during your seven years' wait for her to ripen again, please feel free to avail yourself of more professional services in the interim. Your mission is worthy, and we'll all benefit from your success . . . but you don't have to suffer, *innecesario*. With your capacities, we can gladly join—"

"I'll do my best to hook a brother up," Damali said with a harsh smile. "Thanks just the same."

Gabrielle sighed. "I'll show your entourage to their rooms." She scowled at Tara. "I take it you'll also need a vault before daylight?"

"Please don't let her torch, baby. Make sure she's in a sealed vault—no games. She's an important core for message transmissions," Yonnie said, glancing at Carlos.

"I appreciate the hospitality," Carlos said, moving closer to Gabrielle and stroking her cheek. "Can't have my inner core jacked right through here." He leaned in, winked at Yonnie, and whispered in her ear. "Keep them safe, as well as Damali, and I'll deliver a daywalker councilman's bite . . . maybe me and my boy will come back and do a double visit?"

Gabrielle kissed his cheek and stroked his hair. "Promises like that, Mr. Councilman, will get you everywhere."

"I still don't like it," Damali whispered harshly as she paced about in the plush basement vault. Red velvet and silk were everywhere, and the Louis XIX–period furniture made her want to gag. "I can't believe you told her something like that." She peered around with her hands on her hips. "They've got you in the councilman's blood chamber—I do declare you need to stop frontin', *Mr. Councilman*," she said with sarcastic Antebellum inflection in her voice.

Carlos pulled the black corded tassel to open the bed drapes, sat down hard on the high four-postered bed, and then simply fell back on the goose-down, red silk duvet. The thick comforter poofed up around his body and silk pillows slid from their orderly positions at the intrusion.

"Wall torches, how quaint. I don't suppose any of the bottles on the bar would be regular liquor?" She walked over to the bar, glimpsed the selection, and shook her head. "Not a beer in the house, but they do have old scotch and brandy—should *the councilman* like a shot with a little color. Gimme a break."

She glanced around. No mirrors. Perfect. "Well at least they have a master bathroom and some running water. I guess that's for the girls who work here and still have a pulse." She stomped over to a huge armoire and flung it open, extracting a sheer red teddy, a whip, and a pair of handcuffs. "And here I was hoping for combat boots, jeans, and a T-shirt; how silly of me. Thought I could get rid of the pilgrimage gear and slip into something a little more comfortable, like combat fatigues, and then round out my evening ensemble with maybe a snub-nosed shoulder cannon and a coupla grenades—since I don't have my blades. But nooooo. . . . The girls are servin' all thong!" She flung the hard-play items back into the armoire and slammed the door.

"Girl, I'm so beat up, mentally mangled, and tired, I can't even begin to argue. You're right. I'm wrong. Sorry we have to spend the night in a cathouse, but at least we're alive. *My* bad."

Damali sighed and finally came to his side, sat down on the edge of the bed, and threw up her hands. She had to laugh. It was so insane there was no option. "Yeah. This has been ridiculous."

"I'm just trying to keep Rider from getting smoked in his sleep. Tara could've gotten her throat ripped out by a jealous master, and my boy . . . this whole thing has messed Yonnie up. Rider better stay out of his face, D, seriously, because as fine as Tara is, and being the only available female vamp in the zone—talk to your boy. The only reason we're here is to half baby-sit those three."

"You're right," Damali said, letting her breath out hard. "Baby, I'm sorry I blamed it all on you, but I'm right where Marj is—I just want my life back. This is nuts."

"Tell me about it," Carlos said, closing his eyes. "Half the time I keep forgetting that I can't just go make a playmate for Yonnie to chill him out, or I go to snap my fingers and materialize something and all I get is sound. Then I remember, oh yeah, my shit is changed.

Then I have to concentrate like a schoolkid to throw up a block shield, which leaves me exhausted." Carlos rolled over on his stomach and stretched out his arms. "I must be getting old, baby. I feel all kinds of aches and pains and shit . . ."

Damali crawled toward him on her hands and knees and began rubbing his back. "You're not getting old," she said, chuckling, "just human."

"Please, not so loud," he warned, "especially in here."

"Right, right." She straddled his back and began to work the knots out of his shoulders. Leaning in to whisper in his ear. "Okay. I'm sorry. But look at what you *can* do."

"Like what?" he muttered, wincing as she found a tangle of muscles that were bunched together like walnuts. "When I was on top of my game, you see how smooth the vamp life was and—"

"They can't tell. Did you notice that?"

He lifted his head briefly and glanced at her. "Yeah. Freaky, ain't it?"

Damali kept her face close to his ear. "You've been masked now as a legit vamp. A councilman, at that. That must be a layer of protection you didn't know you had. That'll definitely come in handy if we have to bluff our way out of a corner. Your art of talking trash still holds, that was obvious," she added with a giggle. "Even sunlight couldn't burn that away."

He chuckled and relaxed a bit. He loved the way the heat of her words warmed his ear and her hair brushed the side of his face. "Yeah, but I'ma need more than the gift of gab."

"What about your shield? It held when Tara flipped out, right? And it kept bullets from blowing away the group."

"Yeah . . . it did, didn't it? Damn . . . go figure." He lifted his head and looked at her with a slow-dawning smile. "I must be getting stronger."

"It's getting closer to your birthday."

Carlos turned over so that Damali was sitting on his belly. "It's so wild . . . Yonnie couldn't read my mind—*a master*. He tried to go in and it almost fried his telepathy. Then, when he looked into my eyes to do the solid lock, it burned out his retinas."

"So, if you ever come face-to-face with the chairman . . ."

"I'll smoke his ass."

"Uhmmm hmmm. That's what I like to hear," she said, pecking his forehead with a kiss.

"You ain't half bad yourself, girl. Shape-shifting and whatnot. But you have to come stronger than a sparrow," he said laughing. "You could have gone eagle, falcon, a bird of prey, D, at least."

"Oh, so now you're gonna read a sister for being so freaked out by the prospect of being stranded on the side of a guerrilla-ridden road in no-man's-land that I could only visualize the first thing that came to mind—the last bird I saw. Oh, okay, so it's like that, now?"

He laughed. "Naw, I'm just messin' with you. In fact, I'm jealous," he said, stroking her hips. "I can't shift anymore. But you've got lots of new stuff you can do that's pretty cool."

"I lost my blades, brother. I don't have lots of new stuff. I lost—"

"Yes you do. Like, when we first did the transport together, you only stopped time for a fraction of a second. But in the airport, when it really counted, you did something and froze time for almost five minutes."

"I guess I did a lil somethin' somethin'," Damali said smiling, working on the muscles in his shoulders.

"But that's nothing new," he said, quietly gazing up at her and rubbing her thighs. "You could always do that."

She smiled and bent down to kiss him gently. "So could you."

Carlos traced her cheek with the pad of his thumb and then closed his eyes. "But you should have seen the look on my boy's face when I had to tell him my fangs couldn't . . . he thought . . . He said they'd just retracted because I'd been injured, ya know. I can't—"

She kissed him and stopped his words, her mouth covering the hurt he was trying to confess. She didn't care what the old queens had said about not being with him. There was something profound that happened between a man and a woman, and her man needed his confidence as much as he needed a weapon. *That was his weapon*. The fourteenth gift. Unshakable confidence, and the ordeals he'd faced had shattered it. Without that healed, neither one of them would ever be right. And in her soul she knew that past all the bravado, all the macho bull, she held the key to returning that to him. It was imperative tonight.

"Yes, you can . . . just different than before," she whispered, pulling away from the kiss. "I love you."

His hands found her hair as he pulled back from her kiss. "Baby, listen to me. You've got my maker's mark. From my old life. Your circuitry is rewired to a pattern that I can no longer deliver. You understand?"

"I don't have anything to give you for your birthday, but me," she said, brushing his mouth again. "Why don't you let me be the judge of my circuit board, huh?"

He cradled her face in his palms. "The fact that you're alive and all healed up is enough of a gift for me. I don't want to spoil it by finding out—"

"That I love you, no matter what?"

"I know that, girl . . . and I love you, too, but—"

"Carlos," she whispered. "Listen to me. The one thing I learned through all of this is tomorrow's not promised. There hasn't been a second that's gone by that I didn't wish we had more time, no matter what." She kissed the bridge of his nose. "I wouldn't have traded any of it, if it meant we'd never met." She bent closer, nuzzling the side of his throat and drew a slight shudder from him. "That's still your sweet spot."

He swallowed hard. "Yeah, it is."

"Wanna go exploring? See if the old imprints are still there?"

"I don't know, girl. What if yours are still there? I've got blunt edges, can't even break the skin."

She smiled and stretched out to blanket him. "You did more than just bite me all night."

"I know," he murmured, becoming morose. "That's why I know, it's not going to be the same."

She smiled and let out a weary sigh. "Then I guess I'll just have to go exploring all by myself." She planted a slow kiss on each of his eyelids and traced his jaw with her finger. "Tomorrow, we'll be

back with the group, living from pillar to post, on the lam, in unknown battles, and my man just came back from the dead. I'm
healed and the queens did something that makes me unable to get
pregnant for a while. Do I seem like the kind of woman who is
about to give up and take not-tonight-I-have-a-headache-honey?"

He smiled and rubbed her back. "And do I seem like the kind
of man who wants to have that weird vibe between us with a team
of clerics, a whole band of Guardians, and now some teenagers
looking at us sideways and asking what's wrong?" He rolled her off
of him gently. "Let it rest, D . . . for real. I'm not ready to find out
what I already know."

She lay beside him for a moment, just rubbing his chest in a lazy,
haphazard pattern. "You have a heartbeat now, and a pulse," she
murmured, snuggling up to him. "We never dreamed that could
happen, right?"

"Yeah, but that's different," he said quietly as her lush mouth
found his jugular and gently suckled the sensitive skin surrounding
it. He closed his eyes as she made her jaw softly collide with his to
expose more of his throat.

"I can't drop fang anymore, either . . . but it still feels good
there, doesn't it?" She nipped his neck, making him draw in a sharp
inhale through his nose.

"C'mon, girl, stop playing."

"Okay," she whispered into his ear, then nipped the lobe of it as
her feet slid out of her sandals. She allowed them to hit the floor,
first one, then the other, her eyes hunting his. "I'll stop playing and
be dead serious."

She slid on top of him and lowered her mouth to his, her breasts
barely skimming the surface of his chest as her pelvis stroked a sultry, nonverbal invitation to explore it. Her nipples brushed his,
making the hair stand up on his arms. He allowed his hands to flow
down her shoulders and arms, then her back and the swell of her
hips, like water running over smooth rock, and then he swept the
current of touch up over her buttocks and along her spine, spread-
ing south to north heat, flowing against gravity like his hands were
the Nile.

Oh, yes, she was definitely the motherland, more than mere territory or something to plunder . . . a vast place of mystery and wonder, hardship and pleasure . . . more than a continent to be conquered for resources and black gold; she was his grounding, his center, sacred earth. His body came alive from her patient attention, making him remember the rhythm of the drum. She was a fusion of the past, primitive and unspoiled, and the confusion of everything new and unknown. But, oh, so wise . . . And she was also his woman, who now molded to his body like clay. She was breathing him back to life through deep inhalations and exhalations that matched the pulse of her hips. Her low murmurs of pleasure were like a shaman's incantations . . . *live, love, trust me.* He did.

He deepened their kiss, remembering what she felt like, what she smelled like, and how much he'd missed her, thinking there'd never be another time. Soon what was to be a slow kiss and cautious exploration became a frantic awareness that they'd been given a second chance.

Taking in ragged sips of air, she pushed back and gathered up her lavender robes, and yanked them over her head. She sat on him looking down at him, her partially nude body glistening in the firelight, her breasts rising and falling with every breath. He watched her slowly strip away her panties, one leg at a time, kneeling in a low crouch above him, eyes watching his, all panther. Yet, she was so beautiful, he needed a moment before his hands touched her silken, caramel skin. He reached out to cover her breasts with his palms, and allowed them to hover a millimeter above the soft rise of them, staring at the goddess that straddled him.

That's when he saw it, the sheer silver-gold band of energy that leaked from her pores and covered his hands. He moved them, still not touching her skin, but watching the Light ripple in soft waves and change colors as he disturbed it. She moaned and let her head drop back. Both fascination and desire made him study the phenomena with care.

"You're made of Light," he whispered, cupping her breasts. "Rainbow-colored Light . . ."

The tremor that ran through her registered in the palms of his hands as he circled the heavy lobes, and his thumbs brushed the tiny pebbles that had formed beneath them. He watched her sip air through her mouth as he leaned forward and drew a nipple between his lips, the sound of her voice bottoming out in a low alto moan. Her fingers twined through his hair, oh, yeah, he remembered, but when he drew back to find her mouth, all he could do for a moment was stare.

Every place that he'd once bitten was fired crimson by some strange inner Light she possessed. He leaned up to hold her, tested, explored, finding the hot zones with his hands and landing a kiss against the one that burned brightest—along her throat. Her reaction was immediate, a soft whimper of pleasure and a gentle rake down his back.

Instant recall, snap-flex memory, he flipped her over on her back, shed his cumbersome garb, and knelt between her thighs. Everything within him told him that his control was gone. This first time with her again would be a thunder run. For a moment, he stared down at her, trying to will back a slower pace.

"Can't you see it?" he whispered, looking down at his own arms that were swirling with multihued energy.

She shook her head no as tears glittered back at him. "I just know from touch," she murmured and then leaned up and ran her fingers along his throat and stroked where it made him close his eyes. "Right there," she whispered, "where it's burning up."

He nodded as her touch danced over the perspiration-moist surface. "Yeah, right there."

Her hand slid up the nape of his neck and she gathered his hair into her fist. He could feel his arms trembling when he braced himself above her, waiting for the sudden, impossible strike. When she bit him, he saw stars. Her suckle at his throat felt like it was drawing every fluid in his body into his groin. The unexpected sensation made him cry out and cover her, entering her without warning, moving without patience or control.

His mind fought for distance. This was not smooth or planned; it was pleasure beyond comprehension. Her hand flattened against the base of his spine, bouncing with his ragged thrusts where he could feel her holding an orb of heat as she arched. Yet, he could also feel her control within each agonizing stab of pleasure she allowed. Her legs twined with his and fought his frantic pace. He looked down at her, pained, trying to tell her the quiet truth; he couldn't stop. She felt too damned good. He was now only human. Every stroke was in jeopardy, Russian roulette. She didn't understand and she stared back at him through half-lowered lids, making him close his eyes in shame as his shaft began to fill.

"Take your time," she whispered. "Feel it ripple up your spine one vertebrae at a time," she panted, releasing the hot ball of energy she held, placing a skimming touch at points along his back.

"Oh . . . God . . ." Pleasure thundered up his discs, dredging his scrotum in a dry-heave contraction.

"Uhmmm, hmmm," she murmured. "Let your chakra do the work." Her hands splayed against his buttocks, pulling him against her hard. "Sync up with me. We are one." She knocked his head back with her jaw and bit him again.

It was as though she'd lit a fuse. His arms enfolded her, instinct kicked in, and his jaw collided with hers, seeking her throat. The bite was instantaneous. Her voice hit the vaulted ceiling and bounced off the walls. Beneath tightly shut eyelids he could see her energy rushing, swirling Light, colors moving quickly in elliptical patterns through her veins, coating his insides, and building renewed tidal pressure in his groin. She moved with him, their voices syncopated staccato, tears dripping off the bridge of his nose with sweat as he pulled up from the bite to breathe.

Her stare met pure silver. His eyes were fantastic. *Oh, God . . .* They siphoned sense from her mind and ripped air from her lungs. *Remember to breathe. Right there.* The Sankofa on her spine burned with white-hot pleasure. She held the sides of his face as his lids fluttered shut, drawing another depth-charge release from her womb. He had to stop, her nervous system was unraveling—core meltdown. Only tears and hiccup sobs. *Just. Like. That.* Freefalling so hard she almost bit her tongue. *Don't stop . . .* He was in deep, every rough kiss that landed where he'd once marked her sent her over the spiraling edge while he moved against her and cradled her head. *Yes!* Her hands scrabbled at the duvet. Touching his spine was lethal, it transmitted too much pleasure, another sudden strike made her temporarily go blind.

His hands were tangled in her hair, every pant he took she felt within her lungs. Tremors of pleasure climbed through her finger-tips and crawled up through the soles of her feet, converging be-tween her legs, making every orifice on her body shudder and contract. His face burned against her cheek, his voice turning her mind to jelly, the low baritone resonance of it quaking her from the inside out.

"Yeah, baby, sho' you're right . . . take my time . . . girl, I re-member."

Ecstasy had scorched her windpipe dry. He was talking shit, and there was no way to respond. She no longer owned syntax, just harmonic uttering. He'd driven her so far past the edge that all her tears had fled and were gone. She wept dry-eyed, mild hysteria set-ting in. The only way to repay him was to hold an image in her thoughts . . . the last time, vanishing-point entry . . . and she hurled it against his mind with his next thrust.

The convulsion was so fierce that it made him stop moving for a moment, turn his head . . . open-mouth holler and not a sound came out. Time had stopped, his voice coming after the fact, a de-layed reaction once a pleasure-slam flattened him, sonic boom. The sensation knocked the wind out of him. Her bite, crystal energy, freezing him, then shattering him like glass. Then came the after-shocks, thundering lightning strikes, threatening to snap his neck from shuddering jerks of release, tearing his system into filaments of anguished ecstasy . . . *Dear, God, baby, please* . . .

He lay there for a long time, deadweight on her, waiting for the room to stop spinning, remembering to breathe. Every so often he'd open his eyes, only able to make out the energy outline of darkened objects around them. He was half afraid to look at her, and felt his neck first to see if he had puncture wounds. Slowly he rolled off of her. She covered her neck with her palm and checked for blood, too.

Suddenly she leapt out of the bed, crossed the room, feeling her throat and double-checking her hand for blood. "You *have* to be daywalker," she whispered. "I felt the plunge, and it wasn't a blunt passion nick, brother."

He sat up slowly, and backed away from her, shaking his head. "Girl, you bit *me*—I mean, a *real* bite. I felt two inches open my jugular." A pleasure shiver washed through him and pounded in his erection. He watched it claim her with a shudder that hitched her breath in her throat.

"Stop it," she whispered halfheartedly and briefly closed her eyes. "This is serious."

"I know. Break the connection," he said through his teeth, holding the bedpost for support. "I can still feel you across the room."

They looked away until the connection weakened and ebbed to a tolerable level. Slowly they looked up at each other and lowered their hands from their necks like gunfighters.

"Your eyes finally stopped glowing." Her eyes searched his. "Am I nicked?"

He shook his head no. "D, seriously, did you do me? We'll work it out if you did."

She covered her mouth and laughed and shook her head no. "You're cool. I'm the one who oughta be worried."

"Then what *the Hell* was that?" he whispered, glancing around the room nervously.

"Two Neterus getting a little kinky, I guess," she said in a conspiratorial whisper, giggling and staggering back to bed. "Damn, round one was off da meter."

He edged toward the bed, his legs wobbly as he flopped down on it. "I didn't know . . . humans could . . . I mean—"

"Knowledge is power. Didn't you always tell me that?"

He smiled and came closer to her, touching her with one finger and drawing it back quickly, not sure if it was safe to stir up her energy bands again.

"It *was* awesome, wasn't it?"

For a moment he just looked at her and then smiled. "Damali, there are no words."

"They have some champagne and top shelf over there," she said with a nod toward the bar. "Maybe we can try it again, a little later?" She let her gaze rake his body and land on his crotch. "Or maybe . . . after I've had something to open up my throat a little, I'll work on your femoral—"

"There's blood in those bottles," he said in a tense whisper, drawing away from her again. He sought refuge on the far side of the bed, annoyed that the mere mention of what she might do had sent a contraction through his groin.

She flopped on her back. "I'm not crazy, and not even going there. I'm talking about having a *colorless* glass of wine, or whatever, chilling, and then maybe we can go exploring again." She slung her arm over her eyes. "If you can envision it, you can do it . . . and, baby, can you *ever* do it. That's all I have to say."

"Oh," he said, letting his breath out in relief, and coming nearer to her. He propped himself up on one elbow and traced her inner thigh, remembering what she tasted like, sorry that he'd waxed conservative at an inopportune time.

"You actually thought I bit you?" She shook her head and snuggled up against him. "But you liked it, though . . . Umph. Now I have to worry about my man having a thing for female vamps, and an after-the-fact guilt complex."

He chuckled and stroked her hip, kissing her forehead. "No, baby, trust me . . . female vamps ain't got nuthin' on you." He ran his hand down her inner thigh, loving the smoothness of it and the slick wetness he'd just left there. "And I never felt guilty about getting with you."

She chuckled quietly, thoroughly sated. She could feel him staring at her and she removed her arm from over her eyes. "What?" she said, smiling up at him.

"You ever think about . . . never mind."

Damali let her breath out hard and reached for his cheek, following the subtle curve of it with her hand. "No, I don't think about that," she said softly. "Ever."

"You've never been with anybody else, though. How do you know, if one day, you might wanna just see?"

"They'd have a real tough act to follow," she said with a smile, closing her eyes again and beginning to doze. "Why would I want to ever subject myself to the drama?"

He smiled and lay down next to her, cuddling her against him. "It was all right, then? You okay?"

Damali sighed. She could not believe he was asking her something like that. "No," she said calmly. "In all honesty, I'm really not okay, yet." She felt his body tense and fought not to smile. Why couldn't he just get it through his thick male skull that he'd just rocked her world?

"I'm still disoriented, can't catch my breath, need something to wet my whistle after hollering like a madwoman . . . and making the witches upstairs probably ready to draw knives. But if they bum rush me for you, my legs are jelly and I'm so mellow right about through here that I'd have to just throw up my hands and cry Uncle. No, you messed me up bad, or real good, as the case may be—I'm not all right, yet. I'm devastated. Now go to sleep."

"Oh," he said with a satisfied chuckle and ran his hand down her belly until it found the damp mound of curly hair that hid her bud.

"Go to sleep, man. I need at least an hour before I can go exploring the outer edges of my sanity with you again."

His fingers gently caressed the plump slit, the spill of wetness teasing the tips of them as he remembered her secret earlobe mark and sucked it. "You want some champagne?" he murmured, rewarded by her shiver. "Something to wet your whistle while I find that other old mark on your femoral?"

She opened her thighs against her will, a soft moan escaping her lips under protest. "Stop playing, Carlos . . . I'm only human."

CHAPTER TWENTY-THREE

DAMALI WINCED and chuckled to herself as she stood and yawned. Her bladder was so full it felt like it had been bruised. She glanced at Carlos lying prone, his jaw slack with sleep, as she made her way to the bathroom, scooting quickly into the room and shutting the door. *Dang . . . could ya have eased up on a sister?* She laughed. It was her own fault; she'd started it. But she had no regrets.

She twinkled her toes on the tiles, feeling wobbly and contented, no matter how strange her circumstances. She could temporarily deal with this, if this was her fate. She'd been in worse places, that was for sure. Her eyes almost crossed as water poured from her body and relief wafted through her.

Absently flushing, she went to the sink and washed her hands, smelling the soaps, inspecting now that she was awake and alone. Ethiopia had been profound. The people there had shown her what Marlene said the hidden tribes of Madagascar could do . . . shape-shift, become invisible, move time. East Africa had deep spiritual history, Kemet-Egypt felt like a living, breathing empire within her, not some strange faraway bit of antiquity. The Coptics had made her reevaluate what was possible and what was not. She had three stones, new gifts to explore, and a second chance.

Damali splashed water on her face, and smiled as she heard Carlos gently knock on the door and slip into the red-tiled room with her. She looked up and met his tender gaze. He was so handsome . . . just plain old fine.

"Hey," he murmured. "I missed you."

She grabbed a plush terrycloth hand towel and dabbed her face with the soft crimson fabric. "I was coming back," she said quietly.

"I know," he said, his voice just above a whisper. "But I have a lot of good memories of you in the shower." He gave her an appreciative gaze that made her smile.

She didn't move as he came to her and enfolded her in his arms. His kiss was tender, his hold gentle, as though he were cradling porcelain.

"You wanna see what's been on my mind, and worrying me?"

She touched his face and kissed his temple. "Baby, you don't have anything to worry about."

"Yeah, I do," he whispered. "A lot of things trouble me, especially about living all together with your team."

She hugged him hard, not wanting to hear where he was going with his thoughts, but also knowing that she had to understand in order to dispel his wrong thinking.

"Mind-lock with me like old times, baby," he said upon a deep sigh. "I don't think I can even bring myself to say some of this."

"All right," she said, stroking his hair as she continued to hug him. "Then promise me we can talk about whatever it is?"

He nodded but didn't answer her and simply held the base of her skull as her head found a comfortable place in the crook of his shoulder. They stood like that for a while, naked, belly-to-belly, just breathing and being still. Finally she began to see images roam across the inside of her shut lids. The scenes were so painful that moisture built in her eyes.

She was walking through the compound, laughing with Jose. There were happy times, good times, the house was alive with mundane chaos. Then they were all eating a meal together, Rider was making everybody laugh, regaling them with stories of his bar exploits and holding court at the kitchen table. Soon the team began to disburse, each finding their own room, or a card game—it was an easy time. Jose looked at her for a long time and then slipped off quietly alone.

"Baby, listen—"

"Shush," Carlos said gently, soothing her and rubbing her back. "Let me show you why I'm concerned."

She could feel herself becoming tense, even though she com-

plied and allowed him to continue the shared vision. She remembered that night. It was when she'd thought Carlos was dead.
There had been many nights like that. Even before Carlos had died
and they didn't even know what his fate would be, she remembered
Jose always looking at her that way, wistfully. But then Dee Dee had
joined them and taken up with Jose, which had eased the pressure.
She didn't have to acknowledge the quiet look of longing. Once
Dee Dee had died and Carlos was presumed dead, there was a respectful period of mourning that neither wanted to broach.

"That's right," Carlos whispered, his voice mellow and defeated.
"That's why I asked him to stand in for me, if anything ever happened. If I wasn't here, you know he'd be your choice."

She shook her head and tried to pull out of the vision, but he
held her firm.

"Don't fight it, and I'm not angry. I just want you to be real
about what's going on in the house."

Reluctantly, she settled back against his shoulder. "I know how
Jose felt . . . it's complicated, but he understands and is cool. We're
friends, first and foremost—that's *all*."

Carlos petted her back. "I know he's respectful, but he's still a
man, and he's always loved you . . . from the moment he laid eyes
on you. I was supposed to die back there in Sydney—but I didn't.
That makes it awkward."

She sighed and nodded. What could she say? Only time would
work that out for all of them.

"I know," Carlos murmured, his hand a lazy stroke up and down
her back. "My greater concern is how he makes you feel."

"What?" She pulled back a bit and looked at him.

"Let me finish the vision," he said quietly, hugging her with
care. "Just flow with me for a minute before you get all defensive."

She sighed hard, but couldn't relax within his hold. Even
though she'd complied, a part of her held resistance. She didn't like
what was happening at all.

Soon she was standing in Jose's room, but she knew she was just
a shadow echo, not really there. She watched him stare up at the
ceiling, and then turn his head to look out at the moon. He closed

his eyes, his thick black lashes dusting his cheeks. His expression was so sad that she wanted to go to him and touch his face. Her heart ached—she loved him, this was her friend.

Relief poured through her as she watched him quietly doze off. A slow smile graced his face. That made her happy. He slept as peacefully as a newborn, laughing in his sleep. Then his expression became serious, and alarm bells rang in her head. She shook her head loose from Carlos's hold. "That's enough. This is his personal business."

Carlos let her slip away from him, but the vision held. Her eyes were open but the images still careened past her third eye. She watched Jose take in a slow sip of air, groan, and turn over on his stomach.

"Stop it!" she said firmly. "I want out!" She walked over to the sink and splashed water on her face to no avail. Carlos simply leaned against the door, his expression smug. "I will hate you for this if you don't stop," she said through her teeth. She covered her mouth and shut her eyes tightly as the image blocked out normal vision and she felt it.

In his sleep, Jose had gathered the sheets and pillows into his arms; he murmured her name, moved against the mattress as though she were there. Damali walked across the room, pacing. "Make it stop!"

"You two never talk about it because to do that, you have to acknowledge that it exists."

"Stop it!" she shrieked, her voice climbing in decibel and volume. "Right now, stop this vampiric invasion of my head! His head!"

"Oh, so now you're protecting him? You would call me a vampire; just throw it up in my face at the slightest provocation. Interesting."

"That's not fair," Damali said, trying to regain her former calm. "Stop it, please. This isn't fair."

"Lying to yourself, or him, isn't fair," Carlos murmured. "Especially when seeing him like that for you is turning you on."

"What!"

She started for Carlos to slap his face, punch him, open warfare, it was gonna be *on* in the bathroom—but the phantom sensation of touch rooted her to where she stood on the floor. Now all normal vision was gone, she was in the room, standing by Jose's bed, naked, watching his agonized erotic dream . . . her name on his lips, his hair now matted to his skull by hot sweat . . . it linked her to the memory of her own excruciating years of celibacy, waiting, hoping, yearning for the right one. The sensation crept between her legs, slithering there like a tormented, angry snake.

Jose turned over and sat up as though jolted awake by an electric shock. His eyes were dazed, but he simply opened his arms for her to fill them. "D, I can't keep living like this," Jose whispered. "He's dead. Come to me."

Part of her walked forward. It was as though some force beyond her drew her into his arms. The kiss was so intense and so familiar, but also so very strange. She pulled back from the kiss, even though her legs were still helping her climb into bed with him. "Not like this," she whispered and stroked Jose's cheek. "He's not dead."

"But if he was?" Jose's fingers trembled against her cheek, blurring the line between vision and reality.

Damali covered his hand and kissed the center of it and the touch made Jose close his eyes. "I don't know," she said quietly. "That scares me."

"If he's still alive, he doesn't have to know," Jose whispered, leaning forward to nuzzle her temple. "Just once, so I can put it out of my mind."

"But we'll know," she said, her hand stroking his hair. "And . . ."

"What if we start something in the house that can't stop?"

Tears filled her eyes and she nodded. "I have to go."

"Not yet. Don't go. Stay with me tonight." His eyes held a quiet plea before he closed them and kissed her again, this time with more intensity, his hold on the sides of her face furtive and unyielding. "If he's not dead and is human, then I have a chance. I'll fight for you—fair?" He held her face close to stare into her eyes. "Tell me you didn't feel anything between us, and I'll let you go."

She couldn't answer him.

"Is he dead, really, D? Or alive and human?"

"Let me go, Jose," she said gently. "I have a lot to think about." She covered his hands with hers, but a very wary sensation sparked within her. His line of questioning had been reasonable, true. She'd known he'd felt this way for a long time. It also frightened her to admit that, were Carlos actually gone, he most likely would have been her natural choice. But there was a level of quiet aggression within Jose that was profoundly disturbing, no matter what the situation. This was not like him at all. Something was terribly wrong.

"Let me consider the offer," she said, using evasive tactics to extract herself from his iron hold.

Jose relaxed but his eyes remained cold. "Is he still with you?"

"No," she lied, not sure why.

"Bullshit!" Jose shouted, and she leapt back from his hold and crossed the room. "Is he dead? Did he die in the sun, or did his ass come back as something else?"

"You should know," she said evenly, circling him and glancing around the room for a weapon. "Because you were there. You tell me."

Jose lunged for her and she avoided him, pivoted, and disappeared.

Damali jerked and something sucked her spirit back into her body with a hard snap. She was facing Carlos's sneer with the Jacuzzi between them. She narrowed her gaze and pointed at him. "Incubus! Be gone!"

She watched in horror as Carlos's skin withered and dropped like a dirty towel around his feet. A dark swirling energy created a small funnel cloud where he once stood and began uprooting porcelain, crashing the commode, sink, splintering tiles away from the mortar in rage. Pipes burst and water sprayed everywhere as she avoided the hurling objects. With no weapon in her hand and naked, she panicked and ran toward the door that was sealed shut.

"Lilith hasn't found you, yet. But our realm has," a sinister male voice echoed throughout the room. "You breached our realms with Raven—and she was not a sanctioned assassin!"

A huge pipe went airborne and spiraled toward her chest. Damali ducked and it impaled the door, splintering the wood. As the large, angry entity rushed toward her, its amorphous shape made it impossible to grasp or levy a blow against. Damali swung and her fist went through it, then she felt it pick her up and body slam her to the tile floor. It hovered above her for a second, its eyes green glowing slits of pure venomous rage. Rape was eminent, her hands burned hot, and the moment it thrust her thighs open, she yelled, "Freeze!"

Nothing moved. Tiles hung midair, spraying water held in stasis. She rolled over, pushed herself up, and pried open the door using the pipe like a crowbar.

Carlos chuckled as he felt Damali wrap her legs around his. "Baby, I'm beat. Gimme a few and I promise I'll be back in the saddle in no time."

He heard her giggle and continue to wrap her legs around his. He felt so sleepy it was as though he'd been drugged. She was holding his hands down on the bed now. If she wanted to play rough, that was cool, but he needed a moment to get his fifth wind.

"Right now, I ain't got nothing but love for you, girl," he murmured, chuckling as she stroked his neck. "The well is dry."

When she wouldn't stop, he opened his eyes to find her pouting mouth to kiss away her complaint. But instead of his woman draped around him, he watched in horror as the sheets came alive, strangled his legs, slithered between his thighs, and slid around his wrists and his throat. Instantly the fabric tightened, choking him, pinning him to the bed. Velvet drapes whipped off the poles and took serpentine form, rolling into tight coils that fanned their cobra throats out, hissed, and struck at him.

"Damali!" Carlos yelled, gagging, as the sheets became a noose. He could hear wood splintering and Damali yelling. Something or someone was banging on the door. He was choking to death. The bones in his wrists and ankles began to grind from the suffocating hold of the living sheets. Panic and struggle only tightened them around his body. Then a new emotion claimed him. Fury.

He stared at the offending creatures, his focus singular. Extinction. They had come into his bed, jeopardized his woman's life. Oh hell no. As soon as the thought took root within him, a laser cut the first striking velvet-drape serpent in half. It screeched a horrid death scream and sent plumes of yellow sulfuric smoke onto the air where Carlos's line of vision had severed it. Immediately the sheets uncoiled and slipped under the bed. He sat up and then jumped up, his gaze a torchlike sweep of the terrain halving the armoire, the dresser, cutting a path with silver Light.

Carlos snatched up his pants, pulled the small pocketknife that had traveled with him undetected across the continents from his clothes, and yanked the handle. A dark whirl of energy passed him and he scored it with a golden claw. Billowing sulfur escaped from the deep lacerations. A female demon materialized, and within seconds, her neck was trapped by a chain that sizzled. A head rolled to the floor as Carlos's hands yanked hard. The floor opened and swallowed the carnage.

Damali burst out of the bathroom brandishing a bent pipe. They went back-to-back, circling the room in a fighter's stance, ready. The vault door blew open, and Yonnie and Tara jumped out of Carlos's beam. Porcelain in the bathroom fell and a black tornado whirled past them and exited the room. Gabrielle rushed forward with her coven sisters. Rider came in behind them brandishing a pump shotgun. Carlos turned his head and steadied his breathing until he could glance up without cooking them.

"In my fucking room!" Carlos bellowed, his eyes flickering silver as he snapped his weapon shut. He held the small knife so that it was concealed within his clenched fist.

Yonnie came forward first. "Man, we got set up." He reached for Gabrielle and snatched her across the room into his hand by her throat.

"Let her go," Damali said. "It wasn't her. It was also male— incubus."

Yonnie dropped Gabrielle who skittered away to hug her sisters. "An incubus? That strong? To challenge a councilman?"

"Unheard of," Gabrielle gasped. "My establishment is fortified.

Succubae and incubi don't *dare* tread here unless invited for play. The spell barriers around this place alone would evaporate them." She walked about the room like a detective, fury making her bold. "Look at this mess!"

Carlos glanced around the room at the halved furniture and clean burn lines he'd left. If he weren't so pissed off and unnerved, he would have been pleased.

"Well, looks like you smoked one of them," Yonnie said. "You're definitely back, man."

Carlos nodded, rage still working its way through his system like poison. He glanced at Damali. "Yo, Yonnie. Do me a favor and give her some clothes—combat gear, slayer shit. No gowns. Tims, jeans, and a weapon."

Yonnie gave Damali an appreciative once-over gaze and robed her and Carlos at the same time. He neared Carlos and leaned close to him to speak discreetly as Damali put a nine in the waistband of her jeans and crossed the room.

"While I can tell you were definitely handling your business with the laser, it ain't good for the witches to see you like this. I know you expended a lot of energy before the break-in, and then went into battle on half a tank, but if you can't materialize clothes, man, you're gonna hafta eat right before you lair up with the Neteru in the future." Yonnie kept his voice to a low, private murmur so that only Carlos could hear him. He held Carlos's arm and motioned toward the destroyed bar with his chin. "Whatever's left over there ain't gonna pack the punch. Take any one of the witches or the male Guardian and get your tank right. Feel me. All of them got adrenaline hype. Whoever blew in here on you, man, was strong—so you've gotta be. Lift the ban so we can do this thing, me and you." Yonnie offered a fist pound, but Carlos declined it.

"No. The ban holds. Don't question me on it, I have my reasons."

Damali spun on Carlos and stood between Rider and the witches. "Not here, Yonnie. They're not for feeding to go into battle."

Tara drew away from Rider's side and stood with Damali. "I gave Rider the pump from Gabrielle's artillery. It's loaded with silver shells and packed hallowed earth—just in case some of their clients play a little rough."

"I understand your dilemma, Yonnie," Gabrielle said in an even tone, standing with Tara and Damali so that her coven members were behind her. "We get all sorts in here, occasionally a were-senator becomes overly aggressive, or a lower-level vamp takes it in his head to try an unauthorized flat-line, and one of our girls gets hurt." She opened her black silk robe and stroked a silver dagger and a gleaming Glock nine-millimeter. "Sometimes we have to show them to the door in the morning."

Yonnie opened his arms and smiled. "Baby, it's all peace. We're on the same side."

"Yeah, especially since they've chased your sister and her husband and kids up to Brooklyn," Carlos said, stepping in front of Yonnie. "Let's everybody chill."

"My sister?" Gabrielle said, closing her robe.

"Marjorie Berkfield," Carlos said, trying to end the standoff with information.

"Not Marj," Gabrielle said, nearly growling. "Her daughter is my protégé. Marjorie is the good one, the one in the family who believes in fairy tales and all things beautiful. She had a chance for a normal, placid life. Not her." She walked a hot path to the far side of the room and slid the fireplace mantel back by lowering a torch. "My sister! My lovely, nice sister who wouldn't hurt a fly? First Susan, now they've attacked my establishment and my beloved niece . . . *my favorite niece*?"

The motley group gaped as row upon row of stakes, crossbows, medieval swords, packed shells, every size gun, and ammunition became revealed. Gabrielle snatched down a bazooka. "We take this to the streets."

Damali stepped forward and hoisted down an AK-47 and two ammo clips, and strapped the machine gun over her shoulder. She then took down a silver broadsword. "Now that's what I'm talking about—a woman who handles her business." She and Gabrielle exchanged a glance of mutual respect. "The rest of my team is holed up somewhere in Brooklyn with a trigger-happy old man. We'll have to break diversity to him slowly, but he's on the same mission. Whoever did this waxed his brother."

Gabrielle nodded and glanced at Rider. "The human doesn't look so good."

Rider shrugged and walked toward the ammo wall. "I'm all right. Just a few pints low," he said, offering Tara a strained smile.

"He needs a detox, soon," Tara said, touching Rider's arm as she neared him. "I tried to purge him in the room . . . after," she said, her voice filled with shame. "But I forgot, my bites now— I'm a second." Her gaze searched the women in the room for help.

"I said I'm fine," Rider said with a shiver. "All I need is a shot of Jack Daniels and a gun."

Carlos walked over to Rider and felt his head. "Cold sweats are setting in. This man is dead on his feet, if we don't get him to Marlene soon. She's the only one that I've ever seen purge a high-level bite—"

"She can't do it," Damali said quietly, walking to Rider slowly and swallowing hard. "She could purge me because I had Neteru antibodies. She could bring Jose back because Dee Dee was a third and the connection was the baby, not a bite. Tara's grandmother was working with a fourth-gen." She touched Rider's cheek and then hugged him.

Rider stroked her back and looked at Tara. "Baby, we always knew one day it might come to this, right? Okay. I'm a dead man walking and my number is up . . . but I wouldn't have wanted to get nicked any other way."

Tara covered her mouth and turned away. "Not him and not like this," she whispered.

"Can Berkfield clean this up?" Damali asked, her wet gaze going to Carlos. "Answer me! You guys know how this works!"

"It's all right," Rider said, gently pushing her away. "Let's go find out who we've gotta hot, do the job, and in three nights, I'll need an ambulance."

"No!" Damali shouted. "You get back with the team and see if Medic can do a transfusion. In the meantime, you keep your stubborn ass alive, you hear?" She hugged him hard. "I will kill you if you die on me, Rider. Stop playing."

"Then we'd better get a move on hunting down what caused the problem," Yonnie said, trying to restore the calm.

Damali left Rider slowly and nodded. She went to Tara and hugged her. "It wasn't your fault, and we'll get him cleaned up. I understand. All right?"

Tara nodded. "We'll need strong seers to break their mask."

With a long sigh, Damali walked over to her discarded robes and extracted the three stones from her pocket. "Three with living souls is what we need. I'm one. Who else has the gift?"

Gabrielle stepped forward. "I can astral project and do divination."

Damali nodded. She glanced at the other coven members, but all the women hung their heads. "Then I have to get to Marlene or Father Pat."

"I can see," Carlos said quietly.

"Yeah, man, so can I. But the Neteru said you have to have a soul to break supernatural masks—that's the crux." Yonnie paced over to Tara. "Maybe me and you can get a bead on where the Brooklyn team is and transport them here. Problem is, if they're behind hallowed—"

"I can see," Carlos repeated quietly, walking up to Damali. "I have the visions, too."

"My councilman," Gabrielle said, losing patience. "I know you're very upset, as we all are, but some things are simply beyond—"

"I have a soul," Carlos whispered.

He closed his eyes as a gasp passed through the room and Yonnie came to him slowly.

"What, man . . ." Yonnie said so quietly that his question echoed.

Carlos looked at him sadly. "That's what I've been trying to tell you all along. You just didn't hear me."

"We should be in Brooklyn gathering weapons now!" the rabbi argued. "Not futzing around with this girl in a church. Either she's coming with us to fight or not."

"She's traumatized. Can't you see that?" Marjorie protested. "How old are you, sweetheart? Where're your parents?"

"Still in San Pedro," the young woman said, blowing her nose in a tissue. "We all went there, just a few miles outside of Tijuana, right after Mrs. Rivera and her mother were killed. I thought if I ran far enough . . ." She looked up at Father Lopez and then her gaze lingered on Jose. "I wanted to find his parish. His church. He was the only priest who believed me, didn't think it was all superstition."

She stood up and exited the pew and went to Father Lopez and hugged him tightly. "You came back for me." She sobbed against his shoulder. "Even Jose didn't come for me. I asked them and they wouldn't tell me where you had gone. I stayed at the churches and called the secret number you gave me, but it only rang." Her sobs became more ragged as he rubbed her back and closed his eyes. "You always came before when I called, were always there, I knew if I heard your voice, it would be all right." She looked at Jose hard. "Don't you remember? You were supposed to come back for me, but you didn't!"

"Wait," Shabazz said, glancing at the young woman and then Jose. "You two know each other?"

Jose nodded and looked away. "We go way back. Before her and Carlos. Old history from when we were kids." Sadness registered within Jose's voice. His gaze sought the floor. "Until now, I just didn't remember."

Father Lopez stared at Jose for a moment, as did the others.

"We have to get out of here," the rabbi said, becoming more agitated. "I can feel doom on the way. This girl is like a walking Typhoid Mary! She goes to Philadelphia and stays at a church shelter, and what happens?" He'd asked the question while walking in a circle with his hands clasping his hat. "Disaster. A huge cathedral at Forty-third and Chestnut Streets, she says, has something crash into the southwest tower and bring a stone building down that has stood for over a hundred years. This after a house blows up. This is a bad sign and an omen. Now, she is sitting in another holy place and we're with her? Not good. If this young man forgot her, there is a good reason! My advice to you all is leave the destruction magnet and let us go and fight this fight, then figure it all out. *Later.*"

"There's a lot we have to talk about later," Marlene said in a quiet voice, gaining a nod from Shabazz.

"Let it rest," Jose said, "Later. 'Nita, I'm sorry. Maybe you should stay here until we figure this out."

"I don't want to go with you any more than you want me to, either," Juanita said proudly. "Like I've told you a hundred times, a man picked up the line when I tried to call Padre. He told me to go to the airport, alone, he had a one-way ticket for me, and gave me the address. I was to wait for Padre—that's all he said. Then when the church crumbled they gave me another address and drove me to Thirtieth Street Station, said a prayer, and dropped me off to catch a train to New York. So, I'm not leaving with anyone but him." She held on to Father Lopez tighter and glared at Jose. "*He* never left me. Both you and Carlos did."

Marlene shared a look with Father Patrick, who stood and walked down the long aisle toward the altar with his hands clasped behind his back. Big Mike rubbed his hands over his face and let out a long breath. Marjorie Berkfield and her children shot nervous glances around the team.

"If I hadn't stopped to call into Covenant headquarters from a pay phone, we wouldn't have come here. We wouldn't have known you were here at all," Father Patrick said quietly. "Perhaps I can implore our forces to make weapons available from here."

"But will they have antidemon devices like my brother had developed?" the rabbi said, now stomping his feet.

"If Father Pat makes the call, they know what we're up against. At least this way we'll be strapped en route to your place," Big Mike said calmly. "We'll add what you've got to the stash—so chill."

Shabazz rubbed his hands over his face and stood. "If you've got a specialty, girlfriend, you'd better hone it." He studied Juanita with a hard glare. "We're losing time. We can't leave you here, and if you go with us, you've gotta go packing. Make a decision, sis."

Dan hung his head and spoke in a defeated tone. "Give her time, 'Bazz. I remember what this felt like—having your life change in the glint of a fang. Maybe we can leave her here in Manhattan, go do what we've gotta do, and bring her in slowly?"

"Juanita, baby, you've already told us about what went down in the ambulance. We're here trying to make sure that doesn't happen to you," Jose said as gently as possible.

"We've been here going over this for hours," J.L. said, raking his hair. "I want you to look at Mrs. B. She's got her kids with her, ya know. She has to be terrified, her children are newbies, and her husband was almost slaughtered. I say we take the old core squad out to do this dirty work, then, after the smoke settles, we educate everybody, train the newbies, and give people a chance to adjust." His gaze went to Kristin. "If anything happens to a new, unseasoned Guardian, will any of us ever be able to live with that?"

"I'm with J.L." Berkfield said. "Leave anyone who's new and a civilian in this church with our clerical brothers to bodyguard them, and we take a special forces squad that knows how to handle themselves with weapons up to Brooklyn with the rabbi."

"There is wisdom with that approach," Imam Asula said. "We can guard the three women and the young boy here in the cathedral, while the Guardians bring us back what we'll need."

"Sometimes it is the untried road that is most successful," Monk Lin offered. "We will stay and protect the new ones."

Juanita looked at the others with distrust. "Padre Lopez was the only one who checked on Carlos's family after he had to go into hiding." Her gaze narrowed on Berkfield. "You never came to help his mother. They won't even let me bury his loved ones until they've performed the autopsies—simply because their faces weren't as badly burned as the authorities expected. He helped you, Detective; why couldn't you help him more than you did?"

"I couldn't," Berkfield said without apology. "I would have blown their safe-house cover."

"It's true," Father Lopez said, cupping Juanita's face with his hand. "What they say is true." He allowed his hand to fall away as the group's gaze made him uncomfortable. "Maybe it's a blessing that the funerals had to wait . . . until Carlos could come back and see his family one last time." He reached for her face again and stroked her cheek with trembling fingers. "I won't let anything happen to you, I promise."

Marlene stood, left the disorganized group, and walked toward Father Patrick to privately confer close to the altar.

"Seer to seer, I'm going to ask you one question," Marlene said, staring into Father Patrick's eyes without blinking.

He nodded.

"We've got significant dissention in the ranks, our Neterus in a hot zone where we can't get a lock on them through black-spell barricades, and several serious problems brewing."

Father Patrick's gaze was unwavering. "Ask your question, Marlene."

"This one particular problem that's nagging my mind is very dangerous to our core formation, isn't it?"

Father Patrick closed his eyes. "Yes."

CHAPTER TWENTY-FOUR

CARLOS CHOSE his words carefully as the group assembled around the large oval table in the parlor. He looked at Damali, confused. "You're blocking, baby."

"I'm not," she said, her tone brittle enough to snap. "It's Gabrielle's barriers. I can't connect to the team through it, plus wherever they are is definitely fortified against a transmission coming from this type of location." Damali stood and collected her stones. "We need to go outside."

"Can I talk to you for a minute?" Yonnie said, looking at Carlos.

"Later, man," Carlos muttered and pushed away from the table.

"No," Damali said, stopping at the archway that led to the foyer. "Talk to him now, get it all resolved, so we don't have any issues in the middle of a battle. We need to know who's with us or not."

"I think that would make all of us who still have a pulse feel better," Gabrielle said, standing. "I was willing to be turned, but not flat-lined." She looked at Rider and Tara. "I'm going upstairs to change into some street clothes and will be back in five minutes. I have something he can put on up there, I'm sure—since Yonnie is so pissy with him."

Yonnie snapped his fingers and put Rider in fatigues. "I told you it was peace," he said, his tone low and threatening. "Now, I'd like a word with my councilman—alone. Five minutes."

Rider cocked back the barrel of his pump shotgun. "Thanks. Give the man an audience. In five we move out, like Damali said."

Carlos nodded and the group withdrew to the foyer area to give Yonnie and Carlos space.

Yonnie glanced over his shoulder and walked in close to Carlos. "Is it true?" he asked, his tone nonjudgmental. "It's just me and you. Talk to me."

Carlos nodded. "Yeah, man. I burned in daylight, and came back." He stared at his friend. "I don't expect you to understand it—and if you can't roll with me like this, then, I can respect that. You have to do what you have to do. I have to do the same."

Yonnie shook his head. "No, you're the one who doesn't understand." He swallowed hard and closed his eyes, two quiet tears wetting his face. "Since this happened to me, I always wondered if there was ever a way out of the life." He sighed and opened his eyes, his gaze furtive as it held Carlos's face. "It means there's hope. Even if I go to ash, something could come through the barriers and at least let my soul rest." He walked closer to Carlos. "Two hundred years, man, and I've been living like an animal. But you got out. Tell me how you did it."

"There was a slipup in supernatural law, man . . . I don't know. But—"

"You went down with honor," Yonnie said quietly. "Were always a good man. Had the love of a good woman. Took care of family and pulled yourself out of the bowels." He motioned across the expanse toward Tara with his chin. "She was supposed to be one of yours on the side of Light. Was supposed to guard a Neteru, and not a night has gone by that I haven't felt it in my bones." He paused to steady his voice and force the emotion out of it. "You two have even got the head of a coven sitting up here contemplating change." Yonnie smiled sadly. "The least likely, me, for instance, is standing here wondering what it would really be like to be free."

Carlos nodded and extended his fist, and Yonnie pounded it softly.

"Put in a good word for me when I go down," Yonnie said, his voice far away. "If council is on our asses, sooner or later, you know that's where it ends, right?"

Again Carlos nodded. "My word as my bond, I'll tell them about you, Tara, and Gabrielle. But let's try to get them before they get us. Cool?"

Yonnie began walking toward the group. "Yeah, man, the only problem is, once you blow council chambers, we're ash." He stopped and looked at Carlos, tilting his head. "But I'm okay with that."

Damali stood just beyond the door; her senses keen while contemplating the moon. She hadn't expected her reaction to locking with Carlos. The visit from an incubus had rattled something loose in her confidence as well as her conscience. That type of level-two entity could plant seeds of discontent and confusion, but it had to have something to work with. The private discovery made her shiver. She remembered too many times when things had become awkward between her and Jose, and they'd both been wise enough, or maybe afraid enough, to simply play it off and let the silent tension go undisturbed. And when she thought Carlos was really gone, there had been moments . . .

Damali shook the thought and sealed it away in a silver vault within her mind. Suddenly the early November night felt so cold. She hadn't felt it go down to her marrow like this before, not even in the park dressed in her lightweight African garb. Now she felt every bitter chill in the air. Never again. Never happen. It didn't happen. That was then, this was now. She had to open a channel to Carlos to not only get the mind lock done, but that was part of who they were together. This Jose thing was just a reality specter.

She felt a light touch on her shoulder and knew it was Tara without having to turn around. Without needing to look, she could sense Tara glance back at Rider, who was still in the foyer. Her Neteru instinct was stronger, but her soul heavier. Always the dichotomy of being human and gaining wisdom.

"For whatever it's worth," Tara said quietly, her voice a soothing balm, "I have been there." She sighed as Damali finally glanced at her. "So have they," she said, discreetly motioning with her eyes to the men in the room behind them.

Damali just stared at Tara wondering how she knew.

"It was incubus," she said quietly. "Male energy, and I could trace it by following its illusion." She placed her hand on Damali's arm. "Don't worry. They can't."

Damali let out her breath slowly. "Thanks." She hesitated and then dropped her guard a little more. "But how could it be so strong? Phantoms and poltergeist-type energies are from levels one and two, right?"

"Yes," Tara said, calmly. "If it materialized here, with such force, then something very strong opened their portals and gave them free reign to materialize. Carlos got the female, but the male is still hunting." Her hypnotic dark eyes held Damali's. "But I will answer your real question. You live with unwanted knowledge hour by hour, until it gets further away to become something that you only think about once and a while."

"Thank you," Damali said quietly, and offered Tara an embrace.

Tara was slow to accept it, unsure of hugging Damali back. "You are unafraid of me. I understand your trust of the councilman. He is different now and always loved you. But you're a Neteru, and I am still what I am."

"Yes, you are," Damali said, looking Tara in her eyes. "You are on my team, and in my Guardian brother's heart and soul. Your destiny was to fight with the Neteru. We don't leave our own."

Tara swallowed hard and stroked Damali's arm as she pulled away. "Thank you for that—it is a supreme gift." She clasped Damali's hand. "As we say—until I am ash, I am with you."

Damali touched Tara's shoulder. "Until I am dust, you are with me."

Tara wrapped her arms around herself but continued to stare at Damali. "Live alone for a while. Gabrielle and Marjorie will tell you the same. Neither of us did that before we made our choices. It was a different generation, a different time." She glanced back at the house, noting Rider's shadow behind the foyer glass and Yonnie and Carlos's forms in the parlor. "It is hard to separate from family, especially a mother who loves you. It is even harder to pull away from a man who adores you more than his next breath. But it is far harder to live with yourself never knowing if you can save yourself, stand on your own, be who you must be, and be all right with that."

Tara's hand dropped away from Damali's, but their eyes held

each other's with greater admiration. Thanks wasn't necessary. It was implicit. They both understood.

For what felt like a long time, neither woman spoke. They released their mutual gaze and parted as warriors, both with a cause and a secret bond.

"May I ask you a question?" Tara finally said as she glimpsed Gabrielle coming down the stairs through the glass door.

"Yeah," Damali said, her line of vision following Gabrielle.

"Did you love him back to life?"

Damali stared at Tara. "I don't know, exactly. Maybe?"

"Then I still have hope."

Again, silence draped them under the moon. Both women stood quietly side-by-side, lost in her own thoughts. But when Tara hissed, Damali tensed.

"Succubus," Tara said through her teeth.

Damali touched her shoulder. "I know her."

Tara stared at Damali for a second before her eyes trained on a floating mist near the curb.

"We don't have time," Raven said, her voice lilting on the breeze. "They've followed your essence."

"You double—"

"No," Raven said quickly. "They only know about you, from trailing your essence off of me. We were together, only you and I. Ask yourself, when the incubus attacked, did he still search for Carlos, or did he know he was in the room with you?"

"Something attacked our councilman," Tara said in a snarl, but glanced at Damali, obviously ready to keep the ruse up before a potential enemy.

"It was a restrainer, and then the Amanthras came to finish off the job to be sure he wouldn't intervene. They thought the newly located female Neteru was with just a Guardian, a lover," Raven whispered, glancing around quickly. "Those who hunt him can't identify him. The only reason they got to you is because of our meeting. Ask him if the succubus that came to him spoke, or probed for questions. That's how you'll know."

"I can't ask him that without him wanting to go, too—and he can't." Damali looked at Tara.

"Then it's now or never," Raven urged. "Hurry!"

Damali nodded and stepped forward. Tara bristled.

"Don't trust her after what just happened," Tara warned, her gaze ripping toward the house and then back to Damali.

"Cover me," Damali said, holding Tara's gaze. "I need them blocked for a few minutes so they don't try to stop me."

"Hurry," Raven urged again, beginning to dissolve.

"Where are you going?" Panic widened Tara's eyes and lengthened her fangs.

"To pay Mr. Chairman a little visit."

It was quite possibly the most insane thing she'd ever pulled, but she'd had to leave her weapons on the steps and take Raven's hand. Before Tara could make up her mind what to do, she was being escorted to Hell by a phantom.

Raven's chest heaved like a frightened bird as they landed in the rocky realm of the undead. "Level two, but the one who chased you, is also looking for me. The incubus is—"

Raven instantly dissolved, leaving Damali standing alone.

Punk bitch. Damali shook her head. She could buy the part about the weapons carrying hallowed earth setting off alarms, but this didn't make no kinda sense!

"So, we meet again," a deep baritone voice murmured, its hot breath way too close to her ear for comfort.

"Yeah, we do," Damali said, her night vision sweeping the terrain for something to crush the entity with. "Was looking for you, baby."

The dark form slowly circled her and suddenly materialized with her in its putrid embrace. "And here I thought I'd have to go topside again to find you."

"No," Damali whispered. "You were right. The vision really turned me on, and my old friend, Raven, brought me to you as a peace offering."

The entity's eyes glowed with excitement as a cruel smile

stretched his hideous gray lips into what was supposed to be a grin. "Then I guess I owe her, don't I?"

"Yeah," Damali murmured, stroking his foul cheek. "I know you have to turn me over to Lilith, in order to collect . . . but, uh . . . maybe in an hour?"

"Yes . . ." he whispered. "Maybe in an hour."

Damali motioned toward a cliff side. "Y'all got any flat surfaces around here that might accommodate a sister?"

The entity laughed and transformed into a handsome male that resembled a taller version of Jose. "I see why Lilith is green with envy over you, love. You *are* special." He wafted away from her toward a rock-studded wall and crooked his finger toward her. "I'm very nontraditional. We can do this standing up."

She could feel his magnetic pull forcing her to walk forward. There was nothing to work with, not a loose branch or rock anywhere. Then she smiled. They were beneath the earth's surface, true, but inside the womb of the earth was where the supernatural had taken up parasitic residence. Inside Mother Earth, and she was all natural.

Damali stretched out her arms and closed her eyes. She saw the entity smile in victory, as her outstretched hands seemed to beckon him. "Permission to use you," she whispered.

"Done. Name the shape," he murmured.

"Rock."

Instantly, energy ran though her arms, into her fingertips, and struck the formation the incubus leaned against. He screeched as he attempted to quickly convert his form back into vapor, but the huge boulders that slammed against his humanlike male body sent black blood spewing from his mouth. Damali turned her wrists like she was screwing a faucet, grinding the boulder into his chest cavity, crushing his ribs. His eyes blazed green with rage as the boulder jettisoned off his chest, but his jump forward wasn't fast enough to avoid the razor-sharp stalagmite that took off his head.

Raven was at her side in an instant, coughing through the billowing smoke, her eyes wide. "We have to get you down to three before this crag fills with gangs."

Damali didn't argue, she just grabbed Raven's hand and closed her eyes as a black plume sucked them away into the tunnels.

The wet, dripping, serpentine realms gave her the creeps. When maggots dropped into her hair and cockroaches skittled over her boots and up her pants legs, she covered her mouth to keep from screaming.

"I know. I know," Raven said, breathlessly. "But this is as far as I can go."

Damali refused to look around the writhing swamp and held her breath as the intense, humid funk made her nearly vomit.

"You know the way to the were-realms from here." Raven motioned with her arm and then melted into the wall.

How in the world did Carlos deal with this? She could feel things watching her, the trees moving, and it was time to run. Something huge was uncoiling behind her as she fled through the passageway, seeking the were-demon energies, but when she heard a loud snap, and felt the breeze of a bite at her back, she was liquid motion.

Whatever was on her ass, she couldn't outrun for long. Not through the dense swamp and gnarled, wet tree limbs. She kept losing her footing, falling, and losing valuable distance. She remembered the Amazon and the ridiculously huge serpent that had a head the size of a Mini Cooper.

Tree branches dropped before her with what seemed like a thousand black adders.

"Oh, shit!" Damali covered her head as more bugs and debris fell. Of course the passage between realms would be guarded by whatever level's finest fighting machines! Variable.

Fetid bodies lay strewn and moaning, flesh-rotted skeletal hands grabbed at her, begging for help. She was out. Her legs gave out beneath her, her body hit the floor, and to her amazement she was moving at a dizzying speed over the wet terrain with ease on her belly.

She didn't want to think about it. It was all about motion, snakelike or otherwise. She just hoped that when she came out into the next realm, she could do it again.

When she crested the barrier, snarls and snaps and howls greeted her. This was a bad place for a lady snake to be. But she didn't know how she did the first shape-shift, let alone this one.

Yellow glowing eyes stalked forward in a blackened forest, then disappeared. Beneath her stomach, brittle, sharp gravel dug into her. Then to her horror she realized it was bones! But there was no time to be squeamish with five zone-guard were-wolves moving in.

Images slammed into her mind. The only thing that jumped into it was Carlos. The next thing she knew, she was off her belly, on all fours, with tremendous black paws. Her leap up to a tree branch was so agile she stunned herself. Her roar stilled the howls. The wolves backed up and looked at each other nervously.

"Madame Senator," one of the wolves said, lowering his head in a canine-submissive manner. "We caught the scent of Amanthras at our gate, and saw a black adder slither into our realm. We meant no offense."

Damali could feel her eyes narrow to slits and her tail twitch. "Be gone!" she growled, pacing back and forth on the high limb. "Fools. Why do you think I'm here? I saw it first, and I will deal with it."

When they nodded and apologized for the affront, and then began to back away, she nearly fell off the limb. *Now* she understood, totally, what Carlos had been saying about power. It did have an intoxicating kick to it, and the panther shape was awesome. But she had to focus and live long enough to square off with the chairman.

In one fluid motion, she was down out of the tree, loping toward the last barrier. Level six.

"You let her go where?" Carlos shouted, banging his fist on the door.

Rider yanked Tara's arm. "Are you crazy?"

Yonnie bulked and it stilled the dispute. "If you *ever,* in my presence, grab her like that . . ."

"Easy, man," Carlos said. "Keep your head. The main thing is to find D."

Rider dropped Tara's arm as she snatched it away.

"Raven came to—"

"Raven!" Carlos hollered, stopping Tara's words, and began pacing. "Inside. Everybody!"

The group rushed inside, slammed and locked the front door,
going to the parlor.

"Yonnie, man. Get me down there. My baby's walking into an
ambush."

Yonnie's eyes held so much regret that for a moment he couldn't
respond.

"What do I have to do, beg you?" Carlos shouted.

"I can't. We're topside locked, man. Chairman's orders. We
can't go sub anymore!"

"Oh, shit. Oh, shit." Carlos walked in a circle.

"We've gotta get to Mar," Rider said quickly, holding his gun
on Yonnie and refusing to look at Tara. "She's the only—"

"Marlene doesn't know the dark realms!" Carlos yelled, pounding on the table with both hands. "*I was the master,* a councilman.
I'm the only one who knew the route and had the black blood
strong enough to open council doors, if I went with formal summons! Marlene can't even begin to fuck with my old world!"

"But I can," Gabrielle said, quietly, making everyone in the
room look at her. She nodded and went to her large walnut cabinet
to pull out her crystal ball. "The Guardian mother-seers work with
the Light. They see realms above." She placed the ball that sat on a
dark brass pedestal in the center of the table. "But in order to do
what I do, trust me, I have looked into the dark side."

Her comment drew everyone around the parlor table as
Gabrielle sat down.

"Why'd she do it?" Carlos whispered, as though talking to
himself.

Gabrielle stared up at him. "Do you really want me to tell you
in mixed company—or in private?"

"Just spit it out," Yonnie said, his patience gone along with his
nerves.

"What the fuck," Carlos said, walking between the wall and the
table.

"She did it because Lilith has her egg. Yes, you gave her seed to bring it to life, but what Lilith stole was supposed to grow and thrive in Damali's womb. *This* is the part of the equation that men will never understand." Her narrowed gaze raked Carlos. "This wasn't your fight—this time it was *hers.* This wasn't your vendetta. She will do this or die trying. It is natural law. A mother versus a robber mother. Even the supernatural cannot avert that."

Tara leaned down as she peered at the swirling black smoke that had begun to spiral within Gabrielle's crystal. "It wasn't my place to stop her, and if I could have been her escort to help her smoke that bitch, I would have. If Raven double-crosses her, *she's mine.*" Tara looked up at Rider. "A baby . . . a precious little baby that's only a spec of life now. Do you know what I would give for the chance that Damali was robbed of?" She pushed away from the table and glanced at Yonnie. "None of you will ever experience the loss ache like that!"

The males in the room gathered to one side of the table in a slow, defeated huddle. Gabrielle and Tara glared at them. All eyes were on the crystal ball.

Gabrielle pointed at it and covered her mouth and then laughed. Tara smiled. Yonnie ran his fingers through his Afro as Rider shook his head. Carlos blanched.

All he could do was watch as his baby girl finessed an incubus like an all-pro vamp and slaughtered him. When she went black adder, he almost looked away. The sight of her agile flight at lightning speed on her belly was almost nauseating. But when she shifted and went panther, donning his old form, he had to walk away for a moment to get his head together.

"She's all pro, man," Yonnie said quietly. "She ain't no baby no more, not shifting like that." He shook his head. "Damn, man . . . I've never seen the Neteru work. Now I totally understand."

Carlos glared at him and came back to the table. If he could have still dropped fangs, he would have. But as he watched her cross into level six, everyone at the table sat down slowly.

"Oh . . . shit . . ." Carlos whispered. "She went bat."

Gabrielle nodded as they watched Damali fly in under radar and affix herself to the ceiling, huddling with the swarming masses. "I can try to send her support via a spell, since I do have a willing master vampire in the room with a strong second lieutenant, but then our position will be given away." She shook her head and closed her eyes. "This is suicide."

"Do it," Carlos said. If you can give her a shield, any—"

"I don't know," Gabrielle said as calmly as she could. "I can *see* into the dark realms, not influence events going on there. My spell shields are for topside only."

"But she's gotta watch out for the couriers at the gate!" Carlos paced back and forth like a trapped animal. His heart was pounding so hard that he could barely hear anything else. Then he stopped and his jaw dropped. "A roach?" He ran to the table and clutched the edge of it. "A fucking cockroach, with starving bats all around? Damali, no!"

The moment the aerial assault began, she knew the choice was a bad one. But a mouse was too obvious and was warm blooded, and a roach moved faster, not to mention could better withstand the heat rising off the hot rocks. All she had to do was scurry down the long crag-strewn path and squeeze under one of the doors. But bats dove at her relentlessly. However, the one thing she knew from her days on the streets, a roach was a hard thing to kill.

She scooted over the edge of the narrow path that led to the chairman's front doors and gripped the wall. Hair-raising wails from the Sea of Perpetual Agony echoed up with tortured moans. Molten lava below her made her eyes burn, but the bats avoided her when she squeezed herself into a crack. After each attempt they veered away from the surface as their wings began to smolder, then finally gave up. One tasty little morsel of a cockroach apparently wasn't worth it.

As she righted herself, she tested the air for danger with her antennae, stole under the massive black doors, and then skittered along the edge of the wall like so many vermin probably had done. A mixture of rage and awe temporarily held her transfixed. So this is where Carlos had to run his best game. . . .

The chairman was sitting by himself at his throne, his eyes closed, his gray, bald head slowly throbbing with an eerie pulse of sluggish black blood. She would slaughter this motherfucker in his sleep.

As soon as the thought entered her mind, his eyes popped open, his fangs grew to lengths that were alarming, and he stood. Oh, shit.

Two more councilmen swished into the room from the shadows. Now she had three of these bastards to deal with alone and no weapon. Staying concealed as a roach was no longer an option. It wasn't about coming all this way to be squished like a bug. Damali stood.

They backed up, blinked twice, and snarled.

"You're crazier than he was," the chairman said, holding out his arms so his fellow councilmen didn't lunge.

"Nice to meet you, after all these years," Damali said calmly, looking around the weaponless room. "So. Here we are."

"And to think I've gone to all this trouble to locate you, and you simply waltz into my chambers." He smiled. "Charming."

"I aim to please," she said through her teeth.

The chairman stepped forward. "You must have been magnificent with fangs."

Inside her mind she could hear Carlos yelling for her not to fuck with the chairman and to get out of there. But rather than make her heed his advice, the fact that he'd locked with her during her hit bred an insane level of defiance. "I was," she finally said. "You should have seen me in full bloom." Then it came back to her. *Dananu*.

"You don't know how sorry I am to have missed that," he said with a wicked smile. "Maybe you'll stay a few years so I won't miss it again?"

"Shall we dance?" she said in the mind-bending language. The dark-realm power had her in its grip, and everything from Carlos's old throne was wafting toward her like a toxic gas leak. But it did have the interesting effect of making her bolder.

The chairman cocked his head to the side. The other councilmen's eyes blazed with wonder. "He taught you *Dananu*, too . . . and you understand it?"

"I'm fluent in it, among other things. . . . And can take battle-length in the jugular like a love bite." She leaned her neck over to offer him a tantalizing glimpse of her jugular as a taunt, and then straightened when all three of them licked their lips. "Been a long time since you boys have been topside, ain't it?"

"I can more readily understand Rivera's conflict," the chairman said in a low, seductive tone that had an implicit threat laced within it.

"He was your best, remember?"

"You won't mind if I have a word with the lady alone in chambers, will you gentlemen?"

She could feel Carlos's mind literally catch on fire as the two senior councilmen begrudgingly withdrew.

"We have a debt to settle, it seems," Damali said casually, beginning to walk around the edges of the room, positioning herself for an attack. Who knew what booby traps this old bastard had, and his power was no joke. She could feel it eating at her skin.

He nodded and began to match her moves. "We do, Neteru. But you have always been such a curiosity to me. An enigma. Soft, yet hard. Crazy, yet shrewd. Willing to take a bite all the way to the vanishing point, but then would just as quickly turn around and gore one from our realms. You utterly fascinate me."

"You *thoroughly* disgust me," she said, and like lightning, drew a heavy section of the rock wall away from itself to fly at him.

The chairman ducked, but got up with black glowing eyes, and sent a wall torch toward her. She bent back, but the heat of the flame only grazed her cheek as a warning. She brought her hand to her face. He laughed.

"Six years with you down here will be the best years of my existence."

He raised his hand and a black lightning strike lifted her from her feet and pinned her to the wall. He moved toward her so quickly that he was a mere blur, and instinct made her reach for her hip. He laughed harder.

"What? No Isis, darling?"

His hot, stinky breath covered her throat and made her eyes sting with its fumes. But it was as though she were an amputee, feeling the phantom presence of a missing limb. She stabbed him with whatever had come into her hand and he backed up with a wail, clutching his shoulder.

She dropped from the wall. The combatants parted. He felt the wound and sealed it, his hand coming away with black blood.

"You . . . little . . . bitch!" he yelled, slapping her face from across the room, making her taste blood.

That's when she saw it, the beam of Light in her hand, and she hurled it at him with all her might. He ducked and then turned, trying to save the table. But the Light wand flipped quickly end over end and lodged into the center of the table's crest. Immediately, the other two councilmen reentered the room, and this time they would not be dissuaded.

One flew toward her as the table began to disintegrate. Damali reached for her hip and hurled the tingling sensation at him, dead aim, and he imploded above her, sending cinders to rain over her head. His throne smoked, and her name slowly burned into the stone headrest surface of it. Enraged, the chairman ejected the beam that was festering in his wounded table and hurled a thunderbolt toward her, blowing her through chamber doors.

Falling fast, the heat beneath her brought her to her senses. Strong bird. *Strong bird,* her mind screamed, and she flew at him as a falcon. Wrong bird, when both he and the remaining councilman became huge gargoylelike bats with wingspans that made her look like a sparrow.

Her back to the wall, them moving in rapid blurs, chamber doors open and about to fill with vampire warriors, she hurled rocks to block additional soldiers, and slithered under the table as a snake. When she came up behind Carlos's old throne, she was careful not to touch it.

They were breathing hard, so was she. But the table had been damaged, and they were a councilman short. Unable to measure the impact, she did something that would give them pause. She grabbed their black book from the beneath the broken crest and held it hostage.

"This goes up in flames, if you fuck with me, gentlemen. Try me!"

They stopped circling and stood still.

"If this burns, the harpies will come and ask how I breached your chambers, right?"

The second councilman withdrew. In the standoff she saw an opportunity and took it, spearing him with a wall torch from behind, and then threw a quick Light dagger to implode him. The chairman sealed himself behind a transparent black shield as Damali's name etched into another throne.

"Now it's just me, you, and the history book." Damali caressed the book. "This is closest and easiest to—"

"Stop!" He yelled, as she reached for her hip again to put a Light dagger into the center of the book. "I have something you want, you have something I want," he said in a rasping lisp of *Dananu.*

"What you took from me can *never* be replaced," she said, her voice so low and lethal that it sounded evil to her own ears. "Your head on a silver platter is the only trade!"

"Wait," he said, inching forward and carefully drawing a black vial from the battered table. He stretched out his hand and then jettisoned the object toward her. She caught it and snapped her arm in tight against her body, but never loosened her grip on the book.

"When we bled Carlos out, I kept the last of the *Oblivion* you two made. I was going to give it to Lilith as a surprise when we won the bounty, but, it's not worth the book."

Damali shoved the vial into the front pocket of her jeans with a sneer. "*Oblivion?* Fuck you. Where's my embryo?"

The chairman looked at her hard, his black glowing eyes going red, then gold, and then flickering out to a normal brown. "Embryo? That . . . that was destroyed in my haste, and . . ." He walked in a circle as he spoke, staring at the ground as though about to lose his mind.

"Stop playing with me," Damali shouted. "Not here, not now, and not about that!"

The chairman stopped walking. "Your side never saw its Light flicker out?"

"No," Damali said carefully. "The Neteru queens of old saw it descend and keep going until it hit rock bottom. Level seven."

The chairman de-bulked and walked back to the lopsided table and sat down. "Have a seat," he said too calmly. "Pick a throne, any throne, they're all destroyed."

"I'll stand, thank you," Damali said, unmoved.

"Whatever. But you and I need to have a real discussion, if I think what's happened has."

"She played you," Damali said from across the room, using the available information she had, along with a well-placed hunch. "You fucked her, didn't you, and thought she'd share the bounty with you?" Damali sucked her teeth. "Men are so foolish, especially when there's a baby involved."

The chairman didn't answer. That was all the answer she required.

"She's carrying what's mine," Damali said, seething. "You're her ally, that makes you my double enemy."

"You're lying," the chairman said in a strangled murmur. "I would have smelled—"

"No, you wouldn't," Damali said, renewed rage throttling her. She couldn't even keep up the *Dananu,* she was so furious. "She's stronger than you, which is why she's on seven and not six. And what she stole is normally undetectable to your realms!"

She stepped forward as his stricken expression confirmed her hunch. "Do you think I would have left my own team to tangle with you in your own yard if it hadn't been mission critical?" She could feel herself moving closer to the table on her own volition, the need to wrap her hands around his throat becoming an ache. "Do you think some man is why I'm here? Revenge for a lover? Like some brother would take my mind, the Neteru, like that?"

From the pit of her stomach a war cry fused with the pain in her soul. Before she knew it or the chairman could react, the book was on the floor, her body prostrate across his table, and she had him by the throat. The tussle was futile, but she didn't care. His fangs gleamed and his claws pierced her hands like dangers, but rage had her in a stranglehold, too.

Eyeball to eyeball, they stared at each other, his hands around her throat, hers around his, until they both broke simultaneously and then went at it again, stalemated. When they released each other this time, she pushed back quickly, he zapped the book to his chest, and clutched it, leaving them both breathing hard.

"You're not even strong enough now to rip out my heart," she said, spitting on the floor. "Keep your dusty old book. But you will give me back what she stole!"

He stood and swished away from her for distance, but kept his eyes on her as he pet his book. "You're out of your mind. I'll crucify you on my chamber walls for this affront!"

"No, the fuck, you won't," she said calmly, but evenly, never losing eye contact with him. "You are about to be reduced to an insignificant part of the dark empire, and any remaining vampires along with it, and I'll be unemployed, then dead. Once she delivers the Anti-Christ, we're both history."

Damali swatted dust and debris off her jeans. The chairman smoothed his robes.

"You propose an alliance?"

She laughed. "Maybe I am losing my mind."

"You offered Rivera an alliance, albeit under different circumstances."

"True. Very different. But talk to me," Damali said, following him with her eyes as he walked.

"How do I know this isn't fabrication?"

Damali smiled. "Look at my throat," she whispered, trying to stop the two puncture wounds that had opened in it. "Earlier this evening, I thought . . . never mind. Let's just say I thought there was a little rough love play going on. My Guardian partner felt the bite because we were linked, but now, being down here, *I know* I got bitten. She found me."

The chairman moved forward, but Damali backed up. "I know her signature," he said cautiously.

"Then check it out from where you stand," Damali said, allowing him to see the wound.

He turned abruptly and walked back to his throne, billowing clouds of sulfuric smoke poured from it as he did so, spun, and turned to gaze at her with his eyes glowing black.

"I'll take that as an ID," she said, rubbing the surface.

The chairman sealed the wound with a sweep of his hand, closed his eyes, and trembled as he sat down in his throne. "I will behead her myself," he murmured. "All she wanted me for was bait, knowing we were the most likely ones to detect Neteru essence on the planet, and had your blood samples in our noses." He opened his eyes slowly, composed himself, and nodded. "Since we are being so forthright in this delicate negotiation, and have more pressing matters than old vendettas, I'm going to assume you had *Oblivion* running through you?"

Damali didn't answer, not about to give Carlos's position away.

The chairman sniffed hard and licked his palm where he'd sealed her punctures. "No need to explain. It's running all through your blood." He cocked his head to the side. "But since there was no blood transfer between you two this go round, all she got was yours."

"Would it be enough to spark life?" Damali held her ground, neither admitting to nor denying the chairman's charge.

He stared at her for enduring seconds. "Frankly, I don't know." He made a tent with his hands and allowed his lips to rest against his fingers before speaking. "But what I just tasted running through you, with the adrenaline spike, would make the dead come back to life. You tell me?"

"You know I'm coming for her, then you and I can settle our shit later."

The chairman nodded. "And she's coming for you . . . which, until I know for sure, I cannot allow her to do—my daylight vessel."

Damali's smile was so tight she thought it might crack her face. "Detain me, and I will call down warrior angels so hard, so fast, along with every Neteru queen ever conceived . . . spirits, angels, and a spiritual army to turn this mother out. We can kick off the Armageddon tonight, if you want. Try me."

"You might want an escort, topside, since you seem to be in a suicidal frame of mind." He chuckled and called for a transport cloud. "Or, we can further negotiate over a glass of merlot, then I could take you topside myself as a gesture of our mutual understanding."

"I only traveled with one of you like that, and you fried him."

"But you have obviously brought him back, and are hiding him. I'd like to discuss that, too, one night—but not tonight. It seems moot at this juncture."

"Two seconds longer in here, and I'll find a way to pull your heart into my hand. Do not make me go there in your chambers." Damali began walking away from him. She no longer feared having him at her back. She'd beat his ass down, mentally.

"You're so much stronger now than when you were a little girl."

She stopped walking but didn't turn.

"What you did in here was absolutely phenomenal," he said quietly, his voice a seductive low tone. "The treachery needed to get through all the realms without a master to courier you . . . and the weapons you employed, the shape-shifts. But the thing I respected most about this duel that has come to a draw is that you had no fear. *None.* Your hands around my throat had a singular objective—to blot me from all existence. I could feel it running all through you," he said, his voice now barely audible. "Tell me. Did he teach you that, too?"

She turned slowly to face him, pure hatred cascading through her. "No, baby. That part was all me."

"Thank you, Father O'Dwyer," Father Patrick said, inspecting the heavy artillery that the cleric presented.

"We only had this much, enough to outfit half of your group, but the rest are hand-to-hand combat weapons from the old days," the young priest said.

"Give the newbies the stakes, holy-water vials, anything that's not a projectile," Shabazz said. "If we're out there and they freak, they could blow off one of our heads."

Big Mike nodded and began distributing equipment as Shabazz ordered. "It takes a long time to learn how to fire a weapon properly, when to, and what to target so there's no collateral damage— when civilians and police draw in," he said, tossing a Glock to Berkfield. "Ask him, he knows. Friendly fire is always a problem with the new ones. Even a long blade can be a problem." Mike showed Juanita, Marjorie, and her children how to point the vials toward the ground so they'd quickly burst on impact. "This is for defensive measures only—to back up an attacker, create enough smoke from a singe, and bring us in to finish the job."

"But I have to go with you," the rabbi said, growing agitated. "You won't know where to look."

"You stay here. You'll have a battle-trained policeman, Berkfield, along with the Covenant to guard you," Marlene said. "Give us the keys, tell us where your stash is, and once it's daylight and we get to an area where we can all stay together under barriers that will hold, we'll begin training all you new folks." She nodded toward Shabazz. "You have to learn how to move to be able to hold your position, fire a weapon or swing one, without lopping your teammate's head off with a bad swing. And you have to be able to do it blind, in the dark, sense where they are, where the evil is coming from, because that's where we go—in the dark."

The rabbi nodded and handed Marlene his keys and stepped back to stand with Father Patrick and the other clerics. Satisfied by the terror on the new Guardian's faces, Marlene continued in a matter-of-fact tone.

"I want you afraid so you take this seriously. Fear will keep you sharp, and being sharp will keep you alive. Shabazz has to teach you some break-hold moves—how to fall and get back up without broken bones, how to land blows that will topple an enemy's center of gravity—but for now, your goal is to *run*."

She walked over to Juanita. "Take out all pierced earrings. They can use that to drag you into a feeding den, if it's weres. Down in the shelter section of this church, there's a clothing and food bank. Everybody put on some pants, running shoes, and T-shirts. Nothing they can hold easily to trap you. Hair, same deal. Ponytails are a problem. They're perfect to wind their claws around and snap your neck," she added, demonstrating on Krissy's long tresses. "Cut it, or wind it in a bun that holds."

Marlene paced back and forth, her nerves fraying as she stared at the unready team. Her walking stick clicked on the ground each time she tapped it, creating an eerie echo though the semiempty church. "Let the clerics fan out around you. If one of them goes down, leave him. That's their job. Smudge your throats with holy water and blessed incense. If we're dealing with vamps, that might save your jugular."

"And if you get nicked bad," Big Mike said, "we'll have to do you." He tossed a bowie knife to Berkfield. "Give each of them a short blade with the edges dipped in anointing oil. If it gets hand-to-hand for them, they've gotta go lizard brain."

Berkfield's son slowly accepted the knife. "Dad . . . what's lizard brain?"

"Total instinct, Bobby," Berkfield said. "Military term. When you go totally primal, don't think, just act from that primordial part of your brain, and take out the enemy—kill or be killed. Don't look in their eyes, or even think, just stab whatever's got hold of you and keep stabbing until it lets you go, and then run."

Marlene looked at the stricken expressions on the women's faces. "Lizard brain is not being repulsed by anything you have to do to get free. Gouge out their eyes, bite, kick, scratch, go wild, any part of their bodies is fair game—because yours is, for them. Got it?"

Slow nods answered her, but no one spoke. "Good," she said, pulling on a pair of old jeans and exchanging her sandals for rubber-sole work shoes as she spoke. The men on the squad stripped and dressed in the sanctuary as Marlene continued her lesson, all modesty gone. This was war.

"Not a word," Damali said as a cloud left her in the middle of Gabrielle's parlor floor. "Later, me and you can dissect—"

"Not a word!" Carlos shouted. Was she nuts? He was practically foaming at the mouth with rage. "You coulda—"

"Been smoked," Damali said, leveling her arm at him in a hard snap with her finger pointing toward him so hard that it shook. "But I wasn't, and did what needed to be done. After all the shit you did, double deals, hardball negotiations, and side alliances in Hell, do *not* try to tell me about this situation." She looked at Gabrielle, ignoring the awe on her face, or the outright lust in Yonnie's. Rider she wouldn't even glance at. She settled her gaze on Tara. "Weapons check, then we hit the streets to go find our team. We have much to tell them, the clock is ticking, and girlfriend just got a hit of my blood."

They had concealed their weapons as best they could under long, heavy leather coats as they strolled down the street, seeming like a small group of friends on the way to explore Manhattan's nightlife. The couples paired off and kept their gazes roving. Damali had traded in the bulky AK-47 for a smaller handheld automatic. Rider gave up the pump shotgun for a 380 stashed in his waistband. Gabrielle was strapped with double Glock nines and enough silver to anchor a ship. Carlos was packing twin mini-Uzis, and all had rounds of explosives, bowie knives, and silver daggers. But Damali had insisted on a long blade concealed down the back of her coat. She missed her Isis and still reached for the old girl from time to time out of reflex.

"Still can't pinpoint them," Damali said quietly. "Even outside. Something's wrong."

"We keep moving," Carlos said, passing a crowded bar. "We stay near populated areas and try to pick up the tracer."

Marlene stood outside the cathedral and walked a few paces away from the property boundary. The street was oddly deserted, only a few human passersby walked along, briskly headed to more fascinating destinations deeper within the bowels of the city that never slept.

"You got anything, Mar?" Shabazz asked, coming to stand near her and discreetly cover her. He kept his hand inside his ragged fatigue jacket, poised over his nine.

"Not yet," she replied, her gaze moving along the buildings. "But there's definitely an energy shift." She glanced back at J.L. and Jose. "Formation and fan out." She then nodded toward Dan and Big Mike and they followed suit. Marlene stopped walking and bristled, bringing the group to a halt.

A slow-moving gray mist wafted by and settled several yards

away from them. Marlene held up her hand to instruct the team
not to advance or fire.

"Let it materialize so we know what we're dealing with and
how many. Everybody stay cool."

In agonizingly slow increments, the form filled in, but remained
sheer. Marlene stopped breathing.

"Stay cool, and keep your head, Mar," Shabazz warned. "This
thing is fucking with you. Raven is dead."

"Mom . . ." an echocy voice murmured, making the breeze
amongst the trees whistle as dead leaves swirled on the concrete.
"Mom, it's me, Christine."

"You have to do better than that," Marlene said, fighting the
building tears. "My daughter is dead."

"You don't understand," the entity whispered, its form waffling
and becoming almost liquefied as it struggled to maintain an image. "The portals are all opening . . . level by level. I slipped out to
help you. Come now, so I can bring you to Damali."

Marlene whipped out a holy-water vial and cocked her hand
back, readied for an attack. But when the entity simply wept and
didn't try to take cover or come for her, confusion made her hesitate.

"Do it, please," the entity whispered. "I am so sorry I hurt you
so."

"Do it, Mar," Shabazz said through his teeth. "Raven never
apologized. This is a ruse."

"Noooo. . . ." the ghostly voice wailed. "The talk is everywhere. It is possible to ascend—to change sides. It's not too late. A
councilman opened a gate and Light poured in . . . the warriors
came. I got through the hole because I was never supposed to be
there. Carlos showed us that there's still a path."

"Hold up, 'Bazz," Big Mike said, moving closer. "Even if this is
a game, there's information in it."

Shabazz nodded. The rest of the squad kept their gazes moving
during the standoff, weapons readied. He gave Marlene a sideline
glance. "Make her tell you something good. I'm not down for a
setup."

Marlene stared at what could be a demon posing as her daughter. The sight of her was heartbreaking. Her form moved in a restless state between the old image of her child, and that of a vampire. One moment the entity was a young girl with smooth brown skin, huge pretty eyes filled with tears of remorse. She remembered the thick plaits she used to comb, and the favorite nightgown Christine used to wear when they would cuddle in bed and share stories . . . pale blue. The next moment the adult vixen would take shape, dressed in all-black leather, her form voluptuous and scantily clad, her sad eyes glowing yellow and her fangs razors. But they'd dusted Raven. Damali had levied the deathblow. It tortured her mind to know that her child's soul had bottomed out on the succubae level two.

The test question came to Marlene quickly as she watched the floating entity shift back to her childlike form. "When I used to read stories to Christine, those times were always sealed with prayer before she joined me in bed. Tell me something from that time that is beyond the reach of Darkness."

The child form filled in and began weeping as it hummed the melody of the song, "If I Could." ". . . But I know that I could never cry your tears, but I would, if I could."

Marlene covered her mouth and took in a deep, shaky breath. "If I could, I would always try to shelter you from harm . . ."

The entity nodded. "I know you would . . . if you could."

"I tried, baby," Marlene whispered, her eyes filling. "I tried to so hard."

"Mom, I'm so sorry. I just want to go home," it said, and pointed skyward. "I don't want you to hurt anymore."

"Give that thing another test, Mar," Shabazz said, unconvinced and stepping in front of Marlene.

The city went dark. Every light along the streets—not a massive building in sight had power. Save the moon and stars, New York City was in total darkness.

"Oh, shit!" Jose flung his wool coat back and leveled his weapon at the glowing gray blob that began to dissipate.

The squad drew in close, all weapons revealed and ready to fire.

"The portals are open, you must follow . . . you must follow," the disembodied voice said, leaving a thin gray trail of ether. "There is no time to think."

The group stopped walking. Damali and Carlos pivoted and stared at the blackness of the skyline.

"The lights," Gabrielle gasped. "All of Manhattan?"

People eating at the outdoor cafes stood and shouted. Indoor patrons yelled and screamed and ran outside. Bars emptied. Nightclubs spilled partygoers onto the sidewalks. People rushed from brownstones, apartment buildings, offices, and stores. Those trapped on the upper floors of residences opened their windows and shouted for answers. People trapped behind huge picture windows banged on them in silent terror, their attempts to be seen and heard futile. Chaos rippled down the streets as people fled buildings and filled the streets like panicked lemmings. Cars honked their horns and collisions echoed as traffic ground to a halt.

Rider reached into his coat pocket, pulled out an emergency light wand, and snapped it, spilling eerie blue-tinged illumination over his hands. "There's gotta be people trapped in the subways and elevators all over the freakin' city. You folks with the night vision, can you see anything we oughta be dealing with?"

Carlos and Damali squinted as Tara and Yonnie scanned the terrain.

"Manholes are moving," Yonnie muttered. "You hear it? The metal grating open?"

Carlos and Damali nodded.

"Yeah," Damali said. "Rider, how's your nose?"

"Were-demons," Rider said, pulling out his gun and taking the safety off it. "Wolfen variety."

Gabrielle drew her weapon and wrapped a thick silver band of chains around her fist.

"The vents," Tara said, touching Yonnie's shoulder. "Listen. Slithering."

"Serpents," Damali agreed. "Once you hear it, you never forget it."

"Amanthras," Yonnie confirmed.

"That's every level except six," Carlos said as the team moved with difficulty through the growing crowd toward the subway. "All at the same time?"

The disguised couples pushed their way through the packed street. Frenzied people were rushing everywhere, bumping and shoving, half blind in the dark.

"Yeah," Yonnie said, elbowing his way through the crowd with Carlos. "Only one thing could open all the zones at the same time."

"I know," Carlos said and continued to force his way toward a subway entrance. He fought his way down the yawning black mouth like a salmon swimming against the stream of rushing bodies that bumped and trampled their way to freedom. "Level seven."

CHAPTER TWENTY-FIVE

THE MOMENT they hit the entrance to the platform Damali and her squad were surrounded by pitch blackness. Screams from frightened passengers echoed through the subway cavern and their bodies were bumped and shoved hard as people fled blindly in all directions. Her night vision kicked in and she could see people trampling each other in total panic.

Carlos scanned the mayhem, his vision distorted to only the silvery outline of humans, but when he glanced at Tara and Yonnie, he saw them as a red outline. It took him a few seconds to adjust to his strange new way of seeing in the dark. Light a torch!" he yelled to Yonnie. "We've gotta light a path to get these civilians out of here."

Yonnie complied, materializing two large beacon flashlights. The new illumination seemed to marginally stem the tide of panic as he hurried toward the stairs and shone a light upward. "This way?!" he hollered, making the crowd draw toward the light and out of the team's path.

"Thanks, mister," a man hollered. "You guys cops? What the hell's going on?"

"Power outage," Damali shouted over the din. "Stay cool, get to the top. Follow the light so we can find out the trouble."

Flowing like a living river, the people on the platform rushed up the stairs behind Yonnie. He handed off the lights to the strongest human carriers he could make out and swiftly joined Carlos.

"Watch our backs," Carlos instructed, as he and Damali levered open doors.

"Tara, stay with Rider and you guys get the end cars," Damali said, pushing the end of her blade between frozen car doors and leaning on it like a crowbar. But the moment the doors pried open an inch, she had to yank back her blade and point it upward. Panicked passengers grappled at the doors and leveraged them open and poured out of the trapped cars. She had to press her back against the steel and glass to keep from being trampled or from inadvertently goring a rushing body.

Within minutes all was still underground. Carlos had gotten the conductor out and was working on the front-door exit that led to the tracks. For a moment the team stood still, listening and assessing as the door finally slid back. Yonnie pointed forward with two fingers. She and Carlos could hear it, too, the mild rumbling sound like a slow-moving earthquake shuttering the train with a faint vibration not more than a few blocks away.

Quietly they each made it to the edge of the stalled car and jumped down to the tracks, picking up the pace with a brisk jog, weapons pointed up. When Carlos stopped advancing he hugged the filthy concrete walls beneath the platform, aware of the dangerous third rail that could come back to life at any second when the power returned.

"We can't fire off automatic rounds in here," Damali whispered. "The ricochet alone could kill any of us."

"We need to spot it, bait it, and lure whatever it is up to the streets," Yonnie said, his line of vision trained toward the yawning blackness.

Damali shook her head. "We take a firefight to the streets, with all those people up there, the casualties from our bullets will drop innocent bodies, not to mention give whatever we're hunting body shields and food."

"So what do you propose?" Rider asked, shuddering.

Carlos felt his head and looked at Damali. "This man is ice cold but sweating like a pig. Adrenaline is spiking the virus through his system faster than it should."

"I'm fine. Let's keep moving," Rider said. "I feel stronger, too."

"He can see in the dark," Tara said quietly. "I haven't been leading him, only Gabrielle."

"Will you people give it a rest!" Rider said in a harsh whisper. "I've got at least three nights. We don't have time for this."

Yonnie shook his head and looked at Carlos. "Level seven opened the portals, man. There's no guarantees that his time hasn't sped up. Once the dark current comes up topside . . ."

"I know," Carlos muttered, exchanging a worried glance with Damali. "Rider, if you start getting stomach cramps, you let somebody know. Hear?"

"Whatever," Rider said, spitting on the tracks. "I might be an old man by your standards, but I'm not senile."

Shabazz yanked Marlene's arm hard to stop her as she dashed toward a subway entrance. "Underground we're sitting ducks! You don't even know if we've been set up!"

"Feel it, 'Bazz," she said out of breath. "Tacticals—do you feel a setup?"

Shabazz and Dan stretched out their hands, touching the air, but said nothing.

"Mike, you hear anything up here?"

Mike shook his head no. "Everything is underground. If we're gonna bring it, then we've gotta take the fight to them."

"Jose, track it. Talk to me," Marlene said quickly.

Jose pointed the barrel of his weapon down. "In the tunnels. Just like old times."

"Then she didn't lie," Marlene said, her half-blind gaze hard on Shabazz. "Don't you understand that there's a rip in the whole dark-realm world order? If a soul, like Christine's, that's been damned and committed to an eternal sentence can be reclaimed— this is a serious opportunity. *They messed up* by opening the gates. It's a free-for-all, now. This is the beginning of the big war."

"All right," Shabazz said reluctantly. "Then let's do this."

Mike was out front, using his massive size and bulk to push a wide path open through the bodies so the team could get down to the platform. He produced a flashlight and it made the frightened crowd cheer, then it took almost ten minutes to clear the area and draft marshals that were calm enough to complete the evacuation. Once down on the platform, people who were still stuck in the cars pounded on windows, crying out for help.

"We can't leave 'em, Mar," he said, stopping the team's advance to the end of the platform where they could descend to the tracks. "If something is hunting down here, it'll eat before it fights. You know that."

Every man took a door, using their knives to cut the rubber stoppers and make enough space for their hands to get through. Marlene wedged her stick through a door and leaned on it with the help of passengers inside.

"Follow the lights," she yelled, helping distraught passengers get their bearings to stem their panic.

The team began running, but Shabazz turned back. "Where's Mike?"

A woman was huddled on the floor of the empty first car, her body shielding another one. She looked up with tears streaking her face as Mike shined an emergency light on her.

"She's old," the young woman said. "She fell and was trampled. She doesn't speak English—I think she's Russian, or something."

Mike squatted down as the young woman slowly moved away from a frail, elderly woman who lifted her head and wept.

"I just couldn't leave her, mister," the young woman with braids said, her voice shaky as she tried to stand. "Please. You've gotta help her. She could be anyone's momma."

Mike looked back toward his team. He could hear them calling for him, panicking in the darkness. He put the light closer to the young woman's face. Her big eyes glistened in the eerie bluish emergency-light stick. Her dark brown, round face was gentle, and her hands trembled as they patted the old lady's arm. "Yo!" he hollered. "Back here. We've got injured. Two minutes."

The girl closed her eyes and leaned down to the old woman. "Thank you," she said, glancing up at Mike. "Ma'am, don't worry, this officer is going to help you."

The elderly woman looked up at Mike and smiled a toothless grin. "Bless you," she said. "I'm all right."

Both Mike and the young girl stared at her, amazed as she pulled herself up on a subway pole and they helped her stand.

"C'mon, lady, let's get you up the stairs," Mike said, putting his arm around the old woman.

"But she couldn't speak English," the girl said, her voice filled with awe.

"You two go up to where the guy is with the flashlight. It's dangerous down here. We'll handle it," Mike said, wondering who the sweet sister was who had risked life and limb for a stranger.

"No," the old woman protested, walking quickly. "You must take her with you—she's one of yours. Hurry, before they come."

Mike stood very, very still as the elderly woman walked without assistance, looked both ways as she stepped over the train-door threshold, and quickly paced toward the light. Instantly he pulled a weapon on the girl. "State your business, sis. Fast."

Confusion and terror filled the girl's face.

"Mike, you cool?" Shabazz hollered. "Two minutes is up."

"I'm—"

Before Mike could finish his sentence the train rocked, glass shattered, and the girl in the car with him screamed and hit the floor. Something was moving so fast through the cars, splintering metal doors, taking out poles, and shattering glass, that Mike only got off a short burst of automatic rounds when the huge head struck at him.

He fell back. He could hear people screaming in the distance. A thick, muscular rope of black serpentine body whipped through the car. He rolled on the other side of the pole, dodging the huge razor fangs that dripped acid. The floor sizzled, the young girl shrieked and screamed and balled up in a seat. The long body retracted as the head made another powerful lunge. He heard his teammates rushing toward them. The angry serpent's head collided with the ceiling of the stalled subway car, making metal bend and more glass shatter as it tried to gore Mike.

From the corner of his eye he saw the girl reach into her bag and pull out a switchblade, slashing blindly with her eyes closed as she screamed. She got a deep slice in that drew the demon back for a second, but it redoubled its efforts becoming angrier than before.

The momentary pullback offered him just the opportunity he needed as he sent another controlled burst dead aim into the center of the beast's chest.

A small explosion rocked their car, blowing out the remaining glass and creating a shower of embers as the creature turned to ash and withered.

He was panting, sweat pouring down his temples; his shirt became second skin as it matted to his torso. "C'mon," he yelled to the girl, dragging her by the arm as he heard another slithering sound rocket in their direction.

She was on her feet, stumbling, running. Shabazz had her other arm as the team tried to find the stairs, their light source gone.

"Not the stairs!" Marlene yelled, sending the team in a new direction just as a large head came down the steps.

Jose had fallen on his back and opened fire, sending shells flying as the beast snapped and hissed. The report was deafening and Mike covered his ears as Jose slid across the subway floor. Two beasts twined around the stranded train, crushing it as they looked onward with green glowing eyes, flicking their hideous black tongues, searching for bodies. Dan slung holy-water grenades at the train as the beast Jose battled began to incinerate. The moment the vials exploded, gook splattered the team and plumes of angry, yellow sulfuric smoke choked them. A pair of green eyes opened on the ductwork and electrical cabling over the train and then receded.

Gagging, the team staggered forward. Mike caught the young woman under her arms and held her up as they moved to the end of the platform.

"We have to make it to the next exit," Shabazz sputtered through heavy coughs. "We can't chance this exit, and she can't be left here."

"I wasn't leaving her no way," Mike said, holding the girl close as she clung to his arm. "She saved my life." He looked down at her and gave her a gentle squeeze. "I got you. What's your name, baby?"

"Inez," she choked. "Oh my God, what's happening?"

"Of course it's starting!" the rabbi shouted, his voice echoing through the sanctuary. "This is what I've been trying to tell you all. We shouldn't be waiting here in the dark with only candles like sitting ducks! But that shrew, Marlene, wanted us to just wait."

"Shut up!" Marjorie shouted. "I'm not going out of here with my children. Are you insane? We do what they said and stay here where it's safe!" She stood and hugged her children. "If we had listened to you, we'd probably be out there in the dark, stranded, and killed. You're worried about getting to weapons your brother stashed, but technology didn't save him, did it? Did it?"

"What do you know of my brother?" the rabbi yelled back at Marjorie. "Dr. Ishmael Zeitloff was a visionary who survived Auschwitz—so you will never speak to me about his—"

"If anything, the people or things that killed him are waiting for you to go back there and we would have been set up," Marjorie said, rounding her children and pointing at the rabbi. "Your place is a lure, a death trap. I know it like I know my name—so *shut up* about going to Brooklyn. Not an option or a risk any of us are willing to take."

"How do you live with such a Lilith? You're a schmuck to allow her to take your reason—you're a policeman, do something, shoot something!" the rabbi yelled toward Berkfield. "This screech owl is—"

"What did you say?" Father Patrick shouted, grabbing the rabbi by the arm.

"Unhand me, you old goat! I will kick your ass! I know my rights, this is assault and battery!"

"Hey, old dude, that's my wife—what'd you call her?" Berkfield shouted. "I don't care if you're a—"

"No. Stop it, all of you. Rabbi Zeitloff may have broken the code!" Father Patrick said quickly as the other clerics formed a ring around the growing dispute.

His statement immediately stopped the argument. *"Lilith . . ."* Father Patrick murmured, and then crossed himself.

The others stared at Father Patrick and then the rabbi, who was slack-jawed.

"Lilith?" The rabbi peered around at the group. "The Lilith? The Devil's wife?"

"Oh, shit," Bobby said and stood up. " "Pardon my French, Fathers, but I . . ."

"Yes," Imam Asula said, and then looked at the rabbi. "We can all relate. Explain this Lilith. She's not in our books, Rabbi."

"Adam's first wife—"

"Oh, get out," Berkfield said with a nervous chuckle. "Adam didn't have a freakin' first wife, only Eve . . . and she bit the apple, but hey—"

"That is because you do not know your Torah or the Kabbalah!" the rabbi shouted, smoothing his beard and then calming himself. "She gave birth to hundreds of demons and she divorced Adam and took up residence in a cave on the Red Sea." He looked at Father Patrick. "This is our history, we know her name and your Guardian, Daniel, would agree with me—if he remembers his Hebrew lessons well—which I suspect in his profession, he would. She existed."

"It was all right before our eyes," Father Patrick whispered. "The succubus attacks on the plane. The screech owl–demon presentation . . ."

"That's right," the rabbi said, standing taller. Eerie candlelight glinted off his glasses and made his gaunt face seem longer within the darkened church. The stricken team sat rapt, listening to his words. No one blinked or swallowed as the elderly cleric spoke.

"She would not submit to Adam, and took issue with God, then fled. They sent three angels after her to hunt her down because she fled to Babylon and sucked men's seed from their bodies in their sleep . . . today, the politically correct term is nocturnal emissions. In my day, it was called wet dreams, but I digress. The main thing is that this witch-demon used what she siphoned from righteous men in their sleep to create Hell's army." He shrugged. "She was the Devil's kind of woman and liked to play rough, so he married her.

But there was a truce. The Archangel Michael slayed her progeny to near extinction and she hid what remained beneath the bowels of the earth. She is the forbidden—the creator of lust. She kills babies in the womb, causes miscarriages and stillbirths, because her jealousy over any woman who is with child is so wretched, because of the losses of her own. This demon is almost as bad as Lucifer himself, and I put odds on it that she's even a handful for him."

"We got attacked over the Red Sea," Monk Lin said quietly.

"Our younger Guardians were . . . influenced in their sleep. She tried to pry the whereabouts of the Neterus from them," Imam Asula said, hoisting a machete up tighter in his hand. "They claimed that the succubus was unsuccessful," he added carefully, looking at the other clerics. "But, then again, it is difficult for a man to confess such a compromise in detail, even to his brothers."

Father Lopez looked away. "We've got two teams out there that don't know what they're up against."

"If this is literally the baddest mother in the valley, and our teams are out there possibly stranded," Berkfield said, checking the clip on his weapon, "how do we kill this bitch?"

All eyes went to Father Patrick. He stared at them and then looked toward the altar. "Honestly, I don't know."

Damali and Carlos had stopped walking as soon as the gunfire began in the distance behind them. Yonnie and Tara cocked their heads to one side.

"That was our team," Damali whispered.

Carlos and Yonnie nodded. They all looked down at their feet as vermin squealed and flooded over their boots. Gabrielle closed her eyes and clenched her fists to her sides to keep from screaming. Tara hissed with disgust and hovered just inches above the foul assault.

Rider tilted his head to the side and took in a deep breath. "Everybody stay very still, weapons ready," he murmured. "Werewolves in the house."

Yonnie and Carlos spun at the same time, their gazes going toward the tunnel ceiling. Battle-length fangs ripped through Yonnie's gums. Tara vaporized and took up a position to flank Rider.

Gabrielle pointed her weapon at the fast-moving targets that snarled and then slowed down, assessing their prey as they edged forward. She stood back-to-back with Damali holding her breath, waiting for the attack that was imminent.

The lead beast swayed its huge head, the muscles in its shoulders knitting in readiness to lunge. Carlos's eyes glowed silver as it went into a low crouch against the electrical cable and three more crept down the walls in attack formation.

In a blur, the beasts lunged. Carlos's gaze severed a massive clawed limb that lashed out at Yonnie. Three were-demons went airborne, and Yonnie sucker-punched the one that came at his right, sending it sprawling down the tracks. Rider opened fire, dead aim, incinerating the one that Tara had mounted. Damali ducked, missing a swipe, and her blade connected with a beast's side, opening a horrible gash that spilled black blood. The wounded howled, as Gabrielle and Damali drew their guns in unison and blew off its head. But the huge beast with a missing limb had snatched Rider by the leg.

"Freeze!" Damali shouted, and time crept to a near halt but didn't stop.

Rider unloaded rounds in slow motion, bullets spiraling toward the middle of the beast's huge forehead. Then time snapped back to real time without warning. The massive head exploded in a fiery rain that made Rider protectively cover his face. A half-wounded were-demon rushed Yonnie, and Carlos clapped, opening a shield that the beast moved through too quickly to avoid, leaving a pile of ash. Yonnie spun 360 degrees, his gaze landing upon a huge beast that stalked down the cavern slowly.

The team got Rider to his feet to face the challenger that stood six feet at the shoulders; its head the size of a small chest of drawers. Its matted brown and black fur was crawling with larva and its yellow eyes glowed, creating an eerily hypnotic sight. Yellowed fangs filled its distended mouth, its snout testing the air, making the sound of doglike snuffling reverberate off the walls. The thing before them stopped fifty feet away and the team watched as it drew slow, hard pants into its barrel chest.

"Neterus," it snarled, drooling greenish saliva. "My bounty is won!"

Every trigger finger jerked. No weapons fired. Instant glances of distress ricocheted around the team out of ammo. There was no time to reload. The beast before them was too fast and too strong.

"Senator!" Carlos shouted. "We are to die, but should know our enemy. That is the code of vengeance!"

The were-demon laughed and advanced slowly. "My pleasure, Mr. Councilman." He crouched low for the final attack. "Lilith sent me."

The thing was airborne in seconds. It hurdled forward with such speed that there wasn't even time to duck. But something behind them moved with the same velocity, only slithering speed. The two combatants collided midair above the small squad, sending them scrambling out of the way as the were-demon became ensnared in huge black coils that crushed his bones. The were-demon howled and bit a massive chunk of serpent flesh out of his attacker. They landed with a thud, breaking concrete and bending all rails beneath them.

"The kill is mine," the serpent hissed in a rage-filled sibilance, then reared back its head and stuck the were-demon in the chest, yanking out its heart and entire rib cage before consuming it. Instantly it turned its attention on the scrambling team, patiently drawing the wolfen senator into its viselike jaws. It threw back its head and simply chugged the carcass down, creating a large lump in its side as its head thrashed back and forth.

"Get off the third rail!" Carlos shot his glance to Damali and Yonnie. Tara yanked Rider near her and glanced down, making Rider reach for Gabrielle. Damali was already in safety range as Carlos quickly knelt, grabbed the third rail, released it, and then stared at it. The serpent's huge body moved forward, its width taking up the entire track as its scales scraped along the tiled wall.

Suddenly it stopped, hissed, shuddered, and began to smoke. Its green glowing eyes went silver-blue and its entire body was outlined in silver-white electrical current that arced and made it begin to smoke. It released a hideous scream, twisting and turning and banging its head against the concrete ceiling, sending huge chunks of rock and debris raining down on the team as it burned.

They ran. Behind them was a screeching, jerking menace. Before them was black tunnel, but it was a better option. The blue-white light coming behind them grew hotter and whiter and then came the explosion that threw them forward and skidding dangerously near the hot rail.

"Kill the rail!" Damali shouted.

Carlos covered his head as cement shrapnel hurled toward them. He rolled over on his back and threw up a shield. Rail spikes, bricks and mortar, tiles, and debris flew like rockets toward them, entered the golden glow, and then crumbled to ash.

Silence followed the stench. The lay on their stomachs for a few moments trying to place where they were in relation to the now-live rail.

"Kill the rail, baby," Damali said coughing. "There could be people in the tunnels trying to get out that could get hurt."

Carlos nodded and stood slowly. "It's dead. I'm pretty sure." He stumbled forward and kicked gravel toward it. Then he clapped his hands and tried to summon a shield to no avail. "I'm tapped out for the night."

Yonnie got up slowly, helping Tara and Gabrielle to their feet. "Mr. Councilman, you are still da man."

"No lie," Rider said, struggling to his feet and shuddering hard. "But, guys, seriously. I don't feel so good."

Mike began running first, headed toward the sound of the blast. Shabazz and the others were right on his heels.

Yonnie squinted and looked at Carlos. "Incoming!"

Damali listened hard. "Human. Might be ours."

Yonnie and Tara shared a glance. "We have to feed," Yonnie said and then looked at Rider. "Might have to feed him soon, too."

Carlos caught Rider before he fell. Shivers had replaced the occasional shudder and Rider's face was soaking wet. Damali felt Rider's freezing forehead and looked at his gray pallor, then stroked his hair back.

"We need a medic!" Damali hollered into the blackness, just in case it wasn't her team. Paramedics should have been flooding the tunnels, along with police. That was the best she could hope for.

No one spoke as Carlos hoisted Rider up under one arm and they began a slow run in the direction of the human footfalls.

"Yo, Damali!" Mike hollered. "Hold your fire. It's us!"

Big Mike's call made the two separated squads cover ground quickly. A bouncing dim light came from the direction of Mike's voice. The moment the two teams came together, Damali gasped.

"Inez! Oh, my God!"

"I was trying to find work here," Inez said, hugging Damali hard. "Oh, God, D, what's happening?"

"Where's the baby?" Damali said fast, almost forgetting there was a team. Her best friend, her girl from back in the day, was trapped in this nightmare with her—the only other living soul she knew and would have spared from this life.

"With Momma while I tried to get my finances together. Oh, my God," Inez wailed. "Oh, God!"

"I know, I know," Damali said, soothing her, rubbing her back. "But we have to get out of here to somewhere safe."

"I got her," Big Mike said, extracting Inez from Damali's hold. He glanced in the direction of Jose's light. "But our boy don't look so good." His line of vision settled on Rider and then Tara. "Mar . . . tell me something good."

Marlene shook her head. "Need to get him back to hallowed ground and get to my bag." She looked at Tara and narrowed her gaze. "You're more lethal now that you're stronger. I don't know if I can purge this."

"They're bloody, man," Yonnie said, beginning to shudder. "I've got enough juice left to take 'em to the edge of that property line, then me and Tara gotta do what we gotta do."

"Just take us up to the surface and then go to my house," Gabrielle said. "I have top shelf in there, and my girls will reseal the barriers. It's almost dawn and you have to get inside the vaults."

"Get 'em topside, man," Jose said, looking at Yonnie. "Let's not fuck around with my man's health."

"There's too much adrenaline . . ." Yonnie walked away from the group.

Big Mike held Inez firmly. "Don't freak, be cool. He's all right, just needs—"

"Fresh air!" Yonnie bellowed, and turned to look at Carlos. His eyes were solid red orbs within the darkness, his fangs lowered to attack length. Inez screamed and hid her face against Big Mike's chest. Her fear made Tara and Yonnie's heads jerk toward her.

"I can't transport 'em like this. I'll come out of the cloud with a throat, I know me," Yonnie whispered.

Tara was shivering so hard that Yonnie pulled her to his side and closed his eyes. Rider didn't protest as she tore into Yonnie's throat.

"She's flat-lining," Yonnie whispered, swallowing hard. "She's never fed right, and has to now." He rubbed her back and stroked her hair. "But baby is draining me dry—make a decision."

"You have to pull the cloak," Damali said, touching Carlos's arm. "Now."

He shook his head. "I can't even raise shields."

She grabbed his hand. "Together."

"I've only moved one, me and you, not a whole fucking team, D!"

Yonnie slowly removed Tara from his throat. "Gabrielle, sweetheart," Yonnie said, walking toward her slowly as Tara wiped her mouth with the back of her hand. "Your place is so far away . . . and—"

Carlos's hand reached out and grabbed air. A current ran through Damali's arm, jolting her arm to full extension as her head flung back. The stunned team watched Yonnie make a lunge forward as the drape closed. He fell forward grasping nothing. They landed on the street in a heap.

"Nothing like an emergency to show you what you can do," Damali said, pushing herself up with a grunt.

Carlos's hands were shaking as he stood. He glanced as the sky was becoming light blue-gray. "I hope my brother makes it to the vaults in time," he said quietly. "Been there. Damn he's so low on fuel."

Too stunned too comment, the team slowly stood and brushed themselves off. Jose crouched beside Rider who had begun to go into a mild convulsion.

"Medic!" Jose hollered from the sidewalk. "Dan, J.L., get in there and get Berkfield out. 'Bazz, some-fucking-body go get Marlene her black bag!"

CHAPTER TWENTY-SIX

"WHAT DO you want from me?" Gabrielle shouted as the team that had been hidden in the sanctuary gathered around Rider.

"You tried to bring my children into *this*?" Marjorie shrieked and walked away as Rider raked the floor with his nails. "This is the outcome!"

"Shut up," Marlene said while the clerics kneeled beside the team's fallen man. "Gentlemen. Talk to me."

Imam Asula stood up and shook his head, unsheathing his machete quietly. Father Patrick began performing last rites, as Marjorie forced the teenager's face to her shoulder. Father Lopez guided the new members of the group to faraway pews.

Carlos was on his knees next to Jose. "Oh, shit, man. C'mon. You can shake this thing."

"Let Berkfield try," Jose said, his voice cracking.

"Berkfield's touch will scorch him. It's a weapon, now that the virus is all through him," Marlene said, glancing at Berkfield who was beside Rider on his hands and knees. "He's turning too fast."

Damali walked away and closed her eyes. "No, not Rider," Damali whispered.

Monk Lin touched her shoulder. "We will do it, Neteru. Your affiliation is too close," he said gently. "It will forever haunt you, so let us. That is also why we're here."

Damali shook her head no and went back to Rider when she saw Marlene stand.

"No, Mar! We've got to try—"

"Baby, we've done all we can do." Marlene wiped her face as tears continued to stream down it.

"Damn!" Shabazz said and walked away. He held Big Mike back as he rushed forward to stop Imam Asula.

"Let me do my own man!" Mike hollered, his voice fractured by emotion. "Me and him go back to the beginning. Me, Rider, and Jose—that's the minisquad."

Shabazz released his hold on Big Mike as Imam Asula nodded and passed the weapon to him.

"Get the kids out of here," Damali said with her back to the team. "All the newbies, Dan, too. Nobody will be right after this. Especially not me."

"Aw, shit, Rider!" Carlos said, slapping his hand on the slate floor. "You was supposed to pull through till the end, *hombre*." Carlos stood and paced back and forth. "Not another brother like this."

Slowly the team drew back. Marlene stayed near with Jose.

"I won't let you die alone, old friend," she murmured, stroking Rider's hair as he opened his eyes. But when he presented glittering yellow orbs and hissed at her, new fangs ripping through his gums, Marlene sobbed without censure. "Do it, Mike. Look at him. He's suffering on this church floor. Dawn is going to fry him slow—so do it neat."

She stood up and Carlos and Damali came near, holding up Jose. Shabazz drew Marlene into his arms. Imam Asula put a firm hand on Big Mike's shoulder, nodding that it was time and it was best. Father Patrick's face was stone but marred by streaks of tears. Sunlight was beginning to peek through the clouds, causing the side of Rider's face to sizzle. When he rolled out of the light beam, Rabbi Zeitloff closed his eyes, kissed the Star of David Dan had given him, and whispered, "Shalom, friend."

Berkfield braced himself over Rider's body as Mike lifted the machete. "Please, let me try once! What have we got to lose?"

"You taking a virus into your system that your own blood will attack and torch before it can pass out of your system," Shabazz said flatly, his emotions too raw to cope with. "This is part of the gig. The ugly part that takes your mind one loss at a time."

"What if he just treated the wound site," Damali said, going to her knees beside Berkfield. "He doesn't have to lay on hands, his blood—"

"Baby, stop it. Get up. *Now,*" Marlene whispered as Rider writhed in agony on the hallowed floor. His body began to smolder as he searched blindly and tried to follow the scent of human blood all around him, fangs lowered. "Let him go. We don't know where she bit him, can't even see the puncture marks. She—"

"I can see," Carlos said, his hand hovering over Rider's throat.

Berkfield reached up and Mike lowered the edge of his blade to his wrist. He winced as he slit it. "Show me where," he said, grabbing his wrist as blood spilled and Rider nearly sat up to find it.

Carlos felt his hand go hot over the throat wounds. Shabazz and Jose held Rider steady as he slashed and bit at the bloodied wrist that Berkfield held away from him. He snapped at Carlos's hand and groaned as he pulled it away. All assembled stared at the deep puncture wounds that rose on Rider's throat.

Swollen flesh with bruised, black and reddish-blue rings circled the deep holes in Rider's throat. The unmasked punctures slowly oozed a yellowish blood that gave off the stench of puss. Berkfield held his fist over the foul, torn skin and pumped his fist. As each drop splattered against Rider's throat he cried out and turned away. His skin instantly began sizzling and burning as the blood made contact, emitting crimson smoke as the strongest of the Guardians held him down and kept their distance from his distended mouth and clawed hands.

"It isn't working," Damali said, closing her eyes and beginning to rock. "You're just torturing him."

"Throw me a bowie knife," Carlos said fast. "Hit all the sites." He looked at Shabazz as Jose flipped him a blade. "The femoral arteries before we give up on our brother, okay?"

Damali looked away as Carlos ripped the blade down Rider's pants legs. His cries had turned into beastly shrieks and screams that made the hair stand up on her neck. As she heard a low, demonic voice come out of Rider's throat, she glanced up and for a second her gaze locked with Jose's. He didn't have to say it. She'd allowed her lover to do no less to her, turn her into this abomination for a brief time. But two seconds like this was too long. It wasn't until she watched Rider go through it that the full horror of it gripped her.

The reality made her nauseous, and she sat back on the floor as she watched Carlos and Berkfield work on her fallen brother.

"Damali, make them stop," Rider said in an unnatural voice that made her heart skip.

She couldn't answer him or speak as Big Mike and Imam Asula had to join in holding Rider down. Every cleric in the house of worship had formed a ring around the ordeal, saying prayers out loud in their own religion while new team members sobbed loudly from their fortunately blind positions at the far end of the sanctuary.

"No!" Rider shouted, as Carlos ripped open his shirt and scanned his body, looking for any wound that hadn't been treated. Then he became calm and chuckled low in his throat, his eyes glowing in the shadows as he stared at Carlos. "Mr. Councilman, I'm in your line. You made Yonnie. Yonnie elevated Tara. The sins of the father . . ." Rider hissed and bit at Carlos's searching hands. "You fathered me!" he shouted. His line of vision instantly went to Father Lopez. "Forgive you father for you have sinned." He grabbed the edge of Jose's coat. "And you and I are also in the same line. Make them stop!"

Damali stood up and paced, feeling Rider's eyes on her.

"Baby sis, make them stop," Rider said in a chilling singsong tone. "Do you know how many times she's bitten me over the last twenty-plus years?" He laughed as Berkfield continued to squeeze his wrist over newly erupting puncture marks. "About as many places as Carlos bit you . . . in all the forbidden spots," he said shrieking. "They don't understand what it feels like—not like you and I do . . . so sweetie, make them stop for old Rider. She's right around the corner."

"Keep him talking," Carlos ordered, stripping Rider's shirt off. "He hasn't gone to ash and it's daybreak."

Damali squatted down. "You've got to get the bites out of your system."

"Is it out of yours?" Rider said in a low, threatening rumble. "Is it?" he yelled, his voice suddenly escalating as his eyes flickered brown.

"Let Carlos work on you, honey," Damali said softly. "Tell me where she bit you."

"Everywhere," Rider said, laughing and closing his eyes. "Every-fucking-where."

Berkfield weaved and Jose caught him.

"This man is losing too much blood. Rider needs a freaking transfusion."

"What I need," Rider whispered, as his fangs slowly retracted, "is to be with Tara in a vault before it's too late."

"Shush," Damali said, stroking Rider's hair, tears making his image blurry as she felt human temperature creep back into his flesh. "It's gonna be all right."

Rider stopped struggling. Berkfield pulled back his arm. Guardians relaxed but kept their hold on him firm. Rider didn't open his eyes, just breathed deeply as two tears slipped from beneath his lids and coursed down the sides of his face.

"It's already too late," he said quietly in his normal voice. "He took her back to a lair under battle-feed-then-fuck conditions. She's gone."

Carlos stood and ran his hands through his hair. Jose covered up Rider with his coat and walked away. Big Mike let his machete fall to the floor. Shabazz let go of Marlene and found a vacant pew and sat down. Berkfield went to find his traumatized family. J.L. walked three steps and dropped to his knees, breathing hard. Damali looked at the ceiling, closed her eyes, and asked why.

Damali sat quietly at the long wooden table in the church kitchen. Tea cooled in front of her, but neither she nor the others had any interest in the lukewarm liquid. She placed the three stones she had on the table before her. "So, it has come to this." Her voice was monotone and far away as she made the idle comment. She couldn't even look at Rider as he stared out the window, wrapped in a ragged blanket. Even if they were to get out of New York, where would they go and how would they get there?

The roads were virtually impassable by car. Gridlock ruled as people tried to get out of the powerless city by car or truck or bus. Everything was on the road, and nothing was moving. Trains were dead, the airports shut down, and they couldn't tote an arsenal of weapons through the streets. The compound was gone, and there was nowhere to hide. Even if they could get to Rider's cabin, she doubted he would enter it, given Yonnie and Tara had been there. She couldn't blame him.

Daylight gave them maybe only ten short hours of respite before the next siege.

Carlos was to be rebuilt in seven days, plus seventy days, and the forecasted full team of twenty-one was to be gathered and strengthened within seven months after that, per the old grandfather-seer. But in the last seven days, Carlos had only come into a portion of his power, and they didn't have seventy days to figure out the rest of it. Nor did they have seven months to build a solid squad that was ready. Just like they didn't have time to visit the thirteen countries that had flickered in the lit flags. Time had truncated and run out. Lilith was on their asses. Hell had opened her gates and forced their hand early. Smart move.

"As this team's senior Neteru, what are you thinking?" Marlene asked quietly, making the defeated group momentarily look up.

"I don't know," Damali said, her gaze going around the demoralized faces in the room. "We can't sit here, we have to move, but where?" She sighed and ruffled her perspiration-dampened locks. "Everything that I thought I understood, I don't. Everything that was supposed to be, isn't. Every place that we were supposed to go, we didn't."

"I have a flat roof," Gabrielle said softly. "I have some very influential clientele—human—" she added, glancing at her sister "—who can get you a chopper." She sighed and glimpsed Rider. "That's the least I can do. But we'd have to walk to my place . . . it's not that far."

Gabrielle took off her ring and slid it across the table toward Damali when Rider stood and went to the window. "This is like a pass. The pilots will take you where you wanna go. But I don't think all of you can ride. Maybe just the core team, I don't know how big a helicopter they'll send."

Damali stared down at the tiger's eye stone that was set in platinum. The irony made a bitter smile come to her face. Tiger's eye . . . a cat's eye from a cathouse, but it ruled protection and truth, practicality and courage. She'd also been a cat—a huge one. Now she'd gotten another stone from a very unlikely source. "Thank you," she murmured and added it to her growing collection as Gabrielle sat back.

"Anybody got any suggestions?" Damali asked, absently drawing on the table with her finger. No one answered and she kept swirling the pattern that stuck in her head on the tablecloth. "What are we gonna do with twenty-one beat-up, tired, defeated, scared Guardians, half of whom are new, anyway?"

"How do you do that?" Inez said, her weary voice holding enough fascination to cause the others to look at her.

"Do what?" Damali asked.

"Make that pretty pattern on the table with lights. I always knew you were special, from the first time we laid eyes on each other, but I didn't understand," Inez whispered. "Now that Mike explained, everything you told me and went through makes sense."

Marlene leaned forward and reached across the table to hold Inez's hand. "Honey, what lights?"

"It's the way the lights from the stained glass almost seem to chase her finger," Inez said and yawned. "I'm so sleepy, I'm bleary eyed."

"Get her some paper," Marlene said quickly, looking at Father O'Dwyer. "Please."

The hosting cleric shot out of his plastic chair and rushed to the cupboard drawer, extracted a pencil, and a flimsy telephone notepad. He thrust it toward Marlene, who slid it down the table to Inez.

"Show me what you see when Damali doodles."

Inez chuckled. "I'm no artist."

"Try," Carlos said, coming to stand and peer over Inez's shoulder.

Seeming embarrassed, Inez began to roughly sketch three circles, and then she put arrows next to each direction and looked up.

"Can I see that?" Damali asked in an awed whisper. She studied
the paper and closed her eyes. "It's the formation," she said, filling
in the blanks. "The riddle makes sense. It's everyone that was to
come together." She marked off where each person stood, but
couldn't figure out the team excess.

Gabrielle smiled. "I'm not one of yours, just supposed to help
along the way. Maybe the rabbi is like that, too. Maybe he was just
supposed to tell us about Lilith, and his job is done."

Damali nodded, but she glanced at Marlene and Carlos, and then
over to Father Patrick, who all shared the same frown of uncertainty.

"I'm going home," Gabrielle said, kissing her niece and nephew,
and then slowly touching her sister's hand. "I may not have gone
down the acceptable path, but I am what I am." She hesitated. "I
have backup generators over there, in case the power ever failed. If
they made it to the vaults, the vaults will automatically seal on
timer locks and light sensors." She gazed down at Marjorie. "No
matter what, I love you. I'll get you out of here . . . but life as you
knew it can never be the same now."

Marjorie nodded and stood. She faced her sister and slowly hugged
her. "You saw these things when you were a kid, didn't you?"

Gabrielle nodded. "Your son hears them and uses the music to
drown them out. Your daughter's gifts are like mine, she can see
beyond the grave . . . just like you can, dear sister. Be well."

"Thank you," Damali said, going to Gabrielle to give her a hug.

Carlos stood and extended his hand. "We owe you. Thank you."

Gabrielle just smiled. "Mr. Councilman, you know better than
to tell a witch something like that."

Carlos chuckled. "Debt paid in full in the subway, then. We just
thank you."

"That's more like it," she purred, slinking away. "Gotta keep
you on your toes—words have power. Remember."

Lilith clapped her hands and laughed, rounding the table in council
chambers. "Dante, look at the newspaper headlines. They said I

have a cascading effect on the power grids in the city." She laughed and shook her head.

"Seems like you have a global effect, too. Your portal openings sent shock waves through London and China—"

"I know, but the best part is the competition did exactly what we thought they would—cannibalized themselves. The level-one and two phantoms sent their best and got smoked right in Rivera's vault. They were only supposed to send one, but sent many through the portal instead. It shows that their discipline is weak; their border controls are shaky. Even lower-level ghost gangs have slipped out, forming little cells of uncontrollable bandits that are a nuisance to contain and sweep away. Therefore they lost their shot by a breach of agreement that my husband has taken serious exception to. He hates to be cheated."

"And I'm so sure you told him all." The chairman smiled, his fangs lengthening as he watched her sashay around his table. His need to murder her where she stood was so devastating it gave him an erection. But all he offered her was a sly smile.

"It would be remiss of me to do otherwise."

"And our old friends, the Amanthras?" He made a tent with his fingers in front of his mouth to quell his anxiety.

"Botched the hit, sloppily, just like the were-demons. Their senators couldn't even pull it off." She slid against his throne and whispered in his ear. "So, darling, that leaves just me and you to finish the job."

This was not how he'd ever pictured spending his birthday, much less his life. Carlos stared out of the chopper window as it came to a slow descent over the pier on Delaware Avenue. His family was all gone, he had yet to bury his mother and grandmother and there was no way to access his money from New York during a blackout. The emotions that Damali stirred within him were too numerous to name. He was proud of her, yet furious with her. What she'd pulled off was nothing short of remarkable, but it made him grieve his inability to have done that, too. Everyone said they were equals, she most of all—but at the moment, he sure didn't see it that way. She was the seasoned general. He was the first lieutenant. He hated it.

He couldn't even look Rider in the face; they both knew the deal. Yet he couldn't be mad at Yonnie, either. It was what it was; shit happens and sometimes goes down in a foul way without that being the intent. The thing that truly troubled him, though, was Damali's cool remoteness. True they'd all be wrung out emotionally, but her distance worked his nerves. Never before had she kept secrets—not from him. He had been the one with the black box around portions of his mind; hers was always an open, innocent book. But having a guarded area in his head, he could spot another one a mile away. The stunt she pulled in Hell had caught him blindside, and it told him that there were layers of her he didn't know. He held her hand a little tighter. *Baby, what's wrong? Talk to me.*

So much was going through her mind right now, that all she could do was squeeze Carlos's hand back as the chopper found ground. The riddles were now clear, and she dared not reveal them in front of the group. Big Mike was the tree that a new bird, Inez, would nest in. It was all over the brother's face. Damali sighed. If it was gonna be anybody, then that was cool, she just hated that Inez was part of this insanity. J.L. was already pushing the envelope, having taken too much of an interest too quickly in Berkfield's seventeen-year-old, computer-whiz daughter. The man was a cop. Damali closed her eyes.

Pure drama would shatter the ranks. But with a pending battle, the situation brewing with Father Lopez and Juanita was making her climb out of her skin. There were disapproving brothers of the Covenant on one side, warning dude to honor his vows, Jose on the other, eyeing the new available chick on the team—who, she had to admit, was pretty . . . and who made her bristle when Jose had cozied up to her, which made her really feel weird about too many things to even begin to name them. This new chick was like déjà vu all over again. Damali opened her eyes slowly. Dee Dee.

She would have gasped if Carlos hadn't been sitting beside her. Dee Dee was a tactical sensor. Had she felt something brewing between her and Jose all along? Had she been the thing that had driven the jealous spikes that sent Dee Dee out into the street on her own one night to get nicked?

Guilt stabbed Damali in the side as she wondered if Jose had jumped the gun and messed with Dee Dee as a diversion. She already knew the answer before the thought finished forming, and it only made her shoulders slump. But this time this woman was someone who also used to sleep with Carlos—who, in turn, was trying to be stone-faced about it all . . . while their best buddy, Rider, was literally in mourning.

Truly, she could feel Carlos mourning, too. Not just for the loss of his family, but for the loss of his powers. How long would it take him to see the new ones as an asset, now that she'd just rolled on the chairman like she had—even strangled the old bastard in hand-to-hand combat . . . like she knew her man had wanted to do. Damali cringed. The fact that he'd seen her wheeling and dealing when he couldn't game like that any longer made her stave off a shudder. How did one do damage control on a situation like that?

Damali glanced out the window, wondering how everyone else was faring. Everyone was at the breaking point, mentally. Their own quiet struggles were undermining the whole reason they were here. How were they supposed to go to war as a united front with all this quiet chaos eating them up alive? What if a dag-gone Guardian squared off with a priest over a woman in the heat of battle? Oh, right, and she was supposed to keep a trigger-happy rabbi who wanted to go out in a blaze of glory chilled out. Insane. This is why the ranks had to be tight, and God help them if Yonnie showed back up with Tara at his side. Rider might set off machine-gun rounds trying to kill a master vamp on their side, who could flat-blast everybody before dude wigged and took a clip in the temple by his own hand. Yeah, right, and she was supposed to school a whole new team without even her Isis in her hand!

"You all right?" Carlos shouted as they touched down.

"No," Damali shouted back over the whir of the chopper.

"Tense?"

She laughed. "Understatement."

He nodded and watched the pilot for the signal that it was all right to exit the craft.

This was the most jacked-up set of circumstances he'd ever lived through or even died through. This was the most raggedy-assed team of beat-up warriors he'd ever had the misfortune to have to share a command with—oh, yeah, right, he was a Neteru. If this was what a Neteru was about, they could have the gig, truthfully. Hole up in an abandoned waterfront warehouse space that some witch's John owned and hadn't developed yet, so dude didn't care if they blew it up, or whatever, until he was ready to go condo. Carlos scanned the busted-out windows, weather-chapped exterior, and darkened interior, knowing without having to look that not only was the place impossible to totally secure like a lair or the Guardian's previous compound, but rats, roaches, and every pest in the exterminator's guide also lived there.

And what was wrong with the clerical brothers? What in Heaven's name would make them argue to go to Philly, especially since it had biblical references to the last days? It didn't make tactical sense at all. Their strategy was warped, but he and Shabazz had been outvoted. He hated this democratic bullshit. Nobody took a half-ready team to the fight. The game was to lay low, get strong, then move on whatever had tried to move on you. But, noooo . . . the so-called seers had prevailed. Damali and her impulsive shit had prevailed, which is probably why she didn't have anything to say— girlfriend had made a tactical strategy error and her Leo ass was too prideful to admit it.

Plus, everybody's head was jacked up. Nobody was focused. It was a perfect way to get the whole team smoked.

Carlos watched the white, unmarked delivery vans pull up to the empty warehouse and preapproved drivers begin unloading the equipment and ammunition that Father Pat had ordered. When the clerical team fanned out with Marlene and began setting up prayer barriers, Carlos let out a slow sigh and kept walking.

He wasn't feeling this at all.

"Look, it's late afternoon," Damali said, her voice rising despite her resolve to stay cool. "We could do the loop and get walled back up here by sundown. I think we should go back to where I was, physically go to those same places. If time has truncated on us, then we take everybody back to the art museum, down the steps, past the statues that moved up the parkway—"

"Yeah, and move twenty-two people through the city in this rag-tag group, packing concealed weapons like we're some freakin' tour group?" Carlos leaned across the metal table and stared at her. "No!"

"We've got all sorts of talent on this team. Somebody will pick up a trail, one or many of us could track it, and then—"

"What about no don't you get?" Carlos shouted, as the team looked back and forth between their warring Neterus.

Damali's arm snapped out and shook as she pointed her finger hard. "What about this don't *you* get? They are hunting us already. We are on the run, not on the offense, which I seriously do not like. There is no place on the planet to hide, Carlos, when Hell comes looking to beat your ass down. We have got to make a stand, find its sweet spot before it finds ours. Period. End of story. We do this like I said. I'm not sitting around, lying low, and shaking in my boots while they blow in the front door. Fuck that. I'm trying to find that bitch and smoke her before she comes for me."

"Hold it," he said, rounding the table that was between them. "Are you saying I'm afraid to bring the noise to them? Is that what you're saying?"

She picked up a long blade from the table and threw it to him and picked up a broadsword. "I'm saying that just because you aren't fully ready, doesn't mean that we have to wait—or can wait."

"Oh, Lord . . ." Marlene muttered and pushed back from the table.

Marjorie closed her eyes for a moment and sent her gaze out of a broken window.

"What?" Carlos shouted. "In the subway—"

"You fucking choked, dude." Damali squared off with him. "Yonnie said he couldn't transport, you had seconds to make up your mind, and—"

"I know what the fuck Yonnie said, and I got us out of there—"

"Correction, *we* got us out of there, and that's what's messing with your head. You'd better get used to it: We have to fight together. This is a team, and it's not about—"

Carlos slammed the sword down on the table. "No team went to Hell with you, D! You did that shit solo! No heads-up to any of us, so don't tell me about teamwork, hear?"

"Pick it up," Damali said through her teeth. "Go back-to-back and tell me if you can sense my moves and do so at a split-second pace without lopping off my head or my arm. Because down there, as you well know, you have to be on your best game, and you weren't!"

"I don't have to prove—"

"Do it now! We don't have time!"

Carlos walked away from her. "Fuck you!"

"Oh, so it's like that? You hear some shit you don't wanna hear and it's fuck *me*? Punk!"

"Damali." Marlene was on her feet. "Let's me, you, and Marj take a walk."

"Unproductive," Shabazz said, picking up the castaway blades. "Dangerous, too, since you're concerned about time factors. Becoming a good teacher means you have to be a good student." He shook his head and followed the path Carlos had left.

"Your nerves are fried, mine are fried, the team is going through a virtual meltdown along with a realignment," Marlene said.

"You were right, but they can't take it delivered like that," Marjorie said, glancing over her shoulder. "In front of the younger Guardians was like doing it in front of kids."

"You didn't leave him a way to save face—"

"Fuck his face, Mar," Damali shouted.

"Whatever," Marlene said in a near growl. "Facts being what they are, we need you two working as a well-oiled unit to do this thing. We're wasting time turning on each other. Can't have it."

"Figure out a way to smooth his ruffled feathers so we can do this day trip," Marj said nervously. "It would be best. Been done that way for years. It's practical."

Marlene chuckled. "More efficient than head-to-head—that's why her sister gave you that stone of practicality with the truth."

Although Damali could feel steam coming out of her ears, the old dolls made her laugh.

"I ain't got nothing to say, 'Bazz," Carlos said, walking a hot path across the wide parking lot. Freezing November winds blew off the Delaware River and Carlos set his sights on the Ben Franklin Bridge in the distance when Shabazz's hand landed on his shoulder.

"I came to agree with you, man."

Carlos nodded and walked back and forth, kicking up gravel dust with his Tims. "She makes me so damned mad sometimes I could slap her—but then it would *really* be on. She's so damned stubborn! Always has to have her way, and even when she's wrong, won't admit it!" Carlos slapped his chest. "I know somebody is gonna get hurt like this. I'm no punk, *hombre*. She called me a fucking punk—do you *believe* that shit?"

"*You* know you ain't no punk, *I* know you ain't no punk, and we all watched you walk through the fire."

"Oh, so you're saying she still, after all that, thinks I'm a punk because I'm patient and can wait for the right time to go after the target?" Carlos folded his arms over his chest, the muscles working in his jaw as a new wave of fury threatened to give him a stroke.

"Nope. I'm not saying jack about what she's saying. What I know is this. Her instincts are dead on and—"

"Mine ain't?"

"No," Shabazz said calmly, studying the sky. "Didn't say that, either. You're both right."

"That's some fucked-up logic."

"It's fact," Shabazz said, making Carlos look at him by using a curt tone. "She's right and you know it. To track something, you have to go over a warm trail. We can't go back to the more exotic

places we've been, but Philly gave her the lead—so we start there."
Shabazz nodded toward the river. "Water will be at our backs, and
the museum area is near water. If the lady has a solid hunch, we always play it. That's all I'm saying."

When Carlos looked away and didn't argue, Shabazz pressed his
point. "But we need to do that in broad daylight, then use your
strategy, namely, to get strong, make sure we know what we're dealing with."

Carlos nodded and unfolded his arms, shoving his hands in his
jeans pockets.

"This team is nowhere ready to battle anything," Shabazz said.
"I know it, you know it, and she knows it—but have you ever considered that girlfriend might be scared?"

Carlos looked at him.

"Yeah, that's right. Scared. I said it. Everything around her is
changing, the people she could depend on are nuttin' up. Rider almost bought it, and they took her security blanket, her blades, man.
You think she rubbed your nose in it back there in front of the
newbies, hell . . . I know Damali. When she came back without her
blades, dressed down by the Queen's Council, girlfriend ain't been
right ever since. Her confidence is as raggedy as a bowl of yock.
Plus, now, the clock is ticking on something that could present itself
as her demon child. She's wigging, rightfully so. She ain't got no
diplomacy left in her. Damali is about motion, right through here,
and trying to minimize casualties—you being one of the primary
ones."

"I didn't like the way she was all up in my face, though,
man." Carlos raked his fingers through his hair and let his
breath out hard. "Down in the subway tunnel, I just had a few
seconds to think. I was worried that maybe I try this transport
thing, that's still a little new, and what if it messed up, landed us
in a hot zone, or I dropped somebody? Yonnie's ass was sweating
me and—"

"For two seconds," Shabazz said, looking him in the eyes, "you
got scared." When Carlos looked away, he placed his hand on his

shoulder. "This is me and you talking, nobody else on the team—not even Marlene who I sleep with. Man to man, let's be real, this shit is really fuckin' scary."

Carlos looked up at him and nodded grudgingly.

"It's like having a new car with all these new gadgets on it and having to do a high-speed chase to get away from the cops."

Carlos chuckled with Shabazz.

"C'mon, man, give yourself a break. You can do a lot of the same shit, just in a different way, and your ass is used to being so smooth that what's making you mad is that you don't want to break it out until you know how to use it to the bone. I can dig it, that's a man thing—I understand."

Carlos pounded Shabazz's fist and they smiled.

"Plus, you being a Scorp—y'all are secretive and sly any ole way, dead or alive, and not to be feelin' in total control—to y'all—is a fate worse than death."

"No, lie . . ." Carlos said, letting his breath out hard.

"You're a brother with a lot on his mind," Shabazz said, slinging an arm over Carlos's shoulder and walking him back toward the building. "Been there, ask an old dog how this goes. Your people just crossed over and you ain't even there to bury them proper, you just got out of jail—so to speak, your powers changed, all your friends are either dead or new, your woman is kickin' up the bo bo, your money jacked—that right there would make the average brother intolerable. You've got this new job that you wanna do right, because it's all you got and she's sweatin' you about it. Then, your boy is all messed around by a woman he won by default . . . your other boy is ready to jump off the bridge down the street and you just got pulled into this very wild family that you didn't bargain for. You're in temporary housing that ain't secure or like your old spot, in a brand-new neighborhood—'cause you had to leave all the old people, places, and things in a cosmic twelve-step program, with counselors breathing down your neck, just waiting for you to go back to your old ways . . . and there's times when the old life seemed so much easier, simplistic, despite all the bad—

because you knew that game like the back of your hand. Meanwhile, your body is going through changes because you're about to apex. Sound familiar?"

"It's a lot, all at one time." Carlos said quietly as he stopped walking. "It's total fucking chaos."

Shabazz laughed. "Welcome to married life, my brother." Shabazz shook his head and walked ahead of Carlos. "And y'all wanted a baby right now, too. Madness."

CHAPTER TWENTY-SEVEN

WHEN CARLOS walked back into the ragged warehouse, all eyes were on him. Shabazz monitored the vibe as Damali cut a glare at both of them, but saved the most lethal portion of it for Carlos.

"Since you wanted to step outside," Carlos said evenly, "let's do that."

Stricken glances passed around the group.

Damali flung down the bowie knife and it lodged in the earth with a thump. "Yeah, let's do that."

"Yo, yo, yo," Jose said quickly. "Listen, we're supposed to be fam—"

"This is between me and her," Carlos said through his teeth. "Long overdue, too."

"Definitely long overdue," Damali snapped, her hands going to her hips.

Dan and J.L. started to walk forward, but Shabazz held up his hand.

"They need to get this out of their systems," Shabazz said coolly, his stare forcing the younger Guardians to stand down.

Rider nodded. Big Mike leaned casually against the wall. Berkfield shook his head and let out a breath as he swiped a palm over his balding scalp.

"Girl, don't be crazy," Inez said, her voice a quiet plea for reason.

Damali ignored her, eyes blazing in a challenge as she stared at Carlos. It was on, *for real*. He'd come back in to physically challenge her in front of her team? Had literally squared off on her? Was he outta his mind! She'd wax his ass, if it was the last thing she did—and even if it came to a draw, he'd know he'd been in a serious street fight with someone not to be played with.

"This shit is between man and wife," Berkfield said, and gave his children the "do not move or get in it" eye. He glanced at his wife, Marjorie, who had an unreadable expression of tension on her face.

The clerics all eyed each other, seeming mortified. But Father Patrick slowly shook his head for the others not to intervene. His glance said it all; this had to play itself out.

Jose pushed past Shabazz and Berkfield's verbal barriers, ignoring Father Patrick's silent commentary. "You can't just let 'em rumble out there to settle whatever beef and get all beat up before we—"

"It's between man and wife," Marlene said calmly, echoing Berkfield's words and supporting what Shabazz had said. She raised an eyebrow. Her quiet message was very clear; squash the nonsense going on in the camp. "Let 'em work it out and clear the air, once and for all. Who's gonna lead the teams if our generals don't?"

But there was something in Marlene's firm tone that made Damali glance at her, that bit of gentleness in her voice. True, they had to resolve their conflict, but . . . It annoyed Damali that a slight, nearly hidden smile tugged at Marlene's mouth, and that Marjorie and Marlene exchanged a mysterious glance between them. The older brothers stepped forward and stood between the younger Guardians and the two would be combatants.

Damali bristled. Did the older sisters think it was a joke? That she couldn't hold her own? Did the brothers really feel the need to protect her, yet again? After all she'd been through and proven, and they *still* didn't think she could get the job done? Aw, hell no. Now it was a matter of personal dignity!

"Let's do this," Damali said, and stormed out of the building. She needed to kick Carlos's ass in the worst way. She rounded the building, spun around and pointed her finger in his face Carlos's.

"Let me tell you one damned thing!" she shouted, two inches from his face. "Don't you ever—"

He slapped her hand away and stepped closer. "Don't you put your hand in my face, woman—ever!" he shouted back, now nose-to-nose with her.

Damali cocked her fist back and let it fly.

Carlos caught the punch in the flat of his palm, covered her hand with his fist, and shoved her arm down hard. Then he grabbed her by her arms, hauled her in close, and slammed his mouth over hers in a punishing kiss. When he released her his eyes were blazing silver. "Stop this shit, right now."

"Fuck you—"

"Yeah, and fuck you, too!" he said, kissing her again hard and pushing her against the side of the building.

"You embarrassed me in front of my team," she snapped. "I ain't having it."

"Likewise," he said loudly, breathing hard.

She shoved him back from her. "I don't know who the hell you think you are," she said, tears of rage, nearly blinding her, "but so help me, I'll kick your ass if you keep messing with me. You've been taking me through changes since the day we met! I'm tired of this shit!"

"Well, I'm tired, too, D!" he said, his face close to hers. "You think you can kick my ass? Then do it! I am burnt-the-fuck-out. I'm exhausted, bone weary, and sick of all the drama. And the last thing I'm gonna do is let any woman punk me down in front of a full team of damned Guardians—"

She kissed him hard. He was so angry that he almost couldn't breathe. But he responded by returning the kiss just as violently. When the kiss broke, she slapped his face. He grabbed her jaw hard, the skin whitening beneath his fingertips, and kissed her again. She grabbed his crotch and squeezed hard. They both glared at each other, panting their fury and desire, challenging the other to give in first.

He eased his hold on her jaw. She eased her grip on his crotch. She leaned up and filled his mouth with hers, their tongues dueling in a hot, angry tangle. She moved her hand and gripped the small of his back, gathering up his T-shirt so she could feel his skin. Somehow his hand left her jaw and found the back of her head to hold her hair tightly. His other hand slid to her ass, gripping it.

She was supposed to be pushing him away, so she could kick his ass, but her body wouldn't obey. How her hands had found his zipper was beyond her comprehension. Or why she was holding his hot length in her hands.

She couldn't answer those questions, no more than she could figure out how in the hell her jeans were down around her boots, or why she was outside, behind a building, sweating in the dead of winter, holding onto his shoulders, face buried against his neck as she panted and moaned.

When he bit her and thrust almost violently into her, she gasped and rose to meet him frantically. She bit his shoulder. Carlos moaned like he'd been stabbed.

He was supposed to slap the bullshit out of her for all her offenses, for hitting him first, for trying to sucker punch him, for wounding his pride, for making him worry about her to no end, for not appreciating a goddamned thing he'd ever done. He wasn't supposed to tremble. She wasn't supposed to shudder. She wasn't supposed to fit him like a molten glove. He wasn't supposed to feel her breath hitch when he entered her, not at all.

She leaned her head back and looked at him through narrowed eyes. He stared at her, not blinking, jaw locked tight, moving against her, each hard thrust speaking volumes, cussing her out without words, their gazes locked.

He refused to let her use sex as a weapon. No, he wasn't closing his damned eyes, wasn't feeling how good she felt or remembering shit.

No, she wasn't about to go all soft and croon sweet nothings in his damned ear.

"If you ever . . ." she said through her teeth, meeting his thrusts with fury.

"Don't you ever . . ." he said, his voice hoarse and gravelly as he pumped against her.

Neither would look away. The storm between them gathered. Sweat formed on his brow and began to trickle down his temple.

"I will kick your ass, baby" he murmured.

"And I will slap the taste out of your mouth," she said on a gasp, and turned her face away as her eyes slid closed.

She traced over the tight halves of his ass beneath his jeans and pulled him in closer. He braced one hand against the wall, clung to her waist with the other, his forehead touching hers. She closed her eyes tighter when he shuddered. Intense pleasure flowed over them, blinding them to everything except each other's bodies.

They held each other for a few minutes, breathing hard, recovering, and then slowly pulled away. Carlos straightened his T-shirt and zipped up his pants, not meeting her eyes. Damali yanked up her jeans and fastened them, and smoothed down her shirt.

"Don't say shit to me," she muttered as she shoved her shirt back into her jeans.

"Not a fucking word to me, either," he said, adjusting the fit of his jeans. "Not a word."

"Fine," she said in a testy voice, still breathing hard.

"Fine," he said, glaring at her as he took in deep inhales through his nose.

"Kicked your ass good, though," she said, flipping her locks over her shoulders.

"Yeah, likewise," he muttered, and walked back toward the building.

Carlos watched Damali move the team along the rear grounds of the Philadelphia Museum of Art as though taking their squad on an archeological dig. He hated to admit it, but she'd been right. There was only one sure way to track prey: pick up its trail at the beginning and study its habits. He didn't even want to think about the torrid, angry sex that had gone down. It was too insane, but had definitely chilled them both out.

But the thing that kept nagging him as their team combed the Schuylkill River's edge was, what if this was simply the location of a battle yet to come, not where the thing that was hunting them had been. Though that was very plausible, it was also more than disturbing, especially since they'd been everywhere, pretending to be tourists.

Arriving in an innocuous-looking minivan, clerics had climbed out, seeming to be in a small, eclectic religious group. The young bucks had jumped on motorcycles, and played it off like they were in a group apart from the touring clergymen. J.L. Dan, and Jose had all chosen a bike. Juanita rode with Jose, much to the padre's dismay.

Carlos walked farther down the water's edge, pitching pebbles, and staying as far away from Juanita as possible. Later they'd talk. He owed her that much and more. Juanita had been there for his mother and grandmother, and with them both at the bitter end. Damali would just have to understand theirs was also a friendship with some history, half of which they couldn't go back to—but it was not forgotten, simply something that he and Juanita knew better than to discuss.

Shabazz and Marlene strolled along the East River Drive like a graying couple that didn't know another soul . . . Rider was still stricken, but had blended in with the Berkfields in a Jeep. Big Mike sat on a bench whittling a stick into a stake next to Inez, smiling quietly to himself and seeming like an exhausted jogger—more like a football player—who had just finished a weekend workout. Their white Escalade sat parked.

He and Damali had come to meet them discreetly in a Hummer fully loaded with weaponry like each vehicle had—tags untraceable.

Despite all the equipment, something in his gut just didn't sit right. He and Damali had barely said two words to each other since he'd stormed out of the building, and she'd left it walking hotly behind him, breathing hard with rage. It was all about logistics, professionalism, though. There was no room for personal drama. Period. Everyone was on their mark and on-point. Yet no matter how many of her old stops they scoured, they all came up blank.

Carlos fingered the small knife in his pocket as thoughts tumbled in his brain. From the corner of his eye, he glimpsed Damali walking slowly and scratching her head. Frustration made her bite her lip. Even ornery, she was beautiful. The late-afternoon sun always did something to her skin. But she owed him an apology. The museums turned up nothing. Nary a statue moved or blinked. Not one single flag lit up on the parkway, and nothing mysterious happened in the Masonic Lodge on One Broad Street, even though all these things had happened to her when the sun was out.

Carlos studied the traffic and the tension in the team. The newbies were anxious and picked their way along the back ruins of the museum like frightened deer. Each one of them would take a step or two, then stop, look up, almost visibly sniff the air, and then go back to sensing for danger in the landscape. Older Guardians seemed so weary that he wondered if their sensory capacity wasn't too fried to even register. His was almost there, so it wasn't a slam on their age. Fatigue would do that.

A very fragile part of him wished that she would just look up and squash what had flared up between them.

They glanced up at the same time.

"Look," she said, casting away a stick and walking back toward him. "You were right, okay?"

"That's cool," he said, shrugging and keeping his voice neutral. His pride still stung, but just seeing her come to him with half a bit of contrition helped a lot. "We had to check it out. Made sense."

"Yeah, but we're drawing blanks." She looked out over the water. "I'm sorry I went there like that in front of the team."

He didn't respond, just watched the rose-orange sun fire her cheek his favorite color—sun-kissed caramel.

"You were right about hesitating in battle . . . the thing in the subway tunnel. A split second could cost a life."

"Yeah, but I didn't have to say it that way," she said quietly, looking out at the water.

"Everybody's nerves are on edge."

She nodded. "You think your boy, Yonnie, is gonna come back to our side?"

"I don't know, truth be told. If I were in his shoes, and you needed to feed to live . . . and were dying in my arms—hey, I might have taken a body on the spot. Can't blame the man. I saw him struggling with the decision, he saw me struggling with mine. Rider did, too."

"I know," Damali said. "Half of him wanted Yonnie to take her and save her. Half of him wanted her to burn to ash in the sun, rather than to be with another man. And a crazy bit of hope made him want to go find her in whatever condition she was in, even live in her world, not being able to live in this one alone. God knows I know what that feels like."

"It was futile. He would have turned as a third and went up against a battle-bulked master over a woman he'd marked at the throat. It would have ended badly, plus Rider's soul would have been damned for it all."

"I know," Damali murmured, and touched Carlos's arm. "How do you let something that deep go, once the season for it has passed? I can almost feel her heart breaking, even though she's safe. It was the look in her eyes as we closed the drape, baby. She looked right at him and then shut her eyes . . . like she knew he was turning and with us, we'd have to do him."

"In my old world, that was respect. The closest thing down there that comes to love. To be done by your own, not a competitor—quick, clean, without being maimed and left half alive for the sun to finish you after a fight you'd lost. She knows our way, too, that if he dropped fang, we'd have to take his head . . . and we'd do it out of love, then commend his soul to a place she couldn't. The Light. That's why she let us take him with the clerics and didn't fight with Yonnie in front of us about it. If she's going with him, then she had to make a snap decision, and tried to save both their prides."

What happened outside the warehouse remained off-limits for discussion. Instead, they both danced around it, talking about love and wounded pride in the third person with soft voice—both understanding.

Carlos sighed and looked up to the sky. His distant vampire-blood cousin wore a clerical collar and had a tough decision to make, too. "Choices. Yonnie is choosing to survive in the fucked-up circumstances he's in. If he can pull off a coup, he's the last master standing. Brother won, in many respects." Carlos saluted the sky. "Wise move. If I were backed into his same corner—"

"You wouldn't do that," Damali said, holding his arm. "That was the difference between you and him. You had—"

"A different set of circumstances," Carlos said firmly, allowing his hands to trail down her arms. "Don't ever forget for a moment what I was. I've always told you that. Love can make anybody blind, know that, too. If I were backed into his corner, I'd be thinking that Gabrielle and her girls would make excellent inner-lair protectors. If he can stop his turn blocks, brother has an empire at his feet."

"But what about redemption?" Damali stared at him wide-eyed.

"The last thing on my mind when I was on the run and with you." He kissed her forehead. "My boy just wants a little bit of happiness after living in Hell for years. Tara is his piece of sky. Been there."

The clerical group casually passed by them. The rabbi tipped his hat and kept his voice low.

"We have gone everywhere, and zilch. It is late and we should go back to our base."

"Good afternoon to you too, sir," Carlos said and put his arm around Damali's waist. He glanced at the sky again as they discreetly quickened their pace. The East Coast sun dropped at about four P.M. in the fall. He missed L.A. so much he could cry. Time robbed daylight here. In his old lands, it shone over the ocean and warmed the earth year-round.

The relief of *The Gates of Hell* on the Rodin Museum's wall suddenly tugged at him from blocks away, but he kept walking and nodded to Inez with a smile. He could almost feel the cement breathing; the figures beneath the surface coming alive and making the stone wall turn to rubber against fiendish little claws. Big Mike simply looked up. The Berkfields turned on their motor. Dan shot Jose a look and gunned his engine. J.L. did the same. Berkfield pulled off, he and Marjorie glanced at the van as the clerics got in and slammed the door. Rider never looked up, just sat like a defeated soldier who didn't care if he lived or died.

Carlos opened the Hummer door for Damali. A sophisticated older couple walked by their vehicle. The attractive woman smiled knowingly and tossed her immaculate silver-gray bob over her shoulder as her dark eyes assessed him. Her husband didn't notice, but Carlos did. Damali stared after her, and slowly got into the SUV.

Carlos shook off the sensation of being visually undressed as he gunned the motor. He'd experienced that before, but this time it sent a chill through him. He pulled out of the space and entered the traffic pattern of the wide bending road. He couldn't get her eyes out of his mind. It was an electrifying, horrifying, erection-producing stare from a woman who had to be in her early sixties, her yuppie husband oblivious—but not.

"I know," Damali said.

"Something wasn't right."

"Witch?"

"Possibly."

"What time were you born?"

He glanced at her and sent his focus back to the traffic, spotting the other team members to be sure the group stayed together. "Six P.M. Why?"

"It's almost four."

"We'll be back before full dark. She can't be vamp."

"Lilith isn't all vamp." Damali stared at him. "You said it your-self, level seven ain't no joke. They don't have daylight restrictions, right?" She reached into her jeans pocket and extracted the vial of *Oblivion* she'd scored from the chairman. They both stared at the bait.

He didn't want to think about it. "Yeah."

"None of us know their range of strengths yet."

"I know," he muttered, his gaze drifting to the Rodin Museum as they sped along the parkway toward the expressway.

Damali swept her nose along the edge of Carlos's leather coat and up his neck. He watched her eyes slide shut for a moment. A tremor ran through her.

"You all right?"

She swallowed hard and tucked away the vial. "Not really. Dayum."

"What?" His focus fractured between her and the traffic. "*Obliv-ion* messing with you?" he asked, beginning to panic.

She wiped her face with her hands and opened the window, let-ting in a blast of frigid air. "No. It's not coming from the vial. You smell so good I'm ready to jump your bones in this car. That makes no sense—not given what we're dealing with and . . ."

She stopped talking, pressed the automatic window button, and sat back, calmly closing the window. "Black Jag sedan, three o'clock, the same couple we passed."

"Get the fuck out of here," Carlos said, peeping past Damali as casually as he could. "Oh, shit."

"Oh, shit. Right." Damali lowered her visor and acted like she was fluffing her hair. "No reflection," she said with a sigh and snapped the visor shut. She reached in the glove compartment and withdrew a Glock, holding it down between her legs as she dialed Marlene on her cell.

"Cut the transmission," Carlos said quietly. "If she's with who I think she is, he's Prince of the Airwaves."

Damali nodded and clicked the phone shut. "That's not who it is," she said quietly. "Her husband doesn't know. But you're right about the cell phone. My bad. New plan?"

"Look at the team, baby. Be honest. You think they're ready?"

She shook her head slowly no as every light went red before them.

"We're the bait. Save the team."

He nodded. "This will make the news and toast your career."

"If this goes down fucked up, that's the least that can happen—ash is real likely."

"Old school, like I showed you," he said calmly, waiting on the inordinately slow light. Carlos glanced at oncoming traffic and his team's positions ahead of them.

The light finally changed, the car in front of them moved up. He stepped on the gas as Damali lowered her window, leaned out, and fired two warning shots to shatter the black Jag's window.

Traffic behind them screeched to a halt as the Hummer went over the median and Carlos whipped the vehicle into oncoming traffic. The Jaguar immediately spun and pursued them at a reckless speed. Trees whizzed by, buildings blurred, and that's when Damali saw it in slow motion.

The walls of the Rodin Museum stretched like a thousand

hands were pushing at rubber. Small fissures erupted. She could see it happening in her mind as their Hummer fled along the drive they'd just abandoned, making cars swerve out of their path, the river reflecting the gold setting sun, high rock formations rising along the edge. Boathouses became swift chess pieces, there one moment, gone the next. A vehicle with now-blackened windows spit sparks as the under chassis hit asphalt when they rounded the bend. They didn't know this city. A bridge was strangled with traffic. They had to slow down or bail out.

"We're losing sun!" Carlos shouted. "We can't bail!"

Their minds locked, their movements connected as though they were one. She looked into the rearview mirror. "Oh, no . . ."

The motorcycles had doubled back and were following them. Shabazz had turned the Jeep around. Police sirens were sounding, lights flashing; traffic was snarled. They hit a curb, which made them skid into the side of a building. Damali and Carlos jumped out and began running.

The motorcycles picked them up and took off deep into the park. She clung to J.L. with one hand while firing at the Jaguar with the other. Carlos held on to Dan and leaned into a turn, then pulled the pin on a grenade and lobbed it at the black car.

The explosion simply dented the Jaguar's windshield. Blue-black flames roared over the hood and melted away. The bikes skidded to a slide, gunned in the pivot, and went back the way they'd come, passing cops, dodging stunned drivers, and leaving the Jaguar in the dust.

The van was in sight along with Shabazz's Jeep but headed in the wrong direction. Police helicopters were up, cruising at low altitude, commanding them to stop. But the two choppers pulled up as hundreds of grayish-green entities fought and scrambled along the ground, pouring over the sidewalk from the museum relief. Stony gargoyles bore fangs, and looked up. They angled their gray little bodies at a readied pitch toward the air, spread leathery wings, and took off.

A male voice pierced Damali's mind. "Take her to a clearing." It wasn't Carlos's. The man riding with the woman had familiar eyes.

"Yes, a shield to setting sun, for your locations." Then the message was gone.

Big Mike stood up in the Jeep and leveled a shoulder cannon at the beasts. The rocket missed the chopper by a fraction and splattered some harpies, but that only made the police open fire on their vehicle with an assault rifle.

Within seconds, a black tornado funneled up toward the choppers. Above them, a black triangular formation yawned open in the now-darkening sky. Tiny scavenger bodies shredded themselves in the chopper blades. Carlos and Damali cringed, feeling the blast before it happened.

Helicopter parts flew into buildings. Shrapnel rained on people who ran and took cover. Flames began to climb up the side of an apartment building. The team went over the bridge by the art museum, a black tornado on their tails, rescue units and fire trucks adding to the chaos. New choppers were in the air. News cameras were on the ground and airborne, bearing insignias on the sides of helicopters, adding mayhem that caused near collisions in the streets and skies. SWAT unit vans screeched to the scene. A one-way street cleared as Damali and Carlos zigzagged down it. Murals peeled off buildings and came alive, fighting with phantoms that moved like lightning-fast ether.

She and Carlos hit a wide boulevard, clinging to the backs of the bike drivers. Market Street. Her eyes had tears in them from the whipping winds. Two stone eagles were mounted on either side of a bridge. "Help us," she shouted to the stone, not knowing why. Instinct had led her. The eagles took flight and collided in the air with harpies, protecting their backs. One flew down off the U.S. Post Office marquis. Two huge whales in mural relief leapt off the side of a riverside building, gulping harpies and then sending a tidal wave against the train track–ridden shore.

Their bikes skidded into a turn and went down the pavement, trapped by traffic on one side, the expressway on the other. They looked behind them in horror as the huge superstructure— Pennsylvania Station at Thirtieth Street—filled with darkness.

"She's gonna blow!" Carlos yelled, as the windows groaned,

cracked, and shattered, releasing thousands of harpies in a black rain over the city.

Swerving away from pedestrians and trying not to run over students, they burned rubber through Drexel University's campus. A huge brass dragon leapt down from its pedestal, and until it began gulping harpies, they didn't know if it was friend or foe.

"Bring the art alive!" Carlos yelled over the battle din and motors. "Damali, it's you—this is part of your gifts!"

She nodded and her eyes scanned the blurred terrain for anything useful, blocking the aerial attack of the drivers with all things natural—stone, brick, broken tree limbs—as they hurtled down the streets. But she also kept firing her weapon, one arm reaching back and up.

The motorcycles fled under a train trestle, and passed three large cathedrals.

"Head for hallowed ground," she yelled, holding on tight as her Glock ran out of ammo and clicked dead.

"I can't," J.L. shouted. "They're too close!" He leaned the bike into another radical turn, and left the van and the Jeep, taking the bikes over a high-arched bridge through what seemed to be a college campus. As soon as the bikes hit the apex of the University of Pennsylvania footbridge, they went airborne, and landed with a skidding thud. People fell, screamed, and rolled out of the way. Dirt and debris and leaves churned under wheels and they doubled back, bounced off the curb, and reentered the street.

Father Patrick leaned out of the window of the van. "Take this to open ground, child! People are dying!"

Damali and Carlos watched in horror as a massive winged gargoyle dropped to the white van. She and Carlos both saw it happen in slow motion. Father Patrick turned and screamed no. He threw his body toward Father Lopez, trying to shield the young cleric, who froze for a second, as a razor tail speared the top. The huge winged beast opened the vehicle like it were a tin can, and stabbed its tail in, bringing Father Lopez out with it.

Blood bubbled from his mouth. Carlos slumped against Dan, clutching his chest as the beast screamed and slashed the body back and forth, pitching it in the nearby bushes. Instantly he and Damali both knew that what Carlos had experienced earlier wasn't post-battle shock. It was a premonition.

Rabbi Zeitloff fired a pump shotgun. The priests were backed away by a heavy swarm of incoming harpies and couldn't retrieve their fallen man. Pure darkness fell. The lights down the main streets went black as the cloud passed them.

"Ditch me, kid," Carlos said to Dan, blood oozing from his mouth. "They want me."

"No!" Dan shouted, making another hard pivot.

Carlos dropped from the bike and rolled onto the church steps.

"Take me back!" Damali screamed to J.L. "We don't leave our own."

She turned her head as she saw Imam Asula raise a blade in the bushes. Gargoyles jumped off the sides of buildings. Gray swirling masses of fiendish demons grappled with the clerics. J.L. stopped the bike on the steps of the cathedral on Thirty-eighth Street. The Berkfields drove their Jeep up the other side, missing Carlos and ramming the door. Guardians helped Damali drag Carlos up the steps. It went quiet for a moment, save the trickling water of the ground font. Damali stared at the font inscription for a second. It all became instantly clear as she read the prophetic words from Reve-lations 22:3—A number that made seven: *The Angel showed me the river of the water of life, flowing from the throne of God and the Lamb through the middle of the street of the city*. She knew what she had to do; cut through the city to the park near water.

Sirens neared. Damali stood with her team. Clerics fell into the door.

"We're surrounded," Father Patrick wheezed. "Lopez is gone."

Juanita hid her face in Jose's shoulder. Carlos struggled to his feet.

"The broken-hearted had to make a decision," Carlos gasped. "He was in my line—I felt it."

"Draw the cloak now, baby," Damali said. "Take us to park land, away from civilians."

He nodded and the group huddled between him and Damali. Then they were gone.

The group came to a falling heap in the middle of a green silent valley within Fairmount Park. Silvery water ran near it.

"Formation," Damali said. "Weapons check."

Shabazz checked his Glock. "All out—"

Two huge were-wolves parted the trees before he and Big Mike could get in the protective ring.

"They are out of ammo," one beast snarled. "Let the succubae and incubi squabble over the remains of the priest," it said, issuing an evil snarl.

"Yes . . . all bets are off. To the victor go the spoils," the other said, circling and judging their odds, seeming unsure of Carlos and Damali's capacities. It nodded to Shabazz. "Remember what the incubus said was his greatest fear?"

The other were-wolf nodded. "From prison? Oh . . . yeah . . . Do them both before you do them." It laughed. "Our senator is dead. Make him sorry that he ever taught the Neterus how to raise blades against level five."

"No!" Damali yelled. "Freeze!" She stood wide-legged, a stone in each hand, but the weres didn't slow down. Instead, the trees leaned back and shuddered, stopping the were-wolves' sure lunge.

Two huge, very slow-stalking, sleek jaguar bodies emerged from among the trees and eyed the furious wolfen demons. Their low rumbling growls transfixed the human team while the were-wolves tilted their heads, unsure what to make of the new predators challenging their kill. But the Guardian team could see the lupine-demons assessing the potential strength of the jaguars. Carlos shot a quick glance at Damali. They both knew the big-cat clans on level five occupied a higher rung on Hell's food chain than the wolfen packs.

To everyone, the new, snarling threat was clear; the team remained immobile, not sure which side the new predators were on. The silvery thread within the red thread of their auras made Carlos hesitate. Frustrated confusion forced bluff snarls from the wolfen clan searchers. However, the lupines backed up, fangs drizzling acid drool, their glowing eyes holding a question as they matched the jaguars' menacing, hypnotic circling.

The lead jaguar lowered its head, ears flattening against its massive skull as the muscles beneath its shimmering blue-black coat kneaded in a slow approach, making the beast nearly invisible within the almost moonless night. It glanced up to the slowly eclipsing moon and then narrowed its coppery glowing eyes on Shabazz. "I tol' you if you *ever* put my woman in dis position again, mon, I would come for her."

Marlene's hand went to her chest. Kamal instantly shape-shifted, causing his taller partner, Drum, to do the same. They stood between the were-demons and the Guardian and Covenant teams. Kamal's line of vision held the stunned weres. His shoulder-length locks crackled with angry static charge. His eyes still glowed gold as he spun so quickly that it seemed to be in slow motion, retracted his upper and lower canines, and swept Marlene into his arms, crushing her mouth with a hard kiss. He released her just as fast, leaving her to stumble behind him as he advanced toward the threat with his eyes blazing. Kamal worked the muscles in his neck and shoulders, body-blocking Marlene from a possible attack while tilting his head from side to side as though considering how to dissect the were-demons.

Shabazz moved forward, his locks winding with visible blue-white energy, his hot gaze on Kamal; Big Mike's hand flattened broad across Shabazz's chest, but was knocked away by Shabazz's deft Aikido move. The demons glanced between the near twin images of Shabazz and Kamal, not sure where to begin an attack lunge.

"You had her until she passed the season of childbirth. That is not longer an issue, and you have not protected her!" Kamal shouted. "Her pulse could not be found for almost a week!"

"This is bigger than personal vendettas, were-human!" the lead lupine-demon growled, growing impatient. "The bounty—"

Kamal roared, his canines ripping through his gums again. "After I have tracked her renewed pulse across three continents you won't have a limb left to collect the bounty!" He looked Shabazz up and down with disdain. "Don't try me tonight. Hear?"

"One team!" Carlos shouted, drawing the volatile struggle toward himself and Damali.

Damali's stricken gaze went to Shabazz, begging him with her eyes to stand down, then briefly went to Marlene, unable to witness the shocked pain her eyes held. The rest of the Guardians' eyes revealed confusion, not sure which command to follow—a scenario beyond dangerous. Even the Covenant team seemed unsure. Damali focused on the threat before her. "Let the teams go. Me and Carlos got this."

The were-demons snarled and nodded, their focus on Kamal and Drum. "You see, even the Neterus know it is unwise to split ranks when so much is at stake. Name your price for your cut of the profits; their team was not the objective. Winning the bounty is the prime directive. We could cut a deal, use your capacities for this battle, and be done with this, since we are remote cousins, so to speak. Family."

"The mother-seer's family is *my family,*" Kamal growled low in his throat. "Although I never wanted them to see this."

Upon Kamal's last words, he and Drum shape-shifted so quickly and lunged so fast that the team could barely react. The lupines went airborne within seconds, crossing the expanse to meet Kamal and Drum twenty feet off the ground. Viscous snarls rent the night as flesh-tearing claws gashed battle-bulked forms. Midair collisions thundered through the glen as close-standing trees were decimated and the earth dug up by powerful pivots and clawed landings. Black blood splattered, hunks of fur and meat tumbled against the soaked carpet of grass. But red blood splattered, too. Damali and Carlos's gazes locked. Kamal and Drum would fight to the death— their deaths—but that couldn't happen, not on their watch. The moment the combatants separated to lunge again, Carlos and Damali worked as an instantaneous tag team.

Carlos opened his hands and created a barrier to shield the others standing behind him and Damali, his gaze lethal as it ignited silver. Damali instantly reached for the beam and deflected it to draw a burning line between the weres, Big Mike, Shabazz, Kamal, and Drum, then trapped the were-wolves inside the silvery ring.

"Make 'em talk," she whispered between her teeth.

"Where's Lilith?" Carlos said, walking toward the trapped weres as Kamal and Drum normalized to wounded human forms.

"Let them go," a calm female voice said behind them all, making everyone, even the were-wolves turn.

The trapped demons cowered as the tall, lanky female strode forward, considered them with a smile, and shook her head. She threw her dark, thick tresses over her shoulder and clucked her tongue. "You broke your pact. You were only allowed five to do the job and given moon amnesty regardless of its phase, and you lost. You cannot make good on your hunt, any more than the Amanthras or the ether levels can." Her eyes turned to fire and consumed the writhing entities that charred and smoked on the ground.

"Where's your blade, hon?" she said, laughing as she approached Damali, but stopped as Big Mike and Shabazz scrambled into position. "Dante wants your head on his chamber table for ruining his best man. I agree."

The chairman materialized. Carlos and Damali stared at him. He was just about Carlos's age, wearing a cold-blooded black suit, and a casually sinister smile. Kamal and Drum flanked Marlene and smiled.

"My, this has been expensive." He looked around and chuckled. "I've won, Lilith."

"The team is not in it. This has been me and you for a long time," Carlos said, his gaze locked with the chairman's.

"Let them go, and me and him against you and that bitch," Damali said, easing away from her team. "This has been expensive, as you said." She and the chairman studied each other for a few seconds.

The chairman unsheathed a long, black iron blade and pointed it at Carlos's chest. "You just won't die, neither will she."

Carlos whipped his pocketknife out, making both Dante and Lilith laugh until it extended into the golden hooked talon. He snapped off the handle and brandished the chain between both ends. Damali glanced at him, but kept her focus on their enemies.

Lilith's legs became granite, her wings opened to an impressive twelve-foot wingspan, and her face distorted. "They're just dinner," she said quietly, referring to the teams, as she stared at Carlos. "But you are victory."

She hurled herself toward Damali before Damali could draw a breath. Both women hit a tree and Damali disappeared and came out on the other side of it. The team was frozen, paralyzed as Lilith's spell held them captive. They couldn't even yell out as Carlos lunged for the chairman, missed his blow, but received a deep gash in his back for the effort. The chairman leveled his blade and reached out with a black arch toward Carlos's chest. He deflected it with a gold shield and sliced through the black iron with a searing Light glance and then raked the chairman's face with the golden talon. Dante's wound sizzled as he briefly held his cheek, his hand coming away with black blood. Lilith went airborne and swooped at Damali, missed, and came at her again. But Damali melted into the tree, becoming one with the bark, camouflaging herself, as Lilith rammed it and wood splintered, cracking the mighty oak in half.

The tree hit the ground, causing both the chairman and Carlos to dodge the falling timber. Damali reached out, sending a blue-white arch to the falling wood that raised a hundred stake spikes from it, and hurled it at the chairman and Lilith.

One spike impaled her tail, pinning her to the ground, and she screeched and twisted herself loose, severing her razor-sharp weapon and gushing black blood as she stalked forward.

Fury roiled within the chairman, who opened his arms, released a thousand bats from his chambers, and turned the sky black with their fast-moving bodies as black thunder and lightning shook the earth. Carlos looked up and redirected the lightning. Scorched bat bodies dropped like nasty, shuddering vermin hail. His gaze turned on the chairman as he swung the chain to capture his throat, but he'd already concealed himself and Lilith behind a transparent black barrier.

Winded, Lilith and the chairman stepped back. Carlos and Damali stepped back, breathing hard.

"I don't believe in stalemates," the chairman said, his fangs lengthening as his eyes went from solid red to glowing black.

"Nor do I," Lilith whispered, her tail regenerating as she walked forward. Then she stopped, tilted her head, and inhaled sharply as her eyes slid shut. She shook her head and tried to compose herself for battle, Damali's hand went to her pocket, releasing the black vial in a quick smash against the ground, knowing what the combined effects of *Oblivion* and apexing male Neteru would do— make Lilith strong but sloppy.

Damali leaned her head back and released a battle cry. She and Lilith collided midair. The paralysis around the team fractured. Carlos's shield dropped. Shabazz reached for a shotgun, and the chairman sent a black bolt that summarily snapped his arm, and then sent a shock wave toward Carlos that blew the golden talon out of his hand. Carlos and the chairman locked each other in an energy death grip. The silver beam from Carlos's eyes met the black beam from the chairman's. They released each other and then came together again, twisting, and then repelling each other at equal strength. Big Mike and Dan grabbed a stake from the splintered tree, but as soon as they picked it up, their wrists snapped. Kamal covered Marlene on the ground, using his body to take any debris hurled her way. Drum dropped to his knees, upper and lower canines distended as the loss of blood from his wounds took its toll.

"Keep them out of this!" the chairman yelled.

"Back off," Carlos hollered as Damali and Lilith wrestled each other to the ground exchanging blows.

Lilith's claws hovered a fraction of an inch above Damali's face. Damali held her hands away from her eyes, rolling away from the newly regenerated slashing tail until Lilith cut her own leg and wailed.

"You have what's mine!" Damali shouted.

"Your loss, my gain!" Lilith screeched.

Carlos threw a blow, sending a ball of silver light into the chairman's jaw. He howled and fell back, then got up bigger and angrier than he was before and rushed Carlos, pinning him to the ground, fangs poised over his throat.

"No!" Lilith screeched. She released Damali and rode the chairman's back.

The chairman flung Lilith off, eyed her with a cutting glare, and released Carlos, who quickly rolled away and jumped up.

Yonnie materialized with Tara, and Tara rushed to Carlos,

checked him for wounds, and then bore fangs. Her hiss made
Lilith's gaze narrow and she tried to pull away from the chairman.
Yonnie cocked his head to the side, looked at Carlos, and snarled.

"Man, you oughta be glad we're boys."

Damali's hand went to her hip. Metal hit her hand, warmed it
like a familiar friend. Lilith's skull had hatch marks on it in her
mind. With all her might she hurled the Isis dagger, but Lilith side-
stepped it. The weapon fell at the chairman's feet. Carlos reached
out, but it only rattled on the ground. Damali screamed, "Come to
me," but the weapon lay dormant. The chairman laughed and
lifted it with dark energy, making Lilith lope toward him.

"Finish her off, Dante," Lilith crooned. "But do leave him for a
few hours so we can play." She weaved, high, and chuckled—wiping
her nose with the back of her hand.

The chairman stretched out a shaky finger at Lilith. "You bitch!
You traitorous bitch." He released the dagger and gored her womb.

Stunned, she stood wide-eyed, her legs trembling, her hands unable to touch the sacred metals lodged within her belly as her
mouth filled with black blood and her abdomen smoldered. Bats
stopped flying. Harpies retreated. Damali was on her in seconds,
and yanked out the small Isis blade. Lilith's hands scrabbled at the
gaping wound, but couldn't seal it.

"Finish her," the chairman told Damali.

Holding the blade with both hands, she stared at the offending
demon, the point bouncing. "Give it back," Damali whispered.

A horrid screech felled the Guardians. Big Mike's ears were
bleeding. A blue-white light arced from the tip of the dagger, entered Lilith's body, and blew her womb out her back, bringing
entrails and pieces of her spine with it. Lilith went to her knees,
her eyes glassy and no longer glowing. The twisted organ smoldered, shuddered, and moved like something was crawling inside
it. Damali stepped back as Lilith's body hit the grass at her feet.
Her eyes remained fixed on the gutted organ as it ignited in a
slow, putrid burn. A small white fleck of light exited and shot
skyward as the smoldering organ exploded, sending green gook
everywhere. Damali turned away, knowing what had been hers

and Carlos's was gone. Carlos's eyes remained on the smoldering splatter.

"You only had half of what you needed," the chairman said, looking at Lilith's lifeless body, then at Carlos. "Your blood was never in Damali's veins last night."

Damali stooped to behead Lilith, but just as fast, she was gone. Carlos, Damali, and the chairman backed away. Yonnie and Tara began to move back farther into the shadows.

"She's not dead," Damali told him coolly.

"That was your father's wife," Carlos said carefully. He looked to Yonnie, who confirmed it with a nod.

Yonnie rubbed his jaw. "Mr. Chairman, looks like none of us can go sub anymore. Whatchu gonna tell the man—you was fucking his wife and got mad because she betrayed you by giving away an heir apparent spot that wasn't gonna be yours anyway? That was for him to deal with, the way I see it."

"Run," Damali whispered. "Our side deal is done. Temporarily, we're all even."

For the first time in their lives, Carlos and Damali watched the chairman's expression contain true terror as he backed away from where Lilith had been. In the next moment, he, too, was gone.

Carlos stood very still, his back to the team, his eyes fixed to the spot on the ground that had once been Lilith's womb. The smoke brought tears to his eyes. Perhaps remorse did, too. Then, suddenly, a stream of black smoke wafted toward him, knocked his head back, and entered his nose. The burn stunned him. He turned slowly to stare at the team, but no one seemed to notice what had just happened.

Damali collected her splattered blade and remained squatted, looking at the ground where Lilith's womb had been. She didn't care at the moment where the long Isis might be. She knew it would come when she needed it most. Carlos squatted down beside her, staring at the same spot.

"Let's go home," he said quietly. "Wherever that is anymore."

CHAPTER TWENTY-EIGHT

THE MEDIA called it a wild gangland revenge spree, where many innocent people were hurt, some even killed, with unknown suspects still on the lam. The blackout in New York was a rare "cascading effect" . . . something to do with power companies and fluctuating currents breaking networks and grids. The things in the sky, unexplained black triangles the National Institute for Discovery Science said could be UFO crafts or military tests. Rampaging bats were cited as an anomaly of old building infestation, something bound to happen sooner or later, and of no real consequence to public health. The fact that one of the most popular music icons had her house burn down and she and her band are still missing, kept unconfirmed rumors selling supermarket tabloids.

That this all went down on a rare eclipse of the moon, which lasted three hours and thirty-three minutes to be exact . . . under the sign of Scorpio, keeps the metaphysical communities buzzing and debating. Murmurs ripple through the night. Hell temporarily closed its portals. Too much chaos was bad for everyone's business. The dark realms called a temporary truce by not showing up on anyone's radar. They obviously decided that until their forces regrouped, human beings could create enough mayhem on their own.

"My boy must have repaired their bodies," Carlos said quietly, looking out at the ocean from Venice Beach.

"Yonnie swears he didn't fix their burns. You ever consider that your mom and grandmom were saints?" Damali leaned in to him and picked up his hand. They sat quietly for a while.

"Yeah, maybe," he said after a long while. "Maybe like Padre Lopez."

"Yeah," she whispered, squeezing his hand. "Like Father Lopez."

Damali watched the tide roll in and out, wondering how long the basic rhythm of the universe had kept time by the sea. She had three more stones to collect. Her long Isis blade was still beyond her reach. Her man still had a little less than seventy days to figure out the range of his power. She had even less to figure out hers. Their team was grieving many losses—both in body count and their old ways of life. They had been beat down and were nursing multiple injuries.

Her mother-seer had a serious dilemma that had ironically blindsided a woman with second sight. She couldn't even fathom what was running through Shabazz's or Rider's minds. Damali closed her eyes. Two vampires were also an extended part of her family, along with a Manhattan-based witch and a couple of rogue were-humans from Brazil.

She now had a black box stashed away in her head. The compound had to be rebuilt on new ground, but differently this time. Newbies were at risk and had to be schooled, but the old guard was tapped out. Had problems of their own. Carlos needed his own spot, and she needed hers. Militaristic mad scientists and demons had them all locked in their sights. They only had seven months to hone whatever they had and pull it together. The mess between her and Carlos about her quick trip to Hell without him had yet to be squashed. He still seemed a little distant since the battle in the park. But they'd address that later. The Forbidden was still out there, and carrying a grudge.

She squeezed Carlos's hand tighter and rubbed his back as they stared at nothing and everything under the sun.

"Yeah, I know, baby. We've both got a lot on our minds."

Turn the page for a sneak peek at the next Vampire Huntress Legend novel

The DAMNED

COMING FEBRUARY 2006

Carlos's descent was immediate, but not disorienting like it had been in the past. Nothing reached for him or scrabbled at him as the black siphon pulled him deeper. All it took was his thought, *level six, chambers,* and he landed on his feet just outside the Vampire Council's chamber doors. Not even the bats crowded among the stalactites and stalagmites moved. Hooded messengers bowed and closed their red, gleaming eyes, their skeletal bodies trembling beneath tattered black robes as they lowered their massive scythes. The gaseous fumes that swirled up from the Sea of Perpetual Agony didn't make his eyes water. His nose seemed impervious to the harsh sulfuric blasts. The heat emanating from the bubbling red-orange surface felt like a cool breeze. All moans, shrieks, and wails ceased.

Somewhat bewildered by the reception and his instant adjustment to the environment, Carlos proceeded down the narrow crag and stood before the doors of the council's chambers. He reached for the golden, fanged knocker, expecting the customary entry-check bite, but the demon-headed knocker closed its eyes, retracted fangs, and the door creaked open eerily.

Carlos stood outside the huge black marble double doors, frozen in wonder for a moment. The knockers always did a vamp black blood ID check to be sure no imposter could enter. Not even the chairman had access like this.

After struggling with the conundrum for a bit, he gathered his courage and walked forward, not waiting for the underworld to change its mind. He knew only one thing for sure: power was respected, but only while it lasted. Therefore, whatever the angels had jolted him with, he couldn't waste time thinking about it for too long. The mission was clear: get the book and get out.

As he crossed the familiar marble floor, however, the level of disrepair did give him slight pause. Thrones were overturned and broken; a huge gaping fissure was in the floor. Residue of black blood splatter marred all surfaces, staining everything like it was crude oil goop. Wall torches appeared to have been ripped from their mounts. Rubble and crushed granite were everywhere. It seemed like a veritable war had been fought within the once revered hall. It was obvious that whoever or whatever had been searching for the chairman had exacted serious pain from any entity that had been foolish enough to remain here to try to take a stand.

Carlos glanced around, the eerie desolation unnerving him as he approached the barren, dust-covered, pentagram-shaped table that sat silent and abandoned. No longer could one hear the constant trickle of blood that used to run through it. All motion had ceased; blood was dried and clotted in the veins and arteries of the marble and had come to a dead halt. Inner lair, granite coffins of the councilmen had been reduced to piles of ash and small stones. Mere pebbles represented the once ornately carved caskets now. No respect for the dead resided here. True, Damali had dusted the remaining Council members, except the chairman, but it was also clear that someone or something else had come in there behind her, and it had been very pissed off. Girlfriend didn't do all this damage while she'd been here.

The kingdom of the vampires had obviously heard the death knell. Level seven was in full effect.

Carlos peered down at the crest at the center of the table, wondering. The eyes of the demon head opened slowly and stared back at him. Fear flickered in its red glowing eyes as it submissively retracted one battle-length fang and one broken fang, then shuddered. Carlos glanced back at the chairman's throne. With all the devastation, what if the book had already been stolen? They hadn't considered *that*? Why would it be left here? Clearly, unless the chairman had some serious special power over that artifact, the one who would remain nameless would have already seized the prize and have it in his possession—and there was no way he was going down *there* to retrieve shit.

Carlos wiped at the thin sheen of perspiration forming on his brow. The decision was clear. Report back that the book was gone, and where its probable location was now. Let 'em know the condition of things below, and they could concoct a new plan. That was the ticket. *He was out.*

He began to draw away from the table, wondering if just a mere thought would jettison him to the surface without incident, or if he had to risk calling for one of the trembling messengers? In the few seconds that it took him to draw a rational conclusion, the crest shuddered and yawned open on its own, revealing the vacancy beneath itself. Confirmation. Cool. Even the fucking crest was scared shitless. Obviously it didn't want to be ripped open again and violated. He could dig it. Been there.

As Carlos edged away, stepping over toppled, abandoned thrones with care, and avoiding the chairman's at all cost, memories coalesced within him. Ultimate knowledge lay as rubble at his feet. Carlos hesitated, remembering his old throne. Everything from his line from the beginning of time resided within it, and had offered infinite knowledge. No. He kept edging away. His orders had been explicit.

Before he could clear the circumference of the table, something very odd began to happen right before his eyes. The rubble of the chairman's throne slowly gathered. Carlos was transfixed as stone sealed in upon itself, black marble smoothed, deep crimson velvet rethreaded as though new, dust filtered away, and the chairman's throne righted itself from the floor and regenerated. His first impulse was to run, but a slow trickle of crimson ran down the arms of the throne, pooled at the edges of the demon handgrips, and then dripped to the floor in a long, string of inviting ooze. Then, in a slow, sulfuric burn, Carlos watched his name become etched in the hieroglyphic-like markings at the top of it, replacing the former chairman's.

Blood scent filled his nose, and made him lick his lips. "No," Carlos whispered.

The throne whispered back, its call like a siren's. "Come, and know all." Multiple voices wafted out to him, offering the blood scent as a lure. The slow ooze that had pooled on the floor instantly rippled across the marble to Carlos's feet, covering his Timberlands, circling his ankles. Blood soaked into the hem of his jeans, climbed up his legs, lapped at his thighs, stroked his groin, and then wet his T-shirt to travel up his neck and stroked the place along his jugular until it burned like a lover had caressed him there.

Carlos swayed and caught himself against the edge of the table. The scent was intoxicating, but didn't make him nearly as heady as the hint of power the throne begged to share. He'd always secretly wondered what gave the chairman such absolute reign over the other councilmen. If each of their thrones held the wisdom and collective knowledge of their lines on a given continent, what the hell did the chairman's throne hold?

The blood that teased his throat spread under his nose and across his face in delicate tendrils, licking at his nostrils. Carlos held his breath for a moment, fighting the urge to inhale deeply as he staggered away from the table and kept his lips sealed firmly shut against bloody invasion. He shook his head no as he turned to stare at the throne. No . . . he was out. The book wasn't there.

Carlos was soaked with blood and tears formed in his eyes as his body began to shudder with feed desire. He hadn't sipped in any air, and was suffocating. He angrily wiped the blood away from his mouth, took in a huge gulp of air, and closed his mouth quickly. But the taste in the scent lingered on his tongue . . . made him close his eyes, slowly parted his lips, and a tiny tendril entered his parched mouth where air was allowed to seep in.

Flavors and colors from all the blood consumed from generations of vampires coated his tongue, opened his mouth wider, until the blood ran over his face like a river, pooling in his opened jaw, lowering fangs, and he swallowed.

The throne pulled him blindly as a deep, sensual moan came up from Carlos's abdomen. Blood washed his face; it was impossible to see. The rush of it was so profound that it deafened him, filling his ears, invading every orifice, until he sank against the crimson velvet panting, swallowing, shuddering, crying, laughing, his palms welded to the hand rests.

His body arched as a black electric volt ran through him. It snatched open his third eye, bludgeoning his senses, burning out his cerebral cortex with so much information transmitting so quickly that he sat there like a vegetable, twitching and jerking in the seat. His spine groaned, writhed to the surface beneath his skin, and then snapped, tearing away from tissue anchors and cartilage, making him scream as it became one with the high back marble throne for a moment, and then reentered his body, regenerating with new circuitry and bits of black matter.

Carlos slumped forward, panting, sweat pouring down his frame, his clothes burning away while blue-black flames scorched his skin, but he was unable to move. Then the surface of his skin became suddenly cool. A new torrent of blood filled his mouth, and he greedily gulped it, regenerating more as he did so.

Pain abated. The room again went still. Strength slowly crept into his naked limbs. Fear fled his heart. Knowledge from every throne in the room had a new lord. A sly smile graced his face. Information poured into his mind in streaming, endless still frames . . . then came the pleasure.

Every carnal act that had ever been committed on the planet sent shock waves of ecstasy through him. Depraved or otherwise, it didn't matter. He could feel the impact of it all, every touch, every shudder, every moan, every gasp, every whimper—it all collided and fused as one sensation. He came so hard his heart stopped. His pulse was measured in elongated wails each time his body jerked and emitted thick, black emulsion from his member that wriggled in a slimy wash of tiny black tadpoles over his stomach, lap, and thighs.

Carlos's fingers gripped the armrests; his nails grew, carving into the marble with hooked talons. His eyes were sealed shut, but when he opened them, a ray of darkness shot out, burning and gouging the floor with dark fire where his line of vision went, scorching new sections of marble wherever his eyes looked.

Battle bulked to proportions he'd never dreamed, Carlos stood abruptly. Dark ejaculate slid from his body, splatting to the floor in thick, wriggling plops from his thighs. He stared at it dispassionately as his thighs hardened, a scaled spaded tail swished a razor-bladed tip at what was moving at his feet, making the knots on his spine feel tender as he flexed his spine. Then his toes welded together into gleaming, black, cloven hoofs. *Interesting.* He chuckled, his voice booming like thunder and sending small rocks to the floor from the abraded walls. New, leathery wings unfolded from his shoulder blades and cast a dark shadow from their broad span. He spun to face the throne that had consumed him, fury at the treacherous invasion closing his talons into a fist.

He hurled a punch that exploded against the marble and decimated the throne to bits of stone once more. Breathing hard, he could feel sudden heat flare from his nostrils. He breathed harder and blue flames shot out. "Well, I'll be just damned."

READING GROUP GUIDE

1. What did you think about the various comparisons to the Book of Enoch's seven realms of the Divine as Carlos and Damali learned more about The Light?

2. This particular saga made heavy references to numerology—did it make it more or less interesting for you as a reader?

3. Damali's encounter with the Neteru Council of Queens introduced new characters for the heroine to interact with. Whom do each of these characters represent to you? Would you like to see more or less of these new characters in upcoming books within the series?

4. As Damali comes into her own, how does her evolutionary process as a maturing Neteru mirror the traditional growth path of young women?

5. What did you think about Carlos and Damali's combined quest to gain knowledge from the history of many lands?

6. How do you feel about the new, expanded team with new Guardians? Why?

7. As the team's dynamics change rapidly, so do Damali and Carlos's roles—and their relationship. What do you foresee as potential strengths or pitfalls brought on by these changes?

8. What about the addition of Yonnie, Tara, and Gabrielle to the friendship equation—how do you think this will ultimately affect the team?

9. Discuss some of the heartbreaks and issues besetting the team's older Guardians, such as Rider and Tara (with Yonnie in the equation); Marlene and Shabazz (with the returning Kamal); the loss of father Lopez; and Big Mike's new love interest.

10. Discuss how the clerics' faith was shaken during critical moments, but then strengthened when truly needed. Do you feel this is true to the test of one's faith? In what ways has your faith been tested and what has restored your strength when needed?

11. Did the inconclusive ending disturb you? (Will the Chairman and Lilith surface again? If so, how, where, and as what? If not, why?)

12. Ultimately, would you like to see a Neteru Roundtable of Kings for Carlos?

For more reading group suggestions visit
www.stmartins.com/smp/rgg.html

St. Martin's Griffin